SCOOP

The Truth Only Gets in the Way of a Good Story

To my mentor Jimmy

Will 'Billy' Scott

Love to his trouble+strife
Irene x.

WILL SCOTT

Copyright © 2016 Will Scott
All rights reserved.

ISBN: 1532984170
ISBN 13: 9781532984174

Morgan, thanks for unearthing the rough diamond; Kate Thomas; Bruno; Gaz; Ov and Gandalf, you know why; Emma, sorry for the three year wait; Tommo and Pav, you've both left a gaping hole in the lives of all those who knew you – RIP!

Kitty, my princess and a raison d'être!

Prologue

An autumnal tempest blows outside a Quayside apartment. Trees thrash back and forth violently in the street. The driving rain increases momentum and pounds the pavement, road, cars, and any other animate or inanimate objects foolish enough to brave the unpredictable elements.

The River Tyne malevolently conspires with its tumultuous counterpart below the building as it slashes menacingly at its restrictive riverbanks. The gust finds its legs, accelerates, kicks furiously against the apartment's large lounge window overlooking the riverbank, and causes the double glazing to stretch and strain uncomfortably into the room.

Inside the apartment, "Summer Nights" booms from a treacherously docked iPod on a drinks cupboard, which is situated by a tall glass display unit in a brilliant white-painted room.

Several inebriated twenty-something men and women dressed as *Star Wars* characters sit on an L-shaped leather sofa; they sing and raise glasses to Olivia Newton-John and John Travolta's sexually ambiguous song in a spacious and luxurious lounge area.

A coffee table precariously holds a bowl of crudités, tortilla chips, a half-full bottle of Rioja, a half-empty carafe of chardonnay, and several Budweiser and Smirnoff Ice drinks.

The smooth, polished, charcoal-tiled lounge floor grants permission to three white fluffy Laura Ashley rugs, which are chaotically scattered throughout.

An Andy Warhol picture frame of a flirtatious Marilyn Monroe hangs from one candescent wall; a mocking portrait of the Mona Lisa hangs from another while Botticelli's *Birth of Venus* judges the proceedings from the staircase.

An intoxicated woman in her mid-twenties, dressed in a Princess Leia Organa slave costume, accepts a glass of red wine from Darth Vader. A sip is taken by the princess, who puts it down and stands for several moments observing the scene. The glug of wine appears to have tipped her over the edge of sobriety. She breaks away from the revelry and staggers onwards a short distance away from the lounge area and up several short steps to a mezzanine area cordoned off by a handrail and balustrades three feet above the lounge.

"Watch your step," says Queen Amidala, laughing, as she witnesses Princess Leia sidestep a dining-room table and chair a moment before a collision. Amidala dips her head towards the coffee table and sniffs a line of powder.

"Use the force," quips Obi Wan Kenobi, as Leia ineptly struggles past several inert obstacles. Obi Wan nudges his female friend in the side and indicates for her to move over. He takes a sniff of the powder himself.

"Impressive. Most impressive. Obi Wan has taught you well," adds the menacing tone of Darth Vader as Leia walks clumsily around the furniture.

"Don't get excited," Han Solo quips suggestively.

"Captain, being held by you isn't quite enough to get me excited," snaps Leia flirtatiously to merry laughter and booming music as she approaches a steeper, longer set of stairs ascending up to the roof.

Who is Vader? Leia wonders as she momentarily slips on a tread before regaining her balance. *It's got to be Scotty. He suggested the* Star Wars *theme, and it's not like him to miss a party. But why is he being so mysterious, and why turn up late?*

Intermittently falling on either side of the rising wall and banging her shoulders, Leia continues clumsily up the staircase. She succeeds to the top of the stairs, approaches the bathroom door, and thrusts it ajar. Once inside, she weakly wrestles it in an attempt to shut the door behind her. After three failed attempts to slide the catch into the keep, she submits to defeat and moves towards a mirror above a washbasin. Tired, heavy eyes look back at a five-foot-seven-inch fair-skinned woman dressed in a gold bikini with a red nylon bum and fanny flap lying loosely down to her feet, dark hair curled in a tight bun on top of her head, and a long plait draped on her shoulder. She stumbles awkwardly over to the WC, slumps down on the seat, and pees loudly.

The rain slashes above Leia on the Velux roof-light window, demanding to get in. She turns her head to witness the element's anger.

"Oh no!" she whimpers, looks down, and sees her urine hissing through her skimpy thong. Reaching down, she pulls the underwear elastic to one side and reveals a neatly waxed pubic area. Urine splashes on her hand.

"Shit!" she snaps. "Shit, shit, shit!"

The last couple of urine drops are squeezed out, and she is finished. She reaches over and grabs the toilet roll, wipes herself, and looks at the wet patch on her briefs.

"Thish's no good," she slurs. "They'll 'ave to come, hic, off."

The soiled panties are yanked awkwardly down her legs, and she steps out of her thong.

"Why am I so tired…and drunk? I've not had that mush to drink."

The woman washes her hands in a slovenly manner, dries them, checks herself in the mirror, picks up her underwear, drops it into a laundry basket by the door, and drags her feet wearily through to the master bedroom.

Three strides into the room, and she collapses face forward before the double bed.

Leia is face down on the carpet with her head half under the double bed. She is lying on her right cheek. The left arm is above her head while the right is down by her side. The left leg is half bent while her right mirrors that of her arm. Her bottom is naked and vulnerably exposed to the room.

Vader approaches the inebriated woman, and on closer inspection, he can see the fleshy folds of her genitals. Princess Leia's eyes flash open as she briefly regains consciousness. She feels a weight on top of her and a penetration from behind, but she is helpless to do anything about it. Her mouth opens, and she tries to scream but is powerless as her limp and dead weight of a body does not respond to her brain's instructions.

"You underestimate the power of the dark side." Vader's wheezing words slice through her indolent shell and chill her to the bone. "If you will not fight, then you will meet your destiny," adds Vader, whose words hang portentously in the air as she slips out of consciousness again.

Chapter 1

The curtain is about to be raised on a new football campaign, and here I am, once again, with my fellow members of the TV, radio, and written press at a Middlesbrough Football Club press conference.

Optimism, excitement, and adrenaline may be running at high-octane levels within the football-supporting fraternity, but not with me. Saying that, I bet they're not tripping the light fantastic at the Riverside, either. Teessiders seem to look forward to a new football season in the same way a teenage girl welcomes a kiss from a lecherous uncle on Christmas Day—with dread and anxiety. Yes, the money in a card is agreeable, but is it really worth being groped, fingered, and sexually assaulted for a twenty-pound note?

Boro fans have got to be the most sensible of all the three big North-East football clubs, simply because when they're shit, they'll just not turn up to watch, whereas Sunderland and Newcastle United supporters take some sort of masochistic pleasure in seeing their sides struggle each season.

I greet the new campaign with indifference—you do after several or so years of reporting on the not-so-beautiful game. Nothing's fresh and exciting anymore. It's just another day, in another week, in a season, not a year, at another tedious press conference, where we ask the same patronising questions we've always posed on the eve of a new season.

To be honest, I reckon the manager and players treat us with the same considerable amount of contempt, too, as they reply with the all-too-similarly predictable, dull, and unimaginative answers to complement our condescending questions and shoddy interview technique. And yet some members of the football-supporting fraternity froth at the mouth with excitement when they discover you're a sports reporter or writer. You can be standing at the bar discussing a recent press conference or a football titbit, and some heed-the-ball will interrupt a conversation you are having with a colleague, like this Geordie did last week. The very same radgy had a Newcastle Untied tattoo down his left arm. The illiterate twat!

"So you're a journalist, eh? That must be a great job that, like?"

You don't want to spoil the illusion, so you resist a sarcastic temptation to quip, "No, I'd rather torture kittens with a cheese grater for a living." Instead, you say, "Well, there are worse jobs, I suppose" or "Someone's got to do it" or "Aye, it's not bad when you're getting paid to watch football."

Then there's the pretence of knowing who is leaving or coming to a club when you're asked by football supporters whether the rumours are true or not that a big star has been lined up. You behave like a pundit or revert to Sky Sports–reporter type: "The club has asked permission to talk to him" or "He's asked to leave" or "There are complications" or "There's a get-out clause in his contract." If only they knew the half of it.

Oh, aye, it's a great job, alright—very fucking glamorous! Especially when you've been handed a brief to cover a Johnstone's Paints Trophy Cup tie between Hartlepool and Scunthorpe United at Glanford Park on a freezing-cold December night. It gives me an enormous sense of satisfaction to know my journalism training has not been wasted. All of those nights going through the laborious process of taking notes from shorthand-exercise tapes and swatting up on the machinations of local and central government—it was well worth it. What was the alternative? I could have been out on the piss, of course, or paid a visit to Club Bongo and had some hooker fuck me up the arse with a strap-on for thirty quid.

I love freezing my nuts off in the press box of a self-assembled, MFI-built, flat-pack football ground, soaking up an atmosphere that evokes memories of a funeral service given to a long-forgotten uncle. But that's only half of it. Not only do you have to freeze your arse off while surveying it, but you also have to write about it. Seven hundred words have to be expertly written within fifteen minutes of the final whistle to meet the newspaper's deadline. The sports editor wants you to summarise the wretched excuse of a match and coin some eloquent phrases to make it interesting for the readers while they're burning their tongues on their Pop-Tarts or digesting a healthier option of oatmeal, flaxseed, blueberries, and almonds at breakfast time.

On this occasion, the clock ticks into the eighty-ninth minute. The previous eight-eight minutes have been unremarkable, aside from a deflected own goal, which gave Pools a 1–0 lead. They are coasting to victory. My finger hovers over the send button on my Hotmail account. I have to use Hotmail because our wonderfully skilled and helpful IT department still hasn't worked out how to put the *Post*'s e-mail onto my laptop—useless fuckers. As I was saying, I am just seconds away from filing my match report and fucking off home after a short interview with the manager. It is the most one-sided contest in Johnstone's Paints Trophy history. OK, I can exaggerate at times, but nothing can go wrong, can it?

Fuck! Fuck! Fuck! Fuck! Fuck! Fuck! Fuck! Scunthorpe only equalise in stoppage time against the run of play to send the game into extra time! Bastards! I love it when that happens—as much as I love sitting in my own shit, piss, and vomit after digesting a rancid curry!

That isn't the end of it. It really does get better; the **pièce de résistance** is yet to come.

Ten minutes into the first period of extra time, and the North-East side nets a couple of quick goals and is cruising to victory once more. Top of the pops! It should've been a formality, but no. The useless monkey-hanging bastards decide to make the contest more interesting—for the fucking supporters of the losing side, that is—but it makes my job a lot more frigging difficult than it already is. They allow the opposition to make up the deficit courtesy of some schoolboy defending, and the tie goes into a penalty shoot-out! The good-for-nothing twats! They've always been useless. But when you consider what they're famous for, it is hardly surprising the football team mirrors the town's underachievement and embarrassment.

Hartlepool will be forever known for hanging a monkey during the nineteenth-century Napoleonic Wars. It is commonly accepted that the townsfolk believed that the simian was a spy. Our distant cousin from evolution had washed ashore upon the wreckage of a French ship. So they interrogated it, would you believe? But because the powers that be couldn't get much sense from monkey boy, they hung the poor bastard. They thought the rascal was speaking French, you see.

The town has been mocked ever since. It took nearly two hundred years to live down the shame. But instead of the town trying to bury the bad press, reinvent itself, and play down that embarrassing episode of its inglorious past, the townspeople celebrated their historic bygone days by embracing it and taking a defeat, if you like, and turning it around into a victory. One of those measures of reinvention saw the football club introduce a mascot at the team's home ground, Victoria Park. They called it H'Angus the Monkey. Some pun, eh?

One guy who donned a monkey suit was eventually elected mayor of the town in the early noughties. The irony is overwhelming! His campaign was built on the promises of free bananas for children. But despite the empty promises, he still went on to be re-elected a further two times, three in all. Good to see the locals taking their politics so seriously. They hang one monkey and then elect another into office—you can't make this stuff up, anywhere other than Hartlepool, that is.

Well, they may have redeemed themselves to the rest of the comedy world with that little act of local government, but not in my eyes. So instead of getting away from the ground and into the warmth and comfort of my sliver-grey Skoda Octavia before eleven that night, I spend another hour before I get on the road and head back toward the North East. And is there anywhere better than Scunny to spend a Baltic night in December, witnessing such pitiful entertainment? Watching drunken penguins play Ping-Pong in the Baltic states of northern Europe might run it a close second. But that's about it.

Actually that's quite an interesting concept. I wouldn't mind seeing that at all. Had Kelvin McKenzie put that on his TV channel when he dabbled in the world of satellite television after leaving the *Sun*, he might still be on the TV, because that would have been a sure-fire hit. Where am I? Oh aye, watching a pathetic excuse of a football match and catching hypothermia and frostbite in North Lincolnshire! It's madness; you just wouldn't do it if you were of sound body and mind and in stable mental health, would you?

Talking of people with mental health problems, here's the *Times*'s old queen, Henry Summer. If rumours are to be believed, Summer was caught cottaging on Hampstead Heath a few years back—fucking disgusting at his age. And of all the places to go, he picks the Gay Ham United of homosexual pickup places. The police apparently let him off with a caution. A mate of a mate of a mate's colleague in the force says the copper got a signed Arsenal shirt from Martin Keown for his troubles. Apparently the copper's wife had a thing for the former Gunners' defender! Takes all sorts I suppose.

Wonder what he's doing up here? You rarely see any of the so-called London-based national heavyweights in the North-East, and certainly not at a backwater like Hurworth for a Boro presser. St James' Park and the Stadium of Light, yes, but not in smog land—unless he has a story. Or maybe it's just that he's fallen so far down the pecking order these days that he's been sent to get the football equivalent of a long stand.

You usually get sent for a long stand when you're a young apprentice starting out in a trade. The experienced tradesman will send his young protégé to get a long stand from a work colleague, and the latter will make the precocious wet-behind-the-ears stand for a very long time! Not funny when you're the butt of the joke, but when you're the instigator, it's hilarious. You'll just have to take my word on that. Maybe this is the *Times*'s way of saying to the old bastard, "Fucking retire, and give a younger man a chance!"

He must be about ninety-eight now. That's the trouble with some of these old hacks; they just don't know when to quit and call it a day. They're always hanging around, contributing freelance articles and features and denying youngsters or wannabe reporters a foot in the door, even when they've received a healthy redundancy package.

I've lost count of the number of times the old queen has quoted the Duke of Wellington's "The Battle of Waterloo was won on the playing fields of Eton" or the dozen or so of Oscar Wilde's most famous epigrams. I feel like saying to the old bald bastard, "Henry, fuck off home and let a young 'un have a chance! And while you're there, go and change your pants because you've pissed them again." He's absolutely rank! Stinks the way only old people do—a mixture of piss, shit, and BO. I don't think his suit and coat have been dry-cleaned since the Blitz. And his teeth, Jesus, they're like moss-covered gravestones! They belong in Highgate Cemetery. But it's still not as bad as his breath, for fuck's sake; it's like he lives on cat food!

At Chelsea a couple of seasons ago, the old bastard came into the press room and announced himself in true Wildean style—with a green carnation, fedora, and walking cane. But when he took his plate to the buffet table to get lunch and returned to his chair, the old twat missed it! He fell flat on his back! Needless to say, the casserole had little respect for his exalted position within the sports writers' fraternity and covered him from head to toe in bits of carrot, beef, and gristle. I nearly pissed myself laughing. I had to leave the room while several sycophants rushed to his aid.

Here are a few of the others—and not before time—the presser should have started by now: Steve Doyle from the *Mirror*; Ken Chisholm from the *Sun*, Danny Bew from the *Star*, Will Gibson from the *Guardian*, and Chris Arnott from the *Mail*.

"How are you?" Chris greets me in that low, flat South Yorkshire accent, and he takes a seat by my side.

"I'm fine, mate. You?"

"Well, no, not really. That lazy bastard you work with has pissed me off."

"What's he done?"

"He's only gone and used that Shearer line we were saving."

"When did he use that? This morning?"

"Yeah, and I'm not happy about it."

"Sorry, mate. I haven't seen this morning's paper, and I was off yesterday, so I didn't talk to him to see what he was using."

"Well, if he thinks I'm passing on copy I saved from the England game, he can think again. I'm sick and tired of people not pulling their weight around here. But if that's the way he wants to play it, then fair enough. We'll see how he likes it when he's frozen out."

Jackpot. Saunders is in trouble with the daddy of the North-East sports press pack. It's music to my ears. Saunders calls him the Daily Heil's Minister for Propaganda. But that Marxist wanker would. He is a top, top, top operator, and despite what Saunders reckons, most of us call Arnie 'el Presidente'. He is probably the most experienced of all of the journos on the beat in our region, and he's only thirty-eight.

I'm lucky that Arnie has taken me under his wing. He's a right cunt to other people if he doesn't get his way, mind. And he's had a few scrapes with some of the others, but overall everyone is frightened of him. It's not as if he's a hard bastard or anything—far from it. But he has influence and knows people. He has contacts, and it's in your best interest to get on with him; otherwise, he can make life very difficult for you.

There was one lad from the *Herald*, Mike Jones he was called; he seemed canny enough, quiet, but someone who kept himself to himself. He never really mixed with anyone. He was a bit of a loner, did his work, and just got on with it. Well, there was this time when he missed a group conference between the lads of what and when copy was to be used. And he made the fatal mistake of not checking what copy we were using and saving and used stuff we were holding back. There was hell on!

If you go to press with a story ahead of everyone else, the editors of all the national newspapers want to know why this other guy has the story and you don't. So there is an unwritten rule: we all agree to go to press at the same time with the same story so that no one loses face with superiors. Of course, the tabloids spin the line a bit stronger than the broadsheets. But c'est la vie; that's their prerogative. But in essence, they are the same quotes, and it is up to you how you use them. So because of this, Arnie froze Jones out. He made sure Jones was kept out of the loop and warned all of us that if we cooperated with him, we would get the same. He was stitched up good and proper.

The coward from the *Express* was bullied into sending him made-up quotes from Kevin Keegan. He was chosen, simply because he was the only one who really got on with Jones. And because they were sent from him, they would have been seen as genuine. But the deed only succeeded in generating devastating consequences for the lad when his paper went to press with them.

The stuff sent wasn't that controversial, but they were quotes from Keegan, hinting he was going to sign Thierry Henry from Barcelona. The

Newcastle press office went ballistic, wanting to know where the quotes came from. To Jones's credit, he kept his mouth shut, but it didn't do him any good, because he eventually got sacked. Obviously, unlike a football manager who fucks up at one club yet can still get a job at another, it's not that easy for hacks to get another job once they've been fired. Not sure what happened to him, the poor bastard, although I did hear through the grapevine that he was in the process of writing a novel—a satire or **exposé**—on the wonderful world of sports journalism. The bitter fucker!

So Arnie has taken me under his wing. I realised early on that he was a bit of a nasty bastard, so when I overheard in a conversation that he was a Genesis fan and couldn't get a ticket for a forthcoming Phil Collins concert, I managed to get him one from a distant cousin of mine who worked at the Metro Radio Arena box office. We managed to bond a bit that night. We both like melodic soft rock: Bon Jovi, Europe, Mister Mister, Whitesnake, and Def Leppard, just to name a few. And after a few bottles of alcopops, he admitted to liking Take That and Westlife, whom I can take or leave to be honest. But saying that, I would admit to liking that shit Saunders listens to, the Clash or the Pixies, if it meant I would further my career.

My eventual goal is the *Mail*, not the *Guardian*, *Times*, or *Telegraph*; they're too wordy. No, the only red top with any credibility, principles, and proper agenda is the *Mail*, and that's where I'll eventually end up. First I'll get the chief sports writer's job at the *Post*, and then I'll climb the greasy national's ladder. But I'll not get too greedy just yet, just one step at a time.

Here's Gordon Buchanan now; should be fun. He's one of the quickest wits in football.

"Gordon, a couple of words, please," said one reporter when he was a manager on the south coast.

"Vaginal discharge," he fired back. Brilliant!

Unlike the majority of managers in the Premier League and Football League, Buchanan, Gordon Strachan, Ian Holloway, and Neil Warnock have personality. They will be controversial, say it as it is, and give you an interesting line, unlike the several other bland robots with media training. You don't have to do anything with Strachan's lines, Holloway's quotes, or Warnock's mutterings. They just speak, or rather write, themselves.

Boro's chairman, John Gibside, couldn't make Buchanan's unveiling as Middlesbrough's new manager because he was away on business, so Gibside sent him a good-luck text. The Welshman responded with "Fuck off; I'm watching *Strictly Come Dancing*!" There aren't many managers who could get away with saying that to their bosses.

There are several Buchanan classics out there.

One reporter asked, "There goes your unbeaten run. How are you going to deal with it?"

Buchanan replied, "Probably become a junky and throw myself in front of a speeding car."

Another reporter asked, "Do you think Andy Cole should have had more England caps?"

"I don't care; I'm Welsh," replied Buchanan.

"But if you were English?"

"I'd stab myself."

"Welcome to the south coast, Gordon. Do you think you are the right man to turn things around?"

"No, I think they should have got Gordon Strachan because I'm useless."

Wonder what he's got to say today. He's taken his seat behind the sponsors' board, and this must be the new boy, Nicky Johnson. It's the Welshman's third signing of the summer.

Don't know much about the kid other than he's come from Millwall for about £3.5 million, very expensive for a relative unknown from a League One outfit. Hope it's not a gamble. Johnson's story is a bit of a fairy tale, by all accounts. The lads are firing in the usual questions, and it appears Charlton let him go eleven years ago. He dropped out of football and did several labourer-type jobs before he got a break again.

He played for nonleague Dartford United and helped Macclesfield back into the Football League. Then there was a move to Brentford before a £750,000 move to Millwall. And his goal-scoring talent from midfield has seen him jump a league into the Championship at Boro. Let's hope the fairy tale continues.

"If you stick to it, believe in yourself, and are prepared to work hard, then it shows through," Johnson replies to Danny Bew's question about believing in himself. "I did those things, and I have got back up to the top level. It's hard when you are rejected. You have to go out and find jobs and things like that. I have done a variety of jobs in my time playing part-time football. I used to work as a lifeguard, gym instructor, and taxi driver while I hoped that someone would come in for me and sign me."

"How big is this move?" I interrupt.

"It's a massive move for me," he answers. "My aim is to play as high as I can, and this will help me to do that. I have been here before; there's a lovely hotel and golf course, and everything about it is top quality. It's a massive club, and everything is designed here for the Premier League. It's the dream of every little boy who likes football to play in the Premier League, and mine is no different."

Is that a violin I can hear playing? He'll have me crying in a minute.

Buchanan's not saying much, but he looks smug. His quip about "making the players run around the golf course" rather than play a round with their clubs has brought a few laughs from the audience. But Johnson is still an unknown quantity. Maybe he knows something about this lad no one else does. Up to now, he's brought in nothing more than a bunch of workhorses and grafters. There's not much flair, although you need graft to get out of the Championship, to be fair. But if Johnson can weigh in with a few and if Chris Boys, who signed the other day, can hit the ground running, then they should be in good shape.

Fucking hell, here's the *Echo*'s Billy Ellis. He's left it a bit late, the cheeky bastard.

"Nice of you to join us," quips Buchanan to laughter.

"Sorry, Gordon. Got stuck in traffic," Ellis offers apologetically.

"You should have set off earlier."

Ellis is beaming now—serves the twat right. He goes over to shake Buchanan's hand and says, "Sorry, Gordon, we've never met; my name's Billy Ellis from the *Echo*."

Buchanan takes his hand and replies, "Billy, fuck off!"

The room erupts into laughter while the *Echo*'s man skulks into the corner, out of the way.

Winter, who has been quiet up to now, adds, "Expecting any more new arrivals, Gordon?"

"Two main targets done," he replies. "I would be hoping for more within the next ten days."

And with that, Buchanan gets up and leaves the room.

Not much comedy gold from him today—enough to keep us going until next time, mind, but I'm sure there will be more gems as the season progresses.

"Right, so what are we using, and what are we saving?"

We all turn to face the speaker of those words, Billy Ellis. The cheeky bastard comes in late, and he's trying to dictate what we use.

"What right do you have to say what we do? You came in late, so you don't get any of the Johnson lines," snaps Chris Arnold.

Arnie turns to all of us and adds, "And none of you pass it on."

The *Mail* man turns back on Ellis and spits, "If you can't be professional enough to get your arse down here on time, you don't deserve to be given the copy."

Ellis looks around for support from Steve Doyle, Ken Chisholm, Danny Bew, Will Gibson, me, and Summer, but he gets none. We all avoid his eyes when he looks for help, or we look at the floor and fidget.

"But there was a police incident and a tailback. I had to ditch the car and walk," Ellis protests.

"A likely story," Arnie replies.

"It's true!"

"Yeah, whatever." Arnie turns his back on Ellis and addresses us. "Right, lads, we'll use the Buchanan stuff today for tomorrow, and the Johnson stuff will make a nice Feature Friday for Saturday. Everyone OK with that?"

"Fine by me," Will Gibson replies.

"And me," Ken Chisholm adds while the rest of us acquiesce to Arnold's request.

"I'll transcribe," I chip in. "Henry, give me your e-mail address, and I'll send you the quotes."

"Why, thank you, my dear boy," says Summer, with more than just a soupçon of campiness. "It's henry.summer@thetimes.co.uk."

"No, let Gibbo do it," adds Arnie. "He's bottom of the transcription league from last season, and if he doesn't climb to midtable this term, he'll not get any copy."

We had to introduce a transcription's league because some of the hacks weren't pulling their weight, taking turns in transcribing copy from all the press conferences and the like from player interviews and such. They were quite happy to receive it but not to do any work. So Arnie introduced this league and monitored everyone's input. "Sad and pathetic," Saunders reckoned. Maybe it is, but this way we flush out the bone-idle bastards.

"But—" Gibbo jumps in.

"But nothing," snaps Arnie. "You haven't been pulling your weight, and it's about time you did. We've all got the same lines as everyone else, so why should you ride on our coattails?"

Gibbo sulks at this mini rant.

"What about Stevie Stutter?" I ask in regards to the *Express*'s man, who is missing from the presser.

"Yeah, let him have it," Arnie says, waving his hand insouciantly.

"Well, that's hardly fair," Ellis snaps back sharply. "He's not even here!"

"So fucking what? He pulls his weight when he is here," bites an aggressive Arnold. "You've got a short memory, you have. Stevie tipped us off that Bruce Stephens was getting the Sunderland job. You would have looked a right twat had we not given you that story. So as far as I'm concerned, he gets the copy. Now if you'll excuse me, I have work to do."

Just then I hear the trickle of something dripping. I turn, as we all do, to locate the source of the sound and see Summer slumped in his seat, asleep and pissing himself.

Jackpot!

I've got a feeling this season might be a good one after all.

Chapter 2

Sunday morning, and I'm in the office at work. Sunday, Bloody Sunday! Sunday: the Sabbath, a holy day, a day of worship, and the Lord's day. A day set apart for the worship of God—if you're a Christian, that is—due to the belief in Jesus Christ's resurrection on a Sunday, according to the Gospels.

According to the Gospels. What's that all about?

The life, ministry, death, burial, and resurrection of Jesus Christ. Amen!

Over two thousand years later, and still, deluded imbeciles believe in that fairy tale. He was dead, and then two days later he came back to life from the dead! Aye, righty-ho, your holiness! Next you'll be telling me his father didn't copulate with his mother. What, he didn't? How did the procreation come about, then? Did a stork swoop down from the blue sky and drop him on a doorstep, like in that *Dumbo* cartoon, or was he an immaculate conception?

An immaculate conception: a virgin birth.

A virgin birth! Next you'll be telling me Jesus can raise the dead, walk on water, turn the very same water into wine, feed five thousand people on a couple of cod and parsley-sauce boil-in-the-bags and five Greggs' Stottie cakes! What, he can? Anything else?

He's three people in one.

Three people in one. Who is he, then?

God the father, the son, and the Holy Ghost.

So he's pretty powerful, eh? In that case, I've been a good boy this year; any chance he can fix it for Sunderland to win the FA Cup again, arrange a cosy night in with the latest teenage-girl pop-group sensation, and predict six precious numbers in Saturday evening's Lotto?

No, I didn't think so. Looks like I'll be writing to *Jim'll Fix It* again, although given the circumstances, maybe not. They should bring that programme back, you know. Get another former 1970s Radio One DJ to present it, one who hasn't been under suspicion for historic child-sex offences. That would get tongues wagging. So if Jesus, not Jimmy, can't perform those minor nonleague miracles for me, how does he expect me to believe all that other stuff?

Little wonder my childhood was confusing. I was led to believe that good would conquer evil. But if this is the case, how come Liverpool won all those titles, cups, raffles, and the Co-op Christmas draw, probably, while Sunderland won fuck all? No, you've got no answer to that, have you, Mr. Christ?

I love Sunday mornings, about as much as I would love a red-hot poker up me jacksy! Hello, what have we here? Jackpot. It's Saunders's laptop bag, complete with laptop and Filofax. Wahey! No, I must respect my colleague's personal information and not look through it. Like fuck I will! And what's this? It's only his password and log-in details! Oh, Lordy, forgive me, Lordy, for I have sinned. It's been twenty-five years since my last confession, but don't worry, Lordy, I will say ten Hail Marys and five Our Fathers. I will never doubt there is a God again. Good things do come to those who, eh, wait, scheme, plot, whatever.

The intrigues you've got to devise to get a promotion around here, and the web of machinations you've got to weave to put one over that shitbag Saunders. Well, Mr. Scott, Scottish, snivelling, sycophantic, shitbag Saunders, you may be acting chief at the moment, but you're not going to get the promotion full-time, because I'm going to make sure it is me. You can do all the creeping to Harvey and Cassidy you want to, bonny lad, but it'll do no good.

What a fucking stroke of luck, finding his log-in and password details. Get in the net, my son. But if he's going to be half-witted enough to leave a Filofax lying around with all his personal details, then he deserves everything he's got coming to him. Just as well no one is in at this time.

Right, I'm in. Open e-mail; now whom can I e-mail? Wasn't Saunders supposed to be at that fucking party Lucy held with the news team? The one I suggested to Saunders, who then suggested it to her and took all the credit? And then I didn't even get a fucking invite! Cunt!

To: lucy.bird@northernpost.co.uk
Subject: mmm, last night's party

Hey, doll, what can I say about last night? It was a perfect. Hope we can do it all again.
    Speak soon.

Love,

Scott
xxx

That should just about do it. Right, I need to log out before someone sees me. Oh, fuck, here's Cass! Quick, quick, quick! Shut down, you bastard; shut down! Come on, come on, will you? Good, he's stopped at the top of the office to pick up his post from the mailbox. That will buy a bit of time. Stay there a bit longer, you twat, just a bit longer. Please, stop there! I'll be for high jump, should he find out. And he's just the type to drop me in. Jesus! Come on! Come on! What the fuck's the matter with this thing? Close, for fuck's sake; close! Thank fuck for that. Done; it's shut down. That's a fucking relief. It's a sacking offence to e-mail from someone else's computer.
    This laptop could come in handy. Think I'll take it. I'll slip it into my bag for the time being.
    Here comes Cass. Real name, David Cassidy, like the former 1970s pop star, but better known to me and my fellow colleagues on the *Northern Post* sports desk (but not to him) as Cockney Wanker, Alf Garnett, or Gary Geezer. Says things only people think about saying but can't, for politically correct reasons.

He's old school. Loves his old mum, doesn't he? He's got a picture of his mum on the mantelpiece next to Ron and Reggie Kray, probably. Just like all the East End villains. And the Queen and the Queen Mum, "gawd bless her sowl." Calls a spade a spade, or rather a "black cant"! And when he's trying to be politically correct in front of his more liberal colleagues, he calls black people "coloured." I kid you not. He's a throwback to the good old 1970s, when it was alright for the nation to laugh along with Jim Davidson's Chalky White character and chuckle to Bernard Manning. And a time when you could put your feet up on a Saturday night with a can or two of Double Maxim and a Chinese takeaway and watch *Mind Your Language*, *Love Thy Neighbour*, or *Till Death Do Us Part*—without Ben Elton or any of the other politically correct comedy police saying, "You can't laugh at this; it's racist" or "anti-Semitic" or "homophobic" or "misogynistic."

"They don't make shows like that anymore," he once said. "Fackin' hilarious, they were."

To tell the truth, I thought they were pretty damn funny myself, not that I'd ever admit to it in front of my more liberal-thinking friends. You know the ones, all those right-thinking members of society who believe we should open the gates of England and allow Johnny Foreigner and his tribe of offspring to pollute our green and pleasant land with their radical, religious beliefs and mucky habits. Not only that, but give them a fucking-big house and a grand to spend at Ikea so that they can furnish their dirty, filthy lairs as well. Let's hope the Tory government finally closes the drawbridge and puts a block on it all. I was wandering. How I was going to get through the boredom and hatred of a Sunday? But now it's easy. I can wind up Cass, of course.

"Now then, Cass, how are you this fine morning?" I ask as he approaches the sports desk.

"Fine morning," he spits. "Fine morning! I wakes up this fine morning to find a fackin' chimney pot in my pond. That's what I found this fine morning, thanks to the fackin' storm. Killed all my fish, it did. Gonna cost me a small fortune to fix it. And if I catch the fackin' sootie in the BMW who carved me up at the lights on my way to work, I'll 'ave the geezer's fackin' guts for garters. I'll tell you that for nofin'! On a bloody Sanday 'an all!"

Jackpot! A typical Cass rant. He moves to Newcastle from London to escape, in his words, "all those fackin' foreigners," and a Muslim family move in next door to him; a Polish couple get a house two doors down; some Chinese students move in across the street; and some Pikeys take up residence in the park at the back of his house. But the pièce de résistance has to be our very own Mark "Marty" Martin shagging his teenage daughter! Jackpot!

Marty is Asian, or mixed race. People used to call them half-casts or half-chats when I was a lad. He doesn't know his dad, and he left Halifax to come here after having an argument with his mother's new boyfriend, who was roughly the same age as him, so he says. Apparently she's white but likes black cock. He's not a Muslim or anything, although he says he is for a wind up when someone is being a little racist. It drives Cass up the wall. He's talking about emigrating to Australia. I hope not. It means I'll not be able to ride his missus at our future work soirees or at her salon when she cuts my hair. That reminds me—I need a trim, or in other words, I need her quim.

Mrs. Cassidy is one fit, sexy cougar: a fifty-two-year-old sex bomb, just waiting to explode. Saying that, she generally does when she rides me. All of those hours spent doing yoga and workouts at the gym have been worth it. She has the body of someone twenty years younger. I love a woman who looks after herself.

I remember the first time I saw her in Tiger Tiger, in town. There was a circle of salivating punters letching around her as she danced to that Beyoncé song "Crazy," or something or other. She was doing a kind of slut walk and a twerk. I couldn't take my eyes off her. I wasn't alone. She was stunning in that little white dress, with its plunging neckline, revealing an amazing rack. And the dress showed just enough leg to leave you wanting more.

Her hair was, and still is, platinum white and straight, and it sits seductively on her shoulders. And those shocking scarlet-red, shiny lips that look fantastic wrapped around my throbbing gristle. It makes me horny just thinking about it. Just as well her knight in shining armour was there that night when a drunken tosspot decided to grab her tits. I'm thinking, *I'm not having that. That should be me!*

I couldn't knock over a line of dominoes usually, but this fucker was shit-faced, and I was sober, having just come out. I was on my way to a strip club, as it happens, but thought I'd grab a loosener on the way. Well, I was straight in there with the old one arm around his neck and the other twisted up his back, alerting the two gentlemen at the door, at the same time, of the danger posed by the unruly sex pest. Never thought watching that police-cadet-training programme would come in so useful.

Well, not only was I free to drink in the VIP area all night, as a thank-you from the management for avoiding an explosive situation, but also our damsel in distress was so obliged that I'd saved her from the clutches of the sweaty octopus that after a brandy and Babycham or three, she gave me a blow job in the disabled bog. It was the start of a beautiful relationship.

Nearly shat myself the next time I saw her, mind, at the *Post*'s Christmas party. I didn't realise she was Cass's old lady. In fact, I couldn't remember her name. Just as well the old bastard introduced her.

"Tom, this is my lovely wife, Trudi," he said.

"Nice to meet you, Trudi," I replied as her eyes twinkled at me. And that short gold dress she had on, it wouldn't have looked out of place on my girlfriend's slut of a teenage daughter. My other half, Julie—now an ex as a result of the lies told by her whore of an offspring—was with me, as it happens. They got on like a house on fire. But I was shitting myself that Trudi would let something slip. She had her stocking feet massaging my balls halfway through the starter, the dirty cow. I love stockings and suspenders.

Before the main course arrived, Trudi and I sneaked around the back of the restaurant for a knee-trembler, just so she would stop. We nearly got caught an' all. That stuck-up cow Lucy Look-But-Don't-Touch-Because-I'm-Fucking-Too-Good-For-Anyone-In-This-Office Bird appeared from nowhere. She was only having a sneaky cigarette. I never knew she smoked.

I'd just finished shagging Trudi, bent over a recycling bin, when Lucy lit up. Trudi managed to get away without being seen, unlike me.

"What you doing, sneaking around back there? You nearly frightened the life out of me," said Miss Holier-Than-Thou Posh Bird. Who the fuck did she think she was talking to?

"Thought I heard a dog barking," I muttered under my breath.

"What was that?" she snapped.

"Aye, rightyho, have a good one," I replied and smiled sarcastically as I passed her sour-faced dish. *Oh, take a look at her face. She doesn't like that one little bit. One–nil to Rafferty, methinks.*

"Tom," she called out as I walked by.

"Tom," she repeated.

I pretended not to hear and headed back in to the party. *That'll piss her off.* Everyone in the office bends over backward for the cow.

"Yes, Lucy, I'll make you a coffee," says the serial sycophant, sweaty sock Scott Saunders—my nemesis.

"No, I'll get that," says Marty, who should know fucking better. Even Eric sniffs around her. He's the editor, for fuck's sake!

"You're in early," says Cass, snapping me back to the present. "No big night out in London last night?"

"Nah, didn't fancy it, to be honest, mate. Just went back to the hotel and got started on my copy," I answer.

"Fackin' hell! You're in London, and you don't have a night out? That's not like you; you coming down wivsomefing or summit?"

"Nah, just didn't fancy it, that's all. Thought I'd get an early night and catch the first train from King's Cross this morning so that I can get a flier today."

"So how was Millwall?"

"How was Millwall? Fucking scary, that's how Millwall was, always is."

Millwall, or Bermondsey, must be the only place in England where a street lamp and a discarded traffic cone can look intimidating in broad daylight. *Fantastic, a trip to the New Den! Just the fixture I want to cover.* That's what I thought when Saunders drew up the rota for last week. I fucking love London, me, not!

"Greatest city in the world," said that fucking bucktoothed queer from Hartlepool I worked with in London. Greatest city! My sweaty, pimply backside it is not. I might have to go back there when I get on the *Mail* sports desk.

I was there for a friendly a few years back. When I got to King's Cross and asked the guard how I could get to Millwall football ground, he looked at me as if I were a fundamental extremist. He didn't know. Inquiries to several different people later and I was told by one suspicious Londoner that I "need to get to South Bermondsey, and it's a short walk from there."

"Tube or overland?" I asked.

"Yeah," the helpful geezer grunted.

One tube ride to South Bermondsey later, and I realised it was the overland I should have taken. I got off and found no one around, and it was Spartan. It was like everyone had been wiped off the face of the planet. It was broad daylight, one thirty in the afternoon, and I was starting to get paranoid. It was like I'd walked onto the set of that old film, *Assault on Precinct 13*. I trudged past the shops and looked around. Jesus, those flats looked scary. It's as if they're closing in on me. And if I didn't know better, I could've sworn that streetlight had just threatened to cut my throat. Hang on; there was someone.

"Excuse me," I shouted at a shifty-looking, overweight black girl. "How do you get to Millwall's football ground?"

"Take the P12 bus from over there," she replied in a manner that seemed to question my sanity.

"Can I not walk?"

"You don't wanna walk it," she said, laughing, as if I needed to be sectioned. "You wanna get the bus, doncha?"

"Doncha"? What sort of word is that? Still, I thought I'd better take her advice and take the bus, just in case I got attacked by one of those half-witted inbred Lions' supporters. Talking of half-wits, just before I travelled down to South London for the game, I checked out a fan website and read one of the funniest exchanges on a message board I'd witnessed in many a year.

One supporter, who turned out to be a season-ticket holder at the New Den, was telling the others about how he called the Millwall box office to book his seat for the club's next home fixture. He was told by the lady at the club that the seat he asked for had already been taken. That being the case, he purchased another ticket despite already being the holder of that seat via his season ticket. After several hours of much hilarity and mirth from some of his fellow supporters and head-scratching from the dopey one, his mates finally managed to make him understand that the lady in the box office would not sell him a ticket for the seat he requested because it was his already. All he needed to do was turn up on Saturday, produce his season ticket at the turnstile, and take his seat in the stand. When I tried telling this story to Cass, he said, "You're making it up. No one's that stupid." Fact is far funnier than fiction—this I've found from my experience.

The game, which incidentally finished 1–1, was an uneventful affair, unlike the humorous exchange on the Millwall message board. The famous Lions of Bermondsey spat out their usual bile, vitriol, and hatred, of course: "No one likes us, and we don't care"; "Fuck 'em all"; and "We are Millwall." But I think the hosts' venomous words were wasted on the Teessiders, who didn't really seem to get it or weren't bothered, more like—unlike Charles Dickens, of course. Had Dickens been alive, he would have been proud of the profound and meaningful Lions' words, which were rich in metaphor, alliteration, and symbolism.

There were fewer than six thousand of the baboons at that pointless exercise of a match; fifty-five of those fans had made the trip from Teesside. Now there's loyalty for you. Had my beloved Sunderland been pencilled in for the fixture in South London, there would have been three, four, or possibly even five thousand there despite it being a preseason friendly. And although I hate to admit it, the scum would have brought just as many, whereas Boro supporters, well, they don't deserve a football club or their chairman, for that matter. Bryan Robson took the club to three cup finals: one FA Cup and two League Cups. Fair enough, they lost them all, but it was the first time any manager had taken Boro to a domestic cup final in the club's history. He should be a Teesside legend, but no, most supporters resent him. Likewise with Steve McClaren; he's another who should be celebrated as a legend, but no, he's unpopular because his style of football was not attractive enough.

Even in the most successful spell of Boro's history (a League Cup triumph, a European campaign, and a UEFA Cup final), they still whined on and deserted the club when things went against them.

You could never say that about the Black Cats. Only three cup finals—in 1985, 1992, and 2013—all lost, since the glorious 1973 FA Cup win over the mighty Leeds United, and we still turn up in our thousands despite being up and down the divisions more times than my mother's bipolar disorder.

Saunders has just come in, and he doesn't look too good.

"Fackin' hell, what 'appened to you? Lost an argument wiv a door?" cackles Cass.

Saunders looks like shit. Those piercing pretty-boy blue eyes are black, and his bottom lip has been split. Oh dear, the ignominy, the shame. What will the ladies think of him now?

"Aye, take the piss," the Scottish twat replies in that strong Glaswegian brogue. I think it was Irvine Welsh who said, "If you take away their knives, we could all keep a Glaswegian as a pet."

"What happened?" I jump in.

"No idea," he says. "I was jumped on, knocked unconscious, oot-cawld. Didnae anything aboot it until I came aroond on the Saturday morning."

"Sounds like an episode of *Charlie's Angels*," I quip. "Were you knocked out, and when you came 'round, were your hands tied behind your back, and did you only manage to free yourself by rubbing them against a chair leg?"

Fucking hell, he looks as if he's going to kill me. Whoops, maybe I've said too much.

"What did you say?"

"Nothing, just taking the piss," I say, trying to make light of it.

"Why would you say something like that?"

"Eh? Just taking the piss; lighten up, man."

"This is serious. It wasnae funny. I thought I was going to die."

"You don't 'alf exaggerate sometimes, Scotty," says Cassidy, laughing. "Next you'll be telling us there was a ransom note as well, demanding a year's supply of haggis and deep-fried Mars Bars."

"Go on, take the piss," says Saunders, clearly shaken up from his experience.

"Oh, come on," cackles Cass. "Why don't you admit that some kids from the local primary school beat you up and stop telling tales?

"Fuck off. The only Walter Mitty in here is Raffers, and you know it," he snaps back. "This was real, unlike Raffers's half-baked family-line story, which he claims traces back to Wolf Tone."

"Eh? It does!"

"Bollocks, I asked your mum. She says you're no' even Irish."

"You don't know my...er...I am Irish!"

"No, you're not. Your mum said you once owned an Irish setter. Hardly constitutes being Irish, does it?"

"My mum? I've never had an Irish setter."

"That's what your mum says."

"No, she didn't!"

"Now hang on, or was it an Irish settee?"

"Did you own an Irish settee?" Cass jumps in.

How the fuck did this happen? I'm supposed to be taking the piss out of him, and now he's turned it around.

"You're taking the piss now," I bite back.

"Raffers, I'm more Irish than you."

"Oh, aye, and how do you get that?"

"I've had a pint of Guinness in Dublin's Temple Bar, and, er, I've got a record by the, er, Corrs."

"He's right, you know," adds Cass.

I think, *Cass, you're a cunt! Any guilt I've ever had about banging your missus behind your back has well and truly evaporated.* The Cockney twat generally backs me up, certainly when this pretentious prick gets on his moral high horse.

"That doesn't make you Irish," I snap back. Fuck! I'm snapping harder than a crocodile in an Amazonian rainforest.

"Makes me more Irish than you. You drink Blue WKD; I've seen you," Saunders says earnestly, "which probably makes you homosexual or a girl."

"Yeah, so what are you, a puff or a girl?" quips Cass.

"Fuck off!"

Fucking hell. I'm taking the bait. Stop biting, you moron; stop rising to the bait. I'm better than this.

"Now, now, there's no need to be like that with your work colleagues," says a diplomatic Cass. "We're just saying, sometimes you're a bit slack with your facts. Nofin' personal, gov; we're all on the same side 'ere."

I know he's still taking the piss. I need to change the subject fast. I'm not going to win this one, not when there are two of them.

"OK, you can have that one," I concede bitterly. "So what did the police say?"

"I havnae been to the police."

"You haven't been to the police. Why not?"

"I-I-I just havnae, that's all," he stutters.

"But you've been bleedin' assaulted, you clown," says Cass.

That's better; the equilibrium has been restored. Cass is back on side. Saunders just shrugs his shoulders matter-of-fact-like. And this is the limp-wristed fucker who is the acting chief sports writer. My job! Well, not yet it isn't, but it will be. And if he's easily shaken by a little smack in the mouth, then making the top job my own will be easier than taking the proverbial candy bar from a baby. I haven't even started with you yet, you middle-class tosspot. You can stick your "You can't call travellers Pikeys; that's racist" and "You can't treat all women as sex objects" up your arse. Of course you can't treat all women as sex objects. I mean, there's Ann Widdecombe, isn't there?

So you haven't been to the police yet, my Scottish friend, eh? You've been bound and gagged, and you still haven't been to the police! That's because there is more to this little episode than meets the eye. You're hiding something from us, and I intend to expose it. I'll be like one of those former *News of the World* rats sniffing through his bins to see what sort of drunken debauchery he gets up to in his private life.

I'll uncover his degenerate lifestyle. Saying that, I bet there's fuck all there. He makes Ken Barlow look like Paul Gascoigne. He sipped sparkling water at the last sports department do. Said he was driving and had to be up early for a presser. Lying bastard. He didn't even go; he got the copy sent to him. I can just imagine sifting through his bins and finding a copy of the Liberal Party manifesto, *Gardeners' World*, some Quorn, and some rotten organic vegetables. Maybe there'll be an empty bottle of Ribena and a Milky Bar wrapper. Oh, the shame, having all that dragged out into the public domain. Wherever he goes, people will stop and stand and point at him and go, "Look, there's that boring man, who eats bran flakes."

Another will say, "He doesn't even have the personality to go for something more elaborate, like muesli."

It looks like I'll have to plant half a kilo of smack on the twat to make him look more moderately appealing, well, in a *Coronation Street* Mike Baldwin—interesting type of way at least. OK, son, calm down, deep breaths, change the subject, but subtly wind him up at the same time. Here're the Sunday newspapers; that'll take my mind off things. I pick up the *Sun* on Sunday. This should rile the bastard.

"Hey, Cass, guess what's on the front of the *Screws*?" I shout and hide the paper behind my back.

"Oh, right, let's see," says Cass, rubbing his chin. "It was 'Kerry, My Cocaine Hell' last week, so this week it must be Katie's turn. Mmm, what about, 'I still love Peter'?"

I shake my head.

"No? Of course that was two weeks ago. What about 'I don't love Peter or Dwight or Alex, or anyone now I've got Robbie, my Rampant Rabbit'?"

I shake my head again.

"'Jimmy Saville Looked at Me All Funny'?"

"No, 'My New Breasts Are Ti-Tastic.'"

"She's a disgrace," spits Saunders.

For fuck's sake, here we go again. The country's moral guardian is out to save us all from decadence, degeneration, and Jordan's mammoth breasts.

"Oh, come on, Scotty, she's got marvellous pair of tits; you can't deny that," says Cassidy.

"I find her deeply offensive. She's not only deeply offensive to men but to women, too. She's sent feminism back thirty years."

"Yeah, but I'd bet you'd shag her," I quip.

"Pathetic, the both of you. Little wonder sports writers get a bad name. It's little wonder serious news journalists see us as an unsophisticated bunch of Neanderthals and boneheads."

"What, you'd like to bone her?"

"I'm no' carrying on this conversation with you two, two juveniles," Saunders says indignantly. "Cass, take the PA copy for the Newcastle game yesterday. Obviously I didn't make it. I'm off home 'cause I feel like shite. By the way, anyone seen my laptop? Could've sworn I left it here."

We just shrug, and off he goes. Just like that. He walks off down the office and out. The wanker! I could have done the home game instead of all the hassle of arranging a trip to Millwall! The selfish bastard. You've got more coming to you than a slap around the chops, big man. Don't think that this is the end of it.

Got a text. Wonder who this is from? Fuck! Me mother!

Chapter 3

Humid air hangs heavy on a late-summer August evening in 1981 and suggests a change of fortunes in the climate. The disconsolate sound of "Tainted Love," by Soft Cell, can be heard from a transistor radio.

A little boy of four appears in an untidy kitchen. Piles of pots and pans lie unwashed in a sink full of grimy water. The child has unkempt, wavy, blond hair and wears a *Star Wars: The Empire Strikes Back* T-shirt. His threadbare jeans, soiled with dried mud, hang halfway down his backside, and the jeans are frayed at the bottom. A few paces are trodden before his falling pants are yanked up by the boy. A four-inch scratch to the left side of his angelic visage is violently visible, while a chocolate smudge droops from his top lip. He carries a Luke Skywalker *Star Wars* figure.

The boy rubs sleep out of his eyes and looks at an attractive, slim young woman in her early twenties. The woman has short, blond, bobbed hair, styled similarly to a young Lady Diana Spencer. She reflects by an open rear doorway, which leads into a backyard. A short denim skirt lies just above her knee while a plain white H20 Top Shop T-shirt appears above it. She leans against the right doorjamb with one leg crossed over the other, while her left arm is wrapped around her waist and supports her right arm, which holds a cigarette. The woman stares into the distance, past a small child's bicycle with stabilisers, Legos, and an armless and one-legged Action Man scattered randomly on the concrete surface and at a row of red-brick terraced houses opposite her own dwelling.

A man in his mid-twenties cycles by on a red Raleigh racing bicycle and wolf-whistles at the inviting woman. A welcoming smile reciprocates his gesture. He takes encouragement from her apparently convivial mood, swings the bicycle around, pedals up towards the building, and stops at the three-foot-high brick wall separating them both.

"Hiya," he breezily chirps to the woman standing six feet away, by her doorway.

"Hi," the woman replies flirtatiously, taking a draw from an Embassy Regal cigarette and flicking its ash.

The little lad cautiously approaches his mother while he suspiciously eyes the stranger at the end of his yard. "Great song," says the man.

"Yeah, I like it," she acknowledges.

"I think it's the best single this year."

"Yeah. I like it—like him, very dishy."

"Yeah, I suppose so."

"When's Daddy coming, Mammy?"

"He's not, son."

"He's a little smasher."

"Little sod, more like."

"Why not, Mammy?"

"He's just not," she snaps, agitated. "Go and play in the house!"

The woman walks away from her son's persistent questioning, across the yard, and towards the man.

"So you've just moved here?"

The little boy sets off after his mother, who has stopped just short of the brick wall. She folds her arms in a confident fashion. The little boy tugs on his mother's skirt and asks, "Will he come soon?"

"No! Yeah, about three weeks ago," she says, replying to the boy first and the man second.

"Why not, Mammy?"

"Because!"

"That's good news for me, then?" says the man.

"What's good news?"

"The boy's dad not coming back."

"Oh yeah, and what makes you think I'm interested?"

"Why not, Mammy?"

"Because you're still talking to me, and I'm different than the others."

"Yeah, you all say that."

"Mammy."

The woman turns sharply to her son and slaps him across the head. She screams, "For fuck's sake! He's just not! Do you not hear? So stop asking so many fucking questions!"

The boy bursts into tears.

"Don't be so hard on him." The man smiles at the woman and looks down kindly on the boy.

"He gets right on my tits at times!"

The man raises his eyebrows suggestively at her breasts, and the woman playfully folds her arms across them to prevent him from looking, before lowering them again and smiling.

He laughs and turns his head away from the attractive woman to the little boy and says gently, "So you like *Star Wars*, eh?"

The boy stops bleating for a moment and looks up through his tears at the man on the bike.

"I've got all the *Star Wars* videos in the house. You want to see them?"

The boy nods tentatively.

"You've got a video? Bet it's a rental," the woman playfully accuses the man.

"No, bought it outright. Told you I was different."

"Mmm, and I bet you play video nasties on them."

"Now do I look like the sort of bloke who would be dealing with video nasties?"

"You might be. I don't know. You could be a right perv."

"And so might you!"

"Yeah, well, we'll just have to see, I suppose. Still, you must have money if you have a video, unless it is a rental."

"No, bought it, just like my flat."

"A man of substance, eh? You must be different." The woman looks at him with an element of satisfaction. "What about that accent? It's not from around here."

"I'm originally from Murton, in County Durham."

"Oh, never been that far south."

"You're not missing much. It's a bit of a backwater."

"Yeah, bit like this place."

"Tell you what. Why don't you come around sometime this week, and I'll cook your tea and the little fella's here." He bends down towards the boy, winks, and says gently, "And I'll put *Star Wars* on the video."

The man hands the boy a ten-pence piece. The money is snatched from his hand. The boy hides behind his mother's leg and tentatively pops his head out several times to look at the giver of the gift. "I'll even let you play with my *Star Wars* figures. What do you reckon, little fella?"

"Well, what do you think, Thomas?"

The small child smiles and hides behind her legs once more.

"OK, we'll come for tea. What we having?"

"I'll surprise you."

"Where do you live?"

"Above the village video shop. Knock on the side door, though. Don't go through the front. Otherwise, you'll find yourself in the knitting shop."

The man climbs onto his bicycle and pedals off. The woman watches him as the sky darkens and thick droplets of rain start to slowly splash around her. The sky has become overcast; the drops become more frequent and heavy and begin to soak her T-shirt.

"Thomas, get inside quickly," she instructs, huddling her arms together. She turns to the man. "Hey, I don't even know your name."

"Frank, Frank Rafferty."

"Mary."

"I know."

"How's that?"

"I've been watching you for three weeks!"

Chapter 4

Fucking hell! An apparition of my nemesis, Saunders! Only this time it's real, and I'm not dreaming. It's bad enough having a sleepless night because you've been haunted by the ghosts of your past, but it's another when a spectre of the living is bedevilling you in daylight.

I fucking hate everything about the smarmy bastard. He should have been a catalogue model, not a journalist: just over six foot tall and athletic on account of several gym visits a week—although I don't know where he finds the time. He has dark chiselled features, ebony-black wavy hair gelled back perfectly, blue eyes, designer suits and clothes, and a look of that actor Patrick Dempsey or that 1980s 501 Levi advert gadgy. Nick something or other, eh, he was called. That Madonna was supposed to be shagging him. He had a couple of decent hits back in the day. Not only is he a fucking handsome bastard, but he's nice with it, the wanker! I just know today is going to be shit.

"Scott," I say, acknowledging his presence as we approach the *Northern Post*'s entrance.

"Raffers," he replies, returning my cordial greeting while feasting his face on what looks like a MacDonald's breakfast bun. It wouldn't fill a field mouse, that thing. Always filling his cake hole with those vile saturated products from old Ronald's farm, and yet there's fuck all on him—the skinny bastard.

He's wearing makeup! I kid you not! The nonce is wearing makeup to cover his black eyes. The vain bastard would drown himself in a puddle if he saw his own reflection in it.

We both pick up our morning paper from the newspaper stand, just inside the building, and pretend to read so as not to talk to each other any further. I can only speak for myself, of course. He'd probably want to talk about existentialism or some other pretentious crap. Not today, my son. We walk a few hundred yards further, and we enter the editorial department.

What's that fucking racket? Sounds like Harvey. Fuck me. It is Harvey! And he's back to doing what he does best: terrorising the bejesus out of the news desk. He was given a month off for a stress-related illness. It must have done him the world of good, because he's back at work, in little over a week, giving his heart a full workout by bollocking the news desk's not-so-holy trinity of news editor, John Hardwick; chief sub, Steve Blackley; and chief reporter, Sarah Brownlie. This looks fun. It's always good to see someone else suffer.

Saunders and I look at each other and smirk.

Saunders motions me to stop walking towards the fracas. We observe Harvey draw back his arm and ferociously deliver the *Northern Post* newspaper. It reminds me of a West Indies' quickie in his 1970 or 1980s pomp. The paper hits Hardwick's head. He winces but says nothing. Technically that's assault, but the coward won't do a thing about it.

"A chicken nugget that looks like a fucking sheepdog!" Harvey screams.

Hardwick, Blackley, and Brownlie look at the floor, shuffle in seats, and nervously finger objects on desks.

"A chicken nugget that looks like a frigging sheepdog," Harvey continues. "Is that the best we can do? The biggest-selling daily newspaper in the north of England, and that's the best we can come up with! What next, an elephant-shaped biscuit that can walk a tightrope? A jelly baby that shits jelly tots? Or what about a jumper made out of liquorice? Eh? Eh? Well? What have you got to say for yourselves?"

"It's the way journalism is going," Hardwick feebly protests after a few moments of silence.

"The way!" Harvey splutters, looking as if he is about to self-combust. "Not on my frigging watch, it's not!"

"But the public love this stuff," Hardwick argues weakly. "'The public gets what the public wants.'"

Did he just sing a Jam song? Oh no, don't sing a Jam song, you stupid twat. Eric loves the Jam. Me? I prefer a bit of Dire Straits or Phil Collins, much more melodic and soothing than all that shouting and screaming, but Harvey, he loves all that punk shite. Oh no, too late.

"What?" snaps Harvey, spluttering like an active volcano about to spill its guts over a Pompeian suburb.

"Don't you get funny with me, sunshine, because I'll cut your fucking tongue out with a pair of blunt scissors! I go away for a week, thinking…" Harvey pauses and violently runs his right hand back and forth over a number-four, short-cropped cut of brown hair in animated frustration. "And what happens? I return to chimps having a tea party!"

Harvey has his back to us as Saunders and I walk gingerly past the heated exchange. But the sound of Saunders tearing at his free MacDonald's toy makes Harvey turn.

"Talking of monkeys, Saunders! What you got for the back the morra?" Harvey shouts in that unmistakable and aggressive Geordie brogue.

"The Toon are signing Jonas Perez from Barca," Saunders replies. For a few moments, Harvey is thrown off balance by the weight of the information.

"Perez? Oh, aye, and later tonight I'll be taking new *Pop Factor* sensation Cheryl Mole up the Oxo Tower for a cream pie!"

"Can I come?"

"Not as quick as me, I expect!"

Not sure if Saunders is taking the piss, Harvey does a double take. I don't hang around to find out. I don't want to face the wrath of his tongue. But Perez, what's this all about? He's got to be taking the piss. Perez is one of the best players in the world and well off Newcastle's radar.

Saunders and I walk towards the sports desk and leave Harvey to have his sadistic fun with the news team. We hear him demanding hard news stories for tomorrow's paper or he'll "garrotte the fucking lot of them with a rusty cheese wire." Jackpot!

"What's this Perez craic?" I inquire as we arrive at the sports desk.

"I cannae tell you that, unless I kill you first," quips the Scottish cunt as he picks up the *Daily Mail* lying on the sports desk.

"Come on, I'd tell you."

Cass sits at his workstation, thrashing away at his keyboard. He'll break that fucking thing one of these days.

"Cass," Saunders acknowledges the sports editor's presence. "How are you this morning?"

"Smashin', 'andsome," Cassidy replies without lifting a head from the PC screen.

Saunders continues flicking through the papers and adds, "You mean like the time you tipped me off about Roy Meane quitting Sunderland?"

I shrug. He's got a point, I suppose. I set the Hun bastard up for a fall on the radio that night. The slippery twat still managed to wriggle out of it. He's a jammy bastard. He's the type who could fall into a cesspit and still emerge, despite being covered in shit, with a tray full of prawn kebabs, an Angel Delight, and a bottle of Asti Spumante.

"So then, Scott," said the radio host. "What are your feelings on Roy Meane?"

"Well, Johnny, he will probably take stock at the end of the season and—"

But Saunders wasn't allowed to finish his sentence because the Mackem radio maestro cut in across him.

"Time is something he does not have anymore," said Whitley, Sunderland's encyclopaedic radio man.

Such a shame, given he was on the verge of making a right arse of himself. We knew something was kicking off but weren't 100 percent sure whether the Sunderland chairman was going to fire him or whether Meane was walking out. I told him I would text if any news broke. Sure enough, Meano quit—sorry, left the club by mutual consent. "Mutual consent," my arse. What does that actually mean? And why do clubs actually say that? Why not "We've sacked him; he was shite" or "He couldn't win a raffle. We give him the only ticket in the draw, and he still didn't win the prize." And they trot out and regurgitate the same old press release they've used on the previous five managers: we would like to thank, blah, blah, and wish him, blah, blah, in the future. Lazy bastards!

And what about the undisclosed-fee line? One manager, who shall remain unnamed, said, "Because the pressure is so much greater in the Premier League, I don't want that pressure on the new signing by allowing everyone to know what the exact transfer fee was." What a load of bollocks! It's a tax fiddle; that's what that is. There's no other explanation. Otherwise they would tell us. How are we supposed to do our jobs when they don't give us the facts to work with? And when we do speculate on the price, they say that we're making it up! Of course we're fucking making it up. We have to, if they're not telling us the truth. So Meane walked out. I got a tip-off and, ahem, forgot to tell my so-called colleague. Since then, he's told me fuck all and kept his cards close to his chest. Not that I care.

Here comes Harvey now. Hopefully he's spat out his venom and anger on those hapless news fuckers—a chicken nugget indeed. They're fucking useless news reporters.

"What the fuck happened to you?" Harvey asks Saunders as he gets a closer look at the bruises through the makeup. "Kids from the primary school still beating you up?"

I laugh at this—yes, maybe a bit too deferentially—but it's having the desired effect, winding up Saunders. What a wanker! If it's me or Cass taking the piss, he's telling us to fuck off, but when it's the boss man here, it's "Yes, Eric. No, Eric. Do you want to shaft me up the arse, Eric, or will a nosh do?"

"No, I walked into a door," Saunders explains apologetically.

The lying bastard. Why doesn't he tell him what really happened?

"That's funny, you having a black eye, because a few months ago, I gave my missus a shiner. The police were straight around and asked, 'Why do you keep beating her?' I told them it was 'cause I've got a better reach and a considerable weight advantage.'"

We all laugh at this.

"No, I just lost ma balance," adds Saunders. "There was a cat scootin' aroond in the back alley, and I tripped over and headed the door."

"Clumsy twat! A black cat, you say? I bet it was a black cat, probably sent by Saint Niall, eh? The patron saint of all Black Cats supporters."

Steady on, Eric, there's no need to take the piss out of Quinny. Better not say anything, though; don't want him to know I'm a Rockerite and scupper my chances of promotion. He's just the type to be prejudicial against my faith in all things Wearside.

"I'll be—" I try to speak, but Harvey cuts me off, holding the palm of his hand up in a halt sign in front of my face. The bastard! He's made me look a right tit. I can see Saunders smirking now. Well, I'll show you both, you pair of conniving cunts!

"So what's this about Perez?"

"I can't really give too much away at the minute because I need my source to firm it up."

"Sauce. Who's that then, HP or Heinz?"

Bring it on, Harvey; that's much better.

"Sorry, boss, I cannae, not yet. I should nae've said anything."

"You've got to be taking the piss. There is no way those clowns would pay that money out."

"Aye, but it's no' their investment. The cash is coming from elsewhere."

"Takeover? Give me a clue?"

"I cannae, sorry."

"Aye, well, you'd better be able to stand it up."

"Like a penis on a porn set."

Harvey looks as if he's going to explode. Go on, my son, lamp the Proddy shite. But instead the boss man pauses for a moment and laughs out loud, the obsequious slut! That's not the way. Still chuckling, Harvey takes his leave.

"Penis on a porn set. Very good, Scotty son, very good." And he disappears into his office.

Bloody hell, that's all I need. Our environmental editor, Colin Cartwright, is making his way over to us. What's that wanker want? Obviously enthralled by the gay jousting performance he's just witnessed between Harvey and Saunders. It was like watching Oliver Reed and Alan Bates wrestle in the nuddy in that D. H. Lawrence film adaptation of *Women in Love*. Wankers!

Cartwright could send a glass eye to sleep; he's that dull. He could provide the perfect panacea for insomnia. All we need to do is get the NHS to come down and somehow bottle his boring monotone and sell it across pharmacies nationwide. It could be the saving of the National Health Service as we know it and give the government the boost it deserves in winning the war against the loony left. Cartwright could be held up as a pioneer and saviour of our health service in the same way that Nye Bevan was in postwar Britain. Well, maybe not.

"Hey, Scott," he says tentatively, approaching as Saunders's mobile rings. Saunders puts his hand up to stop him speaking.

"Whatever it is, Colin, I don't wanna know, pal; life's too short," Saunders flippantly replies.

Shite, that means he'll talk to me now! Shit, shit, shit, shit! He's turning to talk to me. Here's Marty. Phew, thank fuck for that!

"Marty," I say, as Mark Martin walks in to save my bacon. "How are you, my friend?"

"Yeah, not bad," he nonchalantly returns my greeting.

Marty's presence is enough to throw off the answer to sleepless nights, and he skulks back to his desk. It doesn't matter how rude and insulting we are to him; he still comes back for more. I feel bad sometimes because he is a decent bloke at heart. But he just brings out the worst in people. Saying that, I think he might be a bit of a racist. I've never seen him converse with the *Northern Post*'s contribution to diversity.

Marty is the editor of the *Post*'s free weekly grassroots sports supplement. He gathers information from the local community on football, rugby, cricket, motorsport, and such, which he receives from contributors via e-mail, fax, or letter. The general public's poor grasp of literacy and grammar frustrates the hell out of the man from Yorkshire and occasionally sends his blood pressure dangerously high. It's led to several hilarious arguments with punters who are dismayed to find their copy has been cut or heavily edited.

"Henry," Saunders acknowledges into his mobile phone. "Aye...Is that right?...No problem. I'll call later...Bye."

Saunders flicks through the morning's papers.

"Who was that?" I ask.

"No!" Saunders theatrically shrieks as if he's been given news some Afghan terrorists driving a Lada with go-faster stripes have murdered his family.

"What?"

"Diana!"

"Diana what?"

"She's dead."

"Eh, I know," I respond, not knowing exactly what he's getting at.

"No!" Marty sarcastically exclaims. "How?"

"Car crash in France!"

"No!" The Asian exaggerates again. This is becoming boring. "Where does it say that?"

"Splashed in the *Mail*! How did we miss that?"

Marty stops typing, looks up at Saunders in mock astonishment, and says, "You mean, the country hasn't gone to the dogs because of all those Pikeys, Sambo nignogs, and illegal immigrants?"

"Don't you worry, my friend. I'm sure the status quo will be resumed tomorra. I've heard Comical Ali isn't dead after all. He's alive, well, and been granted political asylum."

"There are no American infidels in Iraq," lampoons Marty.

Saunders removes his shoe and slaps the desk with it in response, which brings mirth and amusement from all those around the sports desk.

"We shall hit them with our shoes," Saunders satirises.

"Funnier than Michael McIntyre, that one," Marty adds.

"Aye, you can just imagine him on the BBC's *Comedy Roadshow*," says Saunders, mimicking the former Iraqi PR man. "'Bush doesn't even know if Spain is a republic or a kingdom. How can they follow this man? Bush, Blair, and Rumsfeld. They are the funny trio.' Aye, but no' as funny as you, big man."

"You'd think the *Mail* would've dropped Diana stories by now," says Marty.

"Fuck no, what would their readers do without some fucking Diana conspiracy every other day? It was Charles. No, it was the Queen. No, it was Morrissey. No, it was Mr. Kipling. His cakes may be exceedingly good, but not for pissed chauffeurs if it makes them crash because of a bout of indigestion. It was probably the butler that did it, anyway. It's always the butler. Now come on, Marty, tell me, what would they do?"

"Don't know. Maybe lament that the country didn't embrace Mosley's ideology."

"Aye, you've got a point."

And with that comment, smug bastard Saunders goes back to his paper and flicks through pages slowly before adding, "You read this one?"

"Which one?" I ask.

"This one here. The one about the London Olympics. Oh, the outrage, the shame of it all."

"What?"

"Apparently over ninety percent of all novelty gifts from the 2012 games were made abroad," Saunders replies, giggling like a child who has been tickled by his mother.

"I don't know why the paper doesn't just splash a seventy-two-point headline on the front with 'Foreigners, Get Ta Fuck!' And be done with it."

"Hey, you know my favourite bit of that election a few years back?"

"Which one?" I ask.

"The one with that former BNP leader guy—what's he called?"

"Nick Griffin?"

"Aye, Nick Griffin. He was at some party rally or other, but he emerged with the *Mail* tucked comfortably under his arm as he was getting pelted with eggs. Jackpot, as Raffers would say."

The piss-taking cunt!

"Shows exactly what type of character reads their bloody rag. Saying that, the rest of the red tops aren't much better, nor are their Sunday equivalents. The *Star* was backing the English Defence League at one time, until a turnaround a few days later. And we all know the *Star* and *Mail* are the same newspaper group."

"Aye, you could just imagine a job interview for the paper," says Marty. "Do you hate Blacks, Asians, Jews, and every other race other than indigenous English? Yes? Well done, sir, you've got the job."

"I was niver a fan or taken in by Tony Blair, but you cannae argue when he said the paper 'legitimises hatred and prejudices public opinion.'"

What the fuck do they know about these things? Hypocrites! If any of those papers came calling, they'd soon be off. The *Mail* is a top paper!

"But Diana dead! I still can't believe she's gone," Marty laments over dramatically, as Harvey approaches us from his office.

"Aye, I remember the day well," Harvey reflects solemnly, seeming to miss the irony of the situation.

"You a royalist, Eric?" I interject.

"Not at all, bonny lad, not at all. But I had to go to the old doll's hoose for me dinner with wor lass that day."

"Why?"

"The Newcastle versus Liverpool game was cancelled. As I said, a sad day, a very sad day. By the way, you know she died with a Dodi in her mouth?"

And with that shit joke, he tromps off to his office. The rest of them are pissing themselves laughing, while he passes by us without so much as a smile. Don't get it meself, but I join in the merriment as if I do. No sooner has Harvey entered his office, he's back out.

"Hey, Scoop," Harvey addresses Saunders, "the TV people phoned and want you on that Sunday show with the big horse's heed."

"No, I'm no'gaun," the Scot replies.

"You frigging are. Y'not heard? There's a recession. Times are hard, and we need people buying the paper. And you being on TV, bonny lad, will help do that!" Harvey pulls a mock face of astonishment at Saunders.

"I don't mind. I'll do it," I say, offering my services.

"Well, I'd rather Scotty went, to be honest, because he's a pretty boy and, well, you're not."

Harvey doesn't even wait to hear my response, the wanker, and heads into his office. Very funny, boss, very funny indeed. I look around, and there're smirks on Marty, Cass, and Saunders's faces. But they don't say anything. Wankers! I'm never going to get on until I'm lifting my profile on these shows.

"Hey! Watch it," I snap at Hardwick who has bumped into me on the way to Harvey's office.

And no apology, the cheeky bastard.

"Raffers, you putting the kettle on?" Saunders asks.

"Am I, fuck. It's your turn."

"Go'an, and I'll wank you off," he proposes.

"Well, if you're going to toss me off, then it'll be my pleasure," I sarcastically sigh, holding out my hand for the teapot. It'll give me a chance to phone Chris and tip him off about Perez without Saunders's inquisitive looks.

I make a sortie to the kitchen, which is a small seven-feet-by-ten-feet room at the entrance of the editorial department. It has a boiler; microwave; toaster; fridge; sink for washing; and a wall unit for storing cups, plates, and cleaning facilities. I check the milk to see…the fucking thieving news bastards have been at the milk again. I've got a good mind to piss in it one of these days. In fact that's not a bad idea. And if I find out who it is, I'll cut off their fucking balls. I shut the door and lie against it just in case someone tries to gain access. I unzip my fly and pish, as Saunders would say, into the kettle. Rafferty, you're a genius; never forget that. Saunders, that'll teach you to play the big man in front of everyone.

What the fuck! Who is this? Someone's trying to get in. Fuck, it's Noddy. I don't even know his name or what he does here. He's never said a word to me in all the time I've been here. He just nods, laughs, goes about his business, and leaves whatever room he's in, whether it's the kitchen or the pisser. He's like an extra on a film set. Just walks in and walks off. Weirdo.

"Alright, Noddy?" There he goes, nodding, laughing, and uttering incomprehensible monosyllables. There're some queer folk around, I'll tell ya. He washes his cup and exits the room, muttering under his breath, for a change. *Chris Arnott*, I remember. I flip out my mobile and call him.

"Chris?...Aye, fine, mate, fine. Look, you get my text about Perez?... Right, I know, but the sweaty sock is never far away, is he?...Just phone him later and see what he has to say...No, you didn't get it from me! OK, mate, laters, bye."

I've got a text; shit, it's from Millwall Mick. Probably wants his money. I open it; aye, the greedy bastard. We agreed £100, but he wants £150. I'll sort that out later. Oh, look, some old gum and a fag end on the floor. They'll add to the flavour. Give the tea a certain *je ne sais quoi*. I pick up the dump and gum and drop it in the teapot.

I get back to the sports desk as Hardwick, Brownlie, and Blackley emerge from Harvey's office. Looks like they've been bollocked again, judging by their boat races. Saunders starts humming the *Laurel and Hardy* theme tune. We all join in.

"For God's sake, why don't you just grow up?" Blackley bites as he makes his way up the office to his desk.

Saunders responds to this by quickly taking off his shoes, kneeling in them to make himself look like a dwarf, and answering, "I cannae; all that coal I ate as a wain stunted ma growth." Saunders's stunt evokes more mirth and merriment from all but the three news protagonists.

Most of the office staff is now in, and the place is full of activity. One of the cleaners is busy emptying one of the wastepaper bins while Cartwright can be overheard on the phone, lamenting how his friends failed to show up on a planned night out. *It's you, Cartwright,* I'm thinking. *Even your pals find you boring and arranged to meet elsewhere. They'll tell you tomorrow that there was a misunderstanding. Maybe now you'll buy a mobile phone, you tight twat.* I mean, how can a journalist operate without a mobile? It's just as important as your pen and pad or Dictaphone. He's a tit!

Harvey's popped a head out of his headquarters again. He doesn't look too pleased; well, he never does, to be fair. He screams "Blackie!" down the office and follows it up with "Arse! Here! Now!" Blackley tentatively rises from his seat and trudges down to the office. Saunders hums the Death March as Blackley approaches. Marty joins in.

"Piss off!"

Oh dear, he's easily upset, our effeminate and mild-mannered chief subeditor. And the more stressed out he is, the worse his twitch becomes. Apparently he didn't have that nervous tick when he started at the *Post*. But it's obviously been exacerbated by his quick-tempered boss. He's quite an interesting character is Blackley. The office bore, Cartwright, told me he'd had a privileged upper-middle-class upbringing once upon a time but was a disappointment to his family.

Following his graduation from Eton College, Blackley was expected to follow his father into Sandhurst and the upper ranks of the British Army. His homosexuality brought an end to any aspirations his father had for him. His father cut him out his will, according to Cartwright. Blackley's flair for writing and love of the arts, however, saw him rise through the ranks at the *Sunday Times*, from reporter to chief reporter, arts correspondent, chief political correspondent, and finally editor—until a ménage à trois sex scandal with a Tory MP and a rent boy was unveiled by a popular red-top tabloid newspaper and led to his dismissal. He consequently moved north and now lives in Northumberland somewhere with his partner, a psychiatric nurse, who nursed him back to health in hospital while he was recovering from a breakdown.

I don't know why he puts up with Harvey's bullying. He could easily quit and try and make up with his father and say he's had electric shock treatment to cure his homosexuality. I'm sure his old man would believe him. After all, that's what they did to puffs in his day.

Saunders has taken a sip of his tea. He winces.

"Raffers, this tea tastes like pish."

"That's 'cause I pissed in it."

"Aye, I thought so. Bet you used just one teabag an' all."

"No, just the old ones. There is a recession, after all, and we all have to make a sacrifice."

"Think I'll make ma fuckin' ain next time."

Aye, you do that, wanker! Fucking hell, you can hear Harvey screaming from out here.

"Cass, what do you think about Comical Ali?" Saunders asks our sports editor while conspiratorially winking at me as Cassidy focuses on his computer screen.

"Disgusting. No wonder this country's gone to the dogs," says Cassidy as matter-of-factly as a *Mail* headline. "Yet another asylum seeker coming to our country and paid for by the British taxpayer. And he's a fackin' extremist Muslim. I've nothing against Muslims, per se, apart from the bombers and terrorists. But I've got to get out of this country—can't take any more of this."

Cassidy shows no signs of emotion while we're all giggling and laughing.

"Where to then?" I ask.

"Australia."

"Oh, aye, with all your criminal ancestors? You'll fit right in, Cass. Of course, the Aussies are no' bad at sport, so it's no' too bad. But it's ironic really."

"What is?" Cassidy asks.

"The fact the English gave sport to the world so that you could go and thrash those wee colonies you conquered back in the nineteenth century, and now they thrash you," Saunders points out. Cassidy ignores Saunders, whose mobile phone has gone off.

"How's Mr. Mail, the red top's number-one sports writer?"

"Listen to this," Marty cuts in, looking at an e-mail on his PC screen, as I'm trying to listen in to Saunders's conversation. "Brinkpool under sixes are looking for an experienced goalkeeper for the forthcoming campaign."

"No, nothin' at all," says Saunders in answer to Arnie's question. "You?"

"'Experienced!' 'Under sixes!' Their words on this e-mail," says an exasperated Marty.

"No," Saunders replies. "Nothin'…Aye, alright…Aye…Cheerio."

"How much experience does a six-year-old need to play for the mighty Brinkpool?" Cassidy asks.

"Raffers," Saunders shouts. "That was Arnott. Wants to know what Toon line we've got for the morra mornin'."

"Dunno, Champions League should just about do it," says Marty.

"You tell him?" I ask.

"Bollocks! That backstabbing slimy wee bastard can get ta fuck!"

"You know what he's like; you don't want to upset him."

"So what?" Saunders snaps. "When was the last time he gave us anythin' by the way?"

I shrug.

"Exactly. That wee bastard would rape his granny to get on. In fact he probably has; that's a requirement for writing for the *Nazi News*."

"You mean the *Mail*?" Marty adds sardonically.

"Same thing."

"What you on about? The *Mail*'s a fackin' great paper!" chips in Cass.

Good on you, Cass, my son.

"Aye, for wiping your arse," comes Saunders's caustic reply. "You no' hear what we're sayin' aboot this mornin's? Diana, for God's sake! She died ower twenty year ago. Can they no' just lerrit it go?"

"God rest her soul," says Cassidy without a flicker of irony. He really does love the royal family, that fucker.

I don't mind them meself. They bring tourists to the country, which is good for the economy, I suppose, so they have their uses. If you listen to Saunders, they should all be sent to the guillotine and beheaded, French-revolution-style, and the country should become a republic rather than a constitutional monarchy. I mean, what does he want, a police state? Because that's what'll happen should we move away from a constitutional monarchy.

Talking of the police, what do they want? There are two coppers at the top of the office: one older bloke and a younger lass; why is this always the case? Why not two the same age or same sex? They're talking to the editor's PA, who only happens to be his daughter, Sophie. It's not what you know; it's whom you know, at the nepotism *Post*. She's fucking useless, she is. She would struggle to stack a supermarket shelf.

I bleached the kitchen sink and some of the tea-stained cups in the office a few months ago. I know. I'm not always a bastard. Sophie walked in just as I finished and said, "Ooh, they're sparkling! How did you get them so clean?"

"Just a bit of elbow grease," I replied.

"Ooh, where did you get that from?"

I nearly pissed myself.

"Eh, Sainsbury's," I spluttered. "There was a special offer on, two for one." And I walked out before I gave the game away. As I was leaving, I heard her saying she must buy some. She gives dumb blondes a bad name, that girl. I'd still shag it, though.

"Woof! Woof!"

Jesus! I nearly shat myself there. The features editor, Willie Hibbert, has made his usual ostentatious entrance into the office. Father of three, my arse! It's got to be a con. He's never fathered three kids because he's got to be fucking queer. People don't talk like that unless they're shirt-lifters. And he gets on very well with the other office homo, Blackley. Yeah, no doubt about it. Bent as nine-bob note. He sits behind the sports desk. A loud annoying fucker, he is. He's on the phone; well, he's pretending to be. For fuck's sake! That raucous laugh gets right on my tits! I think he only does it to get everyone's attention. "Look at me! Look at me! Everyone, look at me!" He's worse than Lucy Bird. Where is the office princess today by the way? Pulled a sickie, no doubt; she's always pulling a sickie.

The police are coming this way. No one has noticed. Hang on, Saunders has; he doesn't look comfortable with it, either. He looks guilty of something.

"Raffers, looks like the police have found out about your kiddie porn," Saunders shouts out, taking me by surprise.

The fucking shitbag.

"You're still pissed off I haven't given it back. I can tell," I reply, volleying back his first serve. Fucking hell, that was a good return. Don't know where that came from, but I've got him. He stutters. And here's plod now. Quick, serve an ace, son; serve an ace.

"Scott, looks like they've finally caught up with your past of sexual deviancy," I say, just loud enough for the police officers to hear on their way to Harvey's office. I nod in their direction. Both coppers look suspiciously at me and then at Scott, who has gone red with embarrassment. Even Cass and Marty are laughing at his discomfort with the situation. Oh, sweet baby Jesus,

I love you. That was a World Cup–winning moment, an Ian Porterfield FA Cup–winning moment. In fact I think the last time I felt this good was when John Byrne scored the winner for Sunderland in the 1992 FA Cup semi-final against Norwich.

Chapter 5

"I've got a little present for you," says Frank, ruffling the unkempt, dirty-blond hair on the small boy.

"Ooo," gushes the lad's mother as her eyes investigate a spacious lounge area. "What do you say to that, Thomas?" The child looks up at his mother and at the strange man, whom they barely met a few days earlier and who had given him ten pence. Then the boy puts his head down and squeaks a barely audible "Thank you."

"Come on," instructs Frank enthusiastically as he holds out a hand for the boy to take. "Follow me, and I'll show you a surprise."

The boy is reluctant to go at first, but his mum ushers him on by opening her eyes wider and nodding her head forward.

"Mary, there's some beer in the fridge, or cider, if you prefer. Help yourself."

"OK."

Nice flat, Mary thinks to herself, wandering in to inspect a spotlessly clean kitchen. She could imagine herself as the lady of this generous residence. *He seems to like children, too,* she reflects, *which is a bonus. Most blokes run a mile when they discover you have a kid. But this one is making a fuss of mine. This could be the new start we're—I'm—looking for.*

The boy is unsure as he enters the man's bedroom.

"Come on, hurry up," orders Frank, more irritably than before. "Right, take off your top and try this on. Here, let me help." Frank assists Thomas to pull the T-shirt over his head and replaces it with a Sunderland Association Football Club replica jersey.

"Here, let me tuck it in. You'll be just like Sunderland's whiz-kid striker, Ally McCoist."

The older man pulls down the trousers of the child and is about to pull them back up when he pauses to look at the boy's genital area.

"What are you doing in there? What's taking all this time?"

"Just coming," splutters Frank in answer to Mary's inquisition. "Just our little secret, eh, Tom? Just our little secret, son. Come on, we'll show Mum your new shirt. And what about watching *Star Wars* on the video, eh? Would you like that?"

The boy nods as he is led back into the lounge area, where he sees his mother is standing looking out of a large window that overlooks a children's play area.

"Well?"

"Sunderland! Do you not think the kid has enough problems without burdening him with more?"

Chapter 6

Afternoon conference, and I can't wait. They're generally better entertainment than *Live at the Apollo*, an evening throwing darts at dwarfs, or a Gordon Buchanan presser. Harvey's like some drugged-up version of Michael McIntyre on speed or a Basil Fawlty character who has injected a sherbet-based chilli-pepper dip into his veins, especially when the news team come up with a shit story.

Those news reporters wouldn't know a story if it walked up and poked them in the arse with a sharp pencil and said, "Hey, I'm a news story."

They'd probably reply, "How's that?"

"Well, it's not every day a pencil pokes you in the arse of its own accord and speaks to you."

That chicken-nugget line provides evidence of that. A couple of weeks back, one gullible news reporter wrote about an alleged feud between two warring neighbours. In the copy, he quoted one of them as saying, "My next-door neighbour's bush has overgrown, and her back passage is riddled with fungus." He also wrote about a "huge erection in the back garden, which is an unsightly mess." Only it turns out to be a wind up, set up by our rival newspaper to make the gullible twat look like an idiot. They succeeded.

He was also taken in by an alleged female reader who sent in a picture of her kissing a hummingbird. Again our evening-newspaper counterparts revealed that the bird had paid a visit to a taxidermist and was in fact stuffed; the following day we went to press with the story. Another trainee accepted a reader's double-entendre birthday dedication. It read, "To sixty-nine-year-old Miss Connie Lingus, who will celebrate her birthday feasting on my meat and two veg this Sunday. I'm looking forward to when she comes. Ivor Biggin."

Unbelievable.

Fair enough, it's easy to be duped, but that's what happens when you don't go out and get a story. They're just happy sitting on their bone-idle arses in the newsroom and rewriting council and NHS press releases. Read Bill Kovach and Tom Rosenstiel's book, *The Elements of Journalism*, which is supposed to be the journo's bible, if you like. They reckon there are ten fundamentals journalists have to follow for them to fulfil their duty.

1. Journalism's first obligation is to the truth.
2. Its first loyalty is to the citizens.
3. Its essence is the discipline of verification.
4. Its practitioners must maintain an independence from those they cover.
5. It must serve as an independent monitor of power.
6. It must provide a forum for public criticism and compromise.
7. It must strive to make the significant interesting and relevant.
8. It must keep the news comprehensive and proportional.
9. Its practitioners must be allowed to exercise their personal conscience.
10. It's the rights and responsibilities of citizens.

You could follow that paradigm. Me? I prefer to follow the code set by Kelvin McKenzie. I was brought up reading the *Sun*. It was always lying around our house. It didn't seem to matter what bloke my mother was seeing at the time; it always seemed to be the choice of reading material. And as a precocious youngster, I was curious to know about sex. It was probably fuelled by the noises emerging from my mother's bedroom. On several occasions, I crept in, stood at the door, and just watched. She looked in pain most of the time. I couldn't understand it.

I used to hide in her wardrobe or in the washing basket when someone new came around. She was beautiful, my mother. She looked just like

Samantha Fox. I couldn't believe it when I first turned to page 3. I asked my mam what she was doing in the newspaper, and I swear, I couldn't hear in my left ear for a week after that. But it goes without saying that Sam Fox and Debbie Ashby were my favourites. I love big busty blondes.

You couldn't beat the current bun for stories. If you can produce TV shows where women play darts, topless, you've got to have something going for you, haven't you? Then there would be dwarfs bouncing on trampolines and reading the news and stock-exchange reports presented by some bit of totty who would strip naked as she read out the share prices. Genius! The man was way ahead of his time. It's a pity he's not involved in the newspaper industry now.

McKenzie tore up Kovach and Rosenstiel's so-called holy book and re-wrote a new model.

Impartiality, objectivity, political correctness, and fact were replaced in the journo's constitution by personal bias, dishonesty, prejudice and conjecture. Much more flexible, don't you think? The truth may be out there, but, hey, in most cases, it's just an unnecessary obstacle that gets in the way of a good story.

Like the great man said, "When I published those stories, they were not lies. They were great stories that later turned out to be untrue—and that is different. What am I supposed to feel ashamed about?"

Well, you could say "Hillsborough," Kelvin. Your paper was a bit naughty, saying Scousers had robbed from the dead, sexually assaulted them, or, in some cases, pissed on them. But because it's Scousers, we'll let you off.

Boris Johnson certainly got that one right; no one quite does sentiment like Scousers. That was proved following a clamour for Kenny Dalglish's return to Anfield a few years back. I mean, he had done fuck all in the management game since he was at Celtic, about fifteen years, wasn't it? And that role was more as a director than a manager. It was John Barnes who was boss.

I loved that current bun headline, "Super Caley Go Ballistic Celtic Are Atrocious," after the Hoops were dumped out of the cup. Genius! I fucking hate Scousers, me, nearly as much as Geordies. Don't think Sunderland have won at Anfield since 1983 when Gary Rowell netted a penalty in front of the Kop.

"We all live in a Gary Rowell world, a Gary Rowell world, a Gary Rowell world. We all live in a Gary Rowell world, a Gary Rowell world, a Gary Rowell world."

Aye, and that was a proper Liverpool team back then with eleven greats, not like now. And what about the fucking production line of high-profile Scousevile players that seem to end up at Skunk United? Keegan, McDermott, Rush, Barnes, Venison, Beardsley, and Michael Owen? They should be twinned. Scouse Town twinned with Scum City. Still, Kenny Dalglish and Graeme Souness did a canny job of undoing all the good work done at Sid James' Park by King Kev and Sir Bobby Robson. Great term, that. Wish I had coined it. Think it was Will Scott at the *Echo*. He was a bit like that Mike Jones at the *Herald*: loner and also a bit of a wanker—not a bad writer, though.

Then there was Sugar Puffs. Is nothing sacred? I used to love Sugar Puffs until Keegan started promoting them! What's to like about Scousers? Humour? OK, I hold my hands up. Tarby, Ken Dodd, Tom O'Connor, and that John Bishop, they're good but still not as funny as our Kelvin, a comic genius.

McKenzie's newspaper must have been in court for libel, slander, and defamation of character more times than your regular hooker hikes her knickers up and down in a lifetime—and only because he tried to inject a bit of humour into the news.

A million quid went to Elton John. Fair enough, he didn't have underage sex with rent boys. And the story about Elton removing the larynxes of his guard dogs to stop them barking so that he could sleep—absolute genius! You couldn't make it up. Well, you could, and he did! Top of the pops!

Harvey's a bit MKenzian at times. Fair enough, he doesn't like the old quirky chicken-nugget stories or Freddie Star–ate-my-hamster stuff. But he's a right hard bastard. He's fucking great when he's on your side, although a right cunt when he's not. I've been lucky so far. No real bollockings in the time I've been here. He seems to like me, or rather tolerate me, in the same way you tolerate a better-looking mate. You don't really like him, but you'll put up with him because you know it might lead you to a shag somewhere along the line, when you're out on the razzle and he's tapping up a lass who has a mate. Harvey makes the final decision on the promotion, so I'll have to play this one a bit cute. He still doesn't know I'm a Mackem. I can't let that one out the bag; otherwise, I'll never get the post.

Just as well I was born in Scum City and have a Geordie accent. Saunders's got no chance. Fair enough, he writes a decent line and can do all that flowery feature stuff, but I'm the newshound. I'm the one who gets all the exclusives. Well, OK, he's had a few. But just you watch, Harvey will be calling me Scoop soon and not That Swaddler. I'm the best man for the job, you soup-taking cunt! And anyway he's too much of an arse-licker, and Harvey hates that. I just need to make sure I'm on top of my game. A few defence-splitting passes here, a bit of wing-wizard trickery there, and a couple of off-the-ball incidents while the ref isn't looking should seal the deal.

"Alright, alright! Pipe down, children! Pipe down!" shouts Harvey as he returns to his office and takes a seat behind his desk. "Colin, shut that door and keep the bloody draft out."

Cartwright, Blackley, Brownlie, and Hibbert are all present and correct. They look petrified, soft twats. And then there's the lovely Joanne Nicholson, another, like Lucy, with a self-inflated ego, full of her own self-importance. I'm fucking sure Saunders has been there. He denies it, but I'm positive he snaked her at last year's Christmas party. He always denies it. But I know otherwise.

"Right," says Harvey. "News, what you got? And any mention of chicken nuggets, and I'll fucking throw you out of that window faster than you can say, 'Old McDonald has a farm. Ee, I, ee, I, oh.'"

"Residents are still up in arms about those travellers living on the Town Moor," says John Hardwick, almost with a sign of resignation.

"OK, Pikey problems. Anything else?"

"A middle-aged woman has been arrested and refused bail for kidnapping and sexually assaulting a Currys engineer," adds Sarah Brownlie, the office lezza. Not that it's been confirmed, but she did knock me back once. As far as I know, she's never had a bloke, which is hardly surprising, considering she looks like one. She makes Hattie Jacques look positively feminine. Just as well I was pissed. I denied all knowledge the next day when she threatened to tell Harvey I'd sexually assaulted her. I couldn't remember grabbing her tits and feeling her arse. It's just not like me. Anyway I called her bluff, and she did fuck all about it. Suppose she realised no one would believe that a handsome fucker like me would try it on with someone who has a face like a bag of spanners. Saying that, she's a good news journalist.

"Really? Now that's a news story," says Harvey, rubbing his hands together enthusiastically. "You taking note, Hardwick, Blackley?"

They both look blankly at each other.

"Sarah will go far, and one of these days, I can see her sitting here in my seat. So what's the story?"

"The woman called her local electrical store. The engineer went out to check her washing machine in this case. She knocked him out with a big rubber dildo, tied him up, and performed a sex act on him."

"Brilliant!" Harvey laughs. "Headline could be 'Engineer's Gasket Blown!' Or 'Engineer Gets Knickers in a Spin!'"

"It's not the first time she's been in trouble for unlawful sex," Brownlie interrupts. "I did a bit of background research, and she has a history of that sort of thing."

"Such as?" Harvey inquires.

"Five years ago her fourteen-year-old daughter walked in and caught her mother having sex with her fifteen-year-old boyfriend," reveals Brownlie. "The daughter called the police. But when it went to court, it was thrown out because the boy wouldn't testify against her."

"Why wouldn't they believe…" Harvey pauses for a moment. "Nah, forget it. Doesn't really matter. Well done, Sarah. That's a proper story."

"Anything else? Features?"

"Well, em, a series of miracle aids and foodstuffs that are good for your health," Hardwick answers somewhat tentatively.

"Magic mushrooms?"

"Em, no, underwear that prevents high blood pressure, marmalade that eases lumbago, and leek jam that cures hiccups."

"This a wind up?"

"No! Honest," stutters Hardwick.

Hardwick has done well to climb to the dizzy heights of *Northern Post* news editor, considering he was an unremarkable news reporter. But by chance, rather than skill, he's risen through his hometown newspaper's ranks to chief reporter and finally news editor.

Harvey rubbishes most of Hardwick's own concepts, because the boss man doesn't like the novelty, quirky news stories. But to be fair to him, Hardwick is right; for some reason, the public love those chicken-nugget stories—potatoes looking like Santa and, on one occasion, a coal fire in which you could make out the face of Noddy Holder.

"Evidence from a new scientific study says that those things can ease any one of those health problems," Hardwick continues.

"I doubt it," adds Harvey sceptically.

"But you know that nothing gets the public more excited than having new cures for their health problems, and it—"

"Gets people talking and buying the paper," says Harvey, finishing his subordinate's sentence. "There have been times when I've thought, why did I employ you? Especially after the stunt you pulled this morning. Chicken nuggets indeed!"

"But it got record hits on the website for a first-day story," Hardwick responds but is immediately cut short by Harvey, who puts his hand up to prevent him from adding anything else.

"And then you come up with a little gem like this one," Harvey says as he gets out of his chair, walks over to Hardwick, and plants a kiss on Hardwick's forehead. Hardwick blushes.

"That'll keep Tex happy for another week," says Harvey.

"Tex?" Hardwick questions.

"The MD! Wanted to fire you before I went away! Maybe, just maybe, he won't do it this week, eh?"

"Fire, fire me, but why?"

"Because most of the time, you're about as useful as a one-legged chocolate camel in a sun-baked desert! Right. Oot," commands Harvey. "The lot of you! Apart from the wonderful world of sport. I want a word with you."

Harvey waits for the news and features people to leave his office. He walks over and shuts the door behind them. His face shows a look of concern. I look around, and Saunders and Marty follow our editor's movements. I catch Cassidy's eye. We both pull an I-don't-know look while Cassidy also shrugs.

"There's been an incident," says Harvey, with an almost-exhausted sigh. He says nothing for a few moments before announcing, "Lucy Bird has been raped."

You could hear a pin drop. We all look at each other as Harvey walks towards his office window and looks out over the car park.

"The police, as you probably saw yesterday, were in my office for over two hours."

"Where? When? How?" Saunders splutters earnestly, breaking the silence.

"Apparently it was at a house party she arranged a week or so ago. She was drugged, or rather her drink was spiked with...She passed out and... well...the short and narrow of it...She was raped."

Saunders is beside himself; he looks genuinely devastated. I mean, we are all shocked. Not knowing what to do, Cassidy just sits there looking at the floor while I hear Marty mutter under his breath, "I'll kill the bastard."

"Were any of you at the party?"

We all look around at each other.

"Not me," says Cassidy. "I was at home with my old lady. I never get invited to these things."

"I was back in Halifax, seeing friends and family," Marty chips in.

"Me, neither. I was in London. I travelled down on the Friday night for Boro's game at Millwall," I offer as my alibi.

"Scott?" Harvey questions.

"No, no, I didn't make it," says Saunders, who was clearly agitated. "I was invited, but I didn't make it."

"Where were you?" asks Harvey.

"At home...I meant to go. I bought the fancy dress and everything, but..." he stutters anxiously as if he is hiding something.

"Anything to do with the marks on your face?"

Saunders nods solemnly.

"So why didn't you report it?"

"I just thought…what's the point? They'd never find out who did it. And the…incident…was a bit embarrassing."

"In what way?"

"I dinnae wanna discuss it, if you don't mind."

"Well, you'll have to tell someone sooner or later because the police'll be interviewing everyone. Aren't you and Lucy close? Have you not spoken?"

"No, but now I know why," he replies, finding it hard to look at anyone. His eyes are welling up. "I tried to call, text, and e-mail, but she hasn't replied. I thought she must have been ill or on holiday or something. I didn't realise it was this…"

We were all staring at him.

"It was nae me, if that's what you're thinking!"

"Scotty, calm down, son. Calm down," says Harvey reassuringly. "No one is suggesting anything. I've got to talk to everyone in the office about it. I just got you in first, because…well…you lot—aside from Cass, that is—are close to her, from what I've been led to believe. I mean, you go out and socialise after work. I'll talk to everyone when I get the chance…in the next day or so, as will the police. I'm just letting you know. We'll just play everything by ear, I suppose. The police will be contacting each and every one of you in the next few days, I expect. But if anyone knows anything or wants a word alone to discuss anything, let me know. Just try and go about your usual daily business, and try and carry on as normal. That's all…You can go."

We all get up and leave Harvey's office, with the exception of Saunders, who stays behind.

Fifteen minutes pass before Saunders emerges from Harvey's office and returns to his desk in silence. The cocky fucker is usually full of himself, but not now. We're all trying to concentrate on what we're doing, but I catch Marty and Cass both sneaking glances at Saunders as he tidies up his desk.

"Right, lads, I'll see you later," says Saunders sombrely a few moments later as he puts on his coat. "Raffers, can you look after the three clubs today? I've just e-mailed you some quotes for a Newcastle line. You said you've got some Sunderland stuff left over. And you could give Boro a call for an injury round up. That should take care of things. Cheerio for now."

He then slips his laptop bag on his shoulder; it must be borrowed, as his is missing. He trudges slowly and thoughtfully down the office and out of the door.

"You think he did it?" Cass whispers when Saunders is out of ear.

"How could he? Said he wasn't there," says Marty firmly.

"But he looked very uncomfortable in there," I add.

"And so was I," snaps Marty. "Someone I know very well has been raped!"

"I know, but—" I try to say before Marty cuts in.

"You know what?" Marty's terse reply is fired back.

"Eh, nothing, just saying."

"Well, don't. This is fucking serious. It's not fucking, fucking..." he stutters. "A soap opera. It's not *EastEnders* or *Coronation Street*. This is real."

Marty turns back to his screen while Cass and I look sheepishly at each other. I'm not too sure about Marty; he's a right moody bastard these days, looks as if he's going to explode at any minute.

To take my mind off the incident, I check my e-mail in silence. Right, what have we got here? Nothing in my inbox. What about my junk mail? Viagra. Not needed, as I can get a hard-on. Insurance? Nope, sorted on that front. Apartment? Quite happy where I am. Matchmaker? No, still shagging Cass's missus. Well, someone has to, 'cause he isn't. Must get around there today. My balls need massaging, and I need a trim as well.

"NanceeGosmanwuube@hotmail.com wants you to join the group CamWhores." Well, not at work; maybe at home later.

Hello, what's this? "From the desk of Dr. Patrick Uzo, director of foreign operation unit, Central Bank of Nigeria." Jackpot, I love these e-mails. Well, Mr. Uzo, what do you want? Ah, all you need is my full house address, passport number, telephone number, and my bank details, and you'll forward $10 million. I bet you do, my Nigerian fraudster friend. I wonder how many people actually fall for this.

"I'm sure the bastard does this on purpose!" Marty randomly shouts out angrily.

"Who? What?" Cass inquires.

"This fucker from the Micklemoor Martial Arts Club!"

"What?"

"Send me fucking BNP propaganda."

"Eh?"

"You taking the piss?" I join in.

"Why would I take the piss on something as serious as this? What's the matter with you today? Living in some parallel universe where rape, murder, and race-related crime are only a product of our TV screens?"

The fucking wanker! There was no need for that. I was only trying to sound sympathetic. The Paki bastard!

"I've only been included on a BNP mailing list. I bet the bastard is doing it on purpose."

"Really?" Cass asks.

"Yeah, bound to be."

"So who is it?"

"Walter Adams. He supplies copy from his martial arts club, which I don't mind putting in the paper because it's about the kids, right?"

"So how do you get that he's targeting you?"

"Well, the club asked me to come down and present a trophy at its awards ceremony. You could tell he was uncomfortable with me being there. Couldn't look me in the eye. He obviously didn't know I was Asian when he invited me. I think they assumed they were getting a good white boy when he saw my Martin byline in the paper. Had my surname been Patel, Khan, or Kapoor, I don't think they would have asked me somehow. The look on his face said as much. I didn't stop long. The place was dripping with Union Jacks, England, and St George flags and bunting and blokes dressed in Fred Perry with their heads shaved. And as Paul Weller once said, there was a distinct 'smell of too many right-wing meetings.' I presented the trophy and left with our photographer at the first chance. This is the second e-mail I've had since. And it looks as if they've put me on their mailing list to wind me up."

"So what's it about?"

"About some fuckin' rally in Micklemoor on Saturday."

"What's it for?"

"Against the council's decision to allocate a new building to asylum seekers, the racist bastards."

I smile and wink at Cass, who returns my sentiments, while Marty continues to mutter under his breath about how the nation lacks basic grammar and how the country's English teachers should be "fucking strung up and whipped to within an inch of their lives" for "failing to get children a basic grasp on a sentence." I mean, for fuck's sake, Marty, lighten up, will you? It's not Nazi Germany!

Brilliant. Here're Hardwick and Blackley. They've just left Harvey's office, after a bollocking, most likely. Think I need to lighten the mood. All this talk of rape and racism is making me a little happier. I pick up the phone and pretend someone is on the other line.

"Lads!" I shout at Hardwick and Blackley, who both stop and look at me. I talk into the phone as if there's someone on the other end. "What's that you say? Your cat's stuck up a tree? Hang on; I'll put you straight through to news. Lads, hold the front page! There's a cat stuck up a tree!"

"Piss off!" Blackley returns venomously, as we giggle on sport.

"Better still, look," says Cass, pulling out a chocolate biscuit from a packet of Walt Disney cartoon characters. "It's a nice little bow-wow. Now couldn't you just eat the blooming thing?"

"Don't, Cass!" I shout as he promptly bites into the biscuit-shaped Pluto. "They need a pic! Shit, too late! Sorry, lads, you'll have to go with that vandalised Wendy House story at the kiddie's nursery."

"Very funny," says Hardwick. "It's all a big joke to you lot."

"Well, it's better than being a bloody misery like you lot," I say.

"That's because a serious crime has just been committed."

"I wouldn't say a vandalised Wendy House constitutes serious crime now, does it?"

"No, maybe not, but a rape does!"

Bloody hell, I didn't see that coming. Hardwick just stands and glares at us all for a moment. And when he's satisfied that we're not going to come back with any of our usual rapier-like wit, he walks back to his desk. I don't know. You try to lighten the mood, and there's always someone trying to bring it down.

Chapter 7

I'll have to stop appearing on these local radio shows. I initially decided to go on the weekly North-East Sports Show, *Tyne, Tees, Wear, Proud*, because I thought it was a good starting point to boost my profile. Suppose you have to start somewhere, but I don't think I can take any more of the fucking egotist hosting the programme. And it's not like we're inundated with callers. We're lucky if we get one or two callers a show, unless our host blocks them so that he can rabbit on like the gobshite he is.

"Chaps, I'm really enjoying putting the sports world to rights," says our weary Wearside radio-show host, Johnny Elliot, whose droll monotone could send a garden gnome to sleep. He would be more suited to doing voice-overs at the funerals for the families of pet chipmunks. It's about the fifteenth time he's said, "Chaps, I'm really enjoying putting the sports world to rights," in the last five minutes! If he says it again, I swear to God, I'll ram my fist down his throat, pull out his tonsils, wrap them around his throat, and strangle the bastard. He would say he's enjoying it; he's the only fucker talking! As soon as one of us offers a few sentences on a certain subject, he blabs over the top of us. I'm a big Sunderland fan myself, but he should try and maintain some sense of professionalism and give all the North-East clubs a fair proportion of the show. If we do discuss the Geordie scum or the Smoggies, he'll manage to somehow change the subject to when the Black Cats last beat them.

One caller, from Darlington, phoned the show last week talking about Darlo's plight, and our radio maestro missed the whole point of his argument. And he didn't even know they'd been relegated from the Blue Square Bet Premier League. Staggering! I honestly reckon he thought they were still in League Two. And to get off the subject, he remembered that former Sunderland favourites Marco Gabbiadini and Brian Atkinson had both played for Quakers and managed to swing it around to how good they were when they donned the red and white stripes at Roker Park. Unbelievable!

There was one interesting call, however, earlier on this evening. Our radio-show host kept referring to us—Arnie and me, that is—as the show's experts, and someone called in to question what right we had to make that claim. If the Darlington episode was anything to go by, I could see his point. It's just as well that our chat about George Foreman was in private and not on the air. The buffoon was unaware Foreman was actually famous for anything other than his grill. I'm not making this up.

Johnny, usually quite composed and unmoved, to be fair to him, was flapping like a hormonal mother goose trying to protect her young from bird nesters; he was unable to come up with any convincing answers to the upstart's questions.

"So if none of you has played professional football, how can you claim to know the sport?" asked the caller as a follow-up question to a previous inquiry as to whether any of us had been paid as a professional footballer. The call went on for a couple of minutes, and Arnie and I took great delight in seeing the radio man squirm under pressure.

"I mean, when you think about it," the caller went on, "you would never find a butcher's apprentice taking a lead role in a West End stage show like *Swan Lake*, for example. And it would be just as unlikely to learn that a classically trained ballet dancer was running a butcher's shop on Wallsend High Street."

Unable to get a word in edgeways, Elliott was spluttering unpronounceable monosyllables at this point, as the caller continued to talk over the top of Elliott without pausing for breath. To be honest, the caller must have had it all planned and written down, because he was incredibly fluent and articulate.

"I mean, seriously, you wouldn't expect to come across a butcher explaining the intricacies of the Balanchine Method or how to master a *tombé en avant*, would you?"

I hadn't a clue what the fucker was on about, and neither did Johnny Elliot. But on that final word, he cut him off and moved to an ad break. Elliot left the studio as soon as he switched on the jingle to "go to the toilet," but we both knew it was so that he could compose himself. When we went back on air, he made some excuse about losing the caller.

The call momentarily gave me an idea for a new reality TV show. I would call it *The Apprentice Butcher's Ballet* or *The Bacon Butty Ballet*. The idea would be to get your everyday high-street butcher or even a footballer and turn them into ballet dancers. I'd have a panel including celebrity football fans from Newcastle, Sunderland and Middlesbrough. From the Toon, I'd have WorCheryl. I might even forget she's black and white if she agrees to a game of tonsil tennis. From Middlesbrough, I'd probably get Bob Mortimer, and from Sunderland, it would be...eh, let's think. Fuck! Is Steve Cram the only decent celebrity we've got from Sunderland? For fuck's sake, it's either him or Melanie Hill. Aye, well, maybe it'll not work after all.

Could you imagine tuning in to *Match of the Day* or, more appropriately, this week's edition of *Ballet of the Day* on a Saturday night? You'll be settled on the settee, with a chicken tikka masala sitting in your lap, a can of Ace Lager to your right, a naan bread to the left, and a tab in an ashtray by your curry, and you'll wait in anticipation to see what John the butcher, from the Slaughtered Lamb, has to say about the Latvian National Ballet Company's whistle-stop tour of England. And eat your heart out, Alan Hansen; the boy does not disappoint. There's no pussyfooting around here; the bacon boy slices into the postdance punditry and goes straight for the jugular, making Geoff Boycott look like a poor man's Clement Freud.

"So, John," says Gary Lineker, "what did you make of Elza Leimane's performance of the dying swan?"

"Shockingly inept," the sausage maker quickly replies, before waving a hand campily in the air. "And her *pas de bourrée suivi* is more akin to that of an intoxicated bull in a China shop than a prima ballerina. She should be made to sweep up sawdust at the Slaughtered Lamb as a punishment until she perfects Anna Pavlova's ethereal depiction. The piece, originally choreographed by Mikhail Fokine, will have the Russian dance master turning in his grave."

Aye, nice thought, but just wouldn't happen, would it? Nor would you expect to find Leimane on, say, I dunno, *Prime Cut of the Day*, giving viewers expert advice on where to find the best lean cuts on the high street, the best pork scratchings, the best way to cook your turkey giblets, or the only way to enjoy a soft-boiled egg, which is to coat your toasted soldiers with marmite before you plunge them into that soft, gooey, yellow yoke. But I digress; our caller does have a point concerning the paradox. It rarely gets a mention in the field of sports journalism, although I'm sure it is discussed in the changing rooms of most professional football clubs after they've read their morning newspapers.

My fellow sports writers and football scribes are deemed to be experts in their field when, on a whole, they have as much experience of life as a professional footballer as that of John the butcher. But an even bigger paradox probably surrounds the former footballers who have become TV and radio pundits. Footballers and managers dismiss the press as clueless buffoons—and other less-than-savoury words, which wouldn't be suitable for family viewing. Yet the irony of this is that those very same ex-footballers, who once graced some of the finest stadia in the world, all listen to *Sky Sports News*, read copy from my ill-informed colleagues and me, and take our opinion as the gospel according to a football hack—a journalist with no football experience at all.

I met Newcastle midfielder Taylor Ryan outside of work once. Thankfully he didn't seem to recognise me from my picture byline. He was on holiday in Pisa, or rather he was on my flight to Pisa. He might have been going to somewhere in Tuscany, for all I know. Anyway I spoke to him as the bus transferred us from the airport terminal to the hire-car place. I asked him which players Newcastle were intending to bring in after the season ended. He said he "wasn't sure" but added, "I've just read we're after Jermain Daniels," who was the Tottenham striker. I then asked whether United midfielder Joe Marton was going to stay. Again he said he'd "read in the papers they weren't going to offer him a new deal." I questioned jovially, "Do you not talk about things like that in the dressing room?" He admitted they didn't. Staggering!

I've never kicked a football in my life. I couldn't even get a game for Sacred Heart RC Primary School's second XI. Not that they had a second team. But if they did, I still wouldn't have made the team. I was always picked last by the two best players during the school-break and lunchtime kicks around, and then I had to go in goal—the bastards! Yet the wry outcome of this is that former pros believe every word I pen—astonishing! You couldn't make it up. Well, you could, and I do. We all do it if we can't get a decent line.

It's all psychological. If you write it often enough, people will eventually fall into line and believe the hype and clichés you've written. The Tory party has been masters of this for over a century. It doesn't matter whether you're a supporter, an ex-player, the deferential proletariat on the factory floor with no interest in football at all but a desire to get on with his football fanatical boss, or a scheming girl who would fuck a donkey if it meant she could succeed in trapping her intended target into engagement, marriage, babies, and her ultimate goal: making his life one of perpetual misery.

One of my favourite untruths is about the length of time it takes a foreign footballer to settle into the Premier League. If you read my friends in the red tops and broadsheets, they universally agree that it takes a year or a season. Bollocks! If a foreign footballer is good enough, then he'll pick up the pace of the game from the first moment a referee blows his whistle.

One of the greatest urban myths revolves around former French internationals Thierry Henry and Robert Pirès at Arsenal. It has been written and said hundreds, probably thousands, of times that it took a year or more for the pair to settle into the hustle and bustle of the English league's top tier. Readers are quite happy to forget that Henry had always been a winger prior to his move to Highbury and was converted into a striker by his manager, Arsene Wenger. Likewise Pirès spent most of his career as a right-winger or a right midfield player before Wenger swapped him to the left of midfield. If there had been any period of settling in, it would have been becoming acclimatised to their new positions and nothing else. How long did it take for Eric Cantona to settle in? Or David Ginola, Cristiano Ronaldo, Didier Drogba,

Nicolas Anelka, Patrick Vieira, Marc Overmars, Paolo Di Canio, Fabrizio Ravanelli, Juninho, Gianfranco Zola, Gianluca Vialli, Dennis Bergkamp, Jimmy Floyd Hasselbaink, Arjen Robben, JaapStam, Ruud van Nistelrooy, Robin van Persie, Carlos Tevez, and Sergio Aguero? I could go on; the list is endless.

Managers, of course, are quite happy to agree with this line of settling in because it buys them more time in the job if their exotic, new, foreign import is not working out. Another one of my favourites is when a team hasn't played for two weeks because of the weather. Tune into *Match of the Day*, and a sycophantic pundit will say, "Liverpool will be a little rusty for not having played for two weeks." On the other hand, another media expert will say, "Liverpool will be fresher than their opponents for not having played for two weeks." So which one is it? And would they really be rusty? They still train and play football every single day. The statements are paradoxical. But say it often enough, and people will accept it's true, whether it's the average soccer supporter, the ex-football player, or the pundits sitting on the *Match of the Day* sofa or in the *Sky Sports* studio. Yes, your average footballer is an even bigger half-wit than those who pay a fortune at the turnstile. And that is why none of them become football writers. The majority of them are thick as shit and can't write, as my colleague Marty would say, a compound structure of a sentence.

Of course, I'm sure three years as an apprentice in the Slaughtered Lamb might give Leimane a sense of perspective and some expertise on butchery. Likewise John the butcher could take a few ballet lessons before appearing at the Royal Opera House. Then again, they could watch one episode of *Match of the Day* and do a six-month course in journalism, like me and my workmates, and be fully qualified.

My good colleague Scott Saunders eschews this point of view. He would, though; although you think he might want to keep it quiet, he was on the books of Kilmarnock until he was eighteen before being released. You wouldn't want to brag about that, would you, eh? Not being good enough to play in the mediocrity of Scottish football.

I remember an old schoolmate spouting off something similar back in the day at Sacred Heart—Peter Berry, or Bez, as he was called. Best player in the school, he was. Fastest, fittest, strongest, most skilful—he had everything. He could do anything with a ball. Played for England under-fifteen schoolboys and was an apprentice at Newcastle until he suffered a double cruciate injury, similar to the one Michael Owen picked up playing for England in the 2006 World Cup. Tipped to be the next Alan Shearer. Well, that's what happens when you pick me last and put me in goal, you bastard! Call it bad karma or something like that.

Glenn Hoddle was spot on when he said that disabled people were paying for the sins of past lives. Shame he lost the England job because of it. Stitched up by a fellow hack—it was outrageous! The whole country got involved, even the prime minister, Tony Blair. He could have been the best England manager since Sir Alf Ramsey. In fact his win rate as manager is only bettered by Sir Alf. But, no, you can't express such Christian religious philosophy; that would offend the values of other cultures' faiths. If he had been Jewish, Muslim, or Jedi, there would have been no charge of religious discrimination. But because he's a Christian, he should be punished. Saying that, maybe Hoddle had to suffer for past misdemeanours himself. Maybe he ate belly pork on a Friday instead of fish fingers. I do fucking digress at times. Need to try and get a handle on my stream of consciousness and focus; I really do.

But that's what must have happened to Bez. I only wanted to fit in. I only wanted to be his mate. Had he let me knock around with him and his mates, I'm sure he would have been fine.

Still, he wasn't as bad as his mate Graham Hughes. He was a right horrible bastard, always taking the piss, calling me Raggy Raffers and Harry Ramp Rafferty. It wasn't my fault me mam didn't have much money and I had to wear hand-me-downs. She was a single parent, after all. And all of the time, Bez just stood and laughed and never told Hughesy to stop, not once. Well, look who's laughing now boys, eh? I'm the one writing about your beloved game, the one you fought so hard to be a part of. What you doing now, eh? Nowt, I expect—stacking shelves in supermarkets, sweeping roads, and serving burgers. And if you are, then that's bad karma on your wicked lives for making my life a misery.

Well, that was two hours of my life I won't get back. Still, I've got a date with Mrs. Cassidy tonight. That should more than make up for it. Her husband, my boss and friend, has to work late. Thank God for the Johnstone's Paints Trophy. What fool said it was a Mickey Mouse cup? Well, maybe I did, but then I can be as big a hypocrite as the next man. This cartoon cup competition means Cass'll not get away from the office until, oh, nearly midnight. That's plenty of time to fill my boots with rudie Trudi.

Chapter 8

I get to Trudi's shop, Scissor Sister, around seven and am surprised to see she's got a blue rinser under a dryer so late.

"Hiya," squeaks Trudi, with a pitch so high it undoubtedly attracts every stray cat and dog in the neighbourhood to the shop, and beams at me with those big, beautiful pearly whites.

"Come on in. Go in to the kitchen, and put the kettle on while I see to Mrs. Montgomery."

"Hello, Mrs. Montgomery—any relation?" I ask cheekily, as Trudi chuckles.

"No, pet. I think he was a Londoner. I'm from Fawdon," replies the deadpan pensioner.

"No, he's from Sunderland. He made that fantastic double save from Peter Lorimer and Trevor Cherry in the 1973 FA Cup final."

"No, pet, I think we've got our Montgomerys mixed up. The one I was talking about was the commander who led the second battle of El Alamein, in Tunisia, where my husband lost a leg."

"Oh, sorry to hear that, Mrs. Montgomery."

"That's alright, hinny. I just wish they would've taken both his legs and his head—had I known I was going to be a skivvy to him for the remainder of his living days."

"Right."

"To be totally honest, hinny, I never thought he'd come back. I only married him for the pension. But, like a bad penny, he turned up."

Bemused and not knowing whether to laugh or cry, Trudi and I just look at each other and shrug behind her back.

"Is this your boyfriend then?"

"Eee, no, Mrs. Montgomery. I'm a happily married woman."

"And my mother boxed kangaroos in the circus. You must think I was born yesterday."

Trudi beams with embarrassment and continues poking at the old woman's hair with a comb while she tries to remain composed. I clap my hands together at this and mutter, "OK, then, I'll leave you two girls to it, and I'll get myself a coffee."

I go into the back of her salon and switch the kettle on. Boredom sets in quickly, so I rummage around in the cupboards and drawers while I wait for the kettle to boil. Nothing of interest in the cupboards, but, hello, what's this? I find a false bottom in this drawer. Basically it's a removable thin strip of plywood, about an eighth of an inch thick, which is the length of the drawer. I only noticed it because I happened to move a receipt book, which was jammed, and it lifted it up.

What we got here? Passport, chequebook, and some snaps. I take the photos out, and they are pictures of a holiday, by the looks of it. Yep, there's Trudi sitting in the airport lounge with a glass of rosé wine. There're more as she gets off the plane, in the apartment, in evening dress (very sexy), and in the restaurant having a drink. By God, what does she see in that ugly bastard? Hang on, the pics are becoming a little less formal as the evening progresses or, rather, as the fucking lush consumes more rosé or white-wine-spritzer libations. She'd drink a thirty-stone hod carrier under the table, she would. Oh, they're back in the apartment. Her eyes are tired, and her dress is more exposed, showing all of her cleavage. She isn't wearing a bra, so the dress is just covering her nipples. Top of the pops! They're out! Those little puppies are out! She teases the camera, cupping them, squeezing them together, and tweaking those big brown nipples.

Jesus, I'm fucking horny now. I wish she'd get rid of that old wrinkly so that I can fuck her now. Oh, that's it, Trudi love. She's sitting back on the sofa; her tits are completely free now as she lets her dress straps fall by her side. She's pulled her briefs to the side and exposed that lovely neat fanny of hers. It really is a place of heaven on earth. I've never tasted anything as sweet. And aesthetically it's beautiful, all neat and tidy and not like one of those clouts where the labia hang down like a pair of gorilla's arms or a badly packed kebab. On closer inspection, yes, it's waxed—courtesy of her mate Fiona, who runs the beauty side of the business, I expect. Well done, bonnie lass; you've produced a work of art the ancient Greek and Roman gods would be proud of.

Oh my God! There're more! Jesus Christ, there're more! She's only snogging another girl! Trudi, you dirty, dirty cow. I knew you were filthy, but you never let on you liked girls as well. I'll have to bring that up. There are several different pictures with Trudi and this young, slim, wiry, dark brunette. She must be half Trudi's age or younger. She looks like a teenager!

They're kissing, licking, and snorting what looks like cocaine, and bloody hell, I do not want to see that! Cass has taken a photo with him wanking over the girls' breasts. Bloody hell, he looks like a little Buddha! What an image to carry around with me. Urgh, they're sucking him now. Oh well, good while it lasted. I think I'll keep these. No, I'll take the negatives; they might come in useful. I slip them into my jacket pocket and put the drawer back together.

I hear Trudi wishing the old boiler a pleasant evening and locking the door. I quickly slip off my pants, undies, shoes, and socks and sit behind her desk so that I look fully dressed from the waist up, despite being naked from the waist below.

"Now then, lover," she says seductively, "would you like a cut or a blow?" I smile and stand up to reveal my nakedness from the waist. "Oh, a blow it is then, sir. Would you like to come through to the salon?"

She grabs my erection and leads me back into the salon area; she pushes me back into the chair, where only minutes earlier the old lady was getting a different type of blow, and takes my length into her mouth, and within seconds, I've shot my bolt. And despite her obvious delight at first, she is soon disappointed.

"I didn't expect it to end so soon."

"Neither did I, but…it was so good, I couldn't hold back any longer," I selfishly lie.

"OK, you might as well go in that case."

"Eh? Don't be like that."

"Like what?"

"Like that."

"Like you don't care and just use me for a quick jump, you mean?"

"I do care. Come on, that's nonsense."

"Well, that's what it feels like. If I wanted Quick Draw McGraw for sex, I'd just stick to fucking my husband," she snapped acerbically and walked away towards the office area, where I'd recently stolen her holiday negatives. The cheeky fucking cow, I'll, I'll…for fuck's sake, I'll smooth things over. I don't want to spoil a good thing, after all.

"Come here," I say sympathetically, but she just ignores me and continues walking. I catch up with her and put my arms around her waist from behind. "Hey, come on. There's plenty more time; we've got all evening. Tell you what; I was supposed to be meeting up with my mother later. I'll call and cancel, and when we get finished up here," I say as I rub my crotch into her firm behind, "we can go out for dinner. How does that sound?"

She turns to face me, puts her arms around my neck, and looks deep into my eyes.

"You love me?"

Fuck, I wasn't expecting that.

"Of course I do."

"Well, then. You can fuck me over this desk and take me out for something to eat, and then we'll go for a drink."

"Sounds perfect."

"Your mum. I think I'd like to meet your mum."

"No, you wouldn't; she's a Freudian nightmare."

"Interesting."

"Not really, just a schizophrenic." Trudi doesn't hear me say that.

"Well, I'll have to meet her at some point if we're going to move in together."

"So you're not emigrating then?"

"That old fool can please himself. I'm stopping here. I've just started to make the business a success. The foreigners on our street don't bother me the way they do him, and anyway I've got you now."

I think, *Aye, you'll do for now, but I'm only in my midthirties, for fuck's sake, and you're fifty-two. You might be fit now. But in ten years' time, I'll still be a young man, and you'll be, well, it doesn't bear thinking about.*

She manages to get me hard in no time, and I bang her over the desk, on the desk, and in the swivel chair, while she sits astride me, before splashing all over those lovely big tits of hers.

Trudi calls a taxi, and we end up in Sabatini, on the Quayside. I'm halfway through my prawn cocktail when I get a call from my mother.

"Sorry, Trudi, do you mind if I take this?" She shakes her head as an affirmative, because she can't speak with a mouth full of calamari. I leave the table and head out towards the entrance.

"Hi, Mum."

"Where are you? Why haven't you returned my calls? You were shupposed to pick me up from the airport and take your old mum out tonight. Where are you?" She has clearly had a drink and, by the sounds of it, is still in a bar.

"Mum, I texted you saying I couldn't make it."

"Text! Text! You know I can't text."

"Yes, you can; you've been texting me from Ireland."

"No, I haven't; I don't know how to do it."

"Of course...doesn't matter. What do you want anyway?"

"I've losht my pursh and keysh, and—and—and I don't have any money. You'll have to pick me up."

I'm not sure if she's pissed or if I'm talking to a Dutch drag queen.

"But, Mam, I'm already out."

"Out! Out! Already out! How's that? You shouldn't be making arrangmens when you shshould be with your own mum. Where are you…and who are you with?"

"Does it matter?"

"Coursh it matters. Ish it a lady friend? Do you have a lady friend, my little prince? Do you love someone other than your ol' mum, schweetheart?" Not this again.

"Mum, I mean, Mam, where are you?"

"I'd love a gin and tonic," I hear her say to someone in the background. "I'm in the…where am I, darling?" She's obviously talking to some bloke in the background.

"Dog and Parrot," says the man's voice.

"Ther'sh some comedy on sssoon," she slurs. "Why don't you come down? Idle be a laugh." And she bursts out laughing. "Gerritschweetheart… idle be a laugh. Come down 'n have a bit craic wiv your ol' mum. Pretdy please?"

"OK, OK, I'll be down in half an hour."

She's out of control. Not that she's ever been in control in her entire life. Still, she's getting worse with age. And this whole Irish obsession is doing my head in. She's never had an Irish accent, yet every time she comes back from Dublin, Cork, or Belfast even, she lays it on thicker than an Irish navvy drinking Guinness on St Patrick's Day. I tell Trudi the bad news, but she's elated and wants to meet her.

"I don't think that's a good idea," I tell her, but then Trudi starts to sulk. "OK, OK, you can come along."

This is going to be fucking embarrassing. I love my mum, but she always tends to take centre stage and mortify me, whether we're with people we know or strangers. God knows what she'll make of Trudi, given Trudi's old enough to be my mum. I finish my calzone while Trudi polishes off the last of her fish dish. We miss dessert, and I nick the last drop of Trudi's wine, ask for the bill, and take a quick, uneventful taxi up to the Dog and Parrot.

I can't see my mum anywhere and have a horrible feeling she might be upstairs at the open-mic spot. We make our way up the narrow staircase, and sure enough, there she is, Jesus fucking Christ, on the stage.

"And so he came in last night and asked if I wanted some cunnilingus," she says, without the slur that had been evident on the phone earlier. "I said, 'You what? You know I don't like pasta.'" The room laughs enthusiastically. She allows the laughing to subside slightly before she delivers, "But you can go down on me if you like." The room erupts to even harder laughter. There must be about twenty-five to thirty people. A splattering of students, it looks like, but they all seem to be enjoying it.

"That's not your mum, is it?" Trudi asked.

"'Fraid so."

"That was funny. You never said she could do stand-up."

"That's not stand-up. That's what's called showing off and showing me up."

I notice a scruffy, unshaven overweight guy, about thirtyish, at the end of the bar; he talks with a younger barman, probably another student. He says, "She's not bad, and she's fit for an old bird. We should get her back."

Fuck, I hope not. There's no Bud, so I order a pint of lager and a glass of rosé for Trudi. And I can hear that faux Irish accent. "Thank you, boys and girls, you've been great craic. And if you're this nice again, I might even show you it." This gets even bigger laughs, whoops, and whistles than her last joke.

"I'll have to go now; my little boy has just come in. He's a journalist, you know. So your other acts better be good, or he'll be writing bad things about you in his newspaper."

A tall, silver-haired bloke, who must be the compere, enters the stage and says, "Let's give a big Geordie appreciation to Kitty O'Shea! Kitty O'Shea, ladies and gentlemen!"

Kitty O'Shea, you bugger. Well, she hardly had a reputation to be proud of, so probably quite fitting, I suppose—although I think it'll be lost on her that Kitty was English born, or maybe that's her being ironic. I just don't know where she's concerned. She blows kisses to the audience as if she's some star from Hollywood's golden age and wriggles over to me at the bar to more applause and wolf whistles.

"Here's my little boy." She wraps her arms around me and gives me a big hug, ruffles my hair, and kisses me as if I'm still a little boy.

"Not like you to embarrass me, is it, Mam?"

"Oh, be away wityer."

"And what's with the Irish accent?"

She waves her hand in the air nonchalantly and says, "Oh, stop whining. You see the show?"

"Saw the last joke."

"They loved me. What'd you think?"

"You were great, Mam."

"I was, wasn't I? I might just come back and do it again. Think I may have found my vocation after all."

"I thought drinking and getting married was."

"What did you say there?"

"I said, I can just see you on at the Apollo."

"That's enough sarcasm now…You going to buy your mammy a drink?"

"Suppose so," I say and order a gin and tonic.

"Make it a double."

"You sounded sozzled earlier."

"Did I? I feel fine." Mum clocks Trudi. "Is this the friend you were out with?"

"Hi, Mrs. O'Shea," says Trudi, edging into view. "I'm Trudi; nice to meet you."

"Are you, now? And what are you doing with my wee boy? There no men your own age about?"

"Mam!"

"Oh, I'm only messing. What's a matter wit' you, lost your sense of humour? Nice to meet you, too, Trudi. Call me Mary. So tell me, where have you been?"

"Just had dinner at Sabatini, on the Quayside."

"Nice?"

"Fantastic. The fish is to die for."

"I love your hair," my mother says, looking Trudi up and down. "I'd love to have mine like that."

"Why don't you pop into my salon tomorrow, and I'll do it for you?"

"You have your own salon?"

Trudi nods.

"I will. Now, where is it?"

Trudi goes into her bag and pulls out a business card and hands it over.

"In Jesmond, very posh. If you don't mind me saying, you look fantastic for your age."

"Eh, thanks."

"Mam, that's enough."

"Oh shut up, will yer. I was paying Trudi a compliment. I wasn't being a bitch. So what age are you?"

"Mam!"

"Shut it, you."

"Fifty-two."

"You don't look a day over forty, love. A lot better than I do, and I'm two years younger."

"But—"

"Are these real?" And with that, my mother starts feeling Trudi's breasts. "My God, they are! They're gorgeous. Feel mine." And with that, she grabs Trudi's hands and places them on her own. "Not bad, eh?"

"I bet you wouldn't give her a kiss?" a fat bloke shouts over from the end of the bar; he was obviously getting off on witnessing all the fondling.

"Sure I would, but I couldn't take the risk of you coming in your pants. But for your information, I'll be giving them a good ol' squeeze later on when we're alone."

The bloke isn't expecting that response and doesn't know where to put himself, while Trudi gives an embarrassing giggle. "But at least it'll give you some wanking material for the next month, which I'm guessing you'll need… being a fat, ugly bastard an' all."

The man stands up, and I now see that he must be the bouncer, doorman, or whatever bouncers have been rebranded these days—probably gentleman of the door, who sees you to your carriage. Or the assistant landlord, in the same way the referee's assistant has replaced the linesman. He looks furious.

"Slag!" Oh fuck, it's going to kick off! She could start a fight in an empty cupboard, my mother.

"Is that the best you can do, you limp-dicked fucker? You know, you could learn a ting from your parents' mistakes, wee man, and use contraception!"

Obviously she's been learning how to deal with hecklers as well. The bouncer is up now and looking down over my mother, who is remarkably calm in the circumstances. She has not moved from her seat. She stares back at him; expressionless, she's coolness personified.

"Right, sorry about that," I intervene. "We're just leaving."

"You fuck off, shorty."

"Don't you be talking to my boy like that, you victim of incest; otherwise, I'll kick you in the fanny."

I get between the pair.

"Get her outside," I say to Trudi, who looks horrified as the incident looks like turning into a full-blown fracas.

"We're not going anywhere," says my mother calmly. By this time, a crowd has gathered around us.

"I think it would be best if you left before someone gets hurt," the bouncer growls, trying to intimidate us.

"Get hurt. Aw, now would you look at him. A face only a mother could love. It's OK. I'll not hurt you."

The next few moments are a bit of a blur, but my mother manages to edge me out the way, down her gin and tonic in one, pick up what is left of my pint, and empty its contents over him before smashing the glass on his head. He staggers back a step and then launches forward, throws out an arm, and grabs her by the throat. She retaliates by grabbing him between the legs and squeezing—I'm guessing really hard, judging by his high-pitched squeals.

"There's nothing there," my mum declares to the room as he loosens his grip on her throat to move his hands on top of where my mother is squeezing his manhood, or lack of it, according to my mum. She continues to mangle the last vestiges of life out of them. "He does have a fanny. I can't feel a thing."

Those bemused punters observing the surreal scene don't know whether to laugh or call the police. She turns, looks at me, and smiles. "Son, this man has attacked me; you not going to do anything about it?"

I look around and spot a vase on a nearby shelf. I rush over, empty the contents on the floor, and smash it over his head. He collapses in a crumpled heap.

"Come on! Out! Now!" I shout, and the three of us make for the door and head down the stairs. My mother and Trudi and I wail with laughter when we reach the street and head toward Central Station.

"Stop. I've got a stitch," says my mother in between her giggles.

A crowd has tumbled out onto the street behind us, and the bouncer and, I guess, another of his colleagues are after us. They look like a couple of sea lions; although unlike their pinniped counterparts, it's unlikely they would be skilled enough to catch balls on their noses.

"Come on, Mary. Hurry!"

"Quick. Get across the road." I hurry the pair of women, who are still giggling like a pair of adolescents. The bouncers are gaining on us, but I spot a black cab and flag it down. It pulls over, and we get in just as the fat boys arrive. The unshaven one we assaulted bangs on the window and waves his fist violently at us.

"Eh, Monkey Bar, please," I instruct the driver.

"Go'an, feck off, you limp-dicked fecker!" My mother laughs and grabs Trudi's breasts, gropes them, and wiggles her little finger as Fatty looks on, astonished, and the taxi pulls away.

"I've never had so much fun in years," Trudi declares in a fit of giggles.

Welcome to the weird and wonderful world of my mother.

Chapter 9

A woman lies naked on a bed. Her arms are tied to the grilled headboard behind her. Her generously proportioned breasts move up and down intensely—a consequence of a man on top pounding into her. A little boy is confused as he observes the scene from the bedroom doorway. His mother looks to be in extreme discomfort, yet she is encouraging the brute to go "fucking faster" and "harder."

The sight of the boy at the foot of the bed startles the woman, and she roars at him, "Fucking get out! Now!"

The man turns to see what has caused the outburst and witnesses hurt on the lad's face. But rather than feel any sympathy, he mocks the child by allowing a wry smile to hang from his lips. The kid turns around and exits the room.

"Fucking get off me!" the woman screams. "He saw us. He was watching."

"Fuck…off, I'm…nearly…there."

"But…oh," she gasps breathlessly in the throes of passion. "But…oh…God…no…he…was…he…oh…saw…us…oh."

"Because…he's…a…fucking…pervert," puffed the man on the verge of orgasm, "like his mother. Mmm…oh yes! Yes, yes…you…dirty…bitch."

He rolls off the woman, and they lie on the bed, both gasping for a few moments.

"You're a fucking animal," the woman spits bitterly, wriggling out of the dress tie that had bound her to the bed, and begins to gather her clothes and dress.

"Thank you."

"I didn't mean it as a compliment, you prick."

"Who you calling a prick?"

"You, you prick!"

"So I'm a prick and an animal, eh? Kind of ironic, given you like my prick and being done like an animal."

"Fuck off!"

"You fuck off!"

"No, you can fuck off! Thomas?"

"What a lady. No wonder I can't take you anywhere, with a mouth like that. You've got a gob on you worse than a docker's labourer!"

"Yeah?"

"Yeah!"

"Yeah, well you'd…It's a pity you don't fuck like a docker! Then at least I'd get shagged properly!"

"Well, if you're not happy, you and fucking Damien there can both sling your hooks!"

"Oh, don't fucking worry. We will; we are. I'm not putting up with you, your small dick, or any of your pathetic kinky games anymore. I mean, what's the point of them anyway, when your teensy-weensy, sad excuse of a cock shoots its bolt too early? Ever wondered why the girls behind the bar giggle when you're in?"

"Wha—"

"Because I call you Peter Premature, that's why. You're fucking pathetic!"

Incandescent with rage, he glares at her for a moment before vaulting across the bed, grabbing her by the hair, and forcing her face into the bed. "I'll fucking give you pathetic, you fucking slag!"

"Get off!…Ow!…You're hurting me…You bastard!…Get off!"

"I'll fucking kill you!"

The tussle continues with the man struggling to gain control of the slapping, thrashing, and writhing woman beneath him. The rumpus draws the attention of the boy, who enters the room; he's wielding a junior cricket bat. He manoeuvres himself around the bed before smashing the bat against the man's leg as hard as his six-year-old frame will allow him.

"What the...give me that, you little shit!"

The man takes the bat from the child in one hand and, in the sweep of the other, smacks the boy across the face, sending him headfirst into a free-standing wardrobe. The momentary break from the throttling is enough for the woman to compose herself and witness the assault on her little boy. The rage that burns within her could raze the building to the ground. Without a second thought, she's on his back. The weight of her knocks the brute off balance and pulls him to the bedroom floor. Immediately she is on top of him, landing blows to his face as soon as his back hits the carpet. He manages to deflect most of the blows from his face and throw her off, but she isn't finished yet.

Noticing the child's cricket bat, she is up once again and, in one arching swipe, bursts his nose, which makes him fall back once more. Adrenaline, like molten lava, courses through her body, and she feels invincible. She lets out a bloodcurdling scream that not only unnerves the man but also chills him to the bone. He ponders how someone so small could make so much noise. But no sooner has the thought left his depraved mind than the wardrobe crashes down towards him. He catches a slight glimpse of blond hair and a female form behind the heavy-ply, teak-veneered apparatus he hangs his clothes in before it smashes into his fragile frame. The little boy runs towards the cricket bat, picks it up, and begins to hit the prostrate and motionless man beneath the wardrobe.

"Don't you dare hit my mammy! Don't you dare!"

The woman is on her knees and in a trance while the boy continues whacking the man's leg.

"You bastard, you bastard!" the youngster repeats. "How dare you hit my mammy!"

"OK, Thomas, you can stop now," says his mother serenely. "You can stop now, son."

"Is he dead, Mammy? Is he dead?"

Chapter 10

"This is just routine," says the young lady officer, seated to the right of an older male policeman. "You're not under caution or anything, and you are free to go at any time. You're just here helping us with our inquiries. You also have the right to ask for a solicitor if you feel the need to or if you are uncomfortable about any of the questions we ask. We can provide you with one, or you can get your own. But I have to warn you that if you do leave before we're finished questioning, we may have to caution you for obstructing a police investigation and bring you back in. Is that clear?"

I nod and take in the surroundings of the interview room at Newcastle Market Street police station while the two officers settle in with their pens, pads, and question sheet. I'm not comfortable at all. My heart is pounding so hard I'm afraid they'll hear it. *Take a deep breath*, I tell myself. *You'll be OK. They've nothing on you. Think innocent. You're innocent.* I should ask for some water, though; my throat is drier than a camel's flip-flop.

The questioning room is tiny, and the decor, well, Laurence Llewelyn Bowen, eat your heart out! I'm guessing the colour scheme went through a complex interior design process with the TV designer, which followed a systematic and coordinated methodology, with research, analysis, and an integration of the designer's knowledge into the creative process. Unfortunately the police hierarchy must have had the final say and concluded that a dreary battleship grey was the right colour of choice. Saying that, it feels claustrophobic, and I don't suffer from claustrophobia. But I feel as if I can't breathe, as if I'm being asphyxiated. I can't catch my breath. Yawn—that usually does the trick.

The WPC looks up and detects that I'm having difficulty.

"You OK, Mr. Rafferty?"

"Yes, I'm fine, thanks."

Finally I manage to get my breathing right, but I'm getting the odd suspicious look from Juliet Bravo here while they shuffle with their files.

We're seated at a small table, which could sit four people, and I face the officers in charge. There is a black, double-cassette tape recorder to my right, with its back up against the wall.

The lady police is slim, with fair hair in a bob, and, I reckon, in her midtwenties. She is plain with no remarkable features. If she does have any desirable assets, they have been cruelly desexualised by her anodyne uniform.

He is about ten years older, about my age, and a couple of stone overweight. He is balding on top and receding at the sides, which makes him look older, and he has a ruddy complexion, suggesting either too much drink, psoriasis, or an addiction to putting his face in a cow's field full of stinging nettles. To be honest, a month on a health farm still wouldn't be enough for the fat cunt!

You often wonder why people become police or want to become police. To do the right thing, of course: maintain order and keep the peace through surveillance of the public and the subsequent reporting and apprehension of suspected violators of the law. Really? I thought it was all about having unscrupulous power to wield tyrannically over the unfortunate masses and to gain revenge on those members of the public who once bullied you at school or at home. I should become police. I'd be great.

"Mr. Rafferty, can you tell us of your whereabouts on the evening in question?" asks Mr. Shiny Face. He looks familiar, this copper. I'm sure I've seen his face somewhere before. Right, concentrate, be cool and calm, and answer slowly. Look him in the eye and remain composed.

"I was in London," I croak unnaturally, and slightly alarmed, they both look at me. "Sorry, may I have a glass of water?"

The WPC looks at me coldly for a moment before getting up and leaving the room.

"I travelled from Newcastle to King's Cross on Friday evening," I say. My voice is still too high; I need to slow it down.

"And why were you going to London, sir?"

"I was there to cover a Middlesbrough versus Millwall match for the paper." I clear my throat again.

There is a long pause. "But wasn't the match on the Saturday?"

"It was."

Another pause.

"So why did you feel the need to travel down the night before?"

The WPC has returned to the room and handed me a plastic cup with water.

"Thanks," I say and take a drink while the WPC whispers something in Mr. Shiny Face's ear.

"I didn't want to take a risk of the train being delayed on the day of the match and miss it, which has happened before, so I went on the Friday night."

"And you have an alibi to confirm that?"

"I'm sure I can provide several. I have train tickets, somewhere, and there's obviously the hotel, which I checked into on the Friday night. Of course, I was seen at the game, because I submitted a match report. I also interviewed the manager and a couple of players, who, I'm sure, will provide alibis, too."

"OK then, Mr. Rafferty, I think that is all we need for now. We'll need to check out your witnesses, and once we do that, we can eliminate you from our inquiries. You are free to go."

"Thanks," I say, picking up my bag and collecting my coat. "Is it OK if I use the toilet?"

"Of course," the WPC replies and stands up. I can now see that she is hiding big breasts beneath her uniform. Shit, she's caught me looking at them. She gives me a disapproving look. How embarrassing. I can feel myself go red.

I stutter, "Where is it?"

She gives me directions, and moments later I've shat out the runniest of liquid poos. It is more or less water that has been excreted. My nervous system must have taken control of my digestive system, I conclude. Two police have come in, and one of them sounds like Mr. Beetroot Face.

"Yeah, Graham Hughes," says Mr. Beetroot.

"You sure he's done it?"

"Positive. The murdering bastard'll not be so cocky when we dig up the foundations of his conservatory."

"Just seems unlikely, that's all."

"Never underestimate members of the public; they're capable of anything and everything."

"And what about the rape?"

"We're close to solving that one, too. Just been tipped off. There's a warrant out for an arrest and a search warrant to inspect his premises."

And before you know it, they've left the room. Didn't even wash their hands, the dirty pigs!

Search warrant and a warrant for an arrest? Jackpot. It's got to be our case. I haven't heard of another one. But that other name was interesting: Graham Hughes. It can't be the same one, surely? Nah, there's got to be dozens of people with that name. But saying that, he was quite handy with his fists at school. But murder his wife? I wonder if it's the lass he was with at school. Sarah, I think she was called—Sarah Nichols. Gorgeous, she was and knew it. A complete cow as well. Laughed when Graham tripped me up in the school dinner hall while I was carrying a dinner tray. Chips and gravy went all over, and I didn't have enough money to buy some more. Nearly starved to death that day. Now that would be sweet justice if one had been murdered and other sent down for it.

I get outside and walk towards John Dobson Street. There's been some new rain, but it smells quite nice now that the sun is burning it. I switch on my phone, and there's a missed call from Millwall Mick and a text: "You owe me money, you Geordie twat!" I'll call him later.

It's quite busy as it's nearly lunchtime, and there are quite a few cars, buses, and people about. I walk by a scruffy young lad, possibly a teenager, who looks like a homeless, stroking what looks like a goose. There's a bottle of white spirits by his side.

"Y'alright, pal," he slurs. "Wanna stroke me duck?"

"No, thanks."

"Go'an."

"No, you're alright."

"Just a fiver?"

"No, thanks."

"Three pound." He gets up, tucks the bird under his arm, and follows me.

"You're OK."

"Two pound?" God, he stinks of piss.

"No."

"A pound?" I shake my head.

"Wanna wank then?" He hiccups. "I'll do it for a fiver."

I ignore this and continue on.

"Fffourquid? Three quid, me final offer. Alreet, one pound fifty? I canna say fairer than that, can a? We've a deal?" I ignore him. "You wanka! This man has offered money for sex!" he screams at passers-by.

A couple of people turn and look at the commotion. I make an imaginary circle with my finger to the side of my head, which indicates he's a mentalist, quickly get out of the way, and get a step on. A hundred yards on, and I tentatively turn to see he has lost interest and is returning to where I first saw him. I wonder how much he charges for a blow job and speculate on how the others got on. I call Scott, but it goes straight into voice mail. I get Cass, though.

"Cass, how did it go?"

"Just routine," he replies. "I wasn't in there more than half an hour."

"Yeah, me too. You hear anything from the others?"

"Spoke to Marty, and it looks as if it was the same for him."

"Scott?"

"Nah, heard nofing."

"OK, you going into the office?"

"Yeah, I'll have a trip up later."

"OK, catch you then. Bye."

I get lunch from MacDonald's on Northumberland Street (Big Mac, fries, and a coke) and watch people for half an hour. There're some fucking desperate people in here. I've heard that in South Africa, if you leave school without any qualifications, you join the police force. In the United Kingdom, you get gainful employment in this fine establishment, whose cuisine caters for those customers who will accept nothing less than the best for a reasonable price. Not sure which country has its priorities right, but it's fair to say that I would worry if one of these half-wits was given a police uniform and a gun.

Oh, fuck, here's Mickey madman again, with his goose. He's asking if anyone wants to stroke his duck when it's clearly a goose! He's frightening the bloody life out of everyone! There's pandemonium at the entrance of the restaurant. Jesus, it looks like it's bitten a kid—the goose, that is, not mad Mick, who is tucking into the burgers and chips left by those fleeing the place. Staff are running all over the joint, trying to catch the bird, which, like its owner, is in pursuit of abandoned chips, burgers, and chicken nuggets. Whoops, one of the staff slips on some chips and is on his arse. The goose is after a Yorkshire terrier, whose lead has been wrapped around the leg of a chair. The dog manages to unravel the lead and make its escape, but the goose has it cornered.

"Go'an, Donald," the mental cunt shouts, laughing at the ensuing palaver while stuffing his face with leftovers. I'm guessing the duck—I mean goose—is called Donald. Very original. The dog manages to shoot off out the door, and I'm thinking the same. Time for an early exit before I have to give him a wank!

I get to the office, which is busy with the usual suspects, delinquents, and chancers, and both Cass and Marty are in as well. I catch the eye of the office bore, Colin Cartwright, who looks as if he's about to say something, but I look away as Cass opens his mouth.

"You heard then?" says Cass in a whisper, looking around the newsroom as if to make sure no one is listening.

"Heard what?"

"They've charged Scotty."

"Eh?"

"They've charged Scotty."

"They haven't."

"They bleeding well have." I look at an expressionless Marty, who is trawling through his e-mail account, I expect. Cass gets out of his seat. "Here, where we can't be disturbed." I follow him through to Eric's office, where he shuts the door behind us.

"The police arrested him about noon, just after they interviewed him. They got a tip-off before he went in, and a team went around to his flat, kicked the door in, and found all sorts of incriminating items."

"Like what?"

"Like his laptop."

"I thought it had been lost or stolen."

Cass shrugs and pulls an I-don't-know face.

"Apparently there's evidence on there, linking him with it and websites he's visited, which have involved rape fantasy."

"Fucking hell!"

"I know. Staggering, isn't it? It's as if butter wouldn't melt. You think you know certain people."

"How do you know all this?"

"I've got a mate who works for Northumbria Police; he told me. But, hey, listen; there's more as well."

"Like what?"

"Like the fancy dress."

"What fancy dress?"

"The party, you idiot. Lucy's party. It was fancy dress."

"So what?"

"Well, she remembers what everyone was wearing at the party before, eh, she was raped."

"So?"

"They've accounted for everyone. Every fancy dress and each person's costume, apart from the one Scotty was wearing."

"Which was?"

"I'm not sure which one. But they all bought them from the same place, and one was never returned—the one Scotty ordered."

"Right."

"He protested his innocence and said he wasn't at the party, like he did when Harvey asked, but I'm guessing his DNA is all over it."

"But what about that half-baked story about the assault on him?"

"That's what he told the Old Bill, but he doesn't have any witnesses or evidence. Oh, and I forgot to say, they found the drugs—the tablets, the date-rape drug, Rohypnol, he used. He didn't even hide it. As plain as day in his bathroom cabinet. What a fackin' idiot!"

I just look at Cass, and I don't know what to think. I feel elated, relieved, happy. It's brilliant news. The best ever. I can't believe how easy it all was. And with Saunders out of the way, the path to promotion is clear. I feel like singing. I think I will.

"Raffers?"

I'm miles away. "Eh? What? Sorry, I'm just stunned."

"Me too, son. Me too."

"Does everyone know?"

"I told Marty."

"What did he say?"

"Not much, just grunted. You know what he's like—a right moody bastard at times."

"Anyone else?"

"Nah, I'll leave all that to Eric."

"Does he know?"

"Not sure, but he'll find out sooner or later. But who'd have thought it, eh? Scott Saunders? Why would a good-looking bastard like him rape someone? And especially Lucy. They're supposed to be mates. I just don't understand it."

"Me too, mate."

"Didn't you used to go out on the pull with him?"

"I went out with him a few times but only when I first started here and not that often."

"Did he seem like a deviant then?"

"He was never around long enough for me to find out. He'd pull, and then he'd be off. You'd never see him after the first hour. He'd just disappear, with some bird probably."

We ponder this for a while and look out of Harvey's window.

"We'd better get back then," I say to Cass. "It looks like I'll have to take charge of the club lines now the rapist is under lock and key."

"Yeah, looks like it. What you got?"

"Couple of things in the fire, but need to check them out first. After the draw with Wigan and loss to Stoke, it seems the Newcastle chairman is getting a bit edgy. Should the Toon lose at West Ham this weekend, Christian's out."

"Facking hell. He's been through more bosses than I've had hot dinners."

Aye, very original, Cass. I can always count on you to come up with a well-trodden simile.

"To be honest, I think it's a race to see who goes first, Christian or Buchanan."

"Buchanan?"

"Yeah, well, Boro's Welsh army have hardly pulled up any trees since they crossed the Severn into Smogland. And they lost again at the weekend."

"Tell you what, I was listening to that Bernie Strachan on the North-East Legends last night, and he was sticking the boot into Buchanan."

"Yeah, I heard."

"Have they got previous?"

"Not sure. They may have crossed paths as players, but Strachan's still banned by the club, I think, or has refused to go to games out of principle. I think his beef might be with a former ban rather than the manager."

"So what's he been banned for?"

"Telling it how it is. You know clubs don't like hearing the truth, and Bernie is a Boro legend. So he'll sway public opinion and change mind-sets; he's got influence, in essence."

"Right, I'd better draw up the pages. They don't do themselves."

By the time I've rattled out three club lines for Newcastle, Sunderland, and Middlesbrough, Harvey has come in, and it's time for afternoon conference.

But now I'm going in as chief sports writer for the first time—well, acting chief sports writer. I've been in charge when he's been on holiday, of course, but that was different.

All the heads of department start making their way towards Harvey's office, and I get up to join them.

"Where you going?" Marty asks curiously.

"Eh, conference."

"Who put you in charge?"

"Eh, no one. I just thought…"

"Did you now?"

I look at Cass, who detects the dissatisfaction in Marty's tone and pulls a face.

"Don't assume that you're in charge just because Scott's not here."

"I'm not."

"Well, it certainly looks like it."

"I'm not; I just know the club lines, that's all. Thought it would be best if I go in. You go if you want."

"No, you're alright," he says in a much less intense tone. "You go, but I think we need a sports-desk meeting to discuss what's going on."

"Totally agree, mate." Marty turns back to his PC, and I take it as a nod to head into Harvey's office. He's a fucking wanker. Must be having a hard time off Cass's daughter, or rather he's not getting anything.

"Shut the door, Raffers," instructs Harvey as I find an empty chair alongside the already-seated news team. "Right, I want this to be quick, so…where'll we start? Raffers, what's happening in the wonderful world of sport?"

"Got a Sunderland line with the manager telling fans that they should be patient with his young side and that the draws will eventually turn into wins in time. And both Christian and Buchanan are under pressure and will be sacked, should they lose at the weekend."

"Both of them?"

I nod, and he sighs, putting both hands on his face and rubbing up and down. "Len Shackleton was right; football-club chairmen know nothing about the game. OK, that it?"

I nod.

"Oh, where's Scotty?"

I look at him and raise my eyebrows, and he acknowledges after a few moments. "OK, I'll speak to you later."

I get up and leave and hear Harvey scream venomously as I close the door. "So you run an ad on the front page, which offers a free pint or a free glass of wine to every reader, and you lead with a story on binge drinking and the damaging effects it has on our health?"

Binge drinking—now that's a good idea. I think a little celebration is called for. I shut down my PC and start putting on my coat.

"Right, Cass, the three club lines are in the basket. Marty, you need anything for the supplement?"

"Depends. What you got?"

"I've got a story on a one-legged long jumper who has won some paraplegic competition."

"You pulling my leg?" Cass quips and starts laughing.

"You taking the piss?"

"No, serious. I'll write it up tomorrow. Got a picture sent in as well."

He eyes me suspiciously, but fuck him. The less able-bodied athletes deserve some press attention, too, don't they? I head out of the office and across Bigg Market, which is reasonably busy for midweek early evening, and into the Beehive. I order a pint of lager and sit at the end of the bar and reflect on a momentous day. I text Arno the rape news while I sup my pint. His reply is almost instantaneous.

"Fuck! Not surprised, though. Thought there was something dodgy about him."

Aye, you're not wrong there, bonnie lad; you're not wrong there. Still, I could do with celebrating properly. Trudi's away, so I can't fill me boots there. And I'm not paying for it! No, go home, son; have a wank. There's plenty of time for celebrating.

Chapter 11

"**I'm sorry it's** at such short notice," sings the bubbly, young blond girl as she reaches over to touch the headmaster's knee. "But I've just moved to the area and haven't had time to contact the council about…anything, really."

The middle-aged man, who looks much older because of his near-bald pate and the old-fashioned cut of his suit, is enjoying the attention of the attractive, tactile, and youthful woman. More so, when she leans forward, he can clearly see her breasts down the loose-fitting T-shirt. Very large, he thinks, for such a thin girl.

The T-shirt hangs lopsidedly across her shoulders and covers the left, while it exposes the right. And as a consequence of her outfit, the school's head can also see the dark outline of a nipple through the transparent brassiere, not to mention the white cotton briefs when she leans back and crosses her legs.

The close proximity of the girl makes him uncomfortable, more so since the little boy has caught him letching down his mother's top. Yet at the same time, he feels intoxicated. The scent of her perfume—Anais Anais, a fragrance his daughter wears—mixes in with the tang of cigarette smoke and awakens and stirs emotions within him he has not felt for nearly twenty years, or so it seems. He knows it is ethically wrong to go against school procedure, but he feels helpless against her insouciant charms. But what is even more remarkable is that the girl seems unaware of the power she wields. Or maybe he is just reading too much into this? Yes, that's what it is. She isn't a daughter of Beelzebub or some sorceress on a mission to damn or bewitch him. She is just an innocent single parent, who, for whatever reason, hasn't been dealt the best of hands in life, and she needs some help. Her innocence and naivety have been compromised, that he is sure of, while her beauty has become a cross to bear. Such a shame. He must help her, but at the same time, can he really go against protocol?

"Mrs..."

"Miss Connor."

"Miss Connor. I'm not sure I can do."

"Oh, please, Mr. Wilcox," she pleads, leaning over once more and putting a hand higher up his thigh this time. The feeling is electric. He can't remember the last time, or indeed ever, he's felt such euphoria from a single touch. The act makes him erect.

"Oh!" She giggles to hide her uneasiness. The uncomfortable silence is broken when she grabs hold of the situation. "Don't be embarrassed," she says and calmly adds, "It's a perfectly natural reaction. I can be a terrible flirt sometimes. I can't help myself. I think it's because I get nervous. Thomas, can you wait outside the door, son?"

The little boy looks at the flushed face of his future headmaster and jumps ineptly out of his seat, opens the office door, and leaves the room. The awkwardness of the scenario prevents the teacher from returning his soon-to-be pupil's fleeting look.

Through the long rectangle slit of stained glass in the office door, the boy sees the blond hair of his mother, now on her knees, in the lap of the gentleman they have been talking to. He thinks that his mum must have dropped something. Within a few moments, his mother follows him out, shadowed by the headmaster.

"Miss Connor, I'm sure it'll be a formality," he says, clearing his throat, rubbing a damp patch on his trousers, and straightening up his tie. "I'll call the local authorities after assembly this morning, and all being well, young Thomas here can come in tomorrow."

"I really appreciate it, Mr. Wilcox," replies the girl, and she leans up and kisses him on the cheek. He is uneasy about the kiss and looks around to see whether anyone has witnessed the act.

"Bye. Come on, Thomas. We need to get your new school things from the shops."

"Good-bye, Miss Connor."

Chapter 12

What the fuck is that noise?

"There is the final whistle! Ant and Dec, Sting, Alan Shearer, Sir John Hall, Jimmy Nail, Donna Air, Bobby Robson, Robson Green, Jackie Milburn, Tony Blair…can you hear me, Tony Blair? Your boys have taken one hell of a beating."

Ah, Crabbers, a.k.a. Simon Crabtree, former Metro Radio commentator. They were the immortal words muttered, or rather bellowed, following Sunderland's 2–1 victory, in almost monsoon conditions, at Sid James' Park in 1999. It was Ruud Gullit's final match in charge of the club.

That ringtone really cracks me up, although not when it wakes me up at this ungodly hour. I'll have to think and turn it to silent before I go to bed on a night. Who's sending texts at this time? Jesus, is that the time? I stretch over to my bedside table, pick up the phone, and unlock the code by punching in one, nine, seven, three—the year our glorious leader, Bob Stokoe, led us to FA Cup glory.

Bloody hell, I hope not. Buchanan's going to be sacked today! That can't be right; he's spent a small fortune on bringing some second-rate footballers to Teesside from the Scottish Premier League, League One, and the Championship. It doesn't make sense. Aye, fair enough, they've had a shit run of form lately, but you can't just dismiss your manager and start again; it's false economy. It'll cost even more money in the long run. The new manager will want to bring in his own guys, discard players he inherited, and so on and so on. It's not like Steve Gibbons at all. He usually sticks with his managers through thick and thin.

But fuck this for a game of soldiers. I'm going back to sleep. I didn't expect stopping out so late, and hang on—fucking hell, I brought the barmaid back but couldn't get it up because I was pissed. She must have sloped off home. Ah well, you win some, you lose some.

I'd better text a couple of the players and find out if they can back up what my source at the training ground is telling me.

"Alright, mate, have u heard anything about Buchanan being sacked 2day? Raff."

Should I text my colleagues or peers from the nationals? Nah, fuck 'em! What about Saunders? Nah. That information will be of no use to him in prison, unless he tries to file from there. The only file he needs at the moment is of the steel variety, hidden in a big cake, to help aid an escape from his prison cell. I should do stand-up, you know.

I can sit on this for a while yet. I'm the only one who'll have the information, simply because I'm the only one who ever gave Sepi any time. It's nice to be nice, and I am. Fair enough, he's got psoriasis, thinning hair, a gammy leg, and green teeth and looks like he's a paedophile, but it can't be much fun being born a Smoggy. He's probably been fed a diet of worm and maggot sandwiches, served with a polluted-water-based drink from the Tees.

You can just imagine his gin-soaked mother saying, after a night on the game and just before she takes him to the delinquents' school on a morning, "Come on, our Septimus, drink your polluted water; otherwise, you'll never grow that other head. And two heads are always better than one. That's what your uncle Orthus always said, remember?"

Who would call their child Septimus these days? Saying that, who on earth would call their child Septimus in the '60s, 'cause he must be in his forties now? That name had long gone out of fashion when he was born. Aye, the name was popular in the dark ages, but this is the twenty-first century, for fuck's sake. Still, Middlesbrough is more or less entrenched in the dark ages.

If you drive through the town centre, there's a good chance you'll drag down a streetful of washing lines.

Former Prime Minister William Gladstone called Middlesbrough "an infant Hercules," because iron ore and steel was discovered there. It may well have been but not now. Teesside is a dump compared to Wearside. Well, probably, I've never actually lived in Wearside, to be honest, but that's not the point. What is the point? Eh, fuck knows. Well, for one, the people of Middlesbrough can't even spell the name of their town properly; that's the point, probably. They missed an *o* from the name. It's the only borough in the country that is spelt "brough" rather than "borough." Apparently it was the fault of some dyslexic, half-witted councillor, who registered the name incorrectly in the eighteenth century. He'd obviously been to his local alehouse for a rat panini and several pints of water-based grog from the town's river before ineptly registering the town's name into the annals of history. It still makes you wonder why they didn't change it when they learned the error of the councillor's ways. I'm not even sure whether that's true, you know, but I want to believe it.

Christ, is that the time? It's only ten in the morning. I can have another half an hour. I need to get some sleeping tablets from the doctor, that's for sure. I'm not sleeping at all at the minute. I'm sure it's because my mother's back from Ireland. I just don't know what she's going to do next. I've never heard from her since the fracas at the Dog and Parrot. She slept at Trudi's flat that night. And thank God, Cass has said nowt, so it looks as if my secret is safe.

Right, sleep, Raffers. Sleep. It's no good; I can't. Tell you what, son, try and dream about shagging someone; that generally does the trick. Whom, though? Trudi? Fuck, I need to stop thinking about the way my mother was all over her. And I've seen evidence of Trudi's bisexual tendencies. Oh no, I've got a hard-on.

"You sick bastard, Rafferty," my conscience says.

"I can't help it; they're both fit as fuck, for old birds."

"No, it's wrong, you sicko."

"I know. I know."

"You should be ashamed of yourself, motherfucker!"

"I am! I am!"

Right, put those thoughts of Trudi and Mary kissing and licking each other out of your mind. It's not working. Imagine someone you can't have. Who? Britney? Cheryl? Hang on. I know. That stuck-up cow, Lucy Bird. Aye, that's a good idea. Hang on. What's that noise? So she hasn't gone home. The barmaid is still here.

"Hi, just got up for some water," the naked girl from last night says as she gets back under the duvet.

Alcohol has an amazing ability to make people attractive. This is a scientific fact, based on the fucking troll in my bed at this precise moment. She's not my type at all. And it's not just because she's unremarkably plain looking. I prefer a more voluptuous woman with big tits. This one is short and wiry and looks like she has a deep-rooted heroin habit, although I can't see the track marks. Nevertheless, I would hump someone's leg at this precise moment because I feel that horny.

"Think you might be up for it now?"

"Sorry about last night," I laugh, trying to make light of it. "The ale was obviously the boss last night. You kinky?"

"Does a bear shite in the woods?"

She's up for it! Jackpot! Two pairs of handcuffs are rescued from my bedside drawer, and within a minute, she's tied to the rails of my headboard.

"Come on then. Fuck me!"

It would be easier if she would shut the fuck up and didn't look like a little boy! I'll have to imagine shagging someone else. Yeah, Lucy will do. The barmaid's soiled underwear is rescued from the bedroom floor and is stuffed in her mouth. Haha, she doesn't like that at all. Top of the pops!

She's a bit of a hairy Mary, but that doesn't matter, as I imagine riding Lucy. But it's like humping a wellington boot, so after a few minutes, I try her back door. Her disgruntled face, muffled cry, and writhing legs suggest she's not happy with the new arrangement, but who cares? Her legs are over my shoulders, so I'm in control. She struggles at first, and it's tight. She's nipping it to stop me getting in, but I force it in, jackpot! The struggle is turning me on, and oh, fuck, it doesn't take long. I'm coming, oh, yes, yes, yes, yes, oh my, my, giddy grandma. What's-her-name is writhing beneath me after I've slumped on top of her and is making a noise. Don't think she's happy. The knickers are removed from her mouth as I reach over for the keys to unlock the cuffs.

"You cunt!"

Wonder what's up?

"Just let yourself out," I say.

She springs out of the bed like a dirty lop from a freshly laundered bed and grabs her clothes, and within a couple of minutes, I hear the door slam. Might as well get cleaned up and get to the office now.

When I get to the office, there's no sign of Saunders. Why would there be? Cass is in and Marty, as I approach the sports desk.

"Morning, comrades," I say.

"Comrades?" Marty harrumphs sarcastically, whereas Cass gives me a breezy "Afternoon, squire."

Marty's a moody bastard at times. It's not my fault you're black, you stroppy twat! Better give Arnie a call; it wouldn't be wise to leave him out of the loop if he's going to help me get on. Or I could just write a version up for the *Mail* and send it off. Better log on first, though, before I decide. Christ, it's quiet in here today.

"Harvey not in?" I ask.

"Not seen him," Marty responds.

No Harvey, no Saunders, no Hibbert, no Cartwright. Top of the pops! What the hell is the matter with this computer?

"Anyone had trouble logging in?"

"Yeah, think the techies have been updating the system," Cass answers. "You'd better go and see helpful Harry."

Brilliant! I love nothing better than asking the IT guys for help. There'll be the usual refrain of "Have you tried turning your computer off and back on again?"

Tell you what, the lads in our IT department actually show Cartwright in a positive light; they make him look almost charismatic, even. If it was a straight choice between attending the IT Christmas party or having a night out with Cartwright and listening to him drone on about the ramblers' policy on saving the dandelion or the way to tie a multifold overland knot using your shoelaces, my high-tech friends might be disappointed to learn that my date would be with him and not them.

I've made the short journey to the hub of our technical centre, and there's only one in. Shit, I never saw him there. Cass wasn't taking the piss. Hi ho, helpful Harry is in. I say that ironically, of course, because he's anything but accommodating. He's another tick in the diversity box, because, eh, he's a dwarf. And he's a dwarf with a chip on his shoulder—a horrible, arrogant little, bastard. I feel like saying, "It's not my fault you're a short arse. It's your family. There's a genetic defect somewhere, so stop blaming the world for all your problems. Look on the positive side, for fuck's sake. Can any of us get a part in the *Snow White and the Seven Dwarfs* Christmas panto when we're short of cash to pay the milkman? Do any of us get to look up a tasty but failed soap star's skirt when she's playing the lead role? No, exactly, so shut the fuck up, and stop your whining, you short-arsed, poisonous person of restricted growth! And use a stepladder if you can't reach!"

He's got his back to me, and he's playing—surprise, surprise—Dungeons and Dragons. There are stereotypes, and there are stereotypes. And there are some stereotypes you just can't escape from, like Scousers are robbing bastards. I don't care what anyone says. I was in this bar, the King Harry, near Anfield a few years back with some Scousers, and they wouldn't let me put a hand in my pocket all night. What nice bunch, I thought. But then when I left the bar to go for a taxi, I realised why. Someone else had already put a hand in my pocket for me and nicked my wallet! I 'ank you, that was my joke. Michael McIntyre, eat your heart out!

Saunders reckons it's cultural. The know-it-all says that when the Irish landed in Liverpool on the way to America during the diaspora—whatever that is, something about a potato famine or something—he reckons the Irish had fuck-all money or possessions, so they robbed to survive. And, of course, some of them couldn't rob enough money to buy a ticket for the boat to the

United States of America, so they got some scrubber up the duff and stopped on Merseyside.

Apparently my Irish grandparents ended up in South Shields or Hebburn, but my mother said we had to move away because of some row she had with her father, my grandfather. I should ask her about that and find out who my father is at the same time.

Techies might not have a reputation for thieving, but they all possess certain individual characteristics, regardless of colour, creed, height, shape, or weight. To get a job in an IT department, you have to be a wizard on all computer games, have no personality, live with your dead mother, hate your father, have an Oedipus complex, have bad skin, have an obsession with horror movies, cycle to work, be a secret member of the BNP, and play chess with Ku Klux Klan pieces. Well, maybe not the last two.

He's turned his head slightly and knows I'm watching from the door.

"Hiya, Harry, how you doing?"

He doesn't even acknowledge me, so I walk up closer and stand by his shoulder.

"Alright, mate?"

Still no grunt of recognition.

"Harry, if you've got five minutes, can you help me log in? The system doesn't seem to recognise my password."

"You tried switching it off and back on again?" comes the stock IT reply but in a voice so high that it's as if he's taken a deep breath from a helium-filled balloon or been kicked in the bollocks very hard by a lass with stilettos! The wanker! "You tried switching it off and back on again" should be engraved on all technicians' gravestones when they're buried. I remain composed because it is a pointless exercise upsetting these cunts, as they can make your life very difficult.

"First thing I did, mate. But apparently the system has been updated, and we need to update passwords and such."

"Oh, yes, that is correct. Give me a few moments, and I'll be right around."

"You're a star, Harry. Want a coffee from the machine? I'm on my way there now."

"No, thanks," he squeaks, without taking his eyes from the computer screen. The voice would be more suited to that of a prepubescent boy than a man in his, oh, midthirties. I dunno. I've no option but to leave and wait for the little shit.

I wonder what type of dwarf he is and what type of dwarfism he suffers from. I remember seeing this Irvine Welsh play, *Babylon Heights*, about the little people on the set of *The Wizard of Oz*. I'm sure that in the programme notes there was mention of three types of dwarfism…or was it four? I bet he's the type with no sexual glands.

Harvey is at the coffee machine when I get there.

"Morning, Eric."

"Aye, in America," the sarcastic twat replies, looking at his watch. "Any news I need to know then?"

"Yeah, keep it under your hat, though. Buchanan's been sacked."

"Really?"

"Yeah."

"But Gibbons has given him a wad load of cash to bring in all those players."

"Aye, I know. It's not like him at all."

"Who is in for it?"

"Not sure yet, but I'll throw in the usual names: Souness, Hoddle, Houllier, JFK."

"Kinnear! You might as well add Mr. Quick Fit, Mr. Shifter, and P. G. Tips to the list in that case. Has anyone else got the story?"

"No, it's my exclusive, but I might give it to one of the nationals, as a favour."

"Well, don't they just pass it around anyway?"

"Not if I just pass it to one person in particular."

"Not that devious bastard Saunders talks about, is it?"

"Eh…" And before I can answer, he's off.

"In my office in ten minutes to discuss what we're going to do," Harvey shouts back. "I need to see you anyway."

"OK."

I get back to the desk, and Cass and Marty are putting on their coats.

"Where you going?" I ask.

"Union meeting. You forget?" Marty replies.

"Shit, I did."

"You coming then?" Cass adds.

"Send my apologies. I've got to go to Boro."

They both look at me doubtfully, but I blank their stares. As soon as I get my promotion, I'm out of the union. It is a bit shitty, the 2 percent pay rise the management has offered, considering that the VAT rise will wipe out 1 percent. And the request to take a week's unpaid holiday as we fight the recession is a bit hard to swallow, but if it means saving jobs, then surely it is worth it.

Union meetings are as dull as my mother's slate-grey bathroom tiles. Hours upon hours of pointless, amiable chat. Will we ballot for strike? Will we take industrial action? Will we work to rule? Tell you what; these lot make the miners' strike of the mideighties look like Vietnam. No spine, the middle classes. All they want to do is sit around with a rich tea biscuit and a piece of sponge cake or a hobnob and sensibly discuss the wrongs of a capitalist system they are quite happy to exploit when the situation presents itself or suits them. I bet they've all got shares in British Gas, British Telecom, BP, and British Airways. They're fucking hypocrites.

Ten minutes later, and I've told Harvey the Boro crack. I've been tipped off that former fan favourite and Boro legend Tony Clough has been approached to take over rather than the other journeymen bosses. Buchanan was honourable to the last. He approached Gibbons, according to my source, said it wasn't working out the way he had hoped, and agreed to rip up the rest of his contract so that Boro did not have to pay up two and a half years left on his deal. What a man.

So the Welshman is the first manager to go from the North-East's big three, but he'll not be the last. Hugh Christian is under pressure for fielding a reserve side against Man U in the League Cup and being hammered 5–0. There was hell on before the match. Apparently Christian and all the players were having their prematch meal, and *Sky* led with a story that the Londoner's job was under threat despite a home draw against Wigan and an away victory at West Ham prior to the Gunnners' match. The players, obviously thinking it a joke, started taking the piss; only Christian was not amused. He was furious and went to seek out the source of the leak. Given the club's close links with the media outlet, you wouldn't need to be a *Krypton Factor* contestant to second-guess who it was, judging by the behaviour of the club's hierarchy on transfer deadline day.

If Sunderland fans can take any crumb of comfort in the absolute fact that their team has been a parcel of shite in recent years and that Newcastle's fortunes have always fared better than theirs, it's because the clowns running the club of our nearest rivals have always managed to cheer up us Black Cats with their constant meddling. They all should be knighted for making the club the nation's favourite laughing stock: one calamity or catastrophe after another! They're naturals at it.

In the 1990s, Freddie Shepherd and Douglas Hall were caught out by the infamous fake-sheik sting by the *News of the World*. Among several revelations, they were caught mocking Newcastle supporters for spending extortionate amounts of money on club merchandise they buy cheap, calling female supporters dogs, and mocking club legend Alan Shearer by calling him Mary Poppins. And then there were the hookers!

Shepherd then sacked Sir Bobby Robson, the nation's favourite manager. A measure of how popular he was is that even Sunderland supporters loved him. He was replaced by Graeme Souness, who undid all of Robson's good work. A partisan Sunderland supporter couldn't have done a better job. He spent nearly £60 million on the hapless Jean-Alain Boumsong, the hopeless Albert Luque, the mediocre Amdy Faye, and a couldn't-care-a-less Celestine Babayaro. Admittedly Emre, Scott Parker, and Michael Owen were decent, but they hardly pulled up any trees for the club. Owen was the worst of the lot. Fair enough, he had a bad injury, but for £16 million, he did not justify the price tag when he was fit. In essence, Souness did a Dalglish and put a Skoda engine in a Rolls Royce, metaphorically speaking. Newcastle have been on the decline ever since! You'd think Shepherd was a secret Black Cats follower—likewise Souness and Dalglish.

And just when you think it couldn't get any better for us Mackems and worse for them, somebody up there who likes us played a joker, and sports retailer Mike Ashley took over. Reports say he paid £134 million to buy Newcastle or, rather, to buy out the main shareholders, Sir John Hall and Freddie Shepherd. This was the first of several massive faux pas Ashley made, because it was revealed that the businessman failed to do due diligence when he purchased the club. He later discovered that the club owed a further £100 million to debtors, who wanted to be paid at once as soon as the sale of the club went through. Not only that, but there were other outstanding debts he knew little about, such as the payments on transfers that still needed to be settled.

Generally if you buy a player for, say, £10 million, you don't pay it all up front. You pay it off in instalments, like a loan by direct debit—for example, £2 million a year. And United had several players with money still to pay on transfers. Ashley later found, to his dismay, the club's former chairman had spent all the sponsorship money in advance to fund transfers, and Ashley was left to pay it off. Shepherd has always denied this and said that the club was on a sound financial footing and that the Magpies' debt was manageable and structured in the same way as a mortgage.

To be fair to Ashley, he did a lot of good for the club and put them on a sound financial footing. But such was his flippancy that you didn't know what he was going to do next. When he first took over, he installed Chris Mort as chairman. Mort was a lawyer for Freshfields Bruckhaus Deringer. He agreed to take a sabbatical from his law firm to help Ashley smooth over a transition stage on Tyneside. He seemed a sensible appointment and met with supporters, fanzine writers, and journalists to find out what was the best way to take the club forward, and he reported back to Ashley. The result was cheaper season tickets and a singing end, among other things. He even brought back fan favourite Kevin Keegan for a second spell as manager. It looked like a masterstroke, and everything looked rosy in the Magpies' garden. But Keegan was just manager in name. He had little say other than in picking the team. He had no control over transfers and spending. That was left to former Chelsea star Denis Wise, property tycoons Paul Kemsley and Tony Jimenez, and former Luton Town apprentice Jeff Vetere.

Fair enough. Wise and maybe Vetere had some football experience, but Kemsley and Jiminez? And when Mort went back to his former job as a lawyer, Ashley brought in Derek Llambias, a former managing director of the Fifty Club in Mayfair, London. The appointments did not make any footballing sense because they had no historical or emotional links to the club and little experience in running a football club. Ashley might as well have employed Bob the Builder, given the haplessness of their tenure. It all culminated in an unmitigated disaster on August transfer deadline day in 2008, which eventually led to Keegan filing a constructive-dismissal claim.

The catalyst for this was James Milner. According to my source, the club wanted to sell Milner to Aston Villa for £12 million, but Keegan did not want him to go. But the former Newcastle boss was persuaded to allow him to leave because he was given assurances that he could have the money to invest in players he wanted—namely Bastian Schweinsteiger, Olivier Kapo, Sami Hyypiä, and Stephen Warnock. Hardly the Hollywood names the club leaked to the press in an effort to undermine and discredit the ex-England boss. Behind the scenes and behind Keegan's back, the club was also trying to offload big earners Alan Smith to Everton and Joey Barton to Harry Redknapp's Portsmouth.

The former Liverpool and SV Hamburg star had several conversations with the players' agents and wanted to know why there was a hold-up and why the deals were taking too long to conclude. The agents let Keegan know that the players wanted to join the club and that the problem was at United's end. When he investigated this claim, he was told by Denis Wise that the club couldn't conclude the deals. Instead Wise signed midfielder Ignacio González on loan and brought in striker Francisco Jiménez Tejada, a.k.a. Xisco, from Deportivo La Coruña for £5.7 million. Keegan revealed to Wise that he did not know the players, but the diminutive former Blues midfielder told his manager that he could watch them on YouTube. Absolutely staggering when you think about it.

In the tribunal, Llambias admitted to misleading the media and the club's fans as a public-relations exercise. Several key senior staff, including Wise and Llambias, had publicly claimed Keegan had the final word, yet they claimed to the tribunal that this was not, in fact, the case. But the club's signing of González meant that they had violated Keegan's employment contract, which amounted to constructive dismissal.

You would have thought they'd have learned from their mistakes after that, but the fun and frolics continued when they brought in Joe Kinnear as a replacement. Kinnear hadn't managed a club for four years before he was offered the post at St James' Park. He was the last person any of us thought would get it. His first press conference, which I bloody missed because I was on holiday, was certainly colourful. He called one journo a cunt and swore a total of fifty-two times. He gained the JFK nickname—Joe Fucking Kinnear—as a consequence from a popular Newcastle United fan website. As results go, he did OK, but he didn't help his cause by mispronouncing Charles N'Zogbia's name as "Charlie Insomnia" after one match. Later on, he called Yohan Cabaye "Yohan Kebab." Priceless! He suffered a heart attack before they were due to play West Brom at the Hawthorns, a game they won 3–2 with Chris Hughton at the helm as caretaker.

Hughton, of course, was eventually given the Newcastle job full-time after they were relegated. Thanks, Alan. Eight games, and local hero and living legend Alan Shearer couldn't muster up enough points to keep his beloved Magpies in the Premier League. Oh, how I wept—tears of joy and laughter, that is. Oh, how you let down the Geordie nation.

Hughton did well, to be fair to him, by winning promotion and stabilising the club in the Premier League when it looked as if it had been left to sail down the Suwannee River without a paddle and headlong into shit creek. But it was never going to last long, given the idiosyncratic nature of his boss. And with Sunderland due at St James' Park on Sunday, Christian, too, could be joining Hughton out the revolving door by Monday. Well, most probably anyway; Sunderland are overwhelming favourites.

The Wearsiders have started the season better than expected. Bruce Stephens, despite being a Geordie, has won over sceptical fans. So I expect the Black Cats to get their claws into the Magpies and ruffle their feathers in the derby game this week.

The club's new owner, Mike Michaels, is no better. He put forward new plans to build a new one-hundred-thousand all-seater stadium just off the A1 and wants to ground share with Sunderland and Gateshead. Reckons he wants fans of all teams to come to every home game and fill the stadium and support all three sides. That way Gateshead would get to the Premier League. Don't think he's thought it through, the hatred that Geordies and Mackems have for each other or the fixture congestion, to be honest. But he wouldn't, since he comes from the Home Counties. He is also one of those politically correct tits who want more diversity, with woman, black, and disabled people involved in coaching, managing, and physiotherapy. Can you imagine if the physio was disabled in a wheelchair and had to attend to a serious injury on the pitch? Doesn't bare thinking about, does it?

Who would they bring in as Christian's replacement? If I was one of Michaels's advisors, I would suggest Fulchester United boss Tommy Brown. He wouldn't know whether he was real or not. But I'd add, "Mike, he'll not come without his right-hand man and coach, Sid Preston." Brown wouldn't stand for any meddling by Michaels. He'd walk straight into his office and demand hard cash to bring in some of the trusty lieutenants who have served him so well over the years, like Brown Fox, Billy the Fish, Shakin' Stevens, and invisible striker Johnny X. Farfetched? Really? Well, they started it all by bringing in Joe Kinnear! Mike Michaels is as bad as his namesake Ashley.

That was quick. The union meeting is over, and they're all tumbling back into the office.

"Thought you were going to Boro," says Marty doubtfully.

"They've called it off."

Marty looks at me sceptically. The wanker.

"Oh, the Bolsheviks are back," shoots a sarcastic Harvey, who pops a head out of his office and scans the room. "Raffers, I need a word."

I go into Harvey's office and take a seat opposite the three posters of the Jam, the Clash, and the Buzzcocks, which hang on the wall opposite and observe the proceedings. He calls them the holy trinity of punk rock. No

Sex Pistols, mind. The Sex Pistols were up there until Johnny Rotten went on *Celebrity Get Me Out of Here* and did that butter advert. Harvey reckons he sold out and replaced the "Anarchy in the UK" poster with the Jam, the one where they're all wearing black suits with black ties and standing in front of a wall, with "the Jam" in pink graffiti behind them. The one of the Clash shows Mick Jones and Paul Simonon flanking Joe Strummer down a brick alley. Think it must be an album cover. The one of the Buzzcocks is an album cover, too. They're in a studio, with their instruments, and looking at the camera. Don't know what all the fuss is about myself. It's just a lot of shouting and noise.

"Right," says Harvey, who enters the office and takes his seat. "Given what has happened to Scott, I don't think I have any option but to offer you the chief sports writer's position."

Fucking jackpot.

"But only on a temporary basis."

Shitbag!

"I need to find out if you have the necessary qualities to lead the sports desk on a consistent basis, certainly on the written side. Saying that, I have been impressed by the way you've stepped up to the plate since Saunders, eh, well…I still find that hard to believe, to be honest. He just…well…but good work on the Buchanan story, and you're sure it's Clough?"

"Positive. My source said that he overheard a conversation and that the Boro hierarchy is arranging a meeting. If anything changes, you'll be the first to know."

"OK. So Cass will still be in charge of the production side, of course, so you'll have to liaise with him on what goes where and which you think are the strongest stories. Is that OK?"

"Fine, Eric. We get on like a house on fire, so there shouldn't be any problem working more closely than I normally do."

"Champion. Just wanted a quick chat before I get these other clowns in for conference."

Chapter 13

It's a week before the most important fixture known to man—Newcastle versus Sunderland. Calm down, Celtic and Rangers fans, just calm down. The North-East derby is a lot older and fiercer than your Old Firm gig in Glasgow. Our dispute goes back to Oliver Cromwell's times, a lot further than your pithy religious quarrel. Where was I? Oh, aye, John Wayne is dominating the headlines again, and for all the wrong reasons—just for a change. No hookers involved this time, though.

There is no doubt that he is a brilliant footballer on his day, verging on world class. It is hard to ever view England's number-one striker in a positive light following his off-the-field activities. His latest gaff is a petulant threat to quit Manchester United. The sulky striker says he's slapped in a transfer request at Old Trafford because the club lacks ambition. "Man United" and "a lack of ambition" would never sit together in a sentence ever!

Wayne made the announcement on a day when the government revealed that half a million public-sector jobs were being made redundant and that a £160 million fund that drives the national PE and schools-sport strategy was being scrapped. It also financed 450 school-sport partnerships, providing links between schools and professional clubs; in essence, they were some of the biggest cuts to the economy in living memory. Very insensitive of you, John. Whoever was behind the decision, he or his advisors, wants a good hoofing up the arse.

The sorry saga was all concluded, however, when the twenty-six-year-old penned a new five-year contract extension to make him the highest-paid player in the club's history. After he put pen to paper, he said, "I'm delighted to sign another deal at United. I've spoken to the manager and the owners, and they've convinced me that this is where I belong. I am signing a new deal in the absolute belief that the management, coaching staff, board, and owners are totally committed to making sure United maintains its proud winning history, which is the reason I joined the club in the first place."

Cynics among the football fraternity believe that the forward, who already earned a reported £100,000 a week, was contriving a lucrative new deal. His new wage is believed to be in the region of £200,000 a week. Most football supporters won't earn that in a lifetime, never mind a week. Out of touch? Most footballers are!

The outcome of the North-East derby? It was an embarrassment! Men against boys. Sunderland were second best in every department: defence, midfield, and up front. I wouldn't care, as we started well and could have gone ahead early on, but after the first goal went in, we folded like a proverbial seaside deck chair when sat on by a fat lady licking monkey's blood off a ninety-nine ice cream.

Bruce Stephens's side were unbeaten in six and overwhelming favourites to win the contest prior to the match, while Newcastle had recently lost at home to Stoke, had struggled to draw with relegation favourites Wigan at St James' Park, and had toiled to scrape a 2–1 victory at struggling West Ham in their previous three fixtures.

What happened? Did they not read the latest form? At half-time, it is 3–0 to Newcastle, and deservedly so. I leave my seat in the press box to get a cup of coffee and happen to glance up at the radio lads, where a shamefaced former Black Cats legend is sitting with his cocommentator. He looks devastated. I know how he felt.

After the break, we have a player sent off for a rash challenge before the hosts wrap up a 4–0 win. I feel physically sick. And just to rub it in a little bit more, the host DJ plays the Monkees' "Daydream Believer" over the tannoy. Newcastle fans have bastardised the former chart topper on the terraces to disparage former Sunderland boss Peter Reid in the mid-1990s. On this occasion, they insert Bruce Stephens's name instead of Reid. I would love nothing better than to stick the boot in on the black-and-white shit, but what can I do? It's a rout!

The Sunderland manager gives the briefest of post-match interviews and apologises to the club's loyal fans before he skulks off the press-room stage. The partisan Newcastle press are salivating over the result and sycophantically kissing the backside of the under-fire United boss.

I finish typing a 750-word match report and a similar-length quotes piece from the managers and players and send the copy to the sports desk. I pack up and make my way to the exit. Arno and a couple of the others ask if I fancy a post-match drink. I feel like shit, so I make my excuses and get out. I don't want to be surrounded by jubilant Magpies celebrating. I want to be somewhere where I can drown my sorrows or somewhere where I can forget about it.

The texts have already started. "The time is five past Sunderland" is the first one. It isn't even five, for fuck's sake! It's four! The sender? Cass, the Cockney wanker! Obviously he's another one who doesn't know I'm a Sunderland fan, so I have to play along with it. But fuck this; I'm turning my phone off.

I don't fancy going home, but at the same time, I don't want to stop out and witness those marauding morons singing their vitriolic Magpie bile and celebrating a famous victory.

I remember that there's a lovely little pub on Red House Farm Estate, the Piper, hidden away from the main road and in its own private grounds. I head there. It's a black-and-white pub, but I expect there'll be no fans inside. On a day like today, they'll be following the rest of the rats down to the Bigg Market and the Quayside.

I get to the Piper, and my presumption is proved correct. There're about fifteen to twenty people scattered around the pub. Out of that lot, I reckon most of them are couples with the odd barfly and old man sitting on his own. But hang on, what have we here? I don't believe it. Shania—my ex, Julie's daughter—is standing at the bar with a bloke who has got to be ten years older. She's flirting with him big-style, laughing at everything he says. He's got his hand on her arse, and she is playing with his tie. He's smartly dressed in a grey suit. The little prick tease is wearing a little vest top, which displays a bigger bust than I seem to remember, and a skirt so short that had she been in another part of town, there's a chance she'd be arrested for being on the game. By the looks of things, he's swaying a bit and seems a little pissed. The bar staff look concerned, and I'm not surprised. I don't even think she's sixteen yet. No, she must be, as it's over eighteen months since I last saw her, and she was fifteen then. The manipulating little cow blackmailed me for over £200.

I let myself into Julie's gaff this one time when I got finished from work early and she wasn't home. I had honourable intentions an' all. Shania was supposed to be at her friend's after school for tea. I planned to make a romantic dinner for the pair of us. Bought two rib-eye steaks and that rosé wine Julie likes. It's funny how Trudi likes rosé as well. Anyway I thought I'd get changed. I went upstairs and saw that the door to Shania's room was slightly ajar. I looked in, and, blow me, she was only masturbating while having a sunbed. I couldn't help it. I knew I shouldn't have, but it was so erotic. So I whipped out the big fella and started knocking one out.

My eyes were only closed for a few seconds as I came, but before I knew it, Shania was standing in front of me with a towel wrapped around her and screaming that I was a pervert! She was hysterical for a good five minutes before I could calm her down. I was caking it, big-style, pleading with her to calm down and telling her I would make it worth her while if she kept quiet. I started with twenty quid if she kept it as our little secret, but eventually I had to settle for fifty. After that, it cost twenty quid every time I saw the little slag. She'd be making wanking signals behind her mum's back when I was there. I eventually told her to fuck off; she wasn't getting any more money.

But she told her mum, and that was the end of it. Of course, I denied any of it was true. I said that I didn't know she was home and that I had accidently walked in on her. Julie half believed me, but it was no good. It's her daughter at the end of the day. I wouldn't care, but Julie was the best sex I'd ever had. She let me do her up the backside and everything. Never had a lass let me do it up there before. Everyone I've tried a bit of backdoor boogie with since has called me a pervert!

It's payback time, you little slag. And there's something not right about that bloke. I wonder. I take my phone out and switch it back on and take a few snaps of him with his hand on her arse and her whispering in his ear and vice versa. And get in there, son; they're kissing. Jackpot! Wouldn't want these photos to get into the wrong hands, eh?

I follow him to the toilet and take my place in the urinal next to him. I take a sneaky peek at his cock. Jesus, it's bigger than mine. He could do some damage with that. I finish before him and shake and then go to the sink to wash my hands.

"I know you from somewhere?" I question as he approaches the sink.

"You do?"

"Yeah…I know," I pretend to ponder. "You're Julie what's-her-name's bloke…Oh, what is it again?…Julie McCarthy." He looks a bit sheepish. "We met at a ministry Christmas party last year at the Assembly Rooms."

"Did we?"

"Yeah, we were a bit pissed, but I still remember you. I was at the bar, and I bought you a, oh, what was it again?

"Lager."

"Lager it was."

"You work at the ministry, too?"

"I did, but I was only there until I passed my preliminaries to get into the police force. Aye, she was the office babe, Julie, you know?"

"Yeah, she's lovely."

"Do you work with her then?"

"Yes, I'm her boss."

"Is that right? So," I ponder for a few moments, "why are you out with her daughter?" My voice takes an aggressive tone, and it catches him off guard. He looks like a rabbit caught in a car's headlights.

"Don't think she'd be happy to see you here with her daughter."

"Look, mate—"

"And from what I remember, she's only fifteen."

"She's not; she's nearly seventeen," he splutters.

"Not even seventeen, and you're buying her alcohol? I think my colleagues down the station would be interested in talking to you."

"Look, mate, can we talk about this?" He is panicking. "Can I buy you a drink? She was coming onto me. I was in one of the corporate lounges at the match where she works and offered her a lift home and…"

"You thought you'd come to the Piper. It's out of the way. No one will know you, and you thought you'd shag your girlfriend's underage daughter?"

"It's not like that, mate. Honest, it wasn't like that!"

"Well, the photos on my camera don't suggest that."

He's frantic now.

"Look, mate, I'll give you some money."

"So I've got you for supplying a minor with alcohol and bribery? This isn't going to look good on your CV, is it? You'll not only lose your girlfriend, but you'll also lose your job. I can't imagine anyone giving a job to a kiddie fiddler!"

I can't believe how calm I am. But then, again, it is easy to take advantage of someone who is panicking.

"Look, mate, you know I'm not a kiddie fiddler. I know she's young, and I shouldn't be doing this. But please, mate, please, don't do this to me," he cries. Literally he is crying now. And it's as if someone has pressed the fast-forward button the way he's pacing around the toilet. I can't stand seeing blokes cry.

"How much you got in your wallet?"

He quickly grabs the inside of his jacket, pulls out his wallet, and opens it, and there's a wad of cash. I take it all.

"Right, you'd better fuck off and hope I don't say anything."

"Thanks, mate. Thanks, mate," he stammers and makes for the door.

"Another thing."

He stops and turns.

"Straight out the side door. I'll deal with Shania."

He nods.

"And you finish it with Julie."

He nods again, and then he's gone.

I straighten myself up in the mirror. Not bad, son, not bad. You're no Brad Pitt, but equally you're no Billy Bremner. Shania is twirling her drink around with a straw when I approach her. Her face gives off an expression of hate at first, before it turns into panic as she looks past my left shoulder for her mother's boyfriend.

"Now then, Shania, what brings you here?"

"It's got fuck all to do with you!"

"I think I'll be the judge of that." She just glares at me and then starts to pout. "Shall we give your mam a ring?"

"You leave my mam out of it. She fucking hates your guts after what you did."

"Such a lady." I lower my tone. "If you raise your voice once more, I'll take your head off. I think we both know I did fuck all, you lying, conniving bitch."

"Just fuck off, will you? And leave-iz alone."

"I'll do no such thing, and I'm warning you. In fact I think I'll give your mum a call."

"I've told you, man, she fucking hates you, can't stand the thought of you, so I doubt she'll ever speak to you again." Shania looks over my shoulder.

"Don't worry about him; he's not coming back. And I think she will talk to me when I tell her what I've seen tonight."

"What the fuck you on about?"

I pull my phone out and show her the pictures I have taken.

"So what? Like, I'm out with me boyfriend."

"Your boyfriend?"

"Aye, got a problem with that, like?"

"Me? No, but I think your mam might."

"How's that, like?"

"Because it's your mam's boyfriend, isn't it?" She almost shrinks into her glass as the words leave my mouth. "Shall we give her a ring?" Again there is no response other than her looking down into her drink and stirring it even faster.

"Although we could come to some arrangement, where I don't give her a ring."

Shania looks up at this point; she's got almost-pleading eyes.

"What kind of arrangement?" she sheepishly asks.

"Come with me." I set off for the exit, and she follows out of the door. "First of all, you'll tell your mother that your story about me touching you up was a fabrication."

"A what?"

"A lie. I don't care how you tell her, but do it. You can say you were just attention seeking or were jealous of how happy we were. I don't care how you do it. Just do it. And there is another favour."

We reach our destination, my car, which is situated at the back of the car park.

"Get in."

We both climb in, and she puts on her seat belt. I drive to a secluded spot in the far end of the car park. In this light, no one would see anyway. I pull over, undo the belt on my trousers, loosen them, and pull down the zip. She looks at me with a mixture of fear and loathing for a few moments before realising what she's got to do. She undoes her seat belt, reaches over, puts her hand into my underpants, and runs her fingers over my length. I've got a feeling she might have done this before. I ease down my pants and undercrackers to my ankles to give her better access, and within seconds, she has me in her mouth. She may have been reluctant at first, but you can tell she is enjoying it nearly as much as I am. She's running her tongue up and down my shaft and around the head, taking it to the back of her throat. Sixteen years old, and she gives better head than her thirty-five-year-old mother. I try to hold back and enjoy it as much as I can, but it's all over with a minute and a half, I guess. She tries to pull away while I come, but I hold her head down. She quickly opens the passenger door and spits out what she hasn't swallowed. I hand her a paper handkerchief and some water, which she snatches from my hand. She wipes her chin before drinking greedily from the bottle. And when she came up for breath, she snipes, "You bastard!"

"That's what happens to devious little cows like you. You get your comeuppance."

Once again she looks at me through hate-filled eyes.

"Can I drop you off?"

"Home...at the end of the street."

I drop her at the end of the street, as requested, and she jumps out of the car and storms off down the street. Wasn't such a bad day, after all.

Chapter 14

Three consecutive wins over West Ham, Sunderland, and Arsenal, which have Newcastle up to as high as fifth in the Premier League, are followed by two draws and three defeats. It sees the Magpies slump to eleventh, and it is enough to get Christian the sack. Former veteran defender Colin Soloman says that the decision "makes no sense." Ex-player and radio pundit Peter Anderson says he is "devastated and angry," while the players, club captain Kevin Dolan, and Jeff Marton go ballistic with the managing director Derek Lionel after the players call an emergency team meeting.

There is a club statement thanking Christian for taking the club forward and wishing him all the best in the future, while adding that they feel they need an experienced manager to take the club to the next level and that Christian is not that man. By the way, aren't those club statements all worded the same?

There is a definite sense of déjà vu about the dismissal. It is similar in many ways to Chris Hughton's sacking. I find out about Alan Pardew replacing the popular Hughton through a mate of mine who used to go to Derek Llambias's casino, the Fifty Club in London. The former West Ham, Charlton, and Southampton manager was a visitor at the Fifty Club and apparently a friend of Newcastle's MD. I nearly choke on my cornflakes when my pal suggests that he could be the next manager, as it doesn't make any sense to me. But then again, nothing that pair has ever done makes much sense. Don't get me wrong; he has a reasonable CV as a manager, but experience? And could he really do anything more than Hughton? As it happens, he leads the team into Europe before the team struggled again.

Most still believe that the Toon's new deadly duo of Lionel and Michaels is as out of touch with football and its workings as Ashley and Llambias were. They do a Graeme Souness and sign the two younger Nigerian brothers of Jay-Jay Okocha on the back of an anonymous phone call. One of the lads gets tipped off by a club press officer. They give them both a three-year contract! You can't make this stuff up. But they aren't the only ones. Most football club owners and chairman do not understand the game. Yet that has always been the way.

Back in the old days, when football clubs formed, it was the local businessman who ran the club. The town's local butcher, car salesman, or candlestick maker would own the club, and it would be passed down through the family. They certainly weren't Russian oligarchs or billionaires from faraway exotic climes, like today's football-club owners. But it is similar in some ways. It is a throwback to the old class system, with the means of production in the hands of a few middle-class entrepreneurs while the working-class masses worked for their superiors. There is the odd honourable exception, like former Black Cats supporters' favourite Niall Quinn, of course, and Dave Whelan at Wigan. Both of these men played football at the highest level. But they are few and far between.

Lionel and Michaels like to get together with Christian prior to a game and play Fantasy Football. They try and predict what the score of the match will be. Lionel and Michaels feel that Newcastle should have been second in the league prior to his dismissal and aren't happy the team lost home games to Blackpool and Stoke City, while the draws with Fulham and West Brom did not go down too well either. It defies logic to believe football is an exact science and you can predict what happens. Even I know that.

There is the odd protest from Newcastle fans and thank-you banners in support for the popular Christian's tenure at St James' Park. But that is soon forgotten when United spanks Liverpool 3–1. The last goal is superbly scored by Andy Card, who will later be transferred to Chelsea for £30 million despite the club's reiteration he would stay. Christian conducts his press conferences before and after the Reds' victory and insists that Card will not be sold in the January transfer window. I know different.

With Saunders out of the way, I am flourishing in my new role. He wasn't given any bail and is still in jail, although a January date has been set for his trial. I should go and visit him. Marty and Cass have been in and say that Saunders looks like shite; he's lost loads of weight and is barely recognisable. What a shame.

It is amazing how many contacts you pick up and networking meetings you get invited to when you have a "chief" title. It is around this time that I start to think about the next step up the career ladder. Arnie's tip-offs and story leads are beginning to dry up, too. I am supplying him with most of the stories, so I make a conscious decision to drip stories directly to the *Mail*. All I ask is that my byline be a nom de plume and that if I continue to supply the paper with stories, they consider taking me on should a vacancy arise. They give me £500 when I tell them that former player Robert Clark is going to be the new United boss, and they promise more of the same for every exclusive. And when I give them the line that Chelsea has triggered striker Demba Demba's £7.5million release clause and is going to sign, I get a call from a frantic Arnie asking to meet up for a drink.

"They're not going to renew my contract at the end of the season," says a downtrodden Chris Arnold as I take my seat next to him in the Fleet Street pub, in Newcastle's Bigg Market.

"They've told you that?"

He takes a swig from a bottle of Blue WKD as the Cars' "Drive" track clicks on the jukebox and adds to the melancholy. I'm sure he once said it was his favourite song.

"Not in so many words...but I get the picture."

"Why?"

"Don't know. Maybe it's because I haven't had any exclusives lately."

"Right. But what about the Clark to Newcastle story?"

"I never broke that Clark line."

"You didn't?"

"No, and neither did I break the Demba to Chelsea story."

"You didn't? Well, who did?" I try to act concerned, but I'm telling you, there are fireworks of delight exploding inside my head.

"Not sure. Did you not read it?"

"Must have missed it."

"The byline just read 'a sports mail reporter.' Humiliating!"

"Right."

I don't know what to say to him, but it's clear that he's down. I've never seen him like this before. Usually he's assertive, confident, and brash, but he looks broken. And to think I used to look up to this wanker. What a pathetic twat! He is, or was, the biggest bully in the North-East press pack.

"Yeah, so it looks as if I'm out the door."

"Nah, I'm sure you'll be alright. Maybe they're just trying to get you to up your game."

"Up my game! What you talking about? I'm the best news gatherer in the sports business." Well, obviously not now. Looks like I'm stealing that title, you big girl's blouse.

"No, what I meant—"

"No one has broken more stories on my patch in ten years."

"I know, but—"

"There're no buts about it."

He stares at the floor, and I don't say anything for a while.

"You fancy another drink, Chris?"

"No…no, thanks, mate. I think I've had enough. Just wanted someone to talk to, but I've said enough. I'd better be getting off. The wife has been calling all afternoon, and I've been ignoring her calls."

"OK, mate. Look, I'm sure everything will work out." He just looks mournfully at me. "Well, I'll see you at the Sunderland presser—Friday?"

"Yeah, probably."

He puts on his jacket, picks up his laptop, and heads out. I feel like break dancing! Fucking get in there, my son! First I dispose of Saunders. It looks as if Arnie is next on my hit list, and I'm winging it, hot foot, down to Fleet Street—well, you know what I mean. Fucking ironic, don't you think? This calls for a celebration. Think I'll give Trudi a call but not before I call the police and tip them off about Arnie's drink-driving. I whip out my mobile phone and dial one-oh-one.

"Hello, Northumbria Police?...I'd like to report what I think is a man under the influence of alcohol...Yes, he's just nearly knocked me down near the Bigg Market...Yes, I did manage to get his registration. It's *A, R, N, I, E*, one. Yes, that's right. Thanks...No, I'd rather not give my name if that's OK...OK, thanks very much."

From home, I write my three lines, one beauty about how the expectations of Newcastle fans need to be lowered. This always winds them up. I speak to Cass to make sure he's in the office, and I go around to Trudi's hairdressers. She lets a flat out above the shop, but it's been empty for a month or so. It's been quite a convenient meeting place.

I pick up the key she's left under the mat and let myself in.

"In the bedroom, sexy," she shouts. "I've started without you."

She's obviously heard me trudging up the stairs. I strip off outside the door, leave my clothes in a heap outside, and run into the bedroom. She's lying naked and is plunging a Rampant Rabbit into her, the filthy cow! I move myself up towards the pillow and her head and offer myself to her mouth. She greedily takes it and wanks me into her mouth with her spare hand, while increasing the intensity of the vibrator. It doesn't take long, and we both come at the same time—I pull away and splash all over her tits while she eventually slows down the intensity of the vibrator to stop.

"I hope you're not that quick all the time," a familiar voice from behind says. I turn quickly, and I'm shocked to see my mother, dressed in her underwear, leaning against the door. I turn back and look at Trudi, who looks a little spaced out, to be honest.

"What the fuck?" I pull a pillow over my privates.

"Oh, come on, didn't you used to watch me when you lived at home?"

"Fuck! I never—"

"So you did, many a time."

"I fuckin'...did not!"

"Sure, you didn't hide in the wardrobe when you were a teenager then?"

"What the fuck? You...you're sick, mother—fucking sick in the head!"

"Really? Must be a family trait then."

I get up and head hastily towards the door. My mother passes me on the way.

"Mind if I join you, Trudi?"

I turn and see my mother unhook her bra and step out of her knickers and climb into bed beside Trudi. A moment later, and they're kissing and caressing each other. And I run out, picking up my clothes along the way. I make it to the bottom of the stairs before I realise that I'm still naked. I quickly dress, and after a struggle with the latch, I'm out on the street. My head is spinning, and before I know it, I'm on my hands and knees and throwing up.

She's fucking evil! The cow, she ruins everything. Just bulldozes back into my life, at a moment's notice, as if she's never been away and fucks everything up. Well, she's not going to do it this time. And as for fucking Trudi! She's going to get her comeuppance, too. She's as sick and perverted as Mum is!

Need time to think, think things through. I wander towards the shops, and what the fuck! I've been hit. I've been knocked down, and I'm on my back. How? What? Am I dead? 'Course not. I can lift my arm, but what am I doing on the pavement? I look up, and there's an old man looking down on me from a disabled scooter.

"You alright, sunna?"

"Wha...?"

"I said, are you alright?"

I finally realise what has happened.

"Do I look alright?"

"There's no need—"

"No need for what?"

"You just stepped in my way."

"A fucking likely story." I get up and look more closely at the fat old bastard. He must be in his eighties.

"There's no need for language like that."

He's wearing an old cloth cap, a dirty raincoat, and tatty trainers.

"There's every need for language like that when...when a stupid old twat like you runs me down!"

"But you just stepped in my path, son."

"A fucking likely story."

I'm raging, and I don't know what to do. A few old biddies from the nearby shop have now gathered.

"He's right; there's no need for language like that," adds another old wrinkly, sticking her two pennies in.

"Just fuck off, the lot of you!" I turn my back, and all of a sudden, I feel a whack. I turn back, and she's hitting me with a cucumber.

"What the fuck are you doing?"

"Don't you use language like that in front of me!"

"Jesus!"

"Or take the Lord's name in vain!"

And she hits me again. I take the cucumber and throw it across the road, push the old fella off his scooter, jump on, and take off down the street. More people have gathered around the fracas. When I look back, a middle-aged couple helps the old man to his feet. Some of them are waving their fists at me, and I think, *What the fuck am I doing?*

I'm going the wrong way. My car's around the other side of the shops. I turn the scooter around and head back towards them, picking up a healthy ten miles an hour; it feels faster. They're standing there gawping, like, I dunno, docile wildebeests, speechless and rooted to the spot. Not for long, though. They spring and leap to the sides to avoid injury as I drive straight at them while I make my escape. I hear shouts of "Lunatic!" "Idiot!" and "Imbecile!" as I disappear around the corner. I feel much better already. I spot a children's play area and head towards it, and I drive the spacker mobile into the sandpit.

Chapter 15

Beneath the tables of a U-shaped classroom, a note is hastily handed from one pupil to another and from one end of the room to the other. Each student swiftly takes a glimpse at the crumpled message, chuckles, and passes it on in a clandestine, conspiratorial manner as the teacher labours through the correct way to punctuate a sentence.

The tattered correspondence eventually lands in the lap of Thomas, who is concentrating on which nouns need capital letters. He is unaware of the childish cackle building up throughout the room. He looks at the piece of paper resting between his legs and reads it.

Raggy, get a bath. You stink!

Thomas looks up and tries to identify the main protagonist behind the prank. No one looks at him, but the embarrassed and nervous titters coming from his classroom contemporaries cut through him, even more so when he sees a cruel grin on the face of the beautiful Sarah Nichols. He thinks Sarah is perfect; she's got white-blond hair, sparkling blue eyes, alabaster skin, and a beaming smile he wishes would shine on him. And yet it is her heartless, unkind, and almost-brutal smirk that hurts the most. He can just about take the teasing from the others but not from one who looks so angelic, saintly, and immaculate.

Graham Hughes is probably the instigator, Thomas believes. Graham, who sits with his partner in crime, Peter Berry, is seated to Sarah's left. He has teased and bullied Thomas from the first day he started at his new school. And while Peter has been kind to him on several occasions when his mate wasn't around, his association with Graham still makes him as culpable.

The teacher is writing on the blackboard but can hear some of his pupils being distracted and calls out to his class to "keep the noise down." Yet despite his appeal, the whispers, squawks, and chortles continue.

"I said keep it down," he orders once more, turning to face the class. "What is up with you this morning? Rafferty! What is that?...Answer me, boy! What is that?...Cat got your tongue? What is it?"

"A note, sir."

"What does it say?...Come on, boy; read it out...I'm not waiting all day."

"Raggy…"

"Go on."

"Raggy…get a bath…You stink!"

The class, whose giggles had been bubbling beneath the surface prior and during the exchange of language, consequently erupts into riotous laughter as the last words roll off Thomas's tongue.

"That's enough," bellows the teacher as he looks directly into the teary eyes of the classroom victim. "I said that's enough! Quiet, at once!" The roar from the class instructor is enough to finally make the unruly children settle down. "Thomas, go and clean yourself up."

And with that, the eight-year-old gets to his feet and makes for the door.

Chapter 16

I get to the office just before ten in the morning and park in Saunders's old parking bay. Ah, the privileges of being a chief, even if it is acting, for the time being. I could get used to this, and I will.

I issue a breezy good morning to the receptionist, who is called Annie, according to her name tag. She must be new, as I've never seen her before. She has jet-black hair in a bob style and a pretty face for someone who looks to be in her forties. A little bit overweight, but I bet she was a heartbreaker in her day.

I pick up the paper, and on the front, I read about some crazed monster high on drugs and drink who had beaten an old man to within an inch of his life. Fucking disgusting. There's no respect for our old-age pensioners. Hang on…

> A severely disabled war hero was attacked yesterday by a man high on a cocktail of drugs and drink.
>
> George Entwistle, eighty-three, of Acorn Road, Jesmond, was physically thrown off his mobility scooter and verbally abused by a man believed to be in his thirties, while stunned shoppers looked on in horror.
>
> The attacker then drove off in Mr. Entwistle's disability vehicle before attempting to run down shoppers aiding the elderly gentleman. The scooter was later found abandoned in a nearby children's playground.

The incident took place near a popular Jesmond shopping area yesterday afternoon at approximately five thirty.

Mr. Entwistle, a veteran of the Falklands War in the early 1980s, suffered cuts and bruises and was clearly shaken by the episode.

He said, "I saw that the man was in distress on the pavement. So I went over to see if he was OK. I think he must have fallen over drunk. I could smell whiskey on his breath. But he just went mad, shouting and screaming for no reason at all."

Greengrocer Peter Holden said, "I heard shouting, and I went out to see what all the commotion was. And then I saw this madman on a disabled scooter screaming abuse at passers-by, and that's when I called the police."

Inspector Pratt, of the Northumberland police, added, "These are the actions of a very sick and disturbed man. Mr. Entwistle fought for his country during the Falklands conflict, and this is an appalling way to treat one of our war heroes. Deducing from our inquiries, we believe he may be in possession and under the influence of drugs and alcohol and must not be approached. But if you have any information of his whereabouts or his identity, we would appreciate it if you would contact the police immediately."

Police are looking for more witnesses to the incident to come forward as they attempt to apprehend the assailant. He is believed to be in his early to midthirties, with short, blond, mousy hair, a fair complexion, and medium height.

That's the dick splash who interviewed me over Lucy. But high on drugs and drink? I'm not sure a lager top and a dissolvable Disprin count, to be honest. A war veteran who has seen action and yet is shaken by being pushed off a scooter? I've seen more action on a Subbuteo board. No mention that the old bastard ran me down! Who fucking wrote this shite? Ah, the lesbian. Fucking typical. I might have known. I've a good mind to go back and find the old bastard and give him a proper kicking. In fact I will if I'm ever around there again. Although I doubt it…what with fucking…Trudi and my sick mother… It's fucking disgusting.

I get to the sports desk, and Cass is thrashing away on his keyboard. I'm surprised he hasn't broken the bloody thing, the way he hammers it.

"Morning, bonnie lad," he says in a faux Geordie accent, which somehow manages to evoke a mixture of Welsh, Indian, and West Indies inflections.

"Morning, geezer," I return in an even worse Cockney-style twang.

"You see this?" he says, pointing to the front-page story. "Just outside my Trudi's place."

"Aye, so it is."

"Facking disgusting. An old war hero an' all. There's no respect these days. In fact, if this had happened when I was a lad, the whole community would've been out looking for the bastard. And wouldn't have stopped until they found him and strung 'im up."

For fuck's sake, he'll start banging on about how this country's gone to the dogs in the minute.

"This country's gone to the dogs." Here we go. "Did you see *Newsnight* last night?"

"No, why?"

"Them bloody Muslims have got planning permission to build a mosque opposite Durham Cathedral! It's facking disgusting. I'm telling you, my son. I'm off to Australia before long. They don't stand for any of that. You hear what that John Howard said to them, not so long back? He told Muslims who want to live under Islamic Sharia law to get out of Australia."

"Cass, he didn't."

"He bloody did. He told foreigners to adapt to their Western ideals or get out of the country. Told foreigners to learn the language and respect the Christian faith and principles an' all."

I leave Cass ranting and go and make a cup of tea. My phone rings. It's Millwall Mick. I'd better answer this. I've been avoiding him for a while.

"Michael, how's my favourite South Londoner?"

"I'll facking favourite sarf Landoner, you slag. When you gonna pay me for that facking match I did for ya?"

"Sorry, mate. I've just been full of busy and never had a match in London to cover for months, so I've never been down to the Smoke."

"That don't explain why you been ignoring my calls and texts."

"Sorry, mate, I haven't just—well, you know how it is. I'll try and organise a game in London soon, and I'll settle up with you, unless you want a cheque."

"What good's a cheque, you doughnut?"

"Yeah, sorry, mate. I'll sort it out."

"You'd better, or otherwise I'll send the bill to your editor."

Fuck, fuck, fuck!

"Sorry, Mick, I really am. My fault. I'll sort it and bung you another twenty quid for the inconvenience."

"Yeah, well, it's not the money, you understand, but it's been nearly four months."

"I know, mate, sloppy. I'll make it up to you, honest. Look, gotta go. See you soon. Cheers."

"Yeah, you betta."

I'd better sort this out fast. I've been taking liberties with him, to be honest. And I can't have any repercussions or comebacks on that Millwall match; otherwise, I'm fucking done for.

Calm down, son, deep breaths. Things have been getting on top of you lately, what with that sick fucking mother of yours sticking her neb in. You'll be fine; just pay the lad, and that'll be the end of it. That's what I'll do. After Christmas, I'll organise a game in London, and I'll pay the debt and take the fucker out for a curry or something. No, bollocks to that. He's unbearable at the best of times.

Cup of tea? Yeah, cup of tea. I check the fridge for milk. The bastards have been at it again. I marked the bottle before I left last night, and there's half gone. Right, I'll fucking teach you. I take out the bottle and move over to the corner of the kitchen so that no one can see me, whip out big john, and piss in the bottle. That's better. I feel like a new man already. Right, Raffers, come on; you against the world.

We're approaching Christmas, and it's the busiest time of the year for us, what with matches and press conferences coming up thick and fast. I've told

Harvey we need another body in because of Saunders's incarceration, and he's agreed to get a trainee. Not sure who he's got in mind, but I hope it's none of those spanners we've had in on work experience. They've been fucking useless. They love the idea of being a hack but don't want to do the work or put the time in. Most of them are petrified of making a phone call. We've had six in this year, and I've never heard one of them make a call. The one we had in last summer, Jesus, there was more go in a red traffic light.

"Have you phoned him?" I asked him.

"This is one part of the job I hate," he replied.

Staggering when you think talking to people—it's the fucking job! Another said he couldn't get an answer. I sat opposite the twat all day, and he never picked up the phone to dial a number once. One of them said he rang from home when I asked where he got the quotes from. Another one only lasted a day. I took the bone-idle bastard to a Middlesbrough press conference, too. He listened in while I interviewed Gordon Buchanan. Did he realise how lucky he was? I think not! One of the most colourful personalities the game has ever thrown up in the postwar modern era, and he chucked it after a day. Posted messages on Facebook saying he'd made a big mistake. He's the fucking mistake. His father should have had a wank instead.

There're hundreds of journalism-training courses throughout the country and thousands of students in the programmes but few jobs to go to when they've finished. Newspaper sales are down; local newspapers are going out of business because the older generation, who buy the paper, are dying and the younger generation are reading stories online rather than physically buying a paper. In ten years' time, the newspaper industry as we know it will be dead. And yet colleges up and down the country put on these courses. Why? Money, of course. It keeps the lecturers in work and the colleges and universities open for that bit longer.

It's the *Post*'s Christmas party tonight, and I can't be bothered. The rest of the sports desk is going. Cass will be there with Trudi, of course, which is usually fun because I bone her in one of the bogs or in the car park. But I've finished with her after that episode with my mother. My mother has ruined all of my Christmases, and she's managed to do it again. There was generally a new bloke each Festive Yuletide. This year it's a new woman! My fucking woman!

I feel my phone vibrate in my pocket. I don't recognise the number. I generally don't answer numbers I don't recognise, but it can't be more bad luck.

"Hello?"

"Hi, Tom?" I recognise the voice but can't place it.

"Yeah."

"It's Julie."

"Julie?"

"Julie, Julie McCarthy."

Chapter 17

"What can I do for you?"

"I'm sorry, Tom, I'm really sorry."

"About what?"

"Everything. Shania told me everything. That she may have exaggerated about you…well, you know."

I say nothing.

"She says she was feeling left out and jealous of how close we were getting."

"Why now? Why would she confess now after all this time?"

"She told me how you rescued her from Bob."

"Bob?"

"My boyfriend, well, ex-boyfriend now…the guy touching her up in the bar."

"Oh, right." What a lying devious cow her daughter is. Still, she's kept her promise. At least I should be grateful for that. "Don't mention it. It was nothing."

"Nothing? How can you say that? God knows what would've happened had you not been there."

I can guess.

"It was nothing, honestly."

"Well, it is a big deal to me. How can I ever make it up to you?"

"Eh, dunno…Buy me a drink sometime, I suppose."

"What are you doing tonight?" Play hard to get, bonny lad; this could work to your advantage. "Shania's out at the pictures with her friends, so…"

"Got the *Post*'s Christmas do, as it happens."

"Ah, no worries. It was stupid of me to phone. Sorry, I shouldn't have. You've probably got a girlfriend and you're taking her…Maybe another time, eh?"

I pause for a while.

"Suppose I could give it a miss," I say in a bored sigh. "The work parties haven't been as good lately. What you got in mind?"

"Why don't you come over, and I'll cook dinner?"

"Only if it's my favourite," I jovially add.

"What, spaghetti hoops on toast and Angel Delight?" She's laughing now.

"You remembered."

"OK, then, spaghetti hoops on toast and Angel Delight it is."

"You're on! The Four Men of the Apocalypse riding wild horses couldn't hold me back! What about eight-ish?"

"Eight would be fine. See you then. Bye."

"Bye."

I'd better nip down to the supermarket. I wrap up three club lines in a couple of hours. It's getting closer to the January transfer window day, so I write three speculative stories. Or, rather, I make up three yarns, linking an obscure Frenchman to Newcastle, Norwegian striker Peter Lundquist to Sunderland, and former Boro favourite Juninho back to Teesside as a part of a coaching restructure at the Riverside, and I'm on my way home. I'd better have a quick shower and a change of clothes. It's obvious I'll be getting hot, dirty love tonight, and so I'd better give Charlie a good scrub. Maybe she'll let me do her up the jacksy as a way of an apology. I'd better pop into Aldi on the way and buy a bottle of wine to help ease the process.

Julie greets me at the door with a kiss on the side of the cheek; it's like I've never been away. She ushers me through the front door.

"Go through to the dining room; it'll not be long." She goes through to the kitchen and shouts, "Open the wine; the glasses are in the cabinet."

I look around, and it hasn't changed much since the last time I was here, although this cabinet is new. As I slide open the cabinet door and take out the wine glasses, she backs into the dining-room door with two plates of steaming-hot spaghetti hoops.

"The Angel Delight is setting, so you'll have to wait."

"Maybe I could just cover you in it and lick it off?"

"That would be nice," she says, placing the plates on the table, moving over to me, and wrapping her arms around my neck. "Maybe you could dip your dick in it, and I could suck it off."

Before I know it, she's tearing at my jeans, or rather pulling them down, and has me in her mouth while I'm wrenching to get her clothes off as she goes down on me. This fucking bra is a nightmare. She realises I'm having a little difficulty and reaches around and unclips it as I turn her around, bend her over, and start humping her from behind. She's still in good shape for being a mum. Looks a little like Jan Francis off that TV programme *Just Good Friends*: small, brown hair in a bob, wiry body, and small tits with massive nips. Big arse, mind, and that's where I make my deposit. Well, she doesn't have the breasts for it that Trudi has. I collapse on top of her, and we lie in silence for a few moments.

My phone starts ringing from the discarded jeans lying in a heap. It then beeps as it's gone into voice mail. Seconds later we hear the sound of a text buzzing. The phone starts ringing again.

"Someone is desperate to get hold of you."

I get up and see there's one missed call from my mother and one from Trudi, who has also sent a text pleading for me to get in touch, as my mother is in a bad way.

"Anything interesting?"

"It's my mother."

"She's back from Ireland?"

I'd forgotten Julie knew my mother. Met her when we had a weekend in Dublin. My mum insisted we meet down in Temple Bar when she heard I was in the Republic of Ireland's capital. And then she embarrassed me further by squeezing Julie's arse, saying it was a perfect pear shape. Had the whole bar singing along to an X-rated version of Smokie's hit record "Living Next Door to Alice." Julie thought it was great that my mother was still full of beans at her age. Full of shit, more like.

"Yeah, she's been back in Newcastle a couple of weeks."

"That's nice."

"More like a Freudian nightmare." That's what should be written on her gravestone.

"Aw, she was lovely that time in Ireland." I raise my eyebrows doubtfully at her while reaching for my jeans.

"What does she want?"

"The usual, to make my life as difficult as she possibly can, if past experiences are anything to go by…I'm sorry, Julie, but think I'd better go and see what the problem is. It's probably nothing, knowing her, but you never know. It could be serious as well."

"Yes, of course, you'd better find out what's up. Just give me a call, and we can work something out." Julie wraps her arms around me and says, "It's great to see you. I really missed you. I just wish…"

"Ah, forget it. These things happen, I suppose. Glad Shania finally did the right thing. It's been hanging over like a cancerous cloud, to be honest. To think you actually thought I was capable of…that." I shiver to keep the pretence going.

"I know. I know. I'm so sorry for ever doubting you. I'll make it up to you, if you let me." I smile sympathetically and hug her tight.

"I'll call you later when I find out what's wrong with my attention-seeking mother."

Julie sees me to the door and watches as I drive off. In my rear, I can see her wave. I thought I'd be elated, but I feel absolutely nothing for her. At one stage, I thought it was love, but it must have been a phase. To be honest, Trudi and my mother's call give me the perfect excuse to get away. Still, it is Christmas, so I might string it along, at least until the new year. There's nowt worse than spending the Festive season on your own, although I know plenty about that from past experiences.

I'm feeling in a better mood despite the old bag's calls. "A Fairy tale of New York" is on the radio, so I quickly switch over to Heart from Metro Radio. "Best Christmas song ever made," Saunders has always claimed. Is it, shite, not a patch on "Do They Know It's Christmas?" or "Pipes of Peace"? This is more like it: "Simply Having a Wonderful Christmas Time."

I pull over and listen to my voice mail. There is one from Trudi and one from my mother, both telling me we've been invited to Christmas lunch at the Cassidys' house. I get a flashback to Cass shooting his load over that young girl in their holiday snaps, and it gives me a shiver. They're fucking mental. They're all a shrink's wet dream. It would probably turn into an orgy, if previous experience is anything to go by. And I wouldn't be surprised if Cass tried to suck me off! Revolting! No, they can go and get fucked. I'd rather spend Christmas Day watching Noel Edmonds deliver presents to special-needs kids, listening to the Queen's speech, and eating cold ravioli out of a used dog's bowl than go through with that.

I need some groceries, so I head over to the Regent Farm Estate. The only holdup is two young lasses in front of me. They must be about fourteen or fifteen but pretending to be eighteen—classy girls, with their short skirts, vest tops, milk-bottle legs, love bites, and cologne that reeks of greasy chips and cigarettes. A scent that would send any self-respecting adolescent with an electronic tag demented with desire. The checkout girl has chased them after they tried to buy a bottle of Lambrusco Bianco. I would have bought it for them—for a nosh! They only need to ask. They must be fucking freezing dressed like that.

That aside, and I'm in and out in no time. I'm putting the bags in the back of the car when I notice something. It looks like Lucy Bird. Is it? That's her coat, but there are probably hundreds of them like that out there. Could be anyone. She's got her hood up and is walking towards the betting shop and hairdressers. There're two dodgy-looking charvers following her, by the looks of things.

In the time it takes me to close the boot of my car, one of the two tearaways grabs the handbag from her shoulder. He attempts to yank it from her possession. She grabs it, and for a moment, there is a small struggle before the second lad pushes her onto the floor. I'm closing in on them, and the bag snatcher notices my approach.

"Quick," he says to his mate.

"Get off it!" Lucy shouts. But a punch to the face sees her relinquish the grip on the bag as her hands come up to protect her face. I get there just as they run away. But they're too quick for me, and after fifty yards, I give up the chase. I double over and try to catch my breath. I'm wheezing like an old man with asthma. I pull myself around and return to the girl, who is sitting on the dwarf wall opposite the betting shop, her head in her hands.

"Lucy?" I ask tentatively. She looks up with pool-filled, sad brown eyes. She's changed. Lost weight and looks withdrawn and emaciated, but then I guess that's to be expected after what she's been through.

"How…you, OK?"

She nods slowly.

"Sorry, but they got away. Anything valuable in the bag?"

She nods another slow, lamentable acknowledgment.

"Cash, credit card…keys?"

She makes a grunt.

"OK, I'll phone the police, and then I'll see if we can get a locksmith. I thought you lived in town. You live around here now?"

"Uh-huh."

"Do you want to tell me where?" She looks up searchingly, as if asking herself if I can be trusted. "Or do you want to call a locksmith?"

"Can you do it?" she softly speaks. She looks broken, not the confident, vivacious, and ostentatious woman I previously knew.

"Yes, of course, not a problem."

Chapter 18

Most of Christmas Day is spent with Johnny Walker. I get up at eleven in the morning, on account of spending Christmas Eve with Captain Morgan, another fine drinking companion. When I check my phone, I see texts from Trudi, Mum, and Julie, wishing me a Merry Christmas. All three of them had invited me over for lunch, and not one of those invitations felt appealing. Trudi and Mum for obvious reasons, while I did not fancy going over to Julie's gaff to engage in a charade of small talk with her slut of a daughter while I pull crackers and stuff my face with sherry trifle. I ignore Trudi and my mum's texts but reply to Julie, thanking her for the invite, and explain that I can't make it as I am covering the Sunderland match at Old Trafford the following day and stopping at a friend's house in Manchester. This isn't the case, because I am driving down tomorrow—Boxing Day—morning. Seeing Lucy the other day really knocked the stuffing out of me. And ironically, while I am halfway through a delicious slice of toast with brown sauce, another text buzzes on my phone. To my surprise, it is from Lucy and not another plea from that bitch of a mother and her new girlfriend, my slut of an ex.

> Thanks 4 UR help the other night, Tom. Hope U R having a nice xmas day. Lucy x

I feel last night's rum curdle in my stomach and retch, although nothing comes up. I didn't even know that she had my number yet alone that she might use it to get in touch. Not that it would have been hard to get hold of. She could have obtained it from anyone at work. How could anyone do such an awful thing to another human being?

I wonder what she's going through or been through. She's been off work since the, eh, assault in August, and Saunders's trial is booked in for the first week of January, which is…next week. She must be going through, I dunno, hell. I should've done more, called and seen if she was alright or wanted anything. But what could I have done? How could I have helped?

U R welcome. It was nothing. Sorry I have not been in touch, but didn't know what 2 do. Hope U R well. Let me know if I can help in anyway, Merry xmas, Tom x

Fuck! My heart is beating faster than a boy band's drumstick. I need a drink. I check the fridge and cupboards, and there's nothing. There is no beer and surprisingly no spirits. But hang on, there it is, by the peddle bin in the kitchen. A lonely unopened bottle of whisky, which I'd nicked from Lucy's party, stretches out a helping hand, offering to fill the empty void and share the pain of my wretched existence.

"Thanks for the offer, mate. Much appreciated," I tell my new drinking pal. "Don't really care much for Captain Morgan, to be honest, too sweet and sugary."

I settle down with Johnny and watch various Festive cartoons, including "The Snowman" and "Mickey's Christmas Carol," before crying like a proverbial baby to "It's a Wonderful Life" and passing out.

Chapter 19

I remember as a little boy wondering over to a spartanly dressed Christmas tree and staring emotionlessly at its lack of sparkle and splendour and the dearth of presents beneath it. After several moments looking around the cold, dark room, I was aware of a pungent, stale smell of export beer and stubbed-out cigarettes filling my lungs. Dressed in dirty blue-pinstriped pyjamas, I walked over to the television and pressed a button. The sound of an exploding bulb was heard from within the TV while it flashed blue and yellow as it moved in and out of focus before a choir of children singing Christmas carols came into view.

I made my way out of the lounge, up the stairs, which were stifled by a purple paisley floor covering, and into my mother's bedroom. I witnessed her semi naked body lying face down in a state of intoxicated sleep. Her head was cocked to the right and lying in a pool of drool on the pillow, while her right arm and leg were outside the bed covers and flopped down by the side. To her left lay a man on his back, snoring and spluttering.

The export-beer and cigarette odours that polluted the room downstairs were even more conspicuous and acerbic in the main bedroom.

I shook my mum and asked, "Why hasn't Santa been, Mammy? Mammy? Mammy, wake up."

"Ugh. Eh?"

"Why hasn't Santa been?"

"Leave me alo...What?"

"Santa hasn't been."

"Will you tell that little fucker to keep the noise down…or he'll get a hiding," the man shouted.

"He hasn't been?"

"No."

"Well, that's because he doesn't visit naughty boys," she slurred and turned her cheek away to the other side.

You made it up to me on Boxing Day, in the sales, though, didn't you? OK, it wasn't the electric-train Lego set everyone got at school. But at least it was Lego. Everyone seemed to have it when I got back to school, that or Scalextric.

It's the first Christmas Day I can recall, and what a sorry day to remember. My mother lay in bed until midday. Her boyfriend, whose name escapes me, was up and out before she got up. I had to make my own breakfast: Sugar Puffs with water, because there was no milk. I sat and watched Noel Edmonds until her bloke came back pissed up, just as *Top of the Pops* was starting. He caused a row with my hungover mother about spending too much time chatting and flirting with his friends and not paying more attention to him on Christmas Eve, and then he screamed the house down for the lack of a Christmas dinner. Mum told him to fuck off and added that "If he wanted someone to cook and clean for him, he could piss off back to his mother." I crept upstairs to my room as the row ensued and spent the majority of it making a Millennium Falcon out of a Sugar Puffs box and Sellotape.

Mum didn't stay with him long after that. She said he was too possessive and had become tight. Yes, he was a cock, a pervert, and a cruel bastard. And he didn't help to create a warm, pleasant, and merry yuletide when my mum was with him. But he can't be blamed for the abject festive seasons that followed.

I'm not sure if she did it on purpose and out of spite, because of her unhappy childhood. But it was horrible nonetheless. It wouldn't have been any worse had she stopped with him or the other blokes thereafter, although you'd think she would want to put right the bad mistakes or memories of her past. Yet on the other hand, there were years where it seemed as if she did try, only to spoil it by giving me the old England replica kit because it was in the sales and not the new one. It didn't matter when she bought the wrong Sunderland outfits, because no one seemed to be aware of what strip they wore or who their new sponsor was, probably a consequence of neither North-Eastside playing in the same league for much of the '80s and early '90s. But if anyone did notice when we got back to school after the holiday, it would be Graham Hughes. The bastard! It was always Graham Hughes, always taking the piss, always making me look like the pathetic wretch that I was.

"What did you get for Christmas this year, Raggy?" he would mock, much to the merriment of the others. "Last year's latest toy?"

And Chrimbo 1990 when I got the West Germany strip for Christmas, it caused even more mickey-taking, mockery, and skit. I got called Hitler, Adolf, or Nazi boy for most of that year. It was a nice change from being called Harry Ramp, the Tramp, or Raggy Rafferty, mind, but it was still disturbing. I'm sure my mother did it for devilment. And when I complained to the teachers about being bullied, they either said, "You bring it on yourself" or "Stop being so sensitive." So in the end, I stopped bothering. Just kept my head down and tried to avoid trouble when I could.

There were some pathetic presents, though. My mother bought me the first *Now That's What I Call Music* album, which would've been great, had we been in possession of a record player. She'd pawned the bloody thing a week before Christmas to get her gypsy charm bracelet back. One time she wrapped up an opened box of cornflakes and a cold bacon sandwich. She said it was "a special hotel Christmas breakfast." Another time she got her days mixed up, so she popped into the local garage on the way back from a night on the piss and bought some air freshener to go with some bars of chocolate and crisps.

But when I was sixteen, all the pain and suffering ended, or rather that was when she stopped giving me presents. She said I was "too old to be receiving presents" and that "Christmas was for kids." And when I made her aware that Christmas didn't happen for me as a kid in our house, she slapped me across the face and told me, "You aren't too old to be getting a clip around the ear hole for your cheek."

I fucking hate you, Mam! You hear? Fucking hate you!

Chapter 20

"What the fu..." Oh, my fucking neck. What's the telly doing on? Right, must have fallen asleep and left it on. It's fucking freezing, and I feel like shit. And my neck, Jesus! Shouldn't have...Christ, I've...What time is it? Fuck! Need to be quick; otherwise, I'll not make the match.

After a quick shower, I gather my laptop bag, and I'm in the car for ten in the morning and off to Old Trafford for Sunderland's Boxing Day fixture. The weather's not too bad, a bit cold, but that's to be expected this time of the year. At least there's no snow and ice. I take the A69 down to Carlisle and get on the M6 before switching on to the M61 and so on. Much quicker than going down the A1 and M62. Too many traffic jams that way. I've got the *Post*'s pool car, and shit, I just remembered, the radiator's bust. Well, not completely, but it only blows lukewarm air after half an hour of driving. Thank fuck the radio works. That'll take my mind off it—that, and the rape, incest, and fucking murder plans I had yesterday.

It's the usual fare around this time of year. The general football enthusiasts call in to discuss the hosts' topics: a midseason winter break, respect to referees and linesmen—sorry, assistant referees—and video technology.

The Sunderland boss has been quoted before the game, saying he's in favour of a "two-week break" to recharge his players' batteries, although he wants to keep the traditional Boxing Day and New Year's Day fixtures. He doesn't see why the football authorities in England can't arrange it and finish the season two weeks later in May.

This is a typical, lazy, sports-journo question at this time of the year—always a topical question when you're struggling for a line in winter. We hacks generally don't really care, one way or another, as long as the question results in an inside-page lead. And it can be knocked out in less than an hour, in my case. I just hunt out last year's story on it, renose the intro, and stitch in the quotes—and bingo! It means I get to spend more time wanking to bigbaps. com or humping Cass's…bitch! Slut! Focus, Raffers. Focus, son.

Focused. The same goes with the Respect Campaign for referees and video technology, which generally go hand in hand. Back in the day, the video-technology debate always raised its ugly head when a referee and his assistant missed a ball that had crossed the goal line in a game. I don't think video will be reintroduced for anything else other than that. The match official's decision not to award a goal generally resulted in him being harangued by one team, and it, by and large, would go on for a good few minutes after the incident. Two easy questions in one. Jackpot! Needless to say, they're easy to write up, and there's no real conclusion, as I found by listening to the debate.

The video-technology debate is ordinarily split, maybe sixty to forty, in favour of lights, camera, action, while the respect campaign argument was mental. Several callers had little sympathy for the men in the middle if they got their decisions wrong.

One half-wit on the radio suggested a jail term and another suggested castration, while sacking and no voting rights were also quite popular. I think even prisoners who have been incarcerated have those rights. My favourite was some spanner from Darlington who proposed a gladiatorial fight to the death at Wembley with the Premier League's worst referees, to be voted by season-ticket holders only, at every club in the top flight. They would all have to be dressed in regulation kit and have a whistle and pen as weapons in combat against each other, and lions and tigers would also join in the carnage. I think they should be shot myself. With shit.

Whoops. Here we are. I make good time and arrive just after one thirty. I park behind the ground in a huge car park after dealing with some sort of traffic steward. I make my way towards the stadium and pass a sign warning people about unauthorised traders. Hilarious, it's in about seven different

Asian languages. Man United supporters are very sensitive about where the majority of their support comes from. And there have been several surveys in the past that have concluded that they have the most supporters from their locality, whereas others contradict that statement. I guess I would be in the latter camp. Every time the TV cameras arrive outside the historic ground, reporters always seem to find someone with a Cockney accent—either that or someone from China, Japan, or some other nip country. One of the funniest things I saw on TV was while watching Fergie's mob play a Champions League match against Anderlecht at Old Trafford. United scored, and immediately after, a TV camera did a sweep of supporters celebrating the goal. It only found a row of Chinese fans jumping up and down and cheering the effort. Hilarious!

I pass the statue of the Holy Trinity, George Best, Denis Law, and Bobby Charlton and then the one of Sir Matt Busby and Sir Alex Ferguson. Ferguson has his arms folded. They should have cast it with him pointing to his watch. I fucking hate the bastards. Not as much as Liverpool, mind, but nearly as much. Saying that, the ground and tribute to the club's glorious past are something else, certainly when you walk down the Munich Tunnel towards the press room.

There's a plaque to commemorate the fiftieth anniversary, a memorial to the birth of the Busby Babes, and pictures and facts of the team's achievements. The walk up the stairs to the press room is equally impressive. There are life-size pictures of the treble-winning season of 1999, of their first Premier League title, and of other notable triumphs. Then there are the legends who wore the famous jersey: Cantona, Ronaldo, Keane, Beckham, and dozens of other luminaries. I feel star struck by the time I've climbed to the top. And when I enter the press room, I get even more bedazzled by all of the celebrity journos, the hack world's big hitters, the national newspaper's number ones in sport. These are the ones generally seen on Sky, BBC, or special one-off tributes to the sporting world's greats. Most of them even have their own websites. A bit vain and narcissistic, but hey, I'll be quite happy to fall in love with myself once I've climbed the greasy pole. They're all here, from the *Times*, *Telegraph*, *Guardian*, *Mirror*, and *Sun*, and there's the *Mail*'s Matt Kelly.

I need to introduce myself and get networking with him. He's going to be a colleague, after all, if I get my way.

"Hi, Matt," I say, all breezy. He looks at me suspiciously. "Tom Rafferty," I continue. "I work for the *Post* in Newcastle. I'm a friend of Arnie, Chris Arnott."

"Oh, right," he returns, still warily. "Didn't know he had any friends. Bit of a cunt, don't you think?"

"Eh, ha-ha, aye, I suppose so." I laugh sycophantically, as a few heads turn to see what's happening. Kelly has turned away from me and made his way down the room. I follow him.

"What was your name again?" Kelly asks in what sounds like a rather posh Jeeves-and-Wooster type of accent. Think I might have to take elocution lessons.

"Tom, Tom Rafferty."

"Ah, yes. I'm guessing you've heard that the *Mail* isn't going to renew your friend Arnott's contract at the end of the season?"

"Yeah, he told me."

"Just as well really. That unfortunate business outside the Riverside before the Sunderland game a few years ago, added to the drink-driving charge last month."

"Really?"

"Oh, yes, four times over the limit apparently. The editor was livid."

"That, I didn't know. You know who will be taking over his patch in the North-East?"

"Yes, the editor said he did have someone in mind. Apparently he's provided a couple of exclusives from up your way. Not you, by any chance?"

"Well, I don't like to boast, but I'd appreciate it if you kept it under your hat."

"Mum's the word, dear boy. It will be good to have you on board and hear that that ruddy-faced bounder is to walk the plank. We'll talk later, yes? Must prepare for the game."

"Yes, we'll speak after the match and compare notes."

"OK, laters."

I'm feeling great about myself. Things are looking up career-wise. Just need to resolve the Freudian nightmare and the Trudi cougar scenario over the festive period.

I've got about half an hour to prepare and get my facts ready before the kick-off. It isn't half easy when you're handed a stats sheet with your programme and press pass. It's a simple life as a hack. Well, sometimes.

The match as a contest is a non event, to be honest, and not difficult to write up. John Wayne nets a brace for the Red Devils in a 2–0 win. In truth, it could have been seven or eight with no reply; such is the Black Cats' gutless display. You could tell it is a stroll in the park for Man United.

I summarise, "At times, it was like watching a parent scold a child for peeking at his presents before December 25, while, on the other hand, United looked as if they'd been given a new ball for Christmas and weren't letting anyone play with it, such was their dominance."

It's generally standard fare to mention the festive season in a report if it's that time of year. It's the same with Guy Fawkes night or Halloween. You can always stitch in fireworks or spooks or words and phrases associated with the celebration into your match report. Lazy? Aye, I know, but it helps to waste a few lines when you're on deadline at an evening match.

I may have concluded, "The defeat was anything but a disgrace, and the result should be looked at as nothing more than a setback," and added, "Sunderland are still on track to record their best finish to a Premier League season in fifteen years." In truth, I wanted to write, "The players were a fucking disgrace to the shirt, a pathetic excuse for a football team, and undeserving of their supporters," but one has to maintain one's composure in the face of adversity. Hey, look at that; two minutes in the company of the posh lad, and I'm talking like him. I'll be invited to the Bullingdon Club next. Maybe not, eh?

Black Cats boss, Bruce Stephens, comes out to face the written press, something the great Sir Alex Ferguson never did, mind, and trots out the usual injury excuses in mitigation for his side's pitiful performance. Who cares at this stage? All I want to do is write up his defence and file my copy to the sports desk—a task that I accomplish in fewer than thirty minutes.

I swap numbers with Matt before I leave the stadium, and I'm out into the car park and the car at just after seven. I reckon I could be back in the house between ten and ten thirty if there are no hold-ups. I switch my phone back on and call Cass to see if he's received my copy. He acknowledges it has arrived, and I hang up as three text alerts beep on my phone.

The first is from my mum, again, asking for me to contact her.

> Please, son, I feel suicidal. Get in touch, Mum x.

The second—surprise, surprise—is from Trudi.

> Hey, babe, really sorry about the other week. Your mum made some cakes, and I didn't know they were spiked with cannabis. Thought it was all a dream until your mum told me otherwise. Please call. We've got some making up to do. Love you, T xxx

The third nearly knocked me sideways. It was from Lucy Bird.

> Hi, Tom. Can I take u up on offer and meet up for chat? Lucy x

Chapter 21

Ouch! Ow, ow, ow! What the fuck! What's happening? I'm awake…but I can't move. I can't move! I'm paralysed! Disabled! Fuck! I can't move! I've been drugged! I'm lying on my front and…and…someone's on top of me! Fucking me! The pain is excruciating. Who the…it's Cass! The dirty, perverted bastard!

"Alright, my son? Smashing, 'ansome, lurvly."

I can't speak. I want to kill the filthy, gay bastard, but I can't move. I can only make a moaning noise. Where am I? Lucy's flat! What am I doing here?

"Come on, Dave. I want to ride him now," teases Trudi. What the…?

"OK, doll, your turn."

Cass turns me over on to my back, and Trudi lowers herself on top of me. I can't believe it. I've actually got a hard-on. What does that mean? I've been enjoying it? Trudi bucking on top of me feels good, though, even though I feel as if I've been defiled by that debauched cunt. Cass shuffles over on his knees until he's level with my face and offers his long, white, pasty-looking cock. But I can't open my mouth, thank God, so he just slaps it in my face and laughs. It stinks of…shit, ugh. Think I'm going to vomit. I turn my face away and see my mother being ridden over the sofa, doggy-style, by a bloke with silver, wiry hair. He's old enough to be a pensioner. He smiles, waves at me, and says, "You OK, son?"

What the fuck is he on about? Who does he think he is? Looks familiar, mind. I've seen his face somewhere before, but…nah, it can't be. That would make him—oh my fucking God. This is sick. It's Sodom and Gomorrah, a decadent ancient Greek or Roman orgy, or a Catholic priest's enclave.

I notice Marty, who is dressed in a white Ku Klux Klan robe.

"I fucking hate black people, and they hate us," he says to someone who looks like a Jewish rabbi wearing a Newcastle United replica jersey. But it's not; it's Harvey, who is chanting, "Hare, Hare, Hare, Hare Krishna, Krishna, Krishna" and "Keegan, Keegan, Keegan, Keegan Krishna" as Marty slips on the hooded penitent. This has gone beyond mental!

Lucy and Saunders are here…having an argument in the kitchen. She is sitting on the floor and has curled up her knees beneath her chin. Her arms are folded over the knees, and her face is buried into them.

"It was nae me," he protests vehemently. "I would nae dee that to any-wan, niver mind you. I love you."

"Yeah, so you say," she sobs. "I want to believe, but the police have all that evidence."

"It was Rafferty! I know it was!"

"He wasn't even at the party, Scott. How could it be him?"

"He must've been there."

"But he wasn't, was he?"

"Open your eyes, Luce; he was Darth Vader."

"No, he wasn't; that was you. Tom was the only one who—"

"What? The only one who what? He fucking hates you, Luce. Always has."

"No, he doesn't. He chased those thugs away who mugged me. If he hated me, why would he do that?"

"I cannae answer that, darlin'. But I know for a fact he cannae stand you."

"Come on my tits, big boy," Trudi pants breathlessly to Cass, who is wanking furiously over my face.

"Na, I wanna jizz on Tom here."

"Let me help you do it," interrupts my mum, who is now dressed as the wicked queen from *Snow White*. She's so beautiful. She takes Cass's cock and jerks it over her own breasts. Trudi climbs off me and begins French-kissing my mother while they rub their mammaries together.

My head is swimming. Lucy and Saunders are now waltzing to "Summer Nights." Marty and Harvey are goose-stepping to the King, and I and the old man who was shagging mum are talking to a leprechaun—except it isn't a leprechaun. It's helpful Hi-Ho Harry, our IT chief. It sounds like they've inhaled helium, because they sing "Let's Twist Again" like Pinky and Perky.

Boring Colin is here, discussing traffic congestion with Jo Nicholson, but the exchange takes her out, and she falls asleep.

"You see! You see!" screams Colin, punching the air triumphantly. "I can bore people to sleep! I was going to talk about how there are too many black people in the country, but that just gets people annoyed. But the old traffic-congestion conversation has never let me down yet! I could talk a glass eye to sleep! I just need to record my excruciatingly dull monotone and sell the patent to the National Health Service! I'll win a Nobel Prize!"

I know, I think. *That's what I've always said.*

"You going to tell Lucy, or am I?"

"Eh?" It's Millwall Mick.

"Where's ma fackin' dosh, you cant?"

"Next week, Mick. Honest."

"You fackin' bedder, or else I'll squeal to the pigs!"

He makes squealing noises! This is mental.

"Did you, Tom?"

"Wha…?"

It's Lucy.

"Did you do it, Tom?"

"Do what? No, don't know what you're talking about."

It's Bez and Graham, and they're schoolboys, dressed in shorts and a blazer. Bez has dropped his pencil on the floor. Graham has gone to pick it up, and he looks up my mum's dress!

"You boys, what are you like?" asks my mum.

"Sorry, Mrs. Rafferty," Graham responds.

"No, it's OK. You lie on the floor, and you can have a good look. You see, with one of these," she says as she points towards her fanny, "I can have as many of what you've got for the rest of my life!"

"She's such a slut."

"No, she's not, son," says the old fella to my retort. He was banging my mother earlier. He looks something like a sinister Captain Birdseye or a 1970s BBC Radio One DJ. "I taught your mum free love and a liberal attitude to sex."

"Fuck off, you old cunt!"

"Don't be like that, son."

"I'm not your son!"

"Search your feelings, son. You know it's true!"

"Noooooooo!"

Chapter 22

These fucking dreams, nightmares—they get worse. That's the weirdest yet. Not surprised, what with all the fucking baggage I'm carrying around. I've got more than a London airport. Ignore it, son. Just let it go and concentrate on your job. You're doing OK. Focus. The *Mail* job is just about in the bag. Just swim with the tide.

What's this? Aw, no, for fuck's sake! Another Sunderland player has been discovered living in Newcastle—so Twitter has reliably informed me. Or rather, a Car-Toon Army fan has discovered more like, when I've checked my account.

I quite enjoyed jumping on the Twitter bandwagon when it emerged a few years back. It felt great when I built up a huge following and even better when celebs started keeping track of my Tweets. I've never been one of those hacks who Tweets what's going on at a game, for example, when someone scores. What's the point? The BBC and Sky are always all over it, and second, I don't have the fucking time when I'm writing a report. Still, some writers feel compelled to tell you when they fart, never mind share a titbit from a live match. Admittedly it is narcissistic, but who fucking cares? There's a thin line between love and hate, and Twitter gives me the love I've never had. Well, it did; no, it still does to an extent, but every fucking spanner is on it now. Nobodies! Hairdressers, builders, labourers, shop workers, bin men, production-line workers, mentally retarded, and those with clubbed feet and special needs. And as a consequence, the gossip, scandal, and shit-stirring that was exclusively ours, the journos, isn't ours anymore, because everyone's at it. You Tweet a bit of news and tell your audience to buy tomorrow's paper for more information, and they're already out there doing their own research. Before you know it, they've worked out the story, and it's on the web, fucking up your scoop.

Mind you, some of my so-called North-East-based colleagues in the nationals bollix it up as well, Tweeting injury news a couple of days ahead of a game! That's sometimes a back-page lead if it's a big star! The spiteful bastards only do it because they know the story won't go in their paper, because they're competing to get lines in against hacks from the big boys in Manchester, Liverpool, and London. The giants from the capital and North-West usually take precedence over our wee clubs from the North-East. Little wonder no fucker's buying a newspaper these days. That's put me in a good mood, not.

I've not been in the office since about December 23, so that must be nearly two weeks. I get to work and pick up the paper from the front desk. Fuck, yesterday was day one of the rape trial. I quickly flick through until I find it.

Journalist Accused of Rape
By Sarah Brownlie

A local journalist has been accused of drugging and raping a female colleague, on day one of a three-day trial.

Scott Saunders, of Osborne Road, Jesmond, was charged with sexually assaulting a woman and spiking her drinks with drugs at a party.

The jury heard how a woman, who cannot be named for legal reasons, was given a potent cocktail of alcohol and Rohypnol at a house gathering on Friday, August 18, by sports writer Saunders. The thirty-year-old man then took advantage of his inebriated victim and raped her while she was under the influence of the drugs and in an unconscious state.

The attack, which took place in the bedroom of the twenty-six-year-old woman, of Quayside Mews, Newcastle, is believed to have lasted a little over a couple of minutes.

The court also heard how the police, after a tip-off, raided the accused's flat and discovered evidence against Saunders to prove he is guilty as charged. Drugs, S&M pornography, and DNA samples were taken from items of his clothing and matched with that of the victim. A semen sample was also taken from the woman's underwear and was found to match that of Saunders.

The trial continues.

No mention of them working at the *Post*. I can understand it, like. Bad publicity and all that. But fucking hell! He's going down! Going down, going down, going down; going down, going down, go-wing down; going down, going down! Ha-ha, what a result! The day can't get any better! I could do cartwheels through burning hoops of fire.

Cass is full of himself. You'd think he'd be pissed off, working in the office over the Christmas holidays, but no, he's in a chipper mood.

"Fackin' hell!" he shouts out in mock surprise. "Who's this, then—the new starter?

"Very original, Cass. Good Christmas, I'm guessing?"

"Blinding, son, blinding. Trudi had a mate over for Christmas dinner. Fackin' gorgeous, she was."

"Oh, aye," I respond, not really taking much notice and switching on my PC.

"Good holiday?" the office bore, Colin, calls over.

"Eh? Oh, aye, great thanks, Col," I respond with a smile. I see Joanne Nicholson is in when I turn to acknowledge Cartwright. Her eyes are red, which means she's been dumped again or has a cold. Probably the former. Hibbert is in as well. Thank fuck he hasn't started blabbing on yet. God, I hate these fuckers. They'll not be missed when I leave. Neither will Marty, who has just arrived.

"Alright, lads?"

"Don't talk to me, scumbag!"

Fucking hell, there must be bother between Marty and Cass's daughter, judging by that remark.

"She dumped me, Cass."

"Yeah, well. Hardly surprising when you're seen out with Jo there."

Marty just shakes his head. "It's all a misunderstanding. Office night out, and we were the last two standing."

"Yeah, I'm sure it is."

Bloody hell, he's been seeing Nicholson on the side. Dirty dog. I wonder if he's had any more racist propaganda. He-he! Well, he's been logged in for ten minutes, and he's said nowt. So it mustn't have arrived yet.

Hang on, who's this? Harvey has come out of his office with a young lass.

"Right, gather around, boys and girls, and meet the new addition to the sports desk," Harvey says excitedly, slapping his hands together.

Brilliant! It's the new trainee we've been expecting! And it's a fucking girl! That's all I need! She's not much of a looker, either. For fuck's sake! If we're going to have some split arse on the desk, why can't she be a looker? It was the same at journalism college. All the girls on the course looked like trolls, whereas if you had a wander up to the hair and beauty wing of the college, the girls were all stunning. Intelligence in women must make them ugly, I suppose.

"Right, lads," Harvey continues, "this is Keren Veitch, great-granddaughter of the legendary man himself."

I whisper "who" under my breath to Marty, as we all swap handshakes and acknowledge one another. Marty blanks me.

"And another step forward towards diversity," says Harvey. "She's one of God's own, a Geordie, so you might not understand a bloody word she says. But that doesn't matter, because I've been assured she has a GCSE in English and can put words in a sequence commonly known as a sentence. And as we all know, you horrible reprobates, this skill is quite important in the weird and wonderful world of journalism. Right." Harvey claps his hands together again. "I want you horrible lot in my office once the rest of those half-witted muppets you call colleagues are in. We can do all the formal introductions then. Right, fek off!"

Keren looks a little bemused by Harvey's charade and uncomfortable at the same time. Her knight in shining armour will rescue the situation.

"Hi, Keren, just sit here," I say, pulling out a seat. "Here's this morning's *Post*. Just flick through it and familiarise yourself with the style, and I'll try and sort out something for you to do."

"Thanks…"

"Tom."

"Thanks, Tom."

"You're welcome."

Marty and Cass are ignoring her, or maybe they're ignoring everyone after this morning's spat.

I wonder what Andy Grey and Richard Keys would make of it all.

"Women don't know the offside rule." That's what Grey would probably say. Ha-ha! And his sidekick, Keys, would add, "The game's gone mad. Sexist? Do me a favour, love."

What about Monkfish? "Pull your knickers up, love, and put the kettle on."

Cass the misogynist would agree with them, and so do I: Cass, Monkfish, Grey, and Keys.

To be honest, they did make an arse of themselves back in the day with that Sian Massey, when she ran the line in the Wolves versus Liverpool match that time. It was a tight call in the build up to Liverpool's first goal at Molineux, but she got it spot on, to be fair. Well, you do get lucky every now and then, unless she does know the offside rule, Andy son. And then they had a go at Karren Brady. "Do me a favour, love." Ha-ha, not only sexist but condescending as well! Brilliant! Overall, though, what do women know about football? Fuck all, that's what! Ha-ha!

I remember when the incident first came to light. Cass was at his Neanderthal best, whereas the feminist Saunders was unusually quiet while he was ranting. It turned out that Saunders had taped his bombastic blustering and just let him blab on. Saunders then played it back to him, much to our amusement, and did so every now and again for a laugh.

"I'm not sexist," said Cass, which generally means you are when you say something like that. It's the same when someone states, "I'm not racist but…" and then launches into a diatribe about immigration being wrong for the country.

"I love women, me. Love them," Cass continued. "But the world's gone mad. A woman running a line in the Premier League. It's mental, madness, absolute madness."

"A bit like Ginger Spice becoming lead singer of the Clash, eh, Cass?" Saunders chipped in sarcastically.

"Eh? Don't know about that, but it got me thinking. I'll tell you that for nofink. Why the hell do women want to get involved in male-dominated environments? Fair enough, Sian Massey got the offside decision right, but everyone gets lucky once. You've proved your point. So do us all a favour, love. Stop this refereeing nonsense at once, put the kettle on, and make the tea.

"I love women. And I think they are equally important, but we all need to accept that they are very different than men—physically, mentally, and emotionally. So instead of trying to be equal, why don't they just accept these differences and embrace them? I am not for one minute suggesting we go back to the dark ages, when women were treated like second-class citizens, but I do believe we need to redefine the boundaries. Things used to be so much simpler: men went out to work, went down the pub, and then came home for their dinner. The women's job was to look after the children, keep the house clean, and tidy and cook for their husbands and the kids. See, simple, nice, easily defined roles. Children knew where they stood as well. As I say, everything was far more organised, and society was a better place to live as a result. And we had strong female role models like my old mum and nan. Now things are far more complicated.

"Essentially men haven't changed. We still want the same things we did one hundred years ago, but for some strange reason, women want more than being a mother and a wife. They want what we have, and as a result, society has broken down. And do you know who's to blame? Yes, that's right: the likes of Sian Massey. And all because she wants to become a referee's assistant. What next? We've even had to change the name from 'linesman' to 'referee's assistant' because of the bloody women who want to become referees and the likes.

"I blame all the do-gooders who let women become joiners, builders, and painters and decorators instead of traditional female-dominated jobs like cleaners, shop assistants, secretaries, typists, and hairdressers. But we couldn't stop them, could we? Because if we did, we would be accused of being sexist. So now...now we have female builders, female plumbers, and, worst of all, female referees. I'm telling you now. They only got these jobs as a show of tokenism, not because they were any good at them.

"The thing that annoys me is if you speak to any of these women, these so-called feminists, they say how great the female race is and how useless men are. If that's the case, why do they want to be exactly like us?"

"You finished your rant yet?" Saunders asked in a bored voice. "Because I've got a headache."

"Nah, I haven't finished. Name me one traditionally male-dominated occupation that women are now better at. Come on...You can't, can ya? There isn't one. I mean, it's different for men. They can turn their hand to anything. Take cooking as an example. Name me one female chef better than Ainsley Harriet. You can't, 'cause there isn't one."

I laughed at this; surely there are better examples than Ainsley.

"So we get to a situation where we have to have a female referee's assistant at a Premier League match. Football has always been a male-dominated environment, and now we have women trying to be referees. Richard Keys was right: 'The game's gone mad.' It now costs more money because we've had to organise a separate changing area. And we can't swear and have to behave in a totally different way. I mean it's uncivilised. And what about the male referee's assistant who is sitting at home, doing nothing? And what about the woman's child, eh? The child is left with a childminder instead. Ludicrous!

"I think enough is enough. They've made their point. We get it. They wanted to see what it was like being a man, and now they have, they can all go back to being women again. There is no more important role than being a wife and a mother. They should embrace it and enjoy it. They do it so well. At least they used to anyway. And don't believe all that baloney about not being able to afford to live on one income either. If women were out of the male workplace, it would leave more jobs for the men and higher pay as a result. The values we had sixty years ago were far better."

"You finished now? Have you got it all off your chest?" Saunders again asked.

"Yeah, I'm finished."

"Thank God for that."

If women had heard this rant, they'd be coming from both ends of the country to protest, burn bras, and throw themselves in front of the Queen's horse, probably.

"So what made you want to be a sports writer, Keren?" Marty casually asks.

"Just love sport," she says. "Ever since I was a little girl and found out my great-grandfather played for that legendary Newcastle team in the Edwardian age, I fell in love with football." Alright, alright. Calm down, love. "But I love most sports, not just football: golf, tennis, cricket, rugby."

"An all-rounder, eh?"

"Suppose so." Jesus, she's fucking full of it. "Played tennis, rugby, and football for the county and at university."

"What about golf? What's your handicap?"

"I play off nine."

"Bloody hell, I'm off eighteen; you'll have to show me where I'm going wrong." She laughs at this. Don't you just loathe strong, confident women with personality? Hang on, just caught Cass throwing Marty a look of disgust. Brilliant! Go on, Cass son; tell your daughter about his flirting with the new girl.

I need to burst Miss Perfect's balloon.

"Yeah, but do you know the offside rule?" I jokingly but seriously add. She thinks for a moment, screws up her brow, puts a finger in her mouth like that short-arse *Austin Powers* character, and leans her head to the side.

"An ex-boyfriend told me not to worry my pretty little head about such complex issues. I think that's why he became an ex-boyfriend. Let me see. Just say I'm in a shoe shop, second in the queue for the checkout."

Fuck! She knows the joke and is going to make me look like a wanker in front of the whole newsroom. "Heard it," I manage to mouth. But she's talking especially loudly, and no one notices.

"Behind the shop assistant on the checkout is a pair of shoes, which I've seen, and I must have them."

Oh no, the whole office is listening, and she's becoming more theatrical. She's stood up and is using her arms like she's a fucking trolley dolly!

"The female shopper in front of me has seen them as well and is eyeing them up. But we both have a dilemma. We've forgotten our purses. It would be rude to push in front of the first woman since, you consider, I have no money to pay for the shoes. While we're trying to resolve this problem, the shop assistant remains at the checkout and waits for us to make a move. My friend, who is at the back of the shop trying on another pair of shoes, sees my conundrum and prepares to throw her purse to me. Now if she does, I can catch the purse, walk around the other shopper, and buy the shoes! I must remember, however, not to make my move until my girlfriend has thrown the purse, because if I do, I will be offside!"

The whole office erupts into laughter, whistles, and applause. Even Cass laughs—the fucking Neanderthal, fucking shitbag! I'm not even going to look at that smug Paki cunt!

"Keren explaining the offside rule to you, Raffers?"

For fuck's sake, that's all I need, Harvey witnessing the bastard episode.

"It's not an easy concept to get your head around, boss," I reply, trying to make a joke out of it.

"Aye, you're right. But just as well we've brought Keren in here to keep us right, eh? Right, everyone in." Harvey gestures us towards the office, and one by one, we finish what we're doing and follow.

"I suppose we'd better do the introductions before we find out what progress's been made," says Harvey, holding court in his editor's chair. "Right, Keren, I suppose I'd better give you an introduction to your new teammates. Well, Raffers here is Irish, so he claims. He's never lived in Ireland, of course, and neither did his parents. His Irish heritage is purely based on owning an Irish setter."

What the fuck!

"I love Ireland, me, and who wouldn't? The richness of its culture: Guinness, whiskey, Catholicism, womanising, and terrorism, although they never quite got the hang of that one. Could never understand their obsession with bombing London pubs when they could take a tour bus to the House of Commons and Buck Palace. There's one every fifteen minutes, so I'm led to believe. Well, that's the Irish for you. Where was I? Oh, aye, Raffers—he's really from the dark place. He's a Mackem. He thinks I don't know, but nowt gets past me."

Bastard, how did he? Shit! He's only started singing that old American folk classic "He's Got the Whole World in His Hands." For fuck's sake, he's subverted it in to a Sunderland song, the Geordie bastard. Just smile and go with it, like the rest of the daft cunts.

"It's five pound adults. Kids go free. It's five pound adults. Kids go free," Harvey sings.

"I'm not a Mackem," I dispute, but he ignores me.

"Mark here is a Scouser, Keren."

Is he? Fuck! He's from Yorkshire. What's Harvey playing at? I know, showing off to the new girl. Pathetic!

"So make sure you check your change and, em, your fingers when he shakes your hand. And finally your line manager, the sports editor. Not to be mistaken with that annoying twat from the *Partridge Family*, oh no. Our David Cassidy is a cockney, a geezer, who likes nowt better than filling his face full of jellied eels and pie 'n mash. Sometimes it's two pie 'n two mash in fatty's case. Right, enough of the introductions; what has the wonderful world of sport got for me today?"

"The Black Cats today launched a five-million-pound swoop for Tottenham's unsettled striker, Roman Shenkolova."

"Tom, why do you always talk like you're a Sky Sports presenter?"

"Eh, the Magpies have tabled a five-million-pound bid for France under-twenty-one Michael Gallopin."

"Sounds like a racehorse."

"And Boro are launching their brand-new away strip."

"Really? *Hold the front fucking page.* OK, then, I'll leave that all in your capable hands."

We get up and leave, and we all have a smile on our boat races as wide as the Tyne as we exit Harvey's office. Even Cass and Marty cracking on now. The bastards! I'm still being undermined despite the fact that that wanker, Saunders, is locked up.

"Is he always like that?"

"Afraid so," I answer to the new girl, who is clearly amused by Eric's performance.

"I think I'm going to like it here."

Aye, fucking enjoy it while you can. I can add you to the bastard hate list as well, you fucking lesbian.

"Anything for me to do?" Keren asks enthusiastically.

"Suppose you could write that line on Shenkolova to Sunderland."

"OK, are there any quotes to support the piece?"

"No, just write it as a runner."

"Shall I ring the club and get a comment from them?"

"Jesus! No, no, no, what you like?"

"But isn't there a right to reply?"

"Well, you might have learned that at journo college, but we do things differently in the real world."

"Yeah, we bend the rules here, don't we?" Cass pipes in.

"You ring the club, and their press guy will deny it. And we can't have that because we'll not be able to run with the story," I continue. "There's a hole in the paper to fill, and we need to fill it. And we don't have another Sunderland story to go with. When they deny the story the following day, that's when we run a denial line. Two stories for the price of one. Jackpot, eh? See how it works now?"

"So make it up?

"She'll go far, this one." Cass laughs.

"I never said make it up. That would be wrong."

"Right."

"When you've done that, darling, make up a couple of letters. We're short for the 'Sports Feedback' column tomorrow."

"Eh?"

"Look, it's simple," I say, exasperated by her taking the fucking moral high ground. "Write that Shenkolova has had enough of sitting on his arse at Spurs and wants a move."

"Is that not misleading?"

"Aye, no, maybe."

"I'm not too comfortable with doing that, to be honest."

Who the fuck does she think she is? Been here five minutes, and she's calling the shots about what is right and what is wrong.

"Unbelievable," I respond in the voice of former *Match of the Day* pundit Alan Hansen. "As you know, Gary, you have to play percentages in this game." I return to my own accent from the Scotsman's twang and add, "Look, it may be right. Sunderland need a striker, and Shenkolova is one. Earlier in the season, Stephens said he liked him when they were at White Hart Lane. It's an educated guess. Anyway, don't let your conscience get the better of you, my learned friend. We all do it."

"And after three months in this game, you won't have one." Cassidy laughs.

"One what?"

"A conscience." I wink at her.

Miss Prissy Pants isn't happy with this. Well, welcome to the real world, princess. There'll be no fairy-tale ending for you. There'll be no knight in shining armour coming to save you from the ghouls, goblins, and trolls. You're under my spell now, enchanted one.

What the fuck am I on? I need to get a grip on myself or read a self-help book.

I've been told by a few people that self-help books are good, but I've never read any of them. Maybe if I did, I wouldn't be so anxious. But there're so many; which one would I need? *How to Win Friends and Influence People*? Nah, I don't want any friends, and I have enough influence. *How to Stop Worrying and Start Living*? Or what about *Feeling Good*? If my mother wrote self-help books, they'd be called *Give Your Heed a Shake*, *Have a Good Look at Yourself in the Mirror*, and *Have a Word with Yourself, You Daft Twat*. And now I'm back onto that mental bitch. Will she ever just fuck off and leave me alone?

At least I haven't had any texts or calls from her for a couple of days. Wonder why? Shit! Probably because it's turned off. What a tit! I switch it back on. Hello, here's a text coming through now.

Hi, Hope we can sort this out. Miss u Trudi XXX

Does she never give up? I thought my mother was sick, but Trudi! Jesus! She's fucked a mother and son. That makes her more malodorous than my whore of a parent. Well, she can fuck off. Hang on.

"Cass, what did you say earlier about Christmas Day?"

"Which bit?"

"About dinner."

"Oh yeah, Trudi had a mate around. Never met her before. She sounded Irish, but she was a bit tasty. Why do you ask?"

"No reason. Just misheard you, that's all."

My fucking mother, that's who. They probably had a game of naked twister covered in custard while the Queen's speech was on. The dirty perverted bastards!

"I love big tits on a bird, and she had a lovely pair. As big as the old doll's rack, at least."

This cockney wanker gets on my tits, never mind any…for fuck's sake! Just as well Karen and Jo Nicholson aren't here to listen to this. She'd have the fucking union involved. I've got to get out of here. Cass drives me around the bend. And I can't stand the sight of that Paki bastard at the best of times. And then there's the new girl bitch, dullard Colin, the poisoned dwarf, the big-mouthed puff, Lucy, Lucy, Trudi, Mum. Fuck, fuck, fuck! I'm having an anxiety attack. Get up. Get up. Get up, you twat! Go to the kitchen, toilets, anywhere, so that *you can get a grip.*

I quickly get out of my seat and dash into the nearby kitchen. I take deep breaths and try to compose myself. Take a drink of water. Calm, think calm.

Fucking hell, my heart is going to explode! Control, get control! Breathe, breathe, breathe. That's right. Deeper, deeper, and deeper. That's a bit better.

"Are you OK?"

Fucking hell, it's the new girl. Compose yourself.

"Yes, fine thanks. Just nearly choked on some chewy."

"You sure?"

I pretend to cough, and I turn around from facing the window.

"Yeah, thanks, Keren."

"You're welcome. I'm making a brew. You want one?"

"Eh, no, thanks. I've got to go out."

"OK."

She fills the kettle and leaves the room. Aye, that's all you're good for—making tea.

Right, time to address this. I can't put this off any longer. It's eating me up, and it'll not get any better until I face up to it. I take my phone out and type a text out.

Hi, Lucy. I'm free in an hour if you want to meet up. Raff

Chapter 23

I'm on my way to see her, and I am shitting myself! In fact had I not already excreted every loose solid or liquid from my pathetic excuse of a constitution, it would be running down my legs at this very moment. There's a knot in my stomach, so tight that it would restrain a pregnant pig. I feel nauseous as well.

I don't know what to expect. I've never really spoken to the girl before or cared that much for her, for that matter. Yet here I am on my way to meet her. Me, of all people! I've made my dislike of her an open secret. She knows I don't like her. I've made it quite obvious in the past. Why? No fundamental reason really, other than her popularity, designer clothes, model looks, posh car, and apartment bought with Mummy and Daddy's money. That and the way she bounces around as if she's untouchable. Well, that's all changed.

Why hasn't she been in touch with any of her other colleagues or mates? I dunno. Maybe she has. But why does she want to meet me? Yeah, OK, I was there when she was mugged at the precinct, but that was just a coincidence. I acted on instinct. Had I thought about it, I would've just watched, been a voyeur on another crumbling episode of her life. I dunno. Maybe there is some good inside me after all? I doubt it.

There's a coffee shop at Gosforth Regent Centre, opposite the baths. It's reasonably quiet at this time of day, eleven in the morning. Most of the offices have had their early-morning tea break, and it's just before lunch. So there's a bit of a lull and not many people around. A good place to exorcise a ghost? I dunno, but I probably need what the Americans call closure. I dunno. That's probably more psychobabble nonsense. Maybe if I get this sorted in my head, the anxiety and panic attacks will stop, and I'll be able to sleep, free of any nightmares.

I have a copy of today's *Post* with me and quickly flick through the pages.

Accused Denies Rape Charge
By Sarah Brownlie

A thirty-year-old man took to the stand on day two of the three-day trial to deny that he had drugged and raped a female colleague.

Scott Saunders, of Osbourne Road, Jesmond, categorically refuted the charge that he sexually assaulted a woman and spiked her drinks with drugs at a house party.

The jury heard how a woman, who cannot be named for legal reasons, was given a potent cocktail of alcohol and drugs by the sports writer at a house gathering at Quayside Mews, Newcastle, on Friday, August 18. The man, originally from Scotland, was then accused of taking advantage of his inebriated victim and raping her while she was under the influence of drink and drugs and in an unconscious state.

But Saunders told the jury that he was not at the party and did not attack the twenty-six-year-old woman, despite DNA evidence proving he was there. He claims that he was a victim of an assault himself that evening and did not attend the party because of that.

The accused could not explain the bottle of Rohypnol in his medicine cabinet. The drug is widely known as a date-rape opiate, although it was originally prescribed as an antidepressant. Saunders could not explain his S&M pornography or the semen sample taken from the victim's underwear that matched his DNA.

The trial continues.

Here she is, approaching the entrance. She's wearing a knee-length charcoal-grey coat with matching hat and scarf. God, she's pretty. She looks around for a moment, catches my raised arm at the far end of the room, and walks over, confidently enough, which surprises me.

"Hi, Tom; thanks for coming."

I can't make out whether she's being matter-of-fact and upbeat, or if it's a sigh of resignation.

"Don't mention it. Like a coffee or something?"

"A latte would be nice, thanks."

I leave the table to get Lucy's order and observe her at the counter as she meticulously removes the outer clothing she is wearing to protect her from the elements and lays them precisely on the brown-cushioned seat next to her. She fidgets for a few moments, as if checking that everything is in its rightful place, before she settles to stare out of the window. Her head is resting on her hands, which cup either side of her face. She sits motionlessly and observes the passing cars and pedestrians outside the shop.

I stand for a moment, observe, and wonder, what she is reflecting on? She must have caught my watching image through the window. But I anticipate her head twisting around and advance towards the table with her hot drink.

She smiles warmly, which startles me, as I put her coffee on the table.

"Would you like something to eat?"

"No, I'm fine, thank you," Lucy replies politely, fidgeting with the sugar tubes, lollipop-stick spoon, and token ginger biscuit. My heart is pounding. I don't know what to expect. Maybe she knows something. Maybe she is here to blackmail me. Maybe she knows nothing and genuinely wants to see me. Whatever the reason, I am ready, wired, and waiting for her to make a move.

Yet as much as I want to hate and despise her, my antipathy towards Lucy is negated by her striking looks, appealing nature, and overpowering graciousness. I don't know what is going on in her head, but I feel weak and vulnerable at this moment. I am already intoxicated by her fragrance. And when she turns those enchanting, deep, brown eyes on me, I am paralysed, caught in the headlights. I feel like the rabbit in the Cadbury's Caramel adverts—hypnotised and under her spell! It takes me several moments to regain some composure. And when I do recover some poise, she is talking. But not to me. She is staring outside and talking to the plate-glass window.

"I don't really have any memory of it," Lucy reflects, her accentless voice soft and soothing as she gazes through the coffee shop window, at me, at the coffee cup, and outside once again. She repeats this process several times.

"I remember staggering up the stairs...going to the toilet...But after that, nothing...I woke up in total darkness, not knowing where I was or how I got there...Someone must have assumed I was drunk and thrown my duvet over me and slipped a pillow under my head. I went downstairs, and everyone had gone. The shock...it's impossible to describe...I still wake up in a panic sometimes, worried that I won't recognise my surroundings.

"I wasn't sure I'd been raped at first."

God, this is excruciating. I can't believe she's talking about it. This is worse than the police interrogation.

"I just thought it was a bad dream...but then I'd get flashbacks. I felt someone on top of me...in me...then I blacked out. But it somehow didn't feel...real...I knew I didn't have that much to drink. I know...how much I can drink...before I get drunk. I know my own constitution...but I had a couple of blackouts...one in the morning and one in the afternoon. And complete lapses of memory. And I still felt terrible. It was the worst hangover I'd ever had. I called my mum. She came over...helped tidy up. I told her what happened and that I thought...there was a possibility...I'd been raped... It was like I ripped out her stomach. She was sweeping up some mess of the floor when I told her...She dropped the brush...and fell to her knees. It was me who was comforting her at first...Then I curled up in a ball...fell asleep in her arms.

"When I woke, she'd already booked an appointment at a private hospital. She'd seen some TV programme about date rape, where Rohypnol had been used, and the programme said that it stayed in your system for forty-eight hours...They were great at the hospital. No one was patronising or condescending. Everyone was so...kind."

Lucy doesn't speak for a couple of minutes; she just gazes out of the window. I don't say anything during her monologue, just listen and nod. I still don't know how this meeting is going to culminate. It is worse than an episode of *Columbo*. What is she up to? Is she going to reveal that

Saunders is innocent and that I'm the perpetrator? Is this what this meeting's all about? How the fuck was I duped into this? She's going to reveal how I've been rumbled, and she's going to expose me! Fucking, fuckety fucking, *Columbo* bastard and his "Just one more thing, sir." I don't think I can take any more of this. No, no, no, no! Calm, calm down. Stay calm. Take a deep breath; slow it down. That's it. Yes, I'm OK. Wait, she's just realised she's stopped talking.

"I still can't believe it," she continues as she turns to me and then back to the window. "There was no need. He'd had it…could have had it whenever… It doesn't make sense. He's my…*was* my…No, he was more than that. But they found all that evidence. I just…don't know…why."

Lucy turns to look at me once again. Her eyes are burning into me this time. They are intense, questioning, and agitated. "You were close to him, Tom. Did he ever talk about me?"

I am caught off guard momentarily. I can't believe I'm gonna have to talk about the shitbag. Can't really slag him off, though. That would be wrong in the circumstances. Just play it neutrally. Think that's the best idea.

"No, not really, not at all. Scott was a private person, never discussed his private life. I've been out with him a few times. And that was only when I first joined the paper. And on each occasion, he'd disappear before last orders. He was always reluctant to discuss where he went or whom he was with when we ribbed him about his disappearing act."

"Probably coming to see me," Lucy says sadly.

There is another period of silence as she gazes out of the window.

"It's been a weird day," Lucy continues. "I went to the first day of the trial but didn't go into the courtroom. I didn't have to go because I'd already given a statement, and a video of my interview was played. I stood outside. I couldn't face it… or face seeing Scott…after what he's supposed to have done. I'm still numb after all this time. It still feels like it never happened…but it did. Sorry for going on."

"Obviously we're all as shocked…eh…as you about it."

Lucy turns to face me once more, her eyes blazing into me warmly this time. She reaches her right hand over and places it on top of my mine. She repeats this with her left hand.

"Sorry, Tom. I've been going on a bit."

"It's no problem."

"You've been so kind. Thanks."

I've done fuck all. What's she on about?

"Not sure I've done anything really."

"No, you've been really supportive, just listening to me get this off my chest. And when those boys, you know, mugged me. Thanks for that. It really helped."

"It was nothing. I didn't really do anything."

"I know, but you were there and chased them. It was one of only a few times I had left the house on my own. It...I thought it would have knocked my confidence...It did, to a certain extent. But my therapist turned it around and made the experience positive rather than negative. She encouraged me to get in touch with you and others, although I haven't done that yet. I will eventually...I was a bit tentative with you at first because...well, you've never liked me, have you?"

She removes her hands from mine at this point. It's a relief, to be honest. I am a bit uncomfortable with it. But bloody hell, she knows.

"No, that's not true. I just never got the chance to get to know you. In fact I thought it was the other way around, to be honest."

"Really?"

"Yeah, you never seemed to have time for anyone other than a couple of people in the newsroom. You always seemed busy or preoccupied with something every time I was in your vicinity, if you like, and with me working in sport, our paths rarely crossed anyway."

"So you do like me?"

I chuckle nervously at the absurdity of not only the proposition but also the language Lucy uses.

"What's so funny?"

"Sorry, Lucy. I wasn't expecting to be interrogated by a ten-year-old."

She laughs at this, and it seems to lighten the atmosphere.

"I suppose it was a bit adolescent."

"Eh, but to answer the question, I don't know you or ever got the chance to get to know you. So I don't think I've had any chance to like or dislike you."

What a load of garbage I'm talking.

"Sorry, just feeling a bit insecure at the moment. I'm sure you understand."

"Yes, of course I do. Sorry."

"No, there's no need to be." Lucy takes a sip of her coffee. "You have a nice smile, you know."

"Eh?"

"It's not often I've seen you smile, but it's nice when you do."

Oh God! Cupid's arrow has just taken me out!

"How's work?"

Chapter 24

My head feels a lot clearer after seeing Lucy. I got her all wrong. She's the sweetest, kindest, and most forgiving person I think I've ever met. It's made me feel great, the best I've felt in years, probably. And it's set me up nicely for the finest fucking day of the year: January transfer deadline day. I love it! I'm not going into the office today, though. I can run the operation from home. All I need are a phone, laptop, and the pomp, ceremony, and razzmatazz of *Sky Sports News*.

I am up at eight at night and switch on Sky, and they've already been up to Fulham and interviewed Harry Brassneck about possible deals. It'll not be the last time the Sky team stop him today.

They love the wobble-gobbed twat. The cheeky Cockney geezer is always ready to oblige them with a quote or a soundbite. Brassneck has managed clubs on the south coast and in London since he took his first tentative steps into football management two decades ago. Bizarrely he was lined up to take over at Newcastle a few years back, but that was never going to happen. He did agree to take the job, but he was never going to accept it. I reckon he did it to get an improved contract where he was. I bet he's never been further than the Watford gap for more than one night at best. Probably thinks it's beyond the pale, full of northerners walking around in string vests, racing pigeons and whippets, and eating pea soup. He'd be right, of course. Still, I fucking love his craic, me.

Saunders and Cass can't stand him.

"There 'e goes again," Cass would squawk, "talking about his favourite subject: other football club's players."

Saunders would usually tut and nod in agreement. "He does nae even look you in the eye. How can you trust somewan' who'll no' look you in the eye?" The Scottish twat!

Admittedly it does infuriate supporters, opposition managers, and chairman, especially when he lets slip about a release clause in a contract. It has the desired effect—unsettling players. But to be fair to him, he only answers questions we put to him. We'd rather he told the truth than hear a load of lies, half-truths, or sidestepping like other managers.

They're bringing on all the old managers and players to talk about their former clubs and areas that they need to strengthen and such. It's easy to be cynical about it all, but I reckon it's genuinely exciting. I know people who take a day off work to watch *Sky Sports News* on transfer deadline day. It's a fairly uneventful start, but Jim Black hasn't been on yet. You can't get genuinely excited until Jim's there with all the fanfare, party streamers, and kazoos as he shouts, "It's all happening" and "Big news from the North-East!"

I settle down with some toast covered in ketchup and a steaming-hot mug of tea, and in no time, they're back with Brassneck. This time they've stopped him in his car as he is leaving the training ground. He's being interviewed through the car window. The interviewer has mentioned Andy Cornet, Antonio Madrid, Arouna Koney, and Juan Matari, and he's replied either "Yeah"; "I like him"; or "Top, top player"—his standard replies. To be honest, you could make up names—Rubiton Likepolish, Holdin Megroin, or Kris Copafeel—and Brassneck would go, "Yeah"; "Smashing player"; or "Always liked him. He has a good touch."

But the fun and frolics have barely begun. It'll not be long before the texts, calls, Tweets, and message boards go berserk! A few years back, Sky used to bring a football agent into the studio to deliberate with the presenters. He would sit to the side of them and have between six to a dozen mobile telephones in front of him while they blathered on. The television hosts would turn to the agent every five minutes, or so, for an update and ask, "Anything exciting happening?" To which he would reply, "Things beginning to get moving" or "You'll be surprised at what I'm hearing." Turns out, the phones didn't belong to the agent. They were the property of everyone in the studio. The cameramen, presenters, and producers were all asked to put their phones on the desk to make it look as if they had their finger on the pulse. All part of the pantomime, I suppose.

Oh, hang on. What have we here? Sammy the Scouser has just tweeted that Michael Gowen has just got off the train at Liverpool Lime Street Station. I asked him what he was doing.

He replied, "Going home."

"Can you win your England place back?"

"Of course I can."

News like that would fill a page at the *Telegraph* back in the day when Michael Owen played. Talk about taking coals to Newcastle. Fill your boots, lads.

Martini Obafemi has been seen taking two sugars in a cup of coffee in the pub restaurant at the side of a Bolton Travel Lodge. *Sky Sports* understands that he took three in his tea but isn't sure about his sugar intake in coffee. It was believed at one stage that he took artificial sweeteners in his hot drinks, but that turned out to be nothing but hearsay.

Lionel Messi has once been seen in a London East End pie-and-mash shop. He ordered two pie and two mash, but he didn't take a bowl of jellied eels as a side dish. Sky has been led to believe that he was wearing blue jeans, a grey hoodie, and yellow flip-flops on the premises. It is understood that his normal choice of footwear is boots when playing for Barcelona, but clarification is still needed for the usual choice of casual wear on his feet.

Oh, but wait for it! Here he is, the man himself—Jim Black. Cue the kazoos, the canned applause, and the faux excitement.

"Hello, and welcome to *Sky Sports News*," he bellows loudly, without the aid of a loudspeaker. "We have all the big news and stories on Transfer Deadline Day. And why wait any longer? We have sensational news from the North West. It is huge. Sky's Johnny Johnson has heard through the grapevine that an unnamed defender from a London club is moving north. Let us go live to see what he has to say on the matter."

"As you said, Jim, this is unbelievable news," whoop-whoops Johnson. "Everyone I've spoken to can't believe this is happening. It looked like it was going to drag on for days, and Blackburn looked as if they were going to steal the player with a late bid. But it looks as if Bolton have got their man. He'll be joining the Trotters until the end of the season on loan. The fee at the end of the season is believed to be worth in the region of four hundred thousand pounds. The Wanderers' fans will be delighted with the capture and will give him a hero's welcome before this weekend's clash with fierce rivals Burnley. We'll keep you updated with more news on the transfer when we get it, Jim."

"That's right, Johnny. It is a mouth-watering prospect for Bolton supporters. Now let us speak to someone who always has his fingers on the pulse, the *Trotters in the Trough* fanzine editor, Donny Osmund. Donny, what do you think of your potential new signing?"

"Well, Jim, this is fantastic news," replies the enthusiastic gentleman, who is sporting black national-health glasses and an oversized sheepskin coat, complete with a teapot-cosy woolly hat. He looks like a wannabe BBC reporter's special-needs cousin. "This is what we have been waiting for. We've been led to believe that we've beaten Blackburn and Burnley to his signature and that they'll be gutted. Who would've believed he'd choose us over them? It's staggering, Jim, staggering."

"Thanks for that, Donny. Now coming up after the break: more on the biggest transfer story of the day so far."

And so the Sky circus of performers, clowns, and enthusiasts jumps through hoops, walks tightropes, and juggles overhyped stories for the rest of the day. Juggling flour would be more impressive. But it goes on and on and on. Fernando Torres has been seen by a blind man ordering a lamb roghan josh and keema naan from a Manchester takeaway, while a deaf man has heard that Sir Alex Ferguson has been seen with guacamole at Old Trafford. Whether it is a Mexican player or a crudité dip, no one knows. And while those rumours circulate, the Sky boys and girls are backward and forward to Harry Brassneck, who wobbles his chops in a negative or affirmative response. Enthralling television!

I've had several calls from my fellow hacks, and most of them, it appears, are on the verge of a nervous breakdown. They're getting all sorts of grief from their news desks, wanting to know what's going on so that they can plan the following day's pages. Arno, the sad bastard, isn't even a shadow of the man I once respected and admired. He asks if I have any leads. I say I don't, but I've already tipped off his desk with what is happening in the North-East. Another £500 banked for Mr. Rafferty, thank you very much. The *Star*'s Danny Bew, the *Mirror*'s Steve Doyle, and the *Sun*'s Ken Chisholm are all the same. It's as if they have been visited by the ghosts of Christmas past and present and are shitting the proverbial brick. These guys are supposed to have their fingers on the pulse, for fuck's sake. They don't take too kindly to my sunny disposition or my suggestion that they make up something. Don't know why they are being so touchy. It's not like they haven't done it in the past. Well, I couldn't give a Charlie Dickens as to whether or not they keep their jobs or get a story. I've got my lines, but I'm sitting on them until I need to file on deadline. Meanwhile I'll string them all along.

Is the transfer window fair? I couldn't give a monkey's shite, to be honest. The original proposal of having a transfer window was bandied around in 1991 by several of the English league's top-flight clubs. And although observers from outside of the talks felt it was nothing more than empty rhetoric, Division One clubs did put it to a vote. It was narrowly rejected because it was pointed out that smaller clubs, which sometimes need to sell during a season to survive, had little cash to play with in the summer due to the fact there was no one going through their turnstiles.

The idea didn't go away, though. A year later several high-profile managers and senior officials wanted the newly formed Premier League to copy Italy's Serie A model, where, in essence, the transfer shop was closed for the whole season except for a window of a fortnight or three weeks in December or January. Rick Parry, the Premier League chief executive at the time, seemed to be in favour. He backed Terry Venables's idea that managers ought to be coaches, who spend time with their players, making them better rather than looking around for new signings, fighting off agents, or having to deal with unsettled players. That way, they reckoned, would improve the quality of play on the pitch. The small clubs, however, weren't convinced.

The idea had lain dormant until the back end of the 1990s when nine of Europe's top leagues met in Athens to consider and debate the introduction of a transfer window, foreign referees officiating in the Premier League, and even a referee in each half of the pitch. The fear of agents hawking players around Europe seemed to be the catalyst. That and uncertainty about the legality of transfers, following the Jean-Marc Bosman case. Bosman is a former Belgian footballer whose judicial challenge of the football-transfer rules led to a ruling that allowed professional players in the European Union to move freely to another club at the end of their term of contract with their present team. UEFA denied that the Bosman case and the issue of agents were behind their thinking.

UEFA were in favour of a restructure, however, and announced plans in September 1999 for a transfer window, running for six weeks from mid-December to the end of January. A year later the European Commission got involved. They wanted to scrap the entire transfer system because it was accused of breaching the Treaty of Rome. But FIFA stepped in and put forward a three-point compromise package to stave off any dismantling of the system. And one point was the introduction of transfer windows, essentially designed to curb, to some extent, the post-Bosman freedom enjoyed by players, among other proposals.

All European countries and the European Commission agreed to the proposals in order to keep the transfer system intact. Ironically England was the only country to reject the proposition. English clubs decided they were happy with the existing system but, in the end, had it thrust upon them. The yes-no-in-out-shake-it-all-about culminated in 2002–03, when the first transfer window was introduced.

And after all of the drum banging, horn blowing, and feet stamping, it was an exciting day in the North-East compared with the rest of the country. Newcastle sold their star striker again, which is par for the course. Jackpot! Saying that, it was nothing compared to the drama played out at Sid James' Park a couple of years back, with Andy Carroll's £35million transfer to

Liverpool. We all knew he was leaving, but Sky managed to play it out all day like a proverbial soap opera cliffhanger.

That time they would give general news updates, and just before they would break for the adverts, various cheerleaders who were anchoring the programme would bellow, "And back to St James' Park to get the latest update on the Andy Carroll transfer." The cameras would then sweep over to their North-East correspondent, and he would give a blow-by-blow or minute-by-minute account of whether Carroll was staying or going.

They did their traditional vox pops on the street with any spanner-wearing black-and-white shirt. "What do you think about the news that Newcastle are preparing to accept a bid for Andy Carroll?" the rodent-faced Sky reporter asked.

"Typical of this club, man," replied an obese man walking a dog, with a length of orange washing line around its neck as a leash. "They couldn't run a tiddlywinks team, never mind a football team. We'll gan doon, that's for certain."

Another bloke interviewed was quite amusing. He said, "Aye, me sister, like, runs a card shop doon the Toon, like, and Steve McClaren's just been in, like. Aye, he bought one of them good-luck-in-your-new-job, like, cards, like."

Rat Face was speechless and decided he couldn't add anything to having his chain yanked and therefore closed the link by saying, "Back to the studio," just as dozens of feral-looking kids emerged from the back streets screaming, "Keegan"; "Toon Army"; and "We're barmy, salami."

There is still plenty of fun to be enjoyed. Not so much for Cass and Marty, who have to work late. There are several calls from an alarmed Cass. They go something like "Wot the fack is going on now?" and "I still can't put that facking page to bed." Then he asks if I have any work for Keren. I resist, saying, "Tell her to put the kettle on." Instead I say that she could create a file of all the transfer ins and outs. In between that, she could proofread and help out putting captions on pictures.

The Scousers kept increasing their offer for Carroll throughout the day until the Geordie outfit couldn't resist it any longer and accepted £35 million. The wankers, who were guffawing at Darren Bent's £24 million departure from Sunderland to Aston Villa, weren't laughing now. And as per usual, the useless twats didn't have anyone lined up as a replacement. Manager Alan Pardew's statements of "He's going nowhere" turned out to be nothing more than empty rhetoric, and it was a cue for more tumult on the Tyne, courtesy of the United hierarchy. It's a never-ending story, thank God.

It's no different in this window. Yohan Six has just been sold for £25million, and they're trying to bring in French compatriot Michael Gallopin for less than a quarter of the price they've received for the Toon's playmaker. Manager Robert Clark made noises earlier in the week about learning from previous mistakes made in other transfer windows, mistakes where they didn't get someone over the line in time. But they've no chance of signing Gallopin. Not only is he the natural successor to Six in the French national side, but he is also a talent equal to Lionel Messi at his age. If he's going anywhere, it will be Barcelona, Real Madrid, or Bayern Munich—not a small parochially minded backwater of a city like Newcastle, and certainly not for £7million. If Magpies' supporters will be fooled over more "lying as a PR exercise," as was admitted by former managing director Derek Llambias, is anyone's guess. You'd like to think they'd learn after all this time, but they still turn up in thousands.

But just as I'm digesting this good news, I'm hit by a bout of indigestion after hearing that Sunderland striker Darren Kendle has slapped in a transfer request after hearing that West Ham want to sign him. So two loan signings in, several out, and our top scorer is on his way to the East End to roll out the barrel. The fucker! How the fuck are we supposed to not only climb the league and become genuine challengers for European football but also to become cock of the North over those Geordie bastards when this is happening?

This transfer news is typical. It's endemic in the British, European—no, make that the world of—football. Kendle came up here to the North-East; in fact he agitated for a move up here because he couldn't get a game at Chelsea. At the time, he seemed to be the antithesis of the modern footballer: an England international not looking for a large pay increase or a huge signing-on fee. He appeared to buy into the club, its traditions, its history, and its fanatical supporters. That is, at least, what he said to us when we interviewed him. He said he could achieve all his ambitions at the Stadium of Light: win more caps, play in Europe, and, more importantly, lay the ghost of 1973 to rest.

Looking back, he just said what he thought fans wanted to hear. I can't complain about the job he did at the club. He did his job; he scored goals. He netted a goal every other a game. I've just checked the club's website, and yes, they've accepted the Hammers' bid. Bruce Stephens is apoplectic about it.

Stephens has attempted to take the moral high ground and attacked his striker's lack of loyalty. He can fucking talk. He's jumped more ships than a malady-ridden rat! Whether it is for his precious career or for more money remains open to debate. The same goes for Kendle.

But, hey, I'm not going to be a hypocrite. I'm off to the *Mail* at the end of the season where I'll be doubling my salary. Who in their right mind wouldn't? Imagine Mike the mechanic turning down a move to a big car dealer for twice the money because he wants to remain loyal to the owner who gave him his apprenticeship. Would he, bollocks! There is no loyalty in any business. The only loyalty in football comes from the supporters, and the sooner they realise that, the better. The Kendle saga will soon be forgotten, and this time next year there will be another player at another club, showing his contempt for his employers and the supporters by slapping in a transfer request.

What am I talking about? It's like someone has ripped my guts out! I feel physically sick! The greedy black…no, I can't say that, can I?

Right, better get these lines written: Two strikers offski, several loan moves, inski, and a shirt-sponsorship deal for Boro. By the time I've penned my three club lines, the Sky rollercoaster is finally slowing down, despite Jim Black's cries of "It's still all happening"; "There're still deals being pushed through as we speak"; and "Don't switch off just yet; there could be a surprise around the corner."

Can you imagine that fucker at home with his missus while she's in the kitchen? "Mrs. Black has been spotted in the kitchen, a *Sky Sports* exclusive. The clock is ticking, Mrs. Black, and we don't have much time. Hold on to your hats. We can now reveal it's a casserole and not a quiche! Twitter is in meltdown! This is unbelievable news. Mrs. Black is weighing up her options this very moment. Is she going to serve it with white wine or red? The casserole is issuing a come-and-get-me plea at this eleventh hour. I feel like a kid on Christmas Eve."

I shudder to think what he'd be like if he got a shag! And talking of shags, just got a nice surprise text from Lucy.

Hope 2day wasnt 2 stressful. Lunch tomorrow? Lucy x

Fucking hell! That reminds me. It's the last day of the trial! Saunders will have been sentenced! I'll have to read it online because I haven't been into work today.

Chapter 25

Rapist Sentenced for Seven Years
By Sarah Brownlie

A rapist has been sentenced to seven years in prison after an attack on a woman in her own home.

Scott Saunders, thirty, of Osbourne Road, Jesmond, was found guilty at Newcastle Crown Court over the incident, which took place in August last year.

Saunders was among a group of men and women who were drinking at a house party held by the twenty-six-year-old female victim at Quayside Mews.

The woman went to bed, feeling unwell, while the rest of the group continued to socialise. But at some point during the gathering, she was raped by Saunders.

The woman made an appointment at the hospital the day following the party, and tests provided conclusive evidence that she had been drugged by the popular date-rape drug Rohypnol. The hospital then called police, and after making several inquiries, Saunders was arrested and charged with rape after evidence found in the attacker's home linked him with the sexual assault.

Saunders had earlier told the jury that he was a friend of the woman, that he was not at the party, and that he did not attack the twenty-six-year-old, despite DNA evidence proving he had. He claims that he was a victim of an assault himself that evening and did not attend the party because of that. No evidence was provided to substantiate those claims.

The man, originally from Glasgow, denied any sexual contact with the woman and claimed it was "a miracle" that his DNA was discovered on her.

Saunders was at a loss to explain the bottle of Rohypnol in his medicine cabinet, and neither could he clarify how S&M pornography and a semen sample taken from the victim's underwear matched his DNA.

However, the jury at Newcastle Crown Court was unanimous in its decision that he had indeed plotted and then raped the woman.

Judge Kenneth Pickering, QC, told Saunders, "You have been convicted of what was a cowardly attack and, for the victim, a terrifying ordeal.

"This is an assault on a friend and a colleague you have known for many years. She was entitled to feel safe in your company, but she was not."

He added, "Fortunately assaults of this type are rare. But they are treated very seriously by the courts, and you face a long sentence."

Saunders was placed on the sex-offender register.

It's finally over! Ha-ha. Oh my God! The relief! The weight off my shoulders, actually, feels tangible. I've got his job, his girlfriend, and an illuminated path to the *Daily Mail*! If I can just find closure with my mother, Trudi, and that Paki bastard in the office, I'm sure I'll beat the demons and get off my medication.

I couldn't make lunch with Lucy, too much to do. But we're meeting later. One of my leads has just tipped me off that Sunderland have a player on their books with British National Party sympathies.

I'm glad all those hours in the company of Alec Shoulder at journo college have paid off.

He wasn't great on personal hygiene. To be honest, his body odour would have stripped paint off walls. His skin had more craters than Mars, and his teeth wouldn't have looked out of place in a long-forgotten medieval cemetery. But the social misfit always kept us supplied in Midget Gems, wine gums, and toffees, and he also let me copy his exams.

He's now working for Sunderland City Council but helps out at Walter Adams's Martial Arts and Boxing Club, which is really a cover for the club's BNP activities. He was putting out the bunting when he witnessed Black Cats defender Peter Whitworth embrace Adams at the club. He managed to shoot several pictures of them on his phone. One such snap captures them both shaking hands in Adams's office, with a picture of Mussolini in the background. Fair enough if you ask me. Don't see why politics and football have to mix. But I have to put aside my personal opinion and love of everything red and white, as much as it pains me to do so, to be a professional.

Mmm, I wonder what the Leveson Inquiry would make of the culture, practice, and ethics of getting this story. There was no illegal interception of phone messages. There was no unlawful or improper conduct on my part, or on Alec's, for that matter. Is Whitworth a victim of media intrusion? Maybe he is, but we can't have footballers, artists, and celebrities being prejudicial because the colour of their skin is different than others or because they have different religious beliefs. That wouldn't be right, would it? When you're a journalist, you have to have integrity, take the moral high ground, and bring these issues to the attention of the public—more importantly, to the *Daily Mail*. I'll get a couple of grand for this story, with the pictures, ha-ha! Jackpot! Like I give a shit about it. In fact they should send them all back on the banana boats, as one of my mother's blokes once said. Of course I'll bung Alec a hundred quid for his part. It's only right. Not only will I be well rewarded in monetary terms but also this story should just about cement my place next season as the *Mail*'s North-East of England correspondent. Top of the pops!

Things are looking up. Another scoop and no contact from the slut hairdresser and her new mate for a couple of weeks. Lucy wants to see more of me, and my career is about to take off big-style! After I've written the copy and sent it to the *Mail* news desk, I make my way into the office.

I get to my workstation, and the new addition to the sports desk is cracking on like a drug addict with a nervous-system disorder. Faster and louder, and she's getting right on my tits. The gobshite never shuts up. On and on and on about fucking sports trivia: football, golf, cricket, golf, football, tennis, cricket, golf, and even motor sport, for fuck's sake. What's the matter with conversation about hair, cosmetics, earrings, reality TV shows, weight loss, diet, chocolate, diet, hair, chocolate, the cuteness of puppies, and the nice smell of newborn babies?

Cass is in the zone. He has his head focused on the PC screen, while his fingers treat the keyboard with the same respect reserved for a servant of a dominatrix. Marty is patronising the opinionated wench: smiling, nodding, and answering when probed.

"The miracle in Medina, Europe's Ryder Cup victory, or England's rugby World Cup triumph in 2003," Princess Keren Veitch shouts out mischievously at a passing Harvey. "Which one was the greatest?"

"Tough one," he replies, scratching his chin for a moment. "It's like asking to choose between 'London Calling and '(White Man) in Hammersmith Palais.'"

I've no idea what the fucker's on about an' all, so that sorry excuse for a sports writer will be clueless as well.

"I'll, eh, leave that to you, sports connoisseurs."

"Now had you said 'Train in Vain,'" she impishly replies, "I would have said it was tough. But 'London Calling' wins hands down."

"Controversial." Harvey laughs. "I don't think the brotherhood of the Clash would agree, mind."

What a cunt!

"That's why it's always good to debate, don't you think?"

"It certainly is, bonny lass. It certainly is."

What the fuck! Nice to lift the mood with a bit of trivia after a rape story involving a member of staff. I've never known Harvey to be so amiable. I'm not standing for this. Hang on. It looks like the natural order is about to be resumed. The expression on his face goes through the metamorphosis; yep, there it goes from Dr. Jekyll to Mr. Hyde. Champion! And there he goes, off down the newsroom in search of a victim. I mean, someone has to get it. He needs to redress the balance and savage some poor fucker for showing a nanosecond of humanity.

"Tom, what do you think?"

"Eh?" I say distractedly. "I think you should crack on with your work instead of distracting everyone."

She doesn't like that. I've turned her face from summer to winter with one frosty remark. Cass has even lifted his head and furrowed his brow at my insouciant counterattack.

"Right," interjects Marty, shaking a disapproving head at me while trying to save the overly enthusiastic one from further ignominy. "It's about time we make tracks to the Riverside, Keren. You can do the report. I'll do the colour."

They tidy their workplaces, turn off their computers, and stand up in silence.

"How many words, Cass?"

"The usual: six hundred fifty report, four hundred fifty colour, and five hundred quotes piece."

The cheeky fucker. Given my new position, he should be asking me what's needed. I'll cut the fucker some slack this time. Anyway, I fancy a spot of mischievous meddling. The devil will find work for idle hands. The new girl's match report should be a memorable read in tomorrow's *Post*.

The Boro match this evening means that I don't need to worry about a line from them, as the game takes care of that. I just need to trot out a Sunderland and Toon story. I'll hold back the racism story until deadline, which means the *Mail* will be all over it big-style. We'll not have time to do anything with it other than run it in the late edition. I've got some bland quotes from Stephens about how the Mackems will turn around their recent slump and how the Car-Toon Army boss Robert Clark reckons they can play in Europe again despite selling their best player and not replacing him. Fuck off, man!

"Right, that's me, Cass. Two stories in the basket for you. You want a cuppa before I go?"

"Smashin', fanks."

It gives me another excuse to piss in the milk before I leave. Into the kitchen, I go. A quick urine release into the semi-skimmed, and in no time I'm back at the desk with Cass's pissy tea.

"Right then, geezer," I say in my faux Cockney accent. "I'm off to that Kevin Keegan talk-in at the Coxlodge Club."

"I'd love it," Cass replies in piss-taking mode. "I'd love it if I could come."

I arrange to pick up Lucy from outside her flat. Five minutes after I text her from the taxi, she emerges from the block's security door. She bounces towards the cab with that familiar confident swagger that I'd witnessed a thousand times in the *Post*'s newsroom and that I'd grown to loathe. As I jump out of the taxi and open the door, I try to remain composed but feel a pang of anxiety. What the fuck am I doing? She's not royalty or a celebrity!

"Hiya," she greets me with a smile that would illuminate the darkest of alleys or streets. God, she smells fantastic. She's wearing that same charcoal-grey coat, so I can't see what is hidden underneath. But I do see the knee-length leather boots. Oh God! And I've never seen lipstick as red and glossy. She doesn't look or seem damaged in any shape or form. My trousers twitch at the inappropriate thought of her lips wrapped around me. I look back at the fat, middle-aged, bald and scruffy cab driver, and it looks as if he is reading my mind. The dirty old man lasciviously nods his approval in an I-wouldn't-mind-neither-mate type of way. I'm hardly one to take the moral high ground, but it fucking disgusts me that he thinks I am his equal despite the simple fact I am or, probably, even worse.

"Sorry about the delay," she says sincerely, climbing into the taxi, before she spoils the apology by falling into a typical girlie stereotype of "I just didn't know what to wear. I've never been to one of these before. How are you?"

"Great, thanks. You?"

"Had a good day, as it happens."

"Yeah?"

"Yes. Eric called a couple of days ago and asked if I was OK and if he could do anything."

"Did he?"

"It was really thoughtful of him." Harvey, you're one smarmy bastard. "I asked if I could do some work."

"So soon?"

"But it's been nearly six months, and I am going out of my mind, Tom. I'm bored, and I need something to take my mind off what happened. I need closure. I need to stop feeling sorry for myself. I need to get out, like tonight, and face people, although I don't feel ready to go into the office yet. You, my mum, and Eric have all helped. I now need to stand on my own two feet and help those who have helped me. So I'm going to do several features on Refuge."

"Refuge?"

"It's an organisation that helps women and children who have been victims of domestic violence and abuse."

"Oh."

"And they've been great with me, so I thought I'd give something back after all the help they've given me."

Trying to be understanding, thoughtful, and empathetic, I nod as the taxi pulls up alongside the club, but I do my best to block out what happened. After all the trauma in my life, I've become an expert at erasing disturbing events.

As I help Lucy out of the car, I hear what sounds like a club singer belting out an Andy Williams song. I think it's "Music to Watch Girls Go By." It turns out to be a sorry excuse of a transvestite rather than anything coming from outside the club. He, or she, is about sixty, I reckon, and probably dressed in his dead mother's clothes. I don't know what to say, but Lucy finds the charade amusing.

"This way, Luce, before Dame Edna's ugly sister starts asking what shade of lipstick you use."

Lucy chuckles at my quip. I'm fucking funny, me, you know. We pass the club's doorman, who looks familiar.

"Evening, sir, madam."

I nod and recognise who he is. He's that former amateur-boxing champion who got done for possession of drugs with intent to supply. He works at Walter Adams's Martial Arts and Boxing Club. Obviously he's in security part-time. Aren't all former amateur boxers? The world is a one big cliché!

Inside the club isn't much better. At the entrance, there are two pensioners wrestling with each other and turning the air blue with their colourful language. Another elderly fella, probably a committee member, is telling them that they've been warned before and will be barred if they don't stop. The authoritarian club land committee man goes to pick up, with an old handkerchief, a pair of dentures that are lying on the floor. What the fuck have I let myself in for? Just as Lucy and I squeeze past the melee, I hear a familiar voice.

"Granddad, will you behave yourself?"

It's a voice I haven't heard in years. It can't be. I turn around, and it is! Bez! Peter Bez Berry! I can't fucking believe it. But why? Why? Well, he probably still lives around here, obviously; that's why.

"Come on, Tom," Lucy says, pulling at my arm.

Just then Bez looks up, and we catch each other's gaze for a moment. He's trying to figure out who I am and where he's seen me before. But I've got my back to him, and I'm in the function room before the penny drops. I'm happy to sit and get my head down. Not sure whether I'm prepared for any more ghosts from Christmas past. In fact if Bez is here, then so is that cunt Graham Hughes! But then, wasn't he locked up? Lucy is bemused by it all.

"I don't want to sound like a snob, but I've never been to a social club before," she expresses in semi excitement as she looks around the room. "It's so full of life…and characters."

"It's full of characters, alright."

We settle into our seats, unfortunately, too close to the bar. Most of the seating has been taken by the eager beavers keen to see King Kev or their messiah. Sad cunts!

"It's Julie Humble," shrieks Lucy in excitement.

"Who?"

"Julie Humble! We were at journalism college together."

I turn to see an attractive woman with average height, mousy-blond hair, and a nice complexion; she's in her midtwenties. And I guess by her body language that she is arguing with Bez. Oh, fuck.

"She was quite an intimidating woman and a feminist," Lucy continues, delighted to see a familiar face in a room full of strangers. "I started dressing down at college because she didn't approve of the clothes I wore. She said I should dress for myself, not for other people and especially not for men. Part of women's empowerment." And with that, Lucy is out of her seat and over to see Julie.

When Lucy taps her on the shoulder, this Julie person does a double take, and her visage softens slightly from the hard-faced look she previously wore. Bez looks over Lucy's shoulder and directly at me. He takes my partner's intervention as a cue to exit the scene. I make on as if my eyes are policing the room, but I can see that he is heading towards me.

"Tom?"

I turn and look up to a face I have not gazed upon in nearly twenty years.

"Tom Rafferty? It's Bez. We went to school together."

"Ah, yes, that's right." I pretend vagueness, in an attempt to gain the upper hand. "Nice to see you again."

"How are you? What are you up to these days?"

"Good, work for the *Northern Post*."

"*Northern Post*?"

"Newspaper."

"Doing?"

"Writing."

"Ah, so you're a journalist?"

The patronising shitbag!

"Yes."

"Do you specialise in anything?"

"Sport."

"Really?" The cocky cunt starts laughing. "The irony, you were hopeless at school. Sorry, I didn't mean to be…"

"No, it's OK. I wasn't the best, admittedly. On the other hand, you were quite the sportsman; I seem to remember. How did the football career turn out?"

Fucking feast on that, you wanker! He becomes solemn at the thought and stares at the floor. That'll serve the condescending shit right.

"Interior and exterior cruciate ligament injury," Bez reflects. "The same one Michael Owen got when he was at the Toon or rather suffered when on England duty."

"Sorry to hear that," I lie.

"Aye, gutted at the time, but life goes on, I suppose. There were no thousands of pounds available for me to go and see whether Dr. Steadman could fix me up. Old Norman, our trainer, had a go with his magic sponge, mind." He laughed. "But I think he used all the magic dust, fixing a paper cut on Hughesy. Work as a joiner now."

I was starting to feel sorry for the twat. But mentioning his bullying sidekick, Graham Hughes, has dissolved any tablet of sympathy I had for him. What goes around comes around, after all, so the saying goes. Why should I feel sorry for him? It's a dose of bad karma, if there is such a thing. And as if on cue, or through some sort of premeditated act of revenge, here is the tyrannical terror from my past youth himself.

"Hughesy," sings Bez, who is cut from any further conversation as his partner in crime joins us and launches into a tirade of how we live in a corrupt and fascist police state. So it was him that PC Plod was talking about when they pulled me in for questioning. Wonder if he did attempt to kill his wife or girlfriend. If it was that cow from school, she obviously deserved it. Graham finally acknowledges my presence and instantly recognises me. The realisation is enough to take the wind out of his sails, and he stops talking.

"Well, I never," he says. "It's Raggy Rafferty."

Nowt changes. He was a cunt when he was a kid, and he's still a cunt now, clearly.

"You work for the *Post*, don't you?"

He fucking knows. That's a surprise. I nod but don't speak.

"I thought it was your name, and a picture vaguely looked like you by your byline. But I wasn't completely sure. How the fuck did you got a job as a sports writer? I can write all you know about sport on the back of a postage stamp. What a load of shite you write an' all. Ill-informed nonsense. Fucking garbage."

I say nothing.

"Fucking hell, Hughesy; back off, man! There's no need for that! You're bang out of order! Sorry, Tom." Bez turns from Graham to me. I just give a neutral shrug.

"Is there any fucking need for that?"

I'm actually enjoying Bez giving his mate a scolding. It seems that by saying nothing, I'm maintaining the moral high ground.

"Bump into an old schoolmate we haven't seen in about twenty years, and you behave like that!"

"Was never my mate."

"I don't fucking care! You're unbelievable at times!"

"Well, I'm hardly in the best of moods after being locked up for three days."

"And that's whose fault? It's all me, me, me with you! For fuck's sake!"

"Alright, alright, I'm sorry."

"Don't say it to me. Say it to Tom!"

"Sorry, mate, just had a bad week," he says, extending his hand.

I take it and shake it and mutter, "No problem."

Lucy and Bez's girlfriend come over just as the exchange of words finishes.

"Don't start, Julie," says Bez curtly. "I've had enough of Mr. Angry here." Julie is taken aback, while Lucy stands tentatively and tries to ascertain what has been going on.

"Great to see you, Tom. Glad things have worked out for you. If you ever want to catch up and go over old times, we play at the welfare most Sunday mornings. You're welcome to come and have a pint and, eh, give your expert opinion." He laughs at that remark.

"Rather not go over old times, but thanks all the same."

"Ha-ha! No, I understand, mate. You didn't have the best of times at school, did you? OK, mate, the offer still stands. Would be great to catch up."

"Thanks."

Hughesy kind of nods, reluctantly, and the three of them move away from where we were seated.

"What was all that about?" Lucy inquires.

"Ah, just a couple of old school friends."

"Peter seemed nice."

"Yeah, he's OK."

"You don't sound keen?"

"Not really. Bez—Peter—is OK, but I've not got time for his mate."

"Ah, not a nice person, eh? It was great seeing Julie again. She's been offered an assistant editor's position at *Cosmopolitan* magazine in London. Quite exciting, because she gets to travel to America. But she's having problems getting Peter to commit."

"Yeah, he always was a bit of a procrastinator, I suppose."

"They've been together three years, and he's not even asked her to get married."

"Some men are just afraid of commitment."

"But this is a once-in-a-lifetime chance. She's got to go."

"Suppose so. Do you want another drink?"

"Just another tonic water, please."

I wander over to the bar to get away from Lucy's jabbering about *Cosmo* and wonder if she wants a Rohypnol chaser. Never thought *Cosmo* was a feminist magazine. Some people are hypocrites. I see that copper who questioned me at the police station sitting at the end of the bar. Wonder what he's here for. There's a queue a mile long, so I go to the toilet. Shit, Hughesy is at the other end with someone. I turn to go into a cubicle and urinate in there. As I come out, I see that Hughesy has followed me in with this other lad he was at the end of the bar with. They go into the cubicle next to the one I've just emerged from.

"This is top gear, man. Go on; have a line," says the voice of the stranger.

This could be fun. By the time I get to the bar, the queue has disappeared, and I walk up to stand next to the copper and whisper, "Are you one of the security people here? It's just that there're people doing drugs in the toilet."

He looks at me suspiciously, as if he's seen my face before, and then he's off out the door and into the men's bogs. Jackpot! That'll serve you right, Hughesy. Within seconds, there is a fracas around the toilets.

"I wonder what that is all about," says Lucy curiously as I return to my seat.

"Probably druggies. Notorious around here, by all accounts."

I've waited a lifetime to get one over you, Hughesy. My second victory over you, and it's sweeter than the first! Jackpot!

Chapter 26

"Sunderland are shit!" Graham Hughes hisses venomously into Tom's face in the boys' changing rooms.

"Not as shit as Newcastle."

"They are, aren't they, Bez?"

"Aye, they are like, Tom."

"So if they're that shit, how come they beat Newcastle in the play-offs and now play in Division One and Newcastle's still in Division Two?"

"That doesn't make any difference, man."

"It does. Means Sunderland are better."

"Better at being shit!"

"You're talking crap."

"Who do you think you're talking to?" Graham bawls aggressively, pushing Tom to the changing-room floor. Tom gets up and makes an attempt to push the assailant back. Graham is wise to it and sidesteps the challenge. The bully grabs the back of the hapless boy's shirt on the follow-through and launches him through the gap between the pegs and island bench, where several school uniforms hang, and onto the cold floor on the other side. The victim grazes both his hands and knees as a consequence.

"Rafferty! What the hell do you think you're doing, crawling around on your hands and knees in the dirt?" bellows the voice of sports teacher, John Pascoe, as he enters the room and witnesses his student clamber to his feet.

"That's where you'll find all Mackems, sir," quips Graham, just as Tom utters his reply, "Nothing, sir."

"That's enough, Hughes. There are more than enough clowns in the world without you adding to them." The comment brings chuckles and laughter from the group of teenage boys. "Right, get out there, and get warmed up. Two laps of the pitch, you hear?"

Several groans and remarks of "Aw, sir" are made in response.

"Never mind 'aw, sir.' Get out there! Not you, Rafferty. I want a word."

"What is it, sir?"

"What is it, sir? Why don't you tell me? What happened there? You getting bullied?"

"No, sir."

"So you just fell over that bench?"

"Something like that."

"Something like that, eh? You don't help yourself, Tom, do you? And wearing a Sunderland strip to PE is only asking for trouble. You know they're all Newcastle fans, so if you're going to wear it, you've got to expect a bit of stick."

"Suppose so, sir."

"Yes, suppose so, sir. Go on. Get out there, and warm up with the rest of them."

"Yes, sir."

"Yes, sir. And Tom?"

"Yes, sir?"

"Try and keep out of their way, eh?"

"Yes, sir."

Tom runs out of the school building, down by the side of the netball court where the beautiful Sarah Nichols is holding court, and onto the football pitch. He just finishes his second warm-up lap as Pascoe gets onto the playing area.

"Right, Hughes and Berry, pick two teams," instructs Pascoe.

"Who gets first pick, sir?" Berry asks.

"Hughes, for being patient."

"All good things come to those who wait, lad," says the PE teacher. "You should know that by now."

"Thank you, sir," responds Hughes in an ironic sycophantic way. Berry just shrugs and goes along with the comic charade. They both pick players, who all filter behind their respective captains, until Berry is left with Tom.

"Looks like you've got Raggy, Bez." Hughes laughs as he trots away to his side of the pitch.

"Make sure you fumigate your goal."

"Just ignore him, Tom, eh?" says Bez. "You OK to go in nets?"

"Again! Do I have to?"

"Well, just go in for the first fifteen, and we'll see after that."

"You said that last time."

"Sorry, mate. Honest, we'll all take a turn. Hey, apparently Shearer was put in nets when on trial at the Toon."

"How! Bez! We're England, and I'm Gazza," Graham Hughes shouts across the pitch from where his teammates are taking position. "Reet?"

"Aye, fine, we'll be Germany," replies Bez, "and I'll be Lothar Matthaus then. Prepare to get your Limey arse kicked again."

Within minutes of the kick-off, Hughes is on a mazzy run.

"Gazza skips past Thon and Thomas Hassler with ease, while Matthaus is stranded at the other end of the pitch!" Hughesy laughs, doing his best John Motson impression with the ball at his feet. "He nutmegs Augenthala and easily sidesteps Breme. He only has the keeper to beat. Bodo Illgner comes out to narrow the angle, and...the Nazi bastard saves for a corner! Shit!"

The victory is one to savour. Tom never has many, but stopping the bully-boy Hughes from scoring is as good as it gets for the young unfortunate at school.

Chapter 27

There were no earth-shattering stories about Keegan's eventful and colourful return to Newcastle at last night's talk-in, nor were there any groundbreaking hold-the-front-page news headlines. It was pretty tame and bland, to be honest. Nothing new was gleaned or gathered, which was surprising. He more or less went over old ground. Told stories everyone knew or had heard before. It still didn't stop the herds mooing over every syllable or monosyllable or falling over one another to get a picture taken with their messiah. The highlight of the evening for me was undoubtedly getting even with Hughesy. A childhood of bullying erased or exorcised with one timely whisper to a rozzer conveniently standing at the end of the bar. Mind you, the kiss on the cheek when I dropped off Lucy was up there, too. It was uncomfortable for her, but she went through it.

"I'd ask you up for a coffee…but…I don't feel ready," she stuttered and shuffled sadly. Of course, I was the perfect gentleman.

"I totally understand. Don't worry about it. I'm just thrilled you came out with me."

"Tonight was like an adventure. I'm not into sports, but it was a fascinating evening. I got to see an old friend and get out of the house. The last six months have been hard for me. Thanks, Tom, you've been brilliant. I can't thank you enough for all this."

And just as I was adding, "It was nothing," she leaned forward and kissed me on the side of the cheek. There was just enough wetness to provide ammunition for a month's onanism—with the help of some S&M porn on the Internet.

When I get into work the following morning, it's bedlam! Harvey is screaming the house down, and it's all down to my handicraft! Hey, hey! I'd almost forgotten about my meddling after the success I recorded last night. Using Cass's password, I'd managed to log into the company's system at home and change the new girl's copy before it went to print.

I changed it from "City's Brazilian playmaker then turned on the Samba style when he rifled in a tremendous shot from thirty yards to spoil Boro's chances of a third successive clean sheet" to "The Brazilian playmaker then turned on the Sambo style when he rifled in a tremendous shit from thirty yards to soil yet another clean-sheet chance for Boro."

When I pass the news desk, the lezza, Brownlie, tells me to tread lightly. John Hardwick, on the other hand, is enjoying it.

"Rather you than us." He laughs. "It makes a change."

I try not to enjoy the moment more than he is. It'll be tough. The screaming is deafening. The newsroom personnel don't know what to do: be voyeurs to their colleagues' misfortune or ignore the tumultuous proceedings and carry on working.

"Where's fucking Rafferty?" Harvey shouts out. I take off my coat, put down my laptop, and approach the chief's office. Jo Nicholson grimaces as I pass her on the way.

Harvey is pacing the office as I walk in.

"Where the fuck have you been?"

"Eh, on my way in."

Cass is seated and looking straight at the wall on the other side of the room. Our young female sports-writing wannabe, Keren, has her head down and looks distraught, while Marty is expressionless.

"You see this?"

Harvey picks up today's paper and hands it to me.

"Sambo style! Have you ever! The paper's reputation is beyond repairable!"

I have to turn away from him to prevent from laughing.

SCOOP

"We could get away with 'a tremendous shit' as a typo! Because the *i* and the *o* are next to each other on the keyboard. But 'Sambo style'! Jesus fucking Christ! The vowel is at the opposite end of the bastard keyboard…What is the Sambo style anyway? Strolling along…waving your hands…arms down by your side, your head tilted back, singing 'Zip-a-Dee-Doo-Dah,' like a—like a fucking minstrel?"

I'd pay to watch this mad bastard as a stand-up comedian, I would. He's fucking hilarious.

"Why didn't you just write the stereotypical 'Sambo Nig Nogs have got more skill and can run further and faster because of their superior bone structure'? For fuck's sake! They'll all be on the phone: Kick It Out, Anti-Nazi League, Football Unites, Racism Divides, and Show Racism the Red Card! Heads will fucking roll for this. Sure of it. Why was Keren given so much responsibility? She's only been here five minutes."

"I never made that decision," I defend, as the question is directed at me.

"Well, who the hell did?"

There is a moment's silence before Marty interrupts. "I thought it would be a good idea."

"You thought it a good idea to give a trainee the responsibility of a fully qualified sportswriter? It's match facts, players' ratings, and a bit of colour! And I don't mean anything fucking race related when I say that! And that's only if it's a Saturday match, you useless twat! And who made you the boss, by the way?"

Marty shrugs.

"Cass, why is Marty making those editorial decisions? You're the fucking sports editor!"

"Thought she was capable of doing it, so I was happy to accept Marty's proposal," Cass replies matter-of-factly.

"Did you now? Why didn't you ask Tom for his thoughts on the matter? He is acting chief, after all." They all shrug.

"The copy was clean when it came in," objects Cass. "I checked the Word document again this morning."

"Let me see."

Cass and Harvey leave the office. This should be fun. I gained access to the *Post*'s e-mail address and changed the document. Ha-ha! Marty, Keren, and I hear "Idiot!" screamed from outside the office.

"You need to get your eyes tested, you soppy old twat. Stevie Wonder could have done better."

"I swear down. It was clean last night," protests Cass.

"Aye, cleaner than a city-centre window in Mexico City! Go on. Fuck off, the lot of you. I need to think."

We start to make our way out of the room when Harvey calls me.

"Tom?"

"Yes."

"Good work on the Peter Whitworth racist line. Pity we didn't get it earlier. We could have made a bigger fuss of it…like the *Mail*!"

The sarcastic bastard knows I tipped off the *Mail* first. I should have seen that coming.

"Thanks, but I didn't get it until late," I lie.

That *Mail* job is getting so close that I can almost touch it. I need to talk to my contact, who's at the Walter Adams's undercover Nazi party, as it happens.

The newsroom is deathly silent as we return to the sports desk. At least it'll keep that gobshite new girl quiet. She looks all bleary eyed, like she's been crying. I couldn't stand another day of trivia and general positivity. Marty has given her a grassroots sport story to keep her occupied. I'm not going to ask what it is, but I can guess. A blind hurdler, a one-armed golfer, or a legless high jumper.

My mobile phone rings, and it's Millwall Mick. Fuck! I'll answer it. I'm at Fulham this weekend, so I'm planning on giving the racist cunt his money then!

"Mick, me old mate," I sing into the phone.

"Don't 'Mick, me old mate' me, you slag!" he aggressively barks. "Where's me money?"

I move away from the desk and into the kitchen so that no one can hear my conversation.

"Calm down, you muppet," I respond in a cockney twang, trying to take the sting out of the situation. He's just about to launch into another tirade when I jump in. "I'm coming down this weekend to settle up, take you out as a treat, and cover a game in between. But not if you're going to be a stroppy bastard."

"Me stroppy? I've been waiting over six months, geezer."

"I know. I apologise, but I've never had a game down there, have I? I'll sort you out on Saturday, and with a little bit extra so that you can give yourself indigestion filling your face with jellied eels or pie and mash."

"Fak off, you're confusing me wiv West Ham, mate."

"Just winding you up, Mick." I laugh. "Right, I'll see you in the George on Wardour Street about eight bells, OK?"

"You better be! I'm not standing on me Jack Jones all night."

"I'll be there. You can count on it. Speak soon."

"Yeah, laters, Geordie boy."

Geordie boy, the wanker! I'm starving. Think I'll pop out for something to eat and put a call in at the same time.

As I make my way up the street to the Butty Busters sandwich shop, I see, through the inside of a shop window, Blackley taking shelter. He is nervously smoking, which he always seems to do. This should be fun. I creep up on him unawares and scream "Boo!" loudly behind his back. He nearly shits himself, ha-ha! He drops his cigarette and falls to his knees. I walk past, giggling to myself. He's certainly a man with a nervous disposition.

I approach the fried-chicken shop, which is the takeaway two along from my destination, and see they've got a special meal deal on: chicken nuggets, in the shape of farm animals, with chips for £3.99. Ha-ha! Hilarious! Christ, I wonder if the news desk has realised. They must have by now. That chicken-nugget story was months ago. I wonder if Harvey knows they were set up again. If he doesn't, he'll blow his top.

When I get back in the office after a casual stroll around the city centre, there is a bit of a commotion on the news desk. Colin, the office bore, informs me, "Steve Blackley has been rushed to hospital after suffering a heart attack."

Bloody hell! You can't say boo to a goose without repercussions these days. I act concerned. "Really?"

"In the middle of the street, apparently. Reminds me of this time when I was in London."

Oh no, the boring bastard is going to tell one of his sending-a-glass-eye-to-sleep stories. My phone rings. Saved by the bell, literally, thank God. It's Steve Doyle from the *Mirror*. Funny, he's never called me before. Colin sees I've taken a call and turns to Jo Nicholson instead and recites some tiresome tale of how he had to give mouth-to-mouth to an obese man with bad breath, who had collapsed outside Centre Point.

"Hi, Steve, what can I do for you?"

"We're struggling for a Newcastle line, mate. Have you got anything?"

Fucking hell! They're calling me now. They usually call Arnie.

"You not called Arnie?"

"He's on the sick, mate. Has he not been in touch?"

"No, I've heard nothing for a couple of weeks, as it happens."

"He's depressed apparently. This drink-drive charge and the fact the *Mail* aren't renewing his contract have made him suicidal."

"The *Mail* aren't renewing his contract?"

"You not heard about that neither?"

"Heard a rumour, but that's all I thought it was."

"Shadow of the man." He laughs. "You would never think it, would you?"

"No, certainly not, Steve."

If only he knew the half of it.

"Tell you what, though, Tom. There're a few of us relieved to see the back of him, if you know what I mean."

"Aye."

"Well, he was never the most popular among the group, was he?"

"Guess not."

"Bit of a fucking bully, if the truth be known."

"Aye, suppose he was to some. Still, you never like hearing someone has lost his job."

"No, no, know what you mean, but still. Anyway you got anything cooking?"

"I might have. I'll have to get back to you, mate."

"OK, no probs, Tom. It's just our news desks are demanding lines for tomorrow, and we've got nothing on the Car-Toon Army."

"OK, give me an hour or so."

"Cheers, Tom."

"Don't mention it. Bye.

"Cheerio."

Fucking hopeless, the lot of them. Not one of them can come up with a decent line between them. Mind you, I'm struggling with a Toon story myself. But the balance of power is shifting towards me. Glad to hear Arnie is a washed-up deadbeat and the nationals have recognised that I'm his natural successor. The king is dead! Long live the king!

Right, what we got? I know, that Carlos Kickaball they signed on loan on deadline day—Sergio Flores from Racing—could make a line. He can't speak a word of fucking English. I'll give Camp Colin, their press officer, a bell. I make the call in the kitchen. Can't have the rest of the newsroom knowing all my trade secrets, can I?

"Hello, Colin. It's Tom Rafferty from the *Post*."

"Hi, Tom. What can I do for you?" the puff sings.

"I'm short of a Newcastle line for the paper tomorrow. And rather than follow the tabloids' lead and write a negative story about the club's lack of activity in the transfer market, why don't I write a positive line on Sergio? How he wants to make the move to St James' Park permanent and how he wants to follow in the footsteps of Alan Shearer and become a number-nine legend. What do you reckon?"

"Sounds good, Tom, but the bugger can't speak a word of English."

"I'm aware of that, mate. So why don't I just make up a few quotes, and you can run through it before we go to press?"

"Suppose it can't do any harm."

"Mind you, I'll be passing it on to the nationals."

"Only if you make the story as benign as possible. I don't want them bastards spinning it like a fucking burning Catherine Wheel."

"Not at all, Colin. As I say, you can edit the final draft before I give it to them."

"OK then. Look forward to reading it, Tom. Bye."

"Thanks, Colin. Bye."

Flores Plans for Legendary Status
By Tom Rafferty

Newcastle United's new loan signing has made it known that he wants to follow in the footsteps of living legend Alan Shearer.

Sergio Flores arrived on loan at St James' Park on transfer deadline day with a view to a permanent move for £15 million.

The twenty-three-year-old was paraded in front of the press and spoke only through an interpreter. But after two weeks of intense language lessons, the Argentine gave his first interview in English and revealed plans to become a Toon legend.

"To follow in the footsteps of Alan Shearer would be a dream," said an excited Flores.

"He's a legend here. His goal-scoring record speaks for itself. I have heard all about the tradition and history of the famous number-nine shirt, and Alan Shearer is one of the best there has been. He was one of the main reasons I came here. That and because it was the best deal my agent could get me. I know the supporters love strikers, and I hope to be successful while I'm playing for Newcastle."

Flores acknowledged that he knew little of Newcastle while he was a child growing up in Argentina. But once Argentina internationals Fabricio Coloccini and Jonas Gutierrez signed for the club, he became well aware of the club's standing and tradition.

"It's great to be here with Newcastle United," said the on-loan Racing striker. "It's a team with great ambition. It's a team with a great history, and that was a big attraction. I see it as a great opportunity to play football for a club like Newcastle, and I would like to thank the Newcastle manager for giving me this chance at this stage of my career. I'm very excited and have been ever since I was told the deal had been agreed.

"Over the next four months, I hope to do enough to win a permanent transfer and then become a household name. I also want to use the transfer to realise my dreams and play for my country and play in the World Cup."

The story takes little over thirty minutes to write. I e-mail it to Camp Colin, and the pufta replies that he's "delighted" with it and that the copy is safe enough to hand out to "those fucking backstabbing, two-faced cunts who work for the nationals"—his words, not mine. I then e-mail the story on, and Steve Doyle and Will Gibson, from the *Guardian*, send sincere wishes and thanks for the copy. I get fuck all from that cunt Danny Bew at the *Star* or Ken Chisolm at the *Sun*. I'll remember to store that for future reference.

I put the story in the news basket for Cass to pick up for when he's drawing up later. The decrepit old twat is away from his desk at the minute, so I turn to Marty.

"Marty, let Cass know my Newcastle line is in the basket. I'm guessing you got some follow-up from Boro, and there'll be a line from you on Sunderland tonight."

The fucker completely ignores me. "Marty?" He looks up at me and then back to his PC screen. "Did you hear me?"

"Yes, I heard you," he almost spits.

"A bit of an acknowledgment and civility wouldn't go amiss."

He looks at me disdainfully and grunts. If that's the way you're going to play it, then so be it. I switch off my PC, pack my laptop away, and put my coat on.

"I'm not in tomorrow. I'm just going to file from home. Do you all know what you're doing?"

"Yes, Tom," Keren replies, while Marty grunts again. Ah, well, you've been asking for it, you Paki bastard!

As I'm leaving the *Post* building, I take my phone out and call Walter Adams.

"Wally? It's your friendly *Post*-man…I'm good, thanks. Listen, he's going to a Sunderland Community Programme launch at the Academy of Light tonight, seven start. There'll be nibbles and drinks, so I'm guessing it'll run for at least an hour. I'm sure you can take care of things from there…Yeah… OK, mate…No problems…Speak soon, bye…Yeah, bye."

That'll teach the black cunt to disrespect me. Revenge is sweet, sooner or later. It doesn't matter when it's delivered or whom it's for. Lucy, Saunders, Arnie, Hughesy, the new girl, and now Marty. Only the slag mother and girlfriend and Millwall Mick to go. Well, that'll get sorted this weekend.

Chapter 28

There's no news from Wally, as we agreed. I don't want anything relating me to the incident. But I take a call from Cass about a racist attack on Marty. It's pretty horrific, by all accounts. Not only have Wally's mob kicked him to within an inch of his life, but they've also carved *a* and the number eighty-eight into his arms. According to Cass, it is a symbol of "Heil Hitler." They didn't attack him outside the Sunderland Academy. I'm guessing there were too many people around and various CCTV cameras. They followed him home and gave him a hiding there; we know because he was found down a back lane near his gaff by a couple walking home from a chip shop. He's in hospital and in a bad way. Shame, eh? No, not really; he had it coming to him. Hope it's knocked the chip off his shoulder.

Downside to this is that my workload has just increased. Fuck! Fuck! Fuck! I didn't think that one through very carefully.

"Well, you'll have to get one of the subs from news to finish the grass-roots supplement," I tell Cass. "The new girl should be able to write a few stories and do a bit of subbing now, so she can help out there. That'll leave me to concentrate on the club lines, so sorted, eh? Oh, it might be a good idea to start getting a few work-experience guys in to help. Free labour and all that."

Irony or ironies, I get yet another text from Cass's missus, Trudi. I say "yet another text," but it'll be the first one I've had in a month, I reckon.

> I know I've made a mess of everything, but it still doesn't stop me thinking about you. Get in touch, if you want to. Trudi X

If I'm honest, I do miss her—well, shagging her. And I haven't had a shag in ages now. Spend more time shaking hands with Charlie! Thank fuck for xhamster and xvideos. Still, it's all very confusing, and I need to deal with them: Trudi, my mum, and Lucy, I suppose. I feel as if my head is going to explode at times. There's too much going on in there, too much responsibility, and too many schemes and machinations making me ill.

I've already made a conscious decision to burn the bridge I'd rebuilt with Julie. I did enjoy my time with her, and the sex was great. But I can't risk being around her prick-tease daughter. I'd probably end up in jail after abusing her in the most decadent manner possible. And given how I was brought up, what I've witnessed, and what I've put in to practice recently, it doesn't bear thinking about.

I called Julie just after Christmas and told her it wouldn't work out rather than meet up and discuss it in a grown-up, reasonable, and adult manner. I should've just texted, tweeted, or e-mailed her; that's the modern coward's way, after all. See, I must be redeeming myself in some capacity, somewhere…maybe not. Julie took it well and understood when I explained the pressures of my new position, the imminent offer from the *Mail*, and the fact that, more than likely, I'd be moving away. It was a lot easier than I'd expected. Had I made the call to Trudi, she'd be charging around like a cat with vinegar sprayed into its eyes. She's a walking melodrama, that one. Probably due to years of watching *EastEnders*, *Neighbours*, and *Holby City* and reading all those pathetic women's magazines about soap operas.

"Your writing is shit, mate," an accusing voice throws in my direction as I step out of the car. "Call yourself a sports writer! I could write all you know about football on the back of beer mat!"

There're about five or six of them, and they're laughing and mocking me. I can feel another anxiety attack coming on. Need to get into the building and out of their way before they all start to stick the metaphorical boot in—or worse. "A drunken badger would talk more sense," "You're shit," and "My dead grandmother knows more about the game than you" were just three of the tastier insults before they started singing, "Tom Rafferty is a wanker, is a wanker, is a wanker."

SCOOP

My head is throbbing, and I feel sick as I manage to hurry inside the *Post* building before receiving any more abuse. Think I've shat myself. I've followed through.

As I'm scrambling towards the ground-floor toilet, I unfortunately bump into Keren.

"Tom..."

"Two minutes, Keren," I reply, dashing into the bogs to try and compose myself. I splash water on my face and quickly climb out of my trousers and dispose of my soiled underwear. Fortunately there isn't much mess, and after several minutes of breathing exercises, I'm ready to face the world.

"You OK, Tom?" inquires Keren when I get to the sports desk.

"What? Oh, yes, sorry. Thought I was going to wet myself," I lie.

"Terrible news about Marty, Tom."

"Who? Oh, yes, is there any news?"

"Someone's boyfriend finally caught up with him, I expect," Cass spits out bitterly.

Don't think he's forgiven him over the Jo Nicholson episode. I catch Jo looking over and grimacing at Cass's cutting comment. Brilliant.

"I'm going to the hospital after work to see how he is."

"That's great, Keren. Send our regards, and tell him we'll try and pop in to see him later on this week. Are you OK to handle the amateur-sports supplement in his absence?"

"I'll probably need a hand with the subbing, but I can take care of the copy."

"No problem. I'll get one of the news subs to help out. I'll have a word with Eric in conference."

Afternoon conference is getting worse or better, depending on how you look at it or how your humour is. There is no way I could have made it as a news reporter. The stories are getting dafter and dafter. Hardwick is promoting the RSPCA's Cuddle a Cat Scheme, where residents are being encouraged to adopt an abandoned or abused cat or pet. Harvey rolls his eyes. I reckon Hardwick will push Harvey over the edge with his quirky stories one of these days.

"Why not cuddle a tree, a hooker, or a user of amphetamines? I'm sure that will sell more papers than that weak-as-piss story," says Harvey caustically. "Anything else?"

"Government is cracking down on cheap alcohol and raising the unit price," Sarah Brownlie adds. "I'm going to do a feature on it and a vox pop asking local supermarket managers, wine-sellers, and consumers what they think about it."

"Any bloody excuse to increase the levy on booze and fags," says Harvey. "That's why Wetherspoons is my favourite boozer. It's the only pub where you can buy a drink at a reasonable price. Anything else?"

"Oh, the *Mail* is running with 'Are We a Nation of Binge Smokers?' as well. Thought I could follow that up," responds Brownlie.

"Binge smoking! I thought it was binge drinking and chain-smoking. Yeah, whatever, I think I might be out of touch these days. Time to retire, I reckon."

I agree with Harvey. It's similar to when the supermarket chains put up food prices and blame the farmers, a bad harvest, and fuel increases. They never seem to bring the bastard prices down when there's a good summer or when petrol and diesel prices come down.

"Right, go forth and multiply. Tom, I need a word." Once everyone is out, Harvey continues.

"No Scott, no Marty, and no Blackley, for that matter. What's the plan now that we're without those two?"

"Don't worry, Eric; I've got it all in hand. Keren is looking after the grassroots sports supplement, but we'll need a news sub to help out. I'll look after the club lines, and for anything we can't cover, we'll just use Press Association copy. It'll be cheaper in the short term."

"Still looks like I'll have to recruit two, maybe three, new sports-desk bodies. Took a call from the *Daily Mail*...You've obviously caught their eye. Congratulations."

I didn't know what to say. Knew I was close to getting it, but thought they'd tell me first.

"Have I?"

"Fucking come on. Don't play the daft shite with me. I can't stand the fucking paper myself, what with all its right-wing propaganda of 'too many darkies live here' and the perpetual 'Princess Diana farted on this day twenty years ago,' but I do have to keep abreast of what they're writing and who is writing it. I saw that Chris Arnott isn't getting bylines these days and that the stories were coming from somewhere else. Anyway, as I say, congratulations."

"Thanks, boss."

"You've got to work your notice, which will take you up to the end of the football season."

"Yeah, no problem."

"OK, keep me in the loop."

And with that, I leave the office. Calls for a celebration of some sort, but with whom? I'll call Lucy. No, I'll text her.

Just got news of *Mail* offer! Delighted! X

Within seconds, Lucy replies.

Great news. Happy for you. Come around later, about eight, and I'll cook dinner. X

Bloody hell, Princess Lucy is going to cook dinner! She's come a long way from that fateful night. I'm in an extraordinarily good mood. I feel fantastic and even euphoric as I sit and join our depleted sports desk. I've just landed the job of my dreams, and the woman of my dreams is cooking dinner. I'm actually getting to go to the special girl's flat with a genuine invite this time. No need to dress up or go in disguise.

"Did you see last weekend's *Sunday Supplement*, Tom?"

I think, *No, but I'll be on the fucker next season.* "Eh, no, didn't manage it," I reply to Keren's attempt to build what she clearly recognises as a broken bridge between us. "Any good?"

"Not really, or rather I didn't learn anything that I didn't already know."

The fucker's starting to sound like Saunders!

"Which is?"

"The pundits there love hearing their own voice. They're full of their own self-importance, and most of what they say is nonsense, guesswork, or ill informed."

"I've been saying that for years," Cass chips in.

"And what is the obsession the nationals have with the England football team?"

"Yeah, the nationals always get excited about a forthcoming World Cup or European Championship tournament," I add.

"But they actually think England have a chance of winning it!"

"Well, anything can 'appen once they get through to the knockout stages," says an optimistic Cass.

"I can't disagree, Dave," our precocious young sports writer concurs. Dave, you bugger. I've never heard anyone call him Dave before. Cockney Cass, geezer, Alf Garnet, racist cunt, and several other less-than-complimentary names, but never Dave. "But I don't think England will get out of the group stage."

"She's got a point, Cass. And look whom they've got in the draw for round two. Even if they win the group, they've still got to face a South American outfit, an African team, or one of Europe's powerhouses." Can't believe I'm agreeing with the opinionated cow.

"They're deluded," insists a forthright Miss Veitch. "And that guy from the *Telegraph* on the North-East beat, what about him? He's obsessed with the national team, always asking England questions. I've only been to three press conferences with him, and all he's interested in is asking which player is good enough to play for his home country (can he get back in the England squad) or how many caps the individual can go on to win for the Three Lions! Nothing about how the local clubs are going to fair in the domestic program. It's like he's been possessed by the spirits of St George, Sir Arthur Conan Doyle, and Queen Victoria!"

"Ah, you've met Rob Halom then?"

"Unfortunately I've met all of them, and they're a bit of a misogynistic bunch and very childish when they get together."

"You think so?"

"Know so. I tried to mix in with them, but they treated me like some Scarlet Women, a double agent, or some unfortunate with leprosy. When I asked about what copy was being used, they gawped as if I'd spoken some unspeakable language, mumbled something unpronounceable, and huddled into different groups so that I couldn't hear what was going on."

"Yeah, that..."

"I worked for the *Yorkshire Post* a few years ago," interrupts Jo Nicholson, who is ear-wigging into our conversation, "and was at an England Netball World Cup press conference, where several well-known television sports journalists were in attendance, and they blanked me."

"I can understand how that feels, Jo," says her new sister in arms.

"Marty reckons they're socially inadequate," adds Jo. "They don't really have any social skills because they've never really encountered other people outside of their infantile sports-world environment."

Fucking hell, Lucy has just texted to say she's seeing her mum at a women's Refuge meeting tonight and can't make it. Nightmare! These two are starting to get on my tits now. We'll be moving on to the suffragette movement soon.

"The men you mean?" Keren asks.

"Sorry, yes, the men. Marty says most of the men writing about sports have gone straight from school into college or university and then on to working for a newspaper. He believes that they still behave like children because they've had no experience of life outside of school, college, or university. They've never worked on a building site or on a factory floor with real people, so they continue to behave like children."

"Ahem, hang on," I interrupt. "I worked in the building trade for a few years before I became a journalist."

"You must be the exception, Tom," says Keren in a sycophantic tone, although I sense that there's something fucking sinister hidden beneath it. She's not all that whiter than white, if you ask me. "I overheard a couple of the writers say that women shouldn't be writing about sport when they've no experience. But that's bollocks, because none, or very few, of the men writing about sport have any experience, either."

"I agree, Keren," says Jo. "I was sent to this presser because I played netball for England schoolgirls when I was a teenager. So you could say I was an expert to a certain extent. You couldn't say that about the others. In fact they were asking questions that were really only relevant to football, not netball. Weird."

"Jesus, will you two get off your soapboxes? You're giving me a bleedin' headache!" Ha-ha, well said, Cass. It does enough to shut them up.

"Sorry, Dave, just a little frustrated by the general misogynistic attitude towards the few women operating in the sports world. Women's emancipation, to that lot, means little more than having the freedom to choose in which supermarket their wives and girlfriends can buy the Sunday roast. Very childish behaviour and attitudes."

"I agree," says Jo. "They should send them all back to school to study women's emancipation and the Suffragettes."

"Ah, what I wouldn't do to go back to school. You agree, Tom?"

"Do I, buggery—hated every minute of school."

Chapter 29

I left school in 1992, the year Sunderland lost 2–0 in the FA Cup to Liverpool. I'd been ferociously tormented, to put it mildly, for being a Mackem, or rather a supporter of the Wearside team. Graham Hughes and Pete Berry weren't the only two tyrants who made life difficult for me at school, but they were the most threatening. And Kevin Keegan's return as manager early that year had exaggerated the bullies' behaviour towards me even further. I kept my head down and tried to avoid them the best I could, and I concentrated on revising for my GCSE exams. It wasn't too bad, because my tormentor-in-chief, Hughesy, left school in March of that year without taking any exams. And without his sidekick, Bez didn't really take any notice of me.

Newcastle had sacked former World Cup winner, Ossie Ardiles, in January or maybe early February, because the club didn't think he could keep the team in what was the old Second Division. Keegan was brought in to save the Magpies from relegation, which he eventually did on a dramatic last day of the season, thanks to a 2–1 win at Leicester. Sunderland flirted with relegation that year too, but they did just enough to keep the bottom three at arm's length. We finished only one point and two places above the Geordie wankers. However, we had bigger fish to fry.

The FA Cup run was astonishing, and I exulted in all the hate, spite, and abuse that I got at school, as Malcolm Crosby's Rokerites made progress through the early rounds. Although after they plucked the wings of the Canaries, Norwich, in the semifinal, I got little abuse. John Byrne got the all-important winning goal in the first half. And 1–0 was enough to win it after dispatching Port Vale, Oxford, West Ham, and Chelsea, both after replays, in the previous rounds.

Truth be known, I would have been a Newcastle fan. But following the maltreatment I got after foolishly letting a classmate know my mother's boyfriend had taken me to a Sunderland game one weekend, I decided to stick it out and defy the bastards and make them my team. Frank only took me to a couple of games, including the swimming baths, where, I think, he enjoyed giving me a shower more than the plunge. Still, he only did it to win my slut of a mother around. Once we moved in with him, he showed little interest.

Aside from a 2–0 playoff win at St James' Park in 1990, I'd never seen Sunderland beat a Newcastle side. Two weeks after we had triumphed over Chelsea in a sixth-round replay at Roker Park, we lost to a David Kelly goal on Tyneside. It was a starter pistol for more insults, reproach, and vilification. It was the last time, mind. Most people were revising for their exams, and it was a tense period for everyone.

The FA Cup final was a personification of my life at that point: a big disappointment. I wouldn't have cared, but we held our own in the first half. Had John Byrne converted that chance from close range, the outcome could have been different. But once Michael Thomas netted two minutes after the break, it was all one way. Ian Rush compounded the misery with over twenty minutes to go. I didn't bother with the ceremonial presentation of the cup. I went straight back to revising. I had to do well in my exams if I was to escape the wretched existence I had with my whore of a mother.

I got As in English literature and language, a B in modern history, a C in human movement studies, a C in maths, and a D in physics, and I failed woodwork. I hated woodwork, but it was either that, metalwork, or mechanical engineering. You had to take one practical lesson, which involved using your hands. Working with wood was the lesser of the three evils, despite the spelks, the dust in the eyes, and the chisel in the palm of my hand! Just as well I wank right-handed!

The irony of failing woodwork at school wasn't lost on me when one of my first jobs after leaving was for one of my mother's boyfriends, a jobbing builder-carpenter. He was old enough to be my grandfather and my mother's father, I reckoned. Well, he looked it. Na, he couldn't have been. Bob Lee was his name. But he had a fortieth birthday that year. I was sixteen, and my mother was thirty-one, I think. Still, he was shiny bald on top with a shabby silver-horseshoe effect around the back and sides. He was a canny bloke, but my slut of a mother just used him to escape her debts and former boyfriends and as a place to stay until someone, or something, better came along.

They met when he was working on our estate. And my mother, being my mother, used to flirt with the handyman when she saw him pass. But she did this with anyone and everyone, whether it was the postman, binman, paper lad, or milkman. In fact, my first job was as a milkman. Yes—surprise, surprise—with a bloke my mother was seeing. It suited me down to the ground because despite getting up early, or rather not going to bed, I never saw anyone.

Bob came to mend our back door, which was kicked in because of the milkman's jealous rage. All the blokes my mother went out with were the same: jealous and possessive. They were stupid enough to believe that they were the only one she flirted with! Anyway, she gave Bob the typical "all-men-are-bastards" sob story and told him how she was "skint and on the bones of my arse" and what she'd "do to have a proper, solid man" to look after her and "care for my every need." He fell for it hook, line, and sinker. Two days later he turned up in his white van, when the milkman was out, like some evangelical saviour, and moved us out of our rathole into a three-bedroom semidetached house in Coxlodge. I wasn't complaining. I had a decent-sized bedroom with a colour portable TV. Result!

The day of his birthday, I caught her giving him a "special" wank in the kitchen as a compromise for the sex he was pleading for. I overheard the whole conversation. Apparently she'd only let him do it the once, the day we moved in. She was playing the "you're-only-after-one-thing" card. And "I've been taken advantage of at every opportunity." Staggering, really, given she'd spent most of her life as if she had a mattress strapped to her fucking back. Admittedly he wasn't the best-looking bloke, but he was decent enough. Any right-thinking woman would have recognised that and built a life with him.

But bear in mind, my mother had an appetite for destruction, a craving for attention, and an addiction to cheeky cheesy chat-up lines; there was more chance of making a rusty old radiator sing "Bringing in the Sheaves" than that happening!

In 1992, she left him after Christmas for another roguishly agreeable-looking patter merchant with a repugnant aroma of Blue Stratos. He wasn't much older than me. Bob let me stop with him. I think he was hoping that she would come back and that if I was there, it would make her want to see her son. Little did he know that I more or less brought myself up, given her lengthy absences. I gave him plenty encouragement, mind. It was the nicest place I'd ever lived. I didn't want to sacrifice that.

I learned how to hang a front door, toe and heel a double-glazed unit, and ping a plumb line. I also lost my virginity. It was everything I'd expected it to be, although the only experience I'd had was from witnessing the slut with her boyfriends and their dirty videos, which I've still got somewhere.

We'd been working on a house full of double glazing in a townhouse in a leafy Jesmond suburb. We started on the Monday morning and managed to rip out all the windows and fit them within three days. When it came to Thursday morning, we only had the finishing-off work: PVC trim, cleaning, and silicone sealing. It was a balmy Thursday afternoon. Susan Rostron was her name. She was sunbathing in a two-piece bikini in the garden. She was probably in her early forties, I guess, and a little overweight—not fat but curvy. Her tits were falling out of her top; I can tell you that much.

I was sealing the inside of her master-bedroom window when I saw her. Bob had just told me moments earlier that he was off to the builders' merchants for materials. I waited for him to leave and thought I could fit in a quick wank before he came back. As soon as I heard him pull away in the van, I downed the tools and went back to Susan's knicker drawer, which I'd rifled through on day one of the job. I nearly shat myself when she roared, "What do you think you're doing?"

She had a face like thunder, and I was terrified.

"Do you know I work for the police?"

I shook my head hesitantly.

"I could have you arrested, put in jail…and your boss, too!"

I sensed her mood change, but I was still unsure. She eased one of her sliding wardrobes open and pulled out a set of handcuffs. There were several ideas swimming around in my head—one of them to run, obviously—but I was momentarily paralysed. Susan stalked me from one end of the bed to the other like a cat stalking its prey. There was no doubt I was trapped. She slipped one handcuff to my right wrist and hooked it around one post of her luxurious bed. The voluptuous middle-aged woman then made another sortie to and from her walk-in wardrobe with another set of cuffs. She pushed me onto the king-sized bed and cuffed my left wrist to the rail above, as my arms weren't long enough to reach across.

"Terrified" wasn't the word. I don't think I could articulate or measure the ambivalent emotions I was experiencing at that point. I nearly fainted when she let the sarong, which was wrapped around her, drop to the floor and exposed her naked fleshy parts. She seductively looked into my eyes while she unbuttoned my silicone-splattered jeans and pulled down my *Star Wars* novelty boxer shorts. Susan then pulled open a bedside drawer, took out some antiseptic wipes, and cleaned my cock, before her hot, wet mouth swallowed my length. The sensation was euphoric! Just like the cartoons, there were bells, fireworks, and explosions of ecstasy going off in my head and heart. At one point, it felt like I was in danger of a cardiac arrest. Thankfully, less than thirty seconds later, the heart-stopping moment was avoided when she sensed the build-up and withdrew as I exploded on to her tan-lined tits, now fully exposed from the bikini.

"You need to eat more fruit," Susan said matter-of-factly before taking three antiseptic sheets in quick succession from the bedside drawer and wiping both her and me clean. Leaving me cuffed to the bed, she disappeared to the bathroom and returned after a couple of minutes in a creamy white silk dressing robe. Moments later and after a bit of gentle encouragement from hand and mouth, I was hard again, and she lowered herself down on top of me, naked, except for the silk gown, and rode as if her life depended on it. I lasted a little longer that time.

We continued to meet up for nearly a year after that—or, rather, I would go around, and she'd indulge in some kinky stuff while her husband was on different shifts. It was hardly *Lady Chatterley's Lover* or *The Graduate*, although she was older and posher, mind. But following her expert tuition, I was certainly schooled in the art of sex or, should I say, "sexpert." I'm fucking funny when I want to be.

Susan's husband got a new position in London, and so they sold up and moved on. It was around this time that I became depressed. Not that I was the most outgoing of people. I wasn't. My social life outside of work involved accompanying Bob to the Coxlodge Social Club, where he would play darts, dominoes, and cards. I'd sit, nurse a pint of lager, watch him and his mates play, and observe the behaviour of the so-called working classes in their social habitat. The hours of fun they would have pretending to knock over an empty beer glass and watch victims jump back to avoid getting wet, the amusement they would gather from watching a friend tumble to the floor after pulling away a chair as he was about to sit down, and the childish delight of a slurred word or mispronunciation knew no bounds. It was *Groundhog Day* every time I went into that social club.

I eventually stopped going with him, withdrew, and became quite sullen and insular. When I overheard a friend of Bob call me an oddball in the toilet while I was in a cubicle, I became paranoid people were talking about me. As a result, I started suffering from anxiety and panic attacks. At first I thought I was having a heart attack, but I managed to get it under control. They became more frequent when I was at work with Bob. I thought customers or people in builders' merchants were talking about me. I tried to get time off work and made excuses that I was ill. Bob understood at first, but then he said that if I didn't go to work, he would have to sack me and that I'd have to find somewhere else to live.

A visit from my mother, the first time I'd seen her in over a year, was welcome at first, but then her presence only exacerbated the problem. She'd spent the previous twelve months shacked up with some tattooed tough, probably in Ireland. The Emerald Isle was a convenient haven for her. She could foray back and forth across the Irish Sea to her heart's content. And as I later learned, she was generally running away from some tumult she'd obviously caused.

Bob was falling all over her. He showered her with gifts, took her out, and let her stay. But I knew it was only a stopgap. She'd soon be off again when some gentleman mounted a kerb in a vehicle with go-faster stripes and a furry dice muffler. Nevertheless, she did eventually recognise my distress and anxiety after a couple of weeks and gave me some Valium and, later, Diazepam. They felt great. The side effects or hallucinations weren't a problem; they were comforting, cathartic even. I've been hooked ever since.

I suppose it was probably the closest we ever came to bonding as a mother and son. She said she could empathise with my anguish and almost told me who my father was. I'd never seen her cry like that before. I'd seen her shed tears but not in this way. And in the end, she couldn't bring herself to tell me. But just as I was beginning to get to know and like my mum, she disappeared. The following day when Bob and I returned from work, she'd gone, without as much as a Dear John note. Bob was devastated. He didn't speak for a week, which suited me.

Obviously I was never what some people would call "a party animal," but whatever social life I had, I withdrew from even more. I became besotted with football. I'd been interested in football but not obsessed in the way Bez and Hughesy were. Admittedly I was jealous when Bez won that regional penalty shoot-out competition. He got to play keep yuppy with Newcastle's Frank Pingel, but I wasn't addicted. The event was filmed by Tyne Tees Television on Whitley Bay Links. Bez was already one of the most popular kids at school, and after that, he was treated like royalty!

It was hard to take much of an interest in football, however, when the team you supported was shit. I did watch what was to become a familiar cyclical event, an England fiasco at a major European or world championship. This time it was Euro '92. That, of course, was a major disappointment after the euphoria of Italia 1990 and England's glorious failure in losing on penalties to Germany in the semi-final. But what followed the Euros in Sweden was the inaugural season of the newly packaged Premier League, which really captured the nation's imagination. And the fact Bob had invested in *Sky Sports*, prior to the curtain-raiser, meant I never had to leave the house, other than to go to work.

I'd never contemplated a career as a sports writer or journalist. As I'd said earlier, I thought you had to be an expert of some standing or at least had to have played sport at professional or semi professional level. But when I learned that this was not the case, I investigated what qualifications were required. I discovered, to my delight, that two A levels at grade C and above would be enough to get on a journalism course at Darlington College. Unfortunately I had a year in limbo, because I didn't realise that courses at night school or college began in September. But I didn't waste any time. I spent all my nonworking spare time reading football annuals, history books, and other stats. They were tools that would be useful to me when I eventually became a sports writer.

It took another two years to get the A levels, but by the time Sunderland had gained promotion to the Premier League under Peter Reid, I managed to get on a six-month journalism course, courtesy of two Bs in English literature and modern history. The course itself was boring, with modules on central and local government, law, and fucking shorthand! I passed every exam—just—with the honourable exception of shorthand. I just couldn't write one hundred words in a minute. I sat the exam a dozen times until I passed. And I only passed because I'd used a Walkman to tape the reading. Luckily the lecturer needed to leave the exam room for a piss, and I managed to play it back before she came back. I still nearly fucked it up.

I thought that the hard bit would have been passing the exam, but actually it was getting a job. Bob, of course, couldn't understand it. He thought I should know my place and said to me, "Don't get above yourself" and "Those jobs aren't for the likes of us." He said that "being a joiner was an honourable trade" and that I should "be lucky to have one." I don't know how he could say I was a joiner, because I never went to college, like the other lads I met from time to time on different jobs. Bob was just pissed off because he had to find someone else to work with him when I fucked off for six months. I still paid the miserable twat rent. I'd saved enough during the four years or so working with him because I never spent any money other than on comics, science fiction, or porn magazines. The baggy period and Acid House scene passed me by, and I wasn't really into music. I also managed to get a grant to cover the course costs, while I just travelled down to Darlington on the train every day and returned on an evening. I still went back to work for the old fucker until I could get a job in newspapers. It was nearly nine months before I got my break.

I saw an advert in the *Guardian*. Not a newspaper I read, but there happened to be one lying around on a job we were working on. "Trainee reporters required for *Lewisham Gazette*." I couldn't wait for the day to end so that I could write up a cover letter and tidy up my CV. My manipulating of the truth came into its own at this point and has obviously held me in good stead for a life in journalism. The amount of work experience I'd received at newspapers was astonishing—astonishing because I'd never done any. If they'd bothered to check up, I wouldn't have got through the door for an interview. Fortunately the interview went well—better than expected—but then, that was because the assistant editor, who interviewed me, was a voluptuous middle-aged woman, and the attraction was mutual. I was beginning to think that the rozzer's wife, floozy Suzie, was right when she said I had "mother-me eyes."

There was definitely a pattern emerging of the type of women I went for, although at the time I didn't recognise it. Only Julie broke the mould further down the line. But it couldn't have worked out more perfectly. Straight after the interview, I wandered into the nearest Wetherspoons for a Pikey dinner. I thought I'd eat something cheap and filling before I got my train back to Newcastle from King's Cross. I'd no sooner finished my scampi and chips when Sharon Kelly, the *Lewisham Gazette*'s assistant editor, and a couple of her colleagues walked in. Her companions turned out to be Michelle and Darren, two of the paper's subeditors, as I later learned. I watched as they ordered a couple of bottles of Blossom Hill and subsequently made their way to my table.

"Well, hello," said a surprised Sharon. "I thought you'd be away home by now."

"Catching a late train," I replied cheerfully. "Thought it would be best as I didn't know how long the interview would last."

Michelle and Darren eventually buggered off after a couple of hours, and before I knew it, I missed the train and spent the night at Sharon's gaff. I remember getting as smashed as when I was ten years old and experimented with several alcoholic beverages from my mother's drinks cabinet. But other than that episode making me ill, I'd never been drunk until that night. The effect was emotionally dramatic, because it was like I'd swallowed a truth drug. I confessed every wretched moment of my existence to Sharon. Talk about making yourself vulnerable. But she was great. She listened to everything I had to say. She cried, and I cried. And then she shagged me senseless when we got back to her place. It was a lovely two-bedroom first-floor flat in Bromley, not far from the high street and Churchill Theatre. Sharon then banged me again in the morning, made me shower, and cooked me scrambled eggs on toast. She said she preferred her eggs scrambled to fertilised.

I stopped another day and didn't go home until the Sunday evening. Needless to say, she gave me the job before I left. She said she'd look after me and school me in everything about the newspaper industry.

Living in London was brilliant. I could lose myself in the city without raising an eyebrow. It was a great place to reinvent yourself. The shy, paranoid, and introverted individual was reborn into someone more bold, outgoing, and confident. And just as important, before I left the capital to return home and work at the *Post*, I could write quite competently.

I started as a trainee reporter on news and local-council agendas although I got the odd story on sport. The sports desk, as I've come to learn, was suspicious of everyone outside the genre, if you like. The sports desk operated like a newly formed republic created from the disintegration of a Cold War country. When you approached the sports desk with a story, you were treated like a spy, renegade, or anarchist. It was another important lesson I learned and took with me into future jobs.

Sharon used to check the stories I wrote in my personal story basket before I sent them to the news desk to make sure they were up to scratch. We were professional at work. No one knew we were seeing each other, which wasn't that difficult really, as I rarely went out with other members of staff. I was a good loner, despite my new confidence. I'd had years of practice. I could've done it professionally. Working on news stories was tedious, to be honest, and I hated it. But as Sharon said, it gave me a good grounding in how to write for the future.

The old adage of "it's not what you know but who you know" was true as well. My middle-aged lover knew I was desperate to become a sports writer. And with little movement on our sports desk, she used her contacts within the press circle to set me up on a Saturday afternoon working for the Press Association. I'd get sixty quid for filling in statistics, such as corners, free kicks, shots on target, shots off target, and goal scorers for each team, depending where I was sent. It was a piece of piss.

After I'd worked as a reporter on the news desk for a year, a vacancy opened on sport, following an incident where our now former sports writer called a fellow hack a "Paki cunt" at a Millwall versus Charlton football match. He was more or less sacked on the spot. The Asian gentleman had stitched him up over some saved copy he used before he should have. A tactic I was going to be familiar with in the future. In general, I hated my time on news because I had no interest in or enthusiasm for council planning. But there were a few highlights. The sports editor didn't want to take me because he wanted to bring in a mate. But Sharon had the deciding say, and I was in.

My favourite news stories include a dramatic domestic incident involving a chip-pan fire burning a man's wooden leg while he was having a bath, a drunken milkman who'd had one pint too many and crashed his milk float into someone's coy carp pond, and a disabled pensioner on the rampage on a mobility scooter who knocked people down on Bromley High Street as a result of one-too-many whiskey and ginger gargles.

It was one of the weirdest feelings I'd ever had when Sharon pulled me into her office to tell me I would be starting as a sports writer. I could have groped her arse, squeezed her tits, and fingered her fanny then and there, although I don't think it would've gone down well with the rest of the workplace, given that the office was made of see-through glass. But I did manage to get through the holy trinity of sexual assault later at her flat. I also got bum sex for the first time. Well, it was a special occasion, after all.

I fucking loved it. The sports desk was small, with only three people. Understandable given it was a free weekly newspaper. There was Tom Towers, a subeditor, from Petts Wood, just down the road from Bromley. A man of few words, it suited me. Then there was the sports editor, a bucked-tooth cunt from Hartlepool who supported Liverpool, Sunderland, and Hartlepool. I've never understood why people just can't support their hometown team myself. Then I realised that the people from these industrial backwaters have a bit of a chip on their shoulders. They're a bit insecure about their surroundings, so supporting a bigger team boosts their confidence. That, or it makes up for the fact that they have small cocks.

I couldn't wait to get started. At first I kept myself to myself until my face became familiar around the London arenas. One paper, the *South London Press*, I noticed was slapping exclusive on every story it printed. Strange when the quotes it used were from a general press conference everyone attended. It was all part of the learning process. The stories were a mixed bag of amateur you-name-it: athletics, golf, motor sport, martial arts, and disabled quoits. A bit like Marty's brief at the *Post*, really. But Saturdays at the football were something else. Talking to managers and players—well, more like listening to other people's questions and taking notes. I didn't want to make a tit of myself, after all. The London press pack was a bunch of arrogant, stuck-up-their-own-arse, egotistical wankers; saying that, so were their North-East counterparts. Still, I felt comfortable with that because I was growing into it, too. I met Millwall Mick around this time, too.

Chapter 30

I catch the Edinburgh-to-London King's Cross train from Newcastle just after nine in the morning. I buy a standard ticket but travel in first class. The ticket inspector rarely looks at your ticket once it leaves its starting point; he can't be arsed.

David Guest is in the same carriage as me. An intriguing-looking fella, if you ask me. I feel quite unnerved really because he stares at me the whole time. Maybe he is trying to make me feel guilty because first class is full and he'd stood up to give a woman his seat. Very honourable. But fuck them. I paid for my fare, too. Why should I give up a seat for someone as able-bodied as myself? Saying that, it wouldn't have made a difference if the fuckers had walking sticks or crutches or were just lazy bastards with ME. I would've pretended to be asleep.

After an hour or so, I wander down the train to the bogs and find an unattended trolley, so I help myself to some crisps and some beef and horseradish sarnies. Nice. I am looking forward to the Newcastle game at Fulham. I love the walk from Putney Bridge through the leafy park to Craven Cottage. It's very therapeutic in the spring. The pre-summer tweets of the birds and flower fragrances will help take my mind off meeting Millwall Mick after the match.

I first met Mick back in the day when Charlton were an established Premier League outfit. I'd been to a couple of home games at the Valley but just kept myself to myself. I was a bit intimidated, to be honest, what with all those celebrity hacks around. Mick said he'd seen me, although I hadn't noticed him. He asked if I wanted to make a bit of money on the side for a sports agency. Mick couldn't do it because he was going out straight after the match. I wasn't that arsed, to be honest, but I thought it would be good to try and make friends. He got me to copy out all the programme notes from the respective Addicks manager and captain and send them on. Piece of piss, really. Easiest sixty quid I'd ever made. I'm guessing Mick took a cut because it was £120 when I was contacted directly to do it when he was on holiday.

Newcastle play well. It is a comfortable 3–1 victory, but it could easily have been more. Carlos Kickaball nets a brace, and the Toon chief, Robert Clark, is predicting him to follow in the footsteps of Hughie Gallagher, Malcolm MacDonald, and Alan Shearer. The London tabloid press were predicting a return to Europe for the triumphant Tynesiders after the club's recent turnaround in fortunes. The fickle bastards are predicting relegation at the beginning of the season. The Sunday newspaper hacks are running with a story about the Magpies planning an exotic swoop for the Argentine's more illustrious striking partner and apparent best friend. There is more chance of seeing Prince Charles singing, "Yummy Yummy Yummy, I've Got Love in my Tummy," with the Bride of Frankenstein than that happening. But they have to run with something. Me, well, I am happy enough to promote Clark's prediction that the Argentine would be a rightful heir to Shearer's throne and run with the tabloids' Toon for Europe. I need to get done quickly because I have promised to meet my former boss Sharon Kelly for a late supper.

When I told her I was moving back to the Northeast to take up a sports writer's position, Sharon didn't take it very well. I'd spent the best part of five years with her or under her, and I didn't really have a genuine reason to go. My mother was—well, I don't know where she was. I didn't have any family or friends to go back to, nor did I feel any emotional gravity pulling me back home to the North-East. All my experiences of life up north were negative or hinged on hurt and regret. I went because, I dunno, to prove I was worthy, successful, and defiant in the face of adversity. To whom? This is the pathetic part: no one. Yet deep down, I hoped someone from my past would recognise and acknowledge my success. I didn't have any friends. The only people

I knew were Bob and his social-club cronies. Maybe I was trying to make a point to the kids from school who'd made my life a living hell. Whatever, I had the interview at the *Post* with Steve Blackley and John Hardwick, rather than Harvey who was away on holiday, and made a good enough impression for them to offer me the role.

Sharon cried, accused me of betraying her, and begged me to stay, claiming she loved me. There was a lot of guilt thrown my way. I was used to this from my mother, so I wasn't falling for it. Don't get me wrong. I loved all the kinky sex and the fuss and mothering, if I'm honest. But I felt it was time to move on. I was only working on a weekly newspaper, and I needed to make the next step and work for a local daily before I could take the subsequent leap into tabloid journalism. I often visited Sharon when I was in London.

But first Millwall Mick.

I meet up with Mick as planned in the George on Wardour Street, about eight that evening. Already half-cut, he is sitting at the bar when I get there.

"Here he is," he sings, slurring and playing to the Chinese barmaid, who seems bored by the look on her face. "My Geordie pal."

I acknowledge him with a faux subservient "Nice to see you again, mate. It's been too long."

"You can say that a-fackin-gain," says Mick. "You got my money?"

"What you like?" I jest. "I'll get it from the cashpoint when we move on, mate. I don't carry that amount around with me."

"Yeah, OK, sunshine. Tell you what. We'll have a quick one here, and then we'll go to the Ship. Great sounds in there. Better than this." He points to the unintelligible sounds of Bob Marley coming from a speaker at the side of the optics. "Get me a Becks, Geordie boy."

I'll fucking "Geordie boy" the cunt! I order two Becks.

"Good result for your boys today, aye?"

I'm thinking that we lost 1–0 at home to Everton. The inbred still thinks I support Newcastle, despite telling him years ago I was a Mackem. I just go along with it.

"Yeah, three to one flattered Fulham." But he's not listening. He turns back to the pretty barmaid, who humours him.

"So when we going out?" he slavers to the Asian beauty, who just stares at him with a mixture of disdain and disbelief. "Fack me, try a bit of good-humoured banter, and it's like I've asked for anal sex!"

"Short of personality, mate," I humour him. "Come on, drink up, and we'll go to the George."

"We're already in the George, you doughnut!"

"I mean the Ship."

"I dunno. Five minutes outside the comfort of Geordieland, and you're behaving like a muppet!"

I'll fucking "muppet" you, you cunt. We leave the George and make a short sortie to the Ship, only for the stunted fat cunt to mention Lucy.

"Shame about that bird Lucy, aye?"

"Eh? Oh, yeah, shocking, mate."

"I see they got the geezer who did it, aye?"

"Aye, can't believe it to be honest. A lad on the sports desk. Scott."

"Can't believe it was him. Seemed like a nice fella every time I saw him down 'ere on the London beat."

"Just goes to show, though, Mick; you don't know everyone."

"It happened the weekend I did that game for you, didn't it?"

"Yeah."

"Is that why you didn't want to do the game so that you could go to the party?"

Where is he going with this, the scheming shitbag? He is up to something.

"No, mate, I never went to the party."

"Didn't ya? Why's that then? Your workmates think you're a cant an' all?"

"Yeah, something like that."

"Did you have an alibi?"

"Why would I need an alibi?"

"Well, you must've been questioned by the fuzz."

"Yes, but they got the fucker, Mick!"

"Oh, calm down, now. Calm down. You're a touchy fucker, aren't ya? Just saying."

"I don't want to talk about it, Mick. She was a friend of mine, after all."

"I remember you saying you couldn't stand the 'stuck-up cow'—your words, not mine—when we had a drink that time."

"Aye, well, people change and all that, so can you just drop it."

"Yeah, but I'm only saying that it looked suspicious that she got raped and you were—"

"I was what?"

"Not down 'ere, that's all."

"So?"

"Just saying."

I don't reply, because I can feel an anxiety attack coming on.

"Does anyone know you weren't down 'ere?"

"Of course not. Why would they? That's why I paid you."

"What would they say if they found out you weren't down 'ere?"

The scheming cunt is blackmailing me.

"Eh, why? You going to tell someone?" Mick just shrugs at the question but wears a smug look upon his coupon. "Are you winding me up, Mick?"

"Nah, just saying, that's all. If they found out you weren't at the game and yet you told the police as an alibi that you were at the game, what do you think would happen?"

I feel as if I'm going to have a heart attack. This Cockney cunt is going to get it if he doesn't back off.

"What...why...where you going with this? Why would you do that?"

"Just saying. Why lie about being at the game down 'ere if you've got nothing to hide?"

"I'm not hiding anything. I just didn't want to do the game down here, that's all. It was a coincidence, the Lucy thing. I'm hiding nothing. They got the bloke that did it: Scott!"

"Just don't believe he did it, guv. That's all I'm saying. He was down here with that Lucy girl not long ago. I saw them in the Twelve Bar together. He bought me a drink. They looked all loved up. Can't believe he would do it."

"Look, if anyone finds out I wasn't here, I'd lose my job, you fucking fat cunt!"

"Who you talking to, you northern monkey? Watch your fackin' mouth; otherwise, not only will you get a slap, but I also might let your secret slip! Fackin' hell, look at that!"

Mick's suspicions, accusations, and interrogation come to an end when we reach the Ship and he sees a shocking-red Lamborghini parked outside the pub. The South Londoner coos and corblimeys all over it, muttering about 700hp, V12, and 0–62 in 2.9 seconds and costing over £350,000. Admittedly it is a magnificent piece of engineering, but I haven't a fucking clue what he's on about. Carbon-fibre this and monocoque technology that and technical brilliance the other. Wish the loud-mouthed cunt would just shut his cakehole.

"Stand back from the car, please," shouts this big black geezer, who looks as if he's watching it for some gangster.

It's quite dark now, and there are a few people giving the Italian car a look over. I put a hand in my pocket as I approach the entrance of the pub, near the car, and feel my house keys. I go down and pretend to tie my shoelaces. A quick look left and right to see no one is looking, and I manage to get my front-door key out and gorge a line over the wheel arch. I stand up quickly, and I get away with it because the black guy is preoccupied with Mick. He eventually has to physically push Mick away from the motor vehicle.

"I told you earlier to step away from the car!"

"Alright, geezer, keep your hair on! Jesus! What's he like?"

I don't hover to find out the conclusion between the pair; instead I enter the busy bar. I can't get served at first until I move down to the far-end corner of the establishment and catch the eye of a young barmaid, who turns out to be eastern European, and order a couple of Budweisers.

"Cheers, guv," Mick says as I pass him a bottle of Bud. "Fakin' hell, what woz the sooty's problem?"

"Precious about the sports car, I expect. You said it yourself, cost more than a suburban semi in the West End of London."

I'm just happy we're talking about the car and not Lucy, rape, or an alibi. I've got an idea, but I need to get away from him to put it into action.

"I know, but fackin' hell; I've got a good mind to go out and give him a bit of a New Den kicking." I laugh at this.

"I doubt it, Mick; he's about seven foot six, and you're no more than a dwarf."

"You cheeky cant, I'm five foot seven! My ol' mum always said there's good stuff comes in lickle bundles."

What a fucking arsehole he is.

"Here," I say, handing over my beer to him. "I'm going to the bog."

I manage to double back behind without him seeing me and make my way to the entrance, where I approach the black geezer minding the car. "Geezer"! What's all that about? I've been down here fewer than twelve hours, and I'm speaking like a Cockney cunt.

"Look, mate, nothing to do with me, but I've just overheard a chubby bloke bragging to his mate that he's ran a key down the side of the car here."

"You heard...He did what?"

Armed with that information, he's off around the car, checking for marks until he finds the gouge over the wheel arch.

"Who...where is he?" the big brute of a man asks, with his face morphing from concerned and angry into something more ferocious and frenzied-like.

"Chubby bloke at the end of the bar. He's wearing a blue Harrington jacket and said he gave you a piece of his mind earlier."

What happens next is a bit of a blur. The black bloke sets off at a furious pace, and within a couple of seconds, Mick is bundled out into the back lane. I follow behind stealthily, make my way into the toilets, and take a clandestine view of the proceedings from the window. Mick, the stupid cunt, tries to put up a struggle. He screams, "Do you know who you're messing wiv?" He swings his arms all over the place, like an intoxicated octopus, trying to land a punch. But such is his inebriated state that he would've struggled to knock over a man made of marshmallows, never mind a man mountain. He takes a couple of blows from the enormous brute of a black man, who is subsequently joined by another burly bloke, of Caucasian persuasion. "Caucasian persuasion," get me; why not "white bloke"?

The men continue to land blows to Mick's body and face before the black tough guy exits the scene, presumably to guard the car again. To be fair to Mick, he stands up for several minutes before collapsing in a heap upon the ground.

I am shitting myself, just in case I am seen or implicated, but I can't tear myself away from the brutality of the situation. Three more men arrive, and I can hear their accents now; it sounds Russian or eastern European. The muscular oppressors and tormentors continue to land kicks and blows to Mick's listless body in between conversing in their mother tongue.

I feel no remorse as they strike and punch the living daylights out of him. Serves the cunt right for blackmailing me. I make my exit through the throng of revellers, who are unaware of what has just happened. I tentatively stop at the entrance. The car and the bouncer have gone, so I turn right on Wardour Street and make for Tottenham Court Road via Oxford Street.

My heart is still racing as I approach a black man seated in a car parked at the side of the road and ask if he can take me to Bromley for twenty quid.

"I'm not an unlicensed cab driver, mate."

"I'm really sorry, mate. I hope I haven't offended you."

"Don't worry about it."

For fuck's sake! How racist does that make me? Nevertheless, within a few moments, a young black lad in his early twenties, who has heard the exchange, asks where I want to go.

About twenty-five minutes later, I am in the Swan and Mitre. My heart is still pumping faster than a fat lass let loose in a cake shop. Fucking hell. Talking of fat lasses, I see Sharon, and she's not only put on over a stone, but she's also aged considerably since I saw her last year.

"Hiya, Sharon, you look great," I lie.

"Do you think so?"

"Yeah, you've never changed a bit."

"Actually I've put a bit of weight on."

"Well, you can't tell, bonny lass."

After more distracted pleasantries, we spend, or rather I spend, the next couple of hours getting hammered not only because am I trying to forget the consequences of my actions earlier but also because I know she'll be expecting a shag, and I'm not shagging one of the Weather Girls sober!

When we get in, Sharon switches on the TV, and after five minutes of watching *Sky Sports* reporters sensationalising the most trivial of stories, I flick to the Sky news channel. The news on the ticker bar quickly catches my attention. Man beaten to death outside a Soho pub. After several minutes of waiting for the weather, adverts, and a news item on the Middle East to finish, we get to it. The Sky news reporter changes to the recent incident in London's West End. The reporter goes on to explain that a Michael Buckley, commonly known to friends as Millwall Mick, a freelance sports writer, has died after an incident outside the Ship pub in Soho. He adds that the police are looking for witnesses to come forward and help with their inquiries.

I watch the TV and feel totally detached from the incident. I don't suffer anything for the man. I don't sense any sorrow, sadness, or shame for my part in his demise. He was yet another boorish, egotistical wanker of a sports writer in a nation full of boorish, egotistical sports-writing wankers. Another one taken care of, and one less to worry about. Serves the cunt right!

Chapter 31

A fairly uneventful week in the wonderful world of sport culminates with a welcome visit to Lucy's for dinner. Cass does inquire whether I'd had a night out in London and grills me if I knew the sports writer from Millwall who died from the Soho attack. He also lets on that Trudi is being a moody cow and has been since the turn of the year. I make a mental note of his marital problems, but I swerve the Millwall Mick item, saying we'd briefly met, but I didn't really know him. Another bit of good fortune, on my part, seeing as there have been no repercussions from the unpleasant episode. The police have no CCTV footage and no witnesses, and forensics have not returned any evidence. There's nothing to work on, according to several press reports of the incident.

Lucy's two-bedroom flat just off Salters Road is a compact, cosy, and comfortable abode, in contrast to the expansive, impersonal, and almost-palatial quayside apartment she lived in prior to this one. The pretentious artwork has followed her from the former ostentatious dwelling by the River Tyne to this warm, welcoming, leafy suburban accommodation. I feel an overwhelming desire to spray graffiti on them, draw moustaches, or replace the frames with the famous dogs playing snooker—or was it pool? But then I'm not cultured, am I? I'm an uneducated runt in sports journalism.

I feel a little nervous and apprehensive as Lucy buzzes me up to her new residence, which is situated in a block of six similar lodgings. She kisses me on both sides of the cheek when I enter—a bit European, if you ask me. She then sets off with that kind-of-confident catwalk swagger I know so well, loathe, and love at the same time. She's wearing black leggings, a grey skirt cut halfway up the thigh, and a sliver blouse with black pinstripes. The blouse has two top buttons undone, and you can see a welcoming cleavage. Her black-brown wavy hair is parted slightly left of centre, and it hangs down, shaping the curve of her face, and sits on her shoulders.

"Would you like a glass of wine or a beer?"

I think, *Pretend to be sophisticated.* "Yes, red wine would be great. Here, I brought a couple of bottles. I wasn't sure what you liked."

Lucy looks disdainfully at the bottle of **rosé** and Ernst Gallo red I hand to her before she breaks into a smile and says, "Wine not your forte, Tom?"

"Not really."

The patronising cow disappears into the kitchen. "Just go through into the lounge. Hope you're hungry."

"A bit peckish," I shout back to her as I enter the open-plan lounge and dining area. The kitchen has an island where the hob and oven are integrated with other units. At the other end of where the cooking takes place is a bench or dining area, which is already set with cutlery. The harsh brilliant-white decor of her quayside apartment has been replaced with a much more calming and comforting lavender. The soothing ambience is complemented by the music, which my host informs me is Portishead.

Lucy puts down two dinner plates. They reveal a small portion of buffalo mozzarella and beef tomatoes, drizzled in balsamic vinegar and sprinkled with herbs. She lifts her wineglass to mine and clinks it.

"To your new job at the *Mail*."

"I'll drink to that."

I take a sip from the glass. It tastes bloody awful, but I don't let on.

"Like the wine?"

"Yes, it's nice," I lie.

"It's Châteauneuf-du-Pap…I bought it from a vineyard not far from Avignon in the Côte d'Azur about ten years ago. French wines are much nicer when they're older, don't you think?"

I haven't a fucking clue, but there is only one answer to this.

"Totally agree."

"What's your favourite wine?"

"Don't really have one, to be honest. I have a broad range of tastes."

"I'm the same. At first it used to be only European wines, which are probably still my favourite, but my palate has developed over the years, and I can appreciate South American and South African wines more now. Anyway I thought I'd save it for a special occasion."

"Thanks, not sure I deserve this," I say in between wedging a huge cut of mozzarella and tomato into my mouth.

"Oh, come on, Tom. You've landed a job at the biggest-selling daily newspaper in the country."

"Thought that was the *Sun*?"

"No, I'm sure it's the *Mail*. Whatever, it's still one of the biggest in the country. You must be so proud."

"Yeah, I suppose I am."

"Hope you like salmon."

"Yes, great." I've never had it. Once had salmon-paste sandwiches, which I liked.

"I've done salmon with king prawns and tagliatelle pasta in a creamy sauce."

"Sounds delicious." And it is. Never tasted anything like it in my life. I'm not sure what is happening, but as the evening continues, I learn what an incredibly sophisticated, intelligent, and beautiful woman Lucy is—a sharp contrast to my primitive, obtuse, and somewhat-unattractive personality. Yet the irony to this is that Lucy seems to like me. She speaks for what seems like hours about music, culture, and feminist politics. I can see why she got on so well with Saunders. She fucking knows more than the omnipotent Greek god.

I am out of my depth here. I nod and agree with just about every theory, proposal, or hypothesis, despite having no opinion or anything to challenge or add to the topic she is discussing.

The one time I do join in the conversation, Lucy might as well stand me against a wall to face a firing squad. When she switches the conversation to

Bez's girlfriend and the magazine she works for, *Cosmopolitan*, I make a casual observational joke about how women's magazine writers are hypocritical in taking a moral high ground on beauty and obesity when nine out of ten authors who pen these articles are overweight or ugly. I think I'll win her approval. But, no, a miniature feminist rant on how beauty is in the eye of the beholder and how it is every woman's right to choose how she looks or what her body shape is gets thrown in my face. A minor storm in a teacup is avoided when I crack another uncomfortable line about how a visit to Specsavers would resolve it all.

We have retired to the lounge area by this time. We both sit on either end of a charmingly comforting three-seater settee while we quaff half of a third bottle of wine—two Bordeaux have followed the Château whatever-it-is-called, and I am feeling decidedly intoxicated when she turns the conversation onto her parents.

I think she says that they are both doctors or have doctorates or PhDs. I mishear. They are both wonderful human beings, apparently, unlike my slut of a mother. Lucy admits that she was spoilt as a kid, but she was never a brat and appreciates all her folks did for her. She insists, however, that apart from the silver-grey convertible Beetle, which was bought as a twenty-fifth birthday present, everything else has been bought with her own money. Just goes to show, you can't judge a book by its cover, I suppose.

The ambient music and mood are ever changing, and every question about who is responsible for the liberating effect on our evening is met with Massive Attack, Morcheeba, Air, Moby, Jeff Buckley, Sigur Rós, Beach House, Cranberries, and Adele. Adele appears to be the anomaly in this apparent inventory of highbrow, arty-farty evocative listening. But the North London songstress is the one who actually opens the floodgates. "Set Fire to the Rain" lands an uppercut before the Haymaker is delivered by "Someone Like You." I've never felt as pitiful, wretched, and vulnerable in a long time. Lucy notices the welling in my eyes and slides along the sofa to comfort me.

"What's wrong, Tom?"

"Sorry, nothing. I don't know what's up," I say, sniffing and wiping my eyes.

"Have I said something to upset you?"

"No, not at all! Don't know what it is. Just overcome. Probably the unnoticed build-up of stress I've had, and the extra work I've accepted has taken its toll. Just feeling sorry for myself, I think. This is ridiculous, given what you've been through."

"I try not to think about it, Tom. Just try to remain positive and philosophical about things. It still doesn't feel like it happened. That's probably why I've been able to manage."

"Anyway it's still nothing of what you've gone through."

"I'm fine, Tom, honest. I felt sorry for myself for a while, but I think I'm over it. You sure you're OK? I know I shouldn't say this, but it is encouraging to see you cry. There're times when you don't seem human, like you're a robot."

"No, I still have my moments like everyone else. Probably a combination of the wine, sad songs, you, and hearing all those wonderful things you're saying about your parents…I've had none of that…no support from anyone. I've done everything off my own bat…My mother has been a Freudian nightmare all of my life…I've never known my father."

"You poor thing."

Lucy's sympathetic "poor thing" is the catalyst for a tsunami of tears to flood my face, and I am crying like a baby, confessing to the shit life and mental, physical, and sexual abuse I've been subjected to in my dismal, abject life. Lucy starts by holding my hand and then stroking my arm ever so gently while she listens to my confession. But then she edges even closer and begins to caress the nape of my neck and hair on the back of my head. Her fingers are massaging my cranium. It is hypnotic. I can feel her hot breath down the right-hand side of my face as she gets closer, and I am losing control. I feel enchanted, beguiled, and powerless as her soft lips brush my cheek, work their way down to my neck, and then magnetically lock onto my lips when I turn my head. My head is swimming. I drown in ecstasy as my body appears to be besieged by a radiant flush smouldering throughout my constitution. The smaller nibbling kisses gradually become bigger and wetter, and then before I can stop, her tongue is in my mouth and her mouth has enveloped mine.

I can't breathe. I'm drowning. I'm having a heart attack! I've got to get out! I jab Lucy harshly in the shoulder with the palm of my hand and notice her eyes dilate as her mouth opens with the sudden jolt of disbelief.

"What's up?"

My head is spinning one way while it feels as if the room is rotating in the opposite direction. I fall to my knees as I try to get up off the sofa. I can't see and can't breathe, and everything is a blur. I need to get out of here. I can hear Lucy saying, "Tom, Tom, Tom, what's up? What's happening?"

"Need to go. Need to get out," I say. She's grabbed both my arms and is trying to pacify me. "Fuck off! Get off me…you…fucking prick tease!"

"What? Tom, I am not a prick tease! What's happening? Why are you behaving like this?"

"It's a trap."

"A trap! What are you on about?"

Despite my delirious condition, I manage to stagger to the front door, down the staircase, and out of the building, where I fall onto my knees and try to catch my breath. Lucy follows me out and appears to be as distressed as I am. She's crying.

"Tom, Tom, Tom, what's up? Do you need an ambulance? Have you taken something? Why are you behaving like this? Why did you call me a prick tease? Trap, what trap? I don't understand. Please tell me."

I manage to get on to my feet and stumble towards my car.

"Tom, you can't drive in that state. You've had too much to drink, for one."

"Fuck off…bitch, with your mind games."

"What are you on about, Tom? Stop this please! This is upsetting! What have I done? We were having…"

I manage to find my keys, and I'm in the car. I look to see Lucy standing with both her hands, prayer-like, over her nose; mascara is streaming down her face from the tears she is shedding. She appears distressed, hurt, and wounded. I reverse into a car behind me, pull out, and, in doing so, remove the wing mirror of a parked car to my left.

Chapter 32

I awake to several missed calls and texts from Lucy. I can't even remember getting home, although I do recall taking some Prozac. The combination of drink and antidepressant knocked me out. I still feel like shit. I should be flying after my good news and the fact an intelligent, beautiful woman is interested in me. My new contract from the *Mail* arrived on the doorstep yesterday—£60,000 a year, double my *Post* salary. But it hasn't had any positive effect, because in spite of everything, I'm prone to anxiety and panic attacks, despite all of the positives weighing in my favour. I still feel irritable, agitated, and hostile towards everyone and have trouble sleeping. The dreams, or nightmares, are making me even more depressed. The tablets I've been prescribed haven't improved my humour. There are days when I feel as if I can't carry on. I've got no one. It's me against the world, and there's nobody on my side. My fucking mother has a lot to answer for. And as for that fucking slag, Trudi...Yeah, that gives me an idea.

An old laptop, procured from the IT department without their knowledge, will do the job. They'll not be able to track the IP address, so it'll not be traced back to me. I'll just upload these pictures from my memory stick, and bingo! Type a generic e-mail to everyone at the *Post* (while deleting Cass's from the roll), cc everyone from Trudi's client list, and send! Obviously my e-mail address is on the electronic inventory, so I'll get them as well. Wonder what everyone will make of them? Probably shock a few, but I'm guessing most will love feasting their eyes on some magnificent amateur photography.

SCOOP

Thought that would've cheered me up, but I still feel like shit. My head resembles a box of cornflakes in a cereal box. I've got loads on today, what with fucking Marty being out of action, Saunders incarcerated, and a useless fucker of a girl on the desk. Don't know how I'm going to cope. Hang on. It's Sunday. I don't need to go into the office. I've filed all my copy, and I'm off today. For fuck's sake, get a grip!

A text comes through on my phone. It's one of several more from Lucy asking to get in touch. She's becoming as bad as that former slut of a girlfriend and whore of a mother.

Where's that chloroform? Sure, I've got loads left over. Maybe if I inhale it for a few minutes, it'll make me feel better. Apparently it's used as an anaesthetic. Supposed to be banned in the United Kingdom, but it's easily obtained over the Internet. I know it took ages to knock out Saunders, so it should be safe to inhale for a minute or two.

Mmm, I feel a bit better now, a lot less restless. Another text from Trudi; she wants me to call her immediately. But a call from Trudi instantaneously follows. I try to block it, but I accept it by mistake.

"Hello. Tom, is that you?"

After a few moments of silence, I say, "Yes, Trudi, what do you want?" I speak as if I'm bored and with a great deal of indifference.

"I need to see you."

"You've got a fucking cheek. It's over, Trudi. Do you not get it? Did I not let you down gently enough? Can't believe you're still trying after all—"

"I know I fucked up, Tom, and I know you never want to see me. I accept that. It wasn't my finest hour, but I'd still like your help. I'm appealing for you to be the bigger man here. I've somehow managed to make a bigger mess of something."

"Of what?"

"It's embarrassing. Is there any chance we can meet? It's not something I can discuss over the phone. I'd rather talk to face-to-face."

"Where's Cass?"

"He's just left for work."

"If this is a trick…"

"It's not, Tom, honest. I need your help. You're the only one I can turn to. I don't know what to do."

"OK, stop crying. I'm sure it's not as bad as you're making it out to be."

"You don't understand."

"OK, OK, I'll come. Where do you want to meet?"

"The flat above the shop?"

"I hope that slut isn't going to be there!"

"No, eh, she went away for the weekend. I don't know where."

"OK, give me an hour. Leave the door on the latch."

I have a shower, pack a few items into a toilet bag, and make my way to the unusually deserted shopping precinct where Trudi has her shop. I sit for five minutes, observing the curiously quiet area for forms of life. The last time I was here resulted in a tumultuous occurrence. The whole estate was involved. I want to avoid any embarrassing episodes this time around. Well, I certainly don't want to draw any attention to myself.

I'm about thirty yards from Trudi's front door when I hear the voice of an old man calling out.

"Hey! Excuse me, young man!"

I pretend not to hear and get a step on.

"Excuse me. Can I have a word please?"

Out the corner of my eye, I recognise that old cunt on the spacker mobile that knocked me down. I don't fucking believe this. Without missing a stride or acknowledging the disabled fucker, I decide not to go through the front, so I get a move on around the back of the shops, climb a barbed-wire fence (ripping my sweatshirt in the process), and slip away from the old bastard. He follows me around the back, although he doesn't see me.

"I know you're around here somewhere. I recognise you, and I'm going to call the police. Come out; come out, wherever you are!"

He can stop out there all day for all I care. I'm inside Trudi's flat now and ascending the stairs, which lead to the kitchen. Trudi is startled when I enter. She's wearing nothing but a white, tight-fitting cotton vest and matching briefs. Her nipples are erect and poke invitingly through the material. She is unbelievably fit for her age. I wasn't expecting this. It wasn't part of the plan, but I've got to have her.

"Tom" is the only word that escapes her full, red lips because within seconds, I've dropped my bag and am on her, kissing, groping, and rubbing. It doesn't take long to lose the jeans and underwear and pull aside her briefs and penetrate her. Trudi doesn't resist and accommodates my entry by lifting up her right leg and resting it in my left arm. The sensation is incredible. I know it shouldn't be. But the entire erotic nature of this has my head whirling, and I'm on the verge of orgasm. Normally, I wouldn't give a shit. But I don't want this to end too quickly, so I withdraw from her.

"Wait," I say to a confused Trudi. "I've got a stimulant."

"We don't need one," she gasps.

"You'll enjoy this," I say, pulling out the chloroform and a flannel. I douse the cloth in the liquid and put it across my face and inhale.

"What is it?"

"Like poppers."

Initially Trudi looks doubtful, but the dirty cow surrenders as I turn her around and enter from behind. While my left hand grips her generously proportioned breast, the right smothers her nose and mouth, and she has no option but to breathe in the noxious, calming anaesthetic.

"Good?" I ask.

"Mmm."

But I don't last long, and within two minutes, my legs buckle, and I collapse, exhausted. I drop the cloth, and my head rests between her shoulder blades.

"I wasn't expecting that," Trudi says softly.

"Me, neither."

After extricating myself, I sit, fatigued, on a seat by her kitchen table.

"Cold drink?"

"Yes, please."

Trudi pulls a bottle of sparkling water from her fridge and pours two glasses. She excuses herself from the room, and I take the opportunity to slip a drug of my choice into her glass before she comes back. Trudi returns; she's dressed in tight, blue, cut-off jeans and a white, tight-fitting blouse, which accentuates her bust. I should be apologising for forcing myself on her, but fuck it. Why should I, given the consequences of her actions before Christmas? Mind you, had she resisted, I still would have gone through with it.

"I don't know where to start," she weeps, in between sipping water from the glass, blowing her nose, and wiping her eyes. "Some photographs have been e-mailed anonymously."

"Photographs? What photographs?"

"Some holiday pictures…from a few years back…when Dave and I were in Greece."

"What sort of pictures?"

Trudi begins to sob more heavily now. "Let's put it this way, Tom. They weren't your average holiday snaps. They were explicit!"

"Right. And someone has got them how?"

"I don't know how because I kept them at the salon…in a drawer…in my office. No one…God, I feel faint…I don't know…Tom…You often…went in…Really tired…all of a sudden…Need to…lie…down."

"Yeah, you don't look too good, Trudi," I say, watching her eyes become heavier. "Probably a good idea."

I help her through to the bedroom, and within a minute of lying on the bed, she's dead to the world. I prod, push, and grope the prostrate body to get a reaction, but she's out cold. The Rohypnol has done its job. I strip her naked—what an amazing figure aesthetically! She could have modelled, done porn, or become an athlete. How the fuck Cass managed to pull this cracker, I'll never know. But then I'll never understand the complexities of what goes on inside a woman's head. It's not as if Cass has a big cock. Well, not what she told me, anyhow.

I get her tied and bound to the bed, and I take out a marker pen and write "slut" on her stomach. A few pics of this won't go amiss. A nice accompaniment to the aperitif I've already served to the cyber world.

"Thomas! What are you doing, son?"

Fuck! I nearly shit myself. And there she stands at the doorway of the bedroom: the whore of Babylon and the mother of prostitutes. The symbol of deliberate provocation, she's about to bring about an adverse reaction.

"And there came one of the seven angels which had the seven vials and talked with me, saying unto me, come hither; I will shew unto thee the judgment of the great whore that sitteth upon many waters."

"What?" my mother replies.

"With whom the kings of the earth have committed fornication, and the inhabitants of the earth have been made drunk with the wine of her fornication."

"What are you talking about?"

"So he carried me away in the spirit into the wilderness: and I saw a woman sit upon a scarlet-coloured beast, full of names of blasphemy, having seven heads and ten horns."

"Stop it, son. You're scaring me."

"And the woman was arrayed in purple and scarlet colour, and decked with gold and precious stones and pearls, having a golden cup in her hand full of abominations and filthiness of her fornication."

"Stop it, please!"

"And upon her forehead was a name written, mystery Babylon the Great, the mother of harlots and abominations of the earth."

"What's got into you? Why are you behaving this way?"

Those long-forgotten passages come from the biblical book of Revelation. It was something I read years ago; I didn't realise I'd memorised it. It's as if I've been possessed by a spirit. I'm stalking my slut of a mother, and she's backing out of the bedroom and into the kitchen.

"Your face, Tom, it's all contorted. Don't look at me like that. It's scaring me."

"This is all your doing!"

"What is? I don't understand…And what's wrong with Trudi?…What have you done?"

"Nothing, compared to what's coming your way," I growl menacingly.

"Why…what have I done?"

"What have you done? What haven't you done? You're responsible for everything—my mental state, Mother! You're the reason I'm full of…hate…and loathing and—"

"But how? What have I done? I was a good mother. I tried my best."

I laugh manically at this and grab her by the throat. She drops her hand luggage, and her fingers try to release my grip.

"A good mother! A good mother, ha! My childhood was a constant fucking misery, you slut! I was physically, mentally, and sexually abused by you and your…your endless menagerie of so-called boyfriends!"

"Tom…can't breathe!"

"And the perpetual flirting, with builders, milkmen, and…just men in general…even with the teachers and kids who bullied me at school. 'I'd love to fuck your mother,' they'd say. 'Look at the size of her tits' and 'Does she take it up the arse?' and 'I'd love to cum on her tits'!"

"Son…please."

"Don't 'Son, please' me."

"I tried…my best." She's turned on the waterworks now. That'll not work!

"Tried your best? You have got to be fucking joking! That was your best? Really? That was your best? Dragged up! I brought myself up while you were out on the piss with all your…tattooed toughs, cheeky chappies, and blokes with cars with go-faster stripes!" I bang her head against the partition kitchen wall.

"Ow, you're really hurting me, son."

"On one occasion, I had to eat a Sugar Puffs box because there was nothing in the house to eat, while you…you…and your bloke were still out from the previous night. And Christmas! Don't get me fucking started on Christmas. How could you do that to a child, your own son? How could you be so cruel? Why would you do something like that unless…you…you are fucking inherently evil! Myra Hindley would've been a better mother."

I must have relaxed my hold because somehow she manages to garner enough strength to wrestle free and roar ferociously in my face, catching me off guard.

"Don't you take the moral high ground with me, you…you ungrateful bastard! You think you've had it bad, do you? You think you've had it hard! You don't know the half. Ever thought about anyone else aside from your self-pitying self? You think you were dealt a bad hand. Well, what about mine? Eh? What about me? Eh? Fingered and fucked and slobbered on by your father and his mates just after I hit puberty! You think that was a picnic for me? Eh? Do you? Well? Do you? Answer me, Mr. I-Feel-Sorry-For-Myself!

"You've never been through half of what I've had to put up with. All the optimism, dreams, and romance of losing my virginity to a man I love and would eventually marry. The dreams and romance of every young girl…all destroyed by a rapist who had enjoyed an evening drinking one too many pints of Guinness and whiskey chasers! For the best part of two years, it went on. And the abuse only stopped because I got pregnant with you and fucked off! I tried to get an abortion, but it was too late. I was nearly five months gone before I realised. There would've been complications, the nurse said. I could die if I aborted, and by Christ, I seriously contemplated it. My life wasn't worth living."

And while she offloads this dystopian nightmarish diatribe filled full of insufferable revulsion and disgust, I slump to the floor. I am physically and mentally exhausted. My head throbs while my heart thumps so violently that I feel it could be heard three streets away. I am falling headfirst into the abyss.

"That first time…he was pissed when he climbed into my bed after he'd come home from the pub one night. Oh, yes, he was sorry and apologetic the following morning…said it was an accident…and he'd been dreaming. But then a week later he went out and got pissed again. And the abuse started all over. Not long after that, he started to bring his mates back, and they all had a go. Threatened to kill me, they all did, if I said anything about it. And there was no one there to protect me, because I had no immediate family, and my mother had fucked off when I was ten, because she was sick and tired of the violence and abuse. I cried myself to sleep most nights as a little girl, when she was getting her regular beatings, and then I was crying for a different reason not long after that! So don't you fucking stand there and fucking moralise to me about your shit life and being dragged up. You never went through half of my sufferings. Your life didn't turn out too bad though, did it? You work for a fucking newspaper, for God's sake. So stop your whining and your self-pity! Me? I've lived off my wits and tits and the fact that I can fuck and suck...just like the...good whore of Babylon. I had to! It was the only thing I could do to survive. Oh, yes, I hoped to settle down, meet a nice man, and have a nice normal life with a family. But, no, they all could smell that I was a victim, damaged goods, a shag, a mistress, and not girlfriend or wife material."

I manage to whisper, "Father. Who is my dad?"

"Father! Father, you say! Your father was my father, you stupid bastard! Did you not hear what I've just said? Were you not listening to me? Why do you think I behaved like I did? Why I hid behind the party-girl façade and ostentation? To hide the hurting, pain, and wretchedness of my existence! Craving attention...wanting to be noticed...crying for help, but none came... Just more abuse, cruelty, and exploitation. You were...are...a constant reminder of it and that bastard! Why do you think I fucked off and left you behind? I tried to leave you behind! As a baby, I once put you on someone's doorstep and left you. I walked around the block for fifteen minutes before guilt set in and I went back for you. I loved and hated you in equal measures. Still do. You've been a curse on my life. A constant reminder, a jinx or hex on me from...I don't know...I'm too tired...to do this anymore. Don't want to go on."

I try to block out what she is saying. I don't want to hear what she is revealing; it is killing me. I want the pain, hurt, and suffering to end. Then Mary O'Connor, Mary Rafferty, Kitty O'Shea, my mother—or whatever pseudonym, alias, nom de plume, or fictitious character she has used in the past—suddenly stops talking, and her fury subsides. She's let it all out. There is nothing left, and crying, she joins me curled up in a ball. Her arms cradle me; her hands stroke my head and comfort me for what seems like hours. I eventually unwrap myself from her, rise to my feet, and trundle towards the toilet and stairs.

"Son...I'm sorry, son," she whispers, edging her way over to me. Her arms stretch around my neck before her fingers begin stroking my hair, pushing it around my ears. She kisses my neck, face, and then lips. Her hands come up to hold both sides of my face, and she looks deep into my teary eyes with her very own beautiful sky blues. Another kiss delicately brushes my lips before a few firmer nibbles and pecks turn into a full open-mouth affair. Snapping out of the reverie that has bewitched me, I grasp the horror of the situation and push her off. Astonishment and terror become instantly etched on her visage as she stumbles back and begins to fall. Her frantic scrambling arms manage to grab hold of my sweatshirt, as an attempt to break her fall fails, and I go tumbling down the stairs on top of her. My fall is broken, fortunately for me, but regrettably her descent isn't softened by anything other than the rise and fall of the harsh stairs. She lies motionless, her head to the left, her mascara-smudged eyes wide open.

Epilogue

I love *Star Wars*, always have. Still got most of the toys and figures in a box in the garage, and I have the original films on VHS in a bedroom cupboard. I think it's fitting that I watch one: *The Empire Strikes Back*. Probably appropriate that I watch it dressed as Darth Vader, courtesy of the fancy-dress shop on Percy Street. The police and my friends in the media will all appreciate the irony, although the shop might not be too happy when I'm finished with it. It's how they do it in the films, isn't it? Hardly *Seven*, *The Girl with the Dragon Tattoo*, or a complicated John Grisham thriller, I know. Not that I can remember any of them. It was always sci fi, *Home Alone*, or John Hughes movies with the Brat Pack for me. There've been no tangled web or several complex subplots, but people will want to know how I did it.

Right, the video is starting, so I need an aperitif. What have we got here? Jim Beam, gin, Rohypnol, diazepam, cough medicine, and Valium. It's amazing what drugs I've collected from my mother's medicine cabinet over the years. I'll need some bleach, aspirin, and paracetamol, just to be sure. I think I'll have a few whiskys and wash them down with a cocktail of cough medicine, painkillers, and gin, for starters, before I start mixing my drinks and popping some more pills. Urgh! Fuck! Neat whisky is bitter! Should have put a mixer in with it, yuck! Right, where's the laptop?

Dear friends and foes,

I can't do it anymore. The game of life, if that's what you want to call it. I've only ever known deceit, double-dealing, and cruelty in mine, and I've had enough of it.

I want to apologise. What for? Well, I'm going to reveal all of that in this e-mail. I know an apology won't make up for all the wrong I've done to you over the last twelve months, and I don't expect you to forgive me. I'm doing this for me, no one else. The truth be known, I'm not even sure I'm doing it for me at all. I don't give a shit about any of you or myself for that matter, and it won't matter anyway. I'll not be facing up to the consequences of my actions, will I? And it'll be a good way to end it when the movie industry films the story of my life.

Pass this on to the police, and they can release an innocent man, because Scott did not rape Lucy. It was me. Yes, you read that right; it was me. I set him up. Why? Let's just say it was a culmination of being undermined, shut out, and ridiculed behind my back for as long as I can remember. Being sent on a ninety-mile round trip to do a Middlesbrough press conference that Saunders knew was cancelled was the straw that broke the camel's back.

How did I set him up? Easy! I hid behind the bins in the alleyway next to his flat and knocked on his door. When he answered, I came up from behind, and a blow to the head was administered with a baseball bat. A chloroform-filled duster strapped to a mask helped to keep him under. Chloroform is widely available on the Internet, for those of you plotting something degenerate, decadent, or debauched. I then dragged him up the stairs, stripped him naked, bound his arms and legs behind his back, and gagged him before leaving him there in a state of semiconsciousness. A Rohypnol chill pill also helped aid the process when he decided to come around, although still drowsy.

I would like to say I planned it, but I didn't. I just wanted to give him a good kicking. But when I saw he'd been preparing for Lucy's fancy-dress party, that's when my mind went into overdrive.

I left him, took the fancy-dress costume, and went to the party. How did no one recognise me? Easy. Apart from the obvious outfit, the voice box in the costume made me sound like the character. And I didn't stay around long enough to strike up many conversations. The exchanges I made were with people already pissed or high on chemical substances. And because of that, spiking Lucy's drink with a date rapist's favourite aperitif, without anyone seeing, was easy. She was struggling after a short while, so when she went to go to the toilet, I followed. She could have collapsed anywhere. It was just by chance that she did so in her bedroom.

I didn't intend to rape her. I just wanted to frighten her, take photographs of her naked, and send them out to the world. But when it was lying there helplessly on a plate, it was too hard to resist. She is physical perfection, after all.

Why? For the same reason I set up Scott: the opportunity presented itself. Because I could and because I hated her. I loathed the way she looked down on everyone. And when I didn't get an invite to the party, I thought, "Right, you're getting it." It was all too easy. Childish and spiteful? I know.

I returned to Scott's flat, planted the drugs in his bathroom cabinet, and hid some S&M porn under his mattress. I stole, or rather borrowed, his laptop to trawl through rape-fantasy websites and to send an e-mail to Lucy from Scott. I took a spare key from his house, put the laptop back, and tipped off the police anonymously. I even stole a pair—the pair—of soiled knickers Lucy had deposited in her washing basket. And, yes, it was me who wanked you off into them and left the present for the police to find with the other evidence in your washing basket. I think you enjoyed that wank more than you let on, poster boy. Don't deny it; you wouldn't have cum otherwise.

Why didn't they find any DNA on the costume? I was careful throughout; I wiped and cleaned places I might have touched and wore washing-up gloves to avoid fingerprints. A quick sortie back home for some long johns and a long-sleeved T-shirt, as well as a hairnet, ensured that there would be little evidence beneath the costume. I also washed the costume. So while there was a chance of leaving something of me on it, I'd left so much overwhelming evidence pointing in Scott's direction that there was no need for the police to check the costume. Anyway I put him into it after I'd used it, so it would've been crawling in the soup-taker's DNA.

The alibis? Easy! I had train tickets, while an old mate covered the match for a small fee. Simple. The Millwall staff, manager, and players don't know who I am or who he was. Could've been anyone. The only guy there who knew me was from the *Gazette*. I texted him several times prior, during, and after the game and told him I was either running late before the match or sitting several rows behind, before telling him I had to dash and talk to a player after the game. It all went accordingly. It helps he's short-sighted. I got Millwall Mick to wave at him during the match. In fact, Mick was the only one who could've spilled the beans, if you like. Got a bit sloppy a few times because I didn't pay what I owed for the favour. He threatened to spill, but I sorted it in the end, big time. He'll not be blackmailing anyone anymore.

Why did I do it? Well, unlike Shakespeare's villain in *Othello*, Iago, I did have reasons for plotting. It might be a simple reason, but it's a reason nonetheless. I fucking hate Saunders! I loathe every fucking thing about him. He's everything I'm not. I detest his good looks, the odious way he swaggers around full of confidence, and the fact that everyone seems to love him. I did try to be his mate, but he didn't want to know me. I wanted to fit in, and I tried to fit in. It was difficult for me, but he just fucked me off and kept me out of the loop, time after time. I'm glad I stitched him up. He's a Scottish cunt and deserves to suffer. I've suffered, believe you me. Anyway I hope he enjoys his freedom. He's had a small taste in the jail of what I've endured throughout my lifetime. Next time be careful, Scott; be good to your new colleague. Otherwise you might have to suffer your fate once again.

And you can have your CDs back. I took a few when I was around at yours, to see what the fuss was about. You've got a point; you always did, have. And you're nearly always right, Mr. Clever Clogs. Yes, I'm a Debaser, but…Where is my mind? I'm not sure. I've obviously lost it.

Lucy, while I still loathe Saunders, you'll have to believe me when I say the same doesn't apply to you. Yes, I did, not anymore. I'm not trying to justify it. Well, I suppose I am because this is the clearest my head has been for years. Not really. The drugs are kicking in. I've witnessed and felt a lifetime of cruelty and have come to this conclusion: this is how people behave with one another. If you want something, you go out and get it, and to hell with the consequences. But after spending so much time with you, I've realised that you are a good person and not a two-faced cow. You've made me realise that what I've done is wrong and that I'm a worthless piece of shit.

I was always wary that you would find out it was me. I splashed myself with his aftershave and bathed in his shower gel to—literally—throw you off my scent at the party. Despite this, I always thought you'd work it out. Sorry about my behaviour after you cooked dinner. You'll just have to believe me when I say I had the best time ever—until the panic attack.

Too much to confess. Too little time. Better hurry. Cass, it was me who sent these pictures to everyone. Oh, and by the way, when you finish work, you better get yourself along to the flat above the shop. Rudy Trudi is a bit tied up.

Cass, I was shagging your missus before she srted a lesbn relationship with memoher. You'll find her at bottom of stairs. No, didn't kill her; stumbled and fell down them. Marty, it was me who set you up with BNP; it was me who gave Blackley a heart attack, although I never meant it, and it was me who fiddled with Keren's copy. Owt else, aye, fck off, Harvey. You're a cnut!

Feeling drowsy now, drigs and drikn are atking hold. Better send this mmeail befor

What else? Oh, yes, May the Forcshe be wivthYou!

Made in the USA
Charleston, SC
01 September 2016